The MAXWELL *Vendetta*

The Maxwell Family Saga (1)

A Novel by
CARL R. BRUSH

BOOKSIDE Press

BookSide Press
877-741-8091
www.booksidepress.com
orders@booksidepress.com

Table of Contents

Acknowledgement

The Maxwell Vendetta is a prequel to *The Second Vendetta* which was, as is typical in this upside world of mine, published first. But the credit for both novels lies mostly with the same folks. Namely,

Star billing to my wife, Susanne, for her help and support in this and in all other things.

Les Edgerton, Noir master mentor and friend. Your staunch backing and nourishment of this project and of my writing in general gives you a major share in the creation of *The Second Vendetta*.

Nik Morton, Solstice publish editor-in-Chief. You were willing to take a second look, and you are always there with a prompt and patient reply.

Luis Urrea. Super novelist whose writing and workshop tutelage taught me loads about how to make what went on then seem like its going on right now.

Dan Barth for general inspiration for your *Fast Women, Beautiful Horses…*

Finally, my parents, who made sure I had plenty of exposure to outdoor life in Northern California and taught me how to make the most of it.

CHAPTER ONE

S ure, Julian was drunk. It was Friday night, after all, a San Francisco longshoreman's night to howl. And Independence weekend besides. Since when does downing a few too many merit a death sentence? Let alone for a nineteen year old? Nineteen. That's all my younger brother was when he was murdered.

* * *

We'd agreed on a 9:00 p.m. rendezvous at the Fandango Club, an ersatz Mexican dive on Jackson Street famed for Consuela and her Mexican hat dance. Tantalus never yearned for his legendary grapes more than Julian and I lusted after Consuela. Her long legs, angelic ululations, flowing tresses, high-heeled boots clicking like castanets. She'd stroke her bare body with a pair of glittery sombreros that revealed little, but promised the universe.

I was on time, as usual. Julian was not, as usual. He missed these meetings about as often as he kept them, but tonight was special. I'd graduated from the University of California that very afternoon, was ready to celebrate, but by 11:00 p.m., neither Julian nor Consuela had appeared. The night looked like a bust.

A lackluster Mariachi band played a mournful "Oh, Susannah." From time to time someone would yell for Consuela, but she never appeared. The Fandango smelled like most San Francisco waterfront bars—a miasma of liquor and sweat hovering over a rotting marine odor emanating from floors

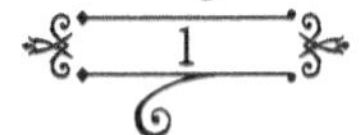

and walls likely salvaged from some shipwrecked hull. I was almost always in a frolicsome humor at the Fandango, so the reek before never bothered me. Tonight it darkened my mood.

I sat on a stool, back to the bar, and took the first swig of my fourth mescal, watched a sultry lass in a black Merry Widow festooned with scarlet ribbons settle briefly on the lap of a deck hand sporting a watch cap and pea coat, then inveigle him into a stroll behind a red curtain near the bandstand. Another lovely headed my way, her third approach, and I'd just about decided to make her my Friday night consolation companion when I heard a "toot, toooot" from the front door. Julian had arrived.

Suddenly the gloom evaporated. When Julian stepped into a room, everyone sought to bask in the sun of his company. Eyes turned toward his sandy hair and beaming smile as naturally as daisies to the sun. Handsome he was, but I always thought his joie de vivre drew people more than his looks. He worked his way through a gauntlet of handshakes like a politician while I ordered fresh drinks. He finally reached me and seized his glass.

"Mud in your eye, Big Brother," he said. We tossed our shots down in a gulp. Julian closed his eyes, shook his head, and blubbered his lips like a horse.

"Again, Dan," he called to the barkeep. "How's tricks?"

"Can't complain, Julian," the bartender said as he poured. "You paying or is Big Brother, here, picking up the tab?"

"Hey, on the cuff."

"No can do, Julian. Cash only till you clear up what's overdue."

"Hear that, Andy? The whole Maxwell empire at my fingertips, and they won't even advance me a jigger of cheap booze."

I flipped the bartender two silver dollars. "That ought to keep our glasses full for a while longer, eh, Dan?"

"Keep the cash coming, Big Brother, and I'll keep pouring."

I turned to Julian. "Glad you made it. Another five minutes, I'd have been in the back with Siren Jenny over there." My prospective date had deserted me for a gent in a threadbare frock coat.

"Oooh," he said, "You're liable pick up some crawly critters from the girls in here."

"I'd name them after you because you kept me waiting so long I turned desperate."

"There's many a slip twixt one bar and the next in these parts," Julian said. "Especially on a Friday night."

"And what slipped you up this time?"

"Andy," he said, "not half an hour ago I had enough cash sitting in front of me to take us both around the world and back again. Just needed an easy-way six. What do I get? An easy way seven. All those pictures in my head of brown women and round coconuts? Poof. Dan, hit us again. We got to use up Andy's money."

My glass barely needed topping off, but Julian's was empty.

"Julian, are you open to a suggestion?" I knew it was a stupid question the second I asked it, but when he got this far into his cups, I somehow couldn't help acting like a parent. A year earlier, Julian had stormed off our Sierra ranch after an argument with Mother and declared his intention to adventure his way over the seven seas. So far, he'd gotten no closer to sailing out the Golden Gate than the wharves, dives, and fleshpots of the Barbary Coast.

"Andy, I know you're gonna tell me I should work my way to Tahiti, but why? Trip of a lifetime and I'll miss the benefits if I'm scrubbing decks." He surveyed the teeming space before us and gestured toward a nearby poker game, one of several scattered among the tables.

"Do you have any idea how much money's in play out there right now, Brother? Thousands. And this isn't even a proper gambling hall. I need only one little jackpot. It'll come. And soon. I can feel it."

"Perhaps if you went back to the Circle M…" Still the parent. Still the fool.

"Those bar girls will be wearing nuns' habits before I go crawling back there, Andy. You know that."

I started to object, swallowed my words. "Forgive me for sounding like Mother?" I lifted my glass.

"And me for playing the naughty child?" We emptied our glasses and turned to Dan for a refill. A grizzled man in a checked shirt and red suspenders sidled between us.

"Evening, Julian," he said.

"Howdy, Mitchell." Julian focused his gaze on the row of bottles behind the bar.

"Time's up, Julian," he said.

"Bad manners, Mitchell," I said. "You want to apologize now?" Julian waved, shook his head.

"I have until Monday," he said. He was smiling.

"I don't trust I'll find you Monday."

"Have a drink on me, Mitchell, and I'll see you Monday noon, Pier Twenty-Three. Set him up, Dan."

"Come on, Little Brother," I said. "Let's go. The Bella Vista or some place that smells better."

"Great idea." Julian shoved away from the bar, yelled "toot, toooot," and plunged back into the crowd like a seal into the waves. I followed in his wake, glanced over my shoulder to find Mitchell hurling a poisonous glare across his free whisky as we ducked through the door, up the stairs, and into the cold murk of July's fog.

"How much do you owe that Mitchell?" I said. Julian teetered a little on the last step up to the boardwalk. I extended a steadying hand.

"The man's only trying to persuade himself he's a hardcase." He regained his balance and stepped to the curbside gaslight.

"I'm sorry to admit it, Julian, but the Bella Vista's beyond my purse. I heard there's a new can-can girl at The Cave down on Kearny—"

I never finished my thought because a huge shadow loomed from the fog and lurched into Julian with such force that he had to grab the light pole to keep his feet.

"Watch who you're pushing around," Julian said. The cone of thin light revealed a man who was big and—judging from the dusky skin and lank, shoulder-length hair—Indian.

"I'll walk where I want to walk," he said.

"Seems to me you haven't learned how to walk at all," Julian said.

Julian was more of an athlete and fighter than I ever was. But he was smaller-boned and shorter, full of drink and in no shape to beat down an opponent several inches taller and thirty or forty pounds heavier. Still, a terrier will attack a mastiff, and Julian shoved the bigger man, who moved not an inch but simply lifted Julian and threw him toward me. I grabbed my brother's shoulders, put him behind me, and stepped between the combatants.

"Hold it. There's no need—" A kick to my privates stopped me mid-sentence, mid-stride, and felled me like a rotten tree. We get tested. Sometimes we pass, sometimes we don't. I failed that night, watched—hurting, helpless, gasping—as the man I would soon know as Michael Yellow Squirrel pulled a knife, rammed it low and hard into Julian's belly, then sliced upwards, the way a man guts a trout. Julian groaned, raised to his tiptoes, and seemed to float for a moment on the point of the blade, a hovering angel.

"Die, you Maxwell son of a bitch," Yellow Squirrel snarled. Then he pulled the knife free and watched Julian crumple silently to the boardwalk. I lifted myself to a knee as the Indian turned my way. Certain I was next, I readied myself to launch toward his knees, though what I would do if I managed to bring him down I still can't say. Luckily, I didn't have to find out. Whistles sounded and two policemen brandishing pistols and nightsticks bounded from the gloom.

"Drop it, redskin. No scalps tonight." The Indian hesitated, then flicked his wrist and sent the knife thunking into the boardwalk, where it quivered beside Julian's trembling foot. Then he raised his hands in surrender.

I scrambled toward my brother. His shirt and flesh were ripped and soaked red, his eyes blank as unminted coins. I looked up and saw Yellow Squirrel smile as the policemen put him in handcuffs.

"You're too damned late," I yelled to the cops as I tried to push together the edges of the bloody crevice in Julian's belly. It was like trying to close the very gates of hell.

JULY 13

CHAPTER TWO

It took me over a week to make my way to San Francisco County Jail to confront Yellow Squirrel. I'd burned to come sooner, but all the arrangements—claiming my brother's body, summoning Mother from the ranch, setting up the funeral—had fallen to me. Now, the days of guilt, grief, anger, and questions chewed my insides as I climbed the jailhouse steps.

Mother had accepted the official explanation of the murder as a chance encounter between a couple of drunks, but I wouldn't. Why had Yellow Squirrel called out "Maxwell"? How did he know Julian? I wanted answers, and my family's name had enough influence in this part of California to buy me ten minutes with my brother's killer even though I wasn't the law or part of his family. I'd been two years older than Julian, but I was more of scholar than a warrior. His killing had changed my attitude, and I was in a hanging mood, for the first time in my life.

I felt somewhat like a prisoner myself when I stepped into the interview room and heard the door clang shut behind me. This was a cell in itself—limestone cold and dank as a cave despite the electric glare of modern lighting, redolent of *The Inferno's* icebound lowest level.

A riveted door swung open and a deputy escorted the Indian in. Even manacled hand and foot, Michael Yellow Squirrel carried himself upright, like a free man. He looked as massive as I remembered, though older—mid-forties, perhaps. His face was expressionless, but his eyes focused steadily on mine. I stared right back. Hard work. The deputy tapped the chair opposite

me with his nightstick. Yellow Squirrel lowered himself deliberately into the seat without glancing away.

"It's ten minutes you'll have now," the deputy said. I heard his brogue, thought to get on his good side.

"Thank you, Sergeant," I answered. "My grandmother's family was from County Cork, by the way. Name of O'Doul." He pulled a silver railroad watch from his pocket.

"I hail from Kerry," he said. "Name of Calhoun, and if I was from Cork, I'd keep it to meself. Ten minutes starts now." He replaced the watch and took up a station near the cellblock door. I placed my hands on the back of my chair and leaned toward the prisoner.

"Let's get right to the point," I said. "This was more than a street fight, wasn't it?"

"You think so?"

"What you said at the end—'Die, you Maxwell son of a bitch.' Explain that." I searched his gaze for hints of nervousness, for any crack I could use to pry my way into his mind. His wide face lay still and opaque as a summer pond.

"Is that what I said? I don't remember." His English was as natural as mine, a contrast to the guttural broken utterings of the Shoshones who frequented the area around the Circle M.

"Oh, you have amnesia now, do you?" I chuckled. "That's rich, isn't it deputy? Killed a man and can't remember." Calhoun smiled slightly.

"Oh, I remember the killing part, Big Brother." He unfolded his arms and leaned toward the table, sneered. His left incisor was missing, other teeth decayed yellow and brown. He smelled moldy.

"What do you have against Julian? Or maybe you have something against the whole Maxwell family," I said. He leaned back. "That's it, isn't it? What did we do to you?"

"You're the scholar. Research it." It appeared the man knew as much about the family as we knew about each other.

"I could, but I don't think I'll have time between now and your hanging," I said.

"You're going to hang me now? Without even a trial?"

"What did you think you'd get? Thirty days? You're an Indian. You stabbed an unarmed white man to death."

His smile disappeared, his cheeks and fists clenched, and he rose. Our faces hovered inches apart.

"Even if it happens, hanging me won't end this, Big Brother."

Sergeant Calhoun rushed over and rapped his nightstick on the table. "That'll do. Time's up."

"Like hell." I turned on him. "This man just admitted he has a vendetta against my whole family. I mean to get to the bottom of it."

"I heard him," the deputy answered. "He's only another liquored-up redskin on his way to hell. Liable to be saying anything to get your goat."

"He's already killed my brother. What does he have to do before you take him seriously?"

"The sheriff said ten minutes, County Cork, and ten minutes you've had."

"I'll be seeing Sheriff O'Neill when I leave here, and if you value those chevrons, Badge Number 609, you'll allow us to finish this conversation. The names 'Maxwell' and the 'Circle M Ranch' mean a good deal even here in the big city."

The sergeant's eyes narrowed, jaw hardened, baton twitched. A small man with too much authority for his own good.

"Yes, sir. Just doing me job, sir. Whatever you say, sir. Five minutes. No matter if your name was Roosevelt." He huffed a few feet off and stood against a wall, one hand on his sidearm, the other on his nightstick.

I turned back to Yellow Squirrel. Tacked in another direction. "I guess I misjudged you, Michael. I took you for a mere brute. Now I see you're quite the tease. All this mysterious talk about life after hanging. Care to let us know who else is in on this? What they might be planning?"

The grin returned. He cocked his head and regarded me as if from behind a tree. "You afraid your brand-new college degree won't protect you from the savages, little white boy?"

"It's all over for you now, my friend, and it won't be long before you and your partners will be cellmates anyhow. Why not save everyone the trouble and spill everything here and now?"

Yellow Squirrel leaned forward and whispered. "Whatever you know, you aren't man enough to do anything about it."

I leaned back in my chair, smiled. "Quite the warrior, aren't you? When your opponent's unarmed."

He stood, slammed his chains on the table. I stayed seated, smiling, taunting, hoping for Calhoun to intercede.

"Amuse yourself now, Andrew Maxwell, but mark these words. Your brother was not the first, and he—will—not—be—the—last. By the next full moon, every last Maxwell, kith and kin, will be dead."

I stood, hoped I appeared resolute even though I felt like a boxer striving to keep his feet after a hard right to the jaw. Kith and kin. If Julian wasn't the first, how far back did all this go? What Maxwells besides Mother and me? Was the original victim someone on the Circle M? My grandparents were dead, but not, as far as I knew, murdered. My vanished father? Someone before that?

"Are you going to let these threats pass, Sergeant?" I said.

"What do you expect him to do?" Yellow Squirrel said. "Arrest me?" I swear the guard stifled a laugh as he jabbed Yellow Squirrel in the back with a nightstick.

"This one ain't going to do no harm to no one else." Calhoun rapped twice on the chair. "We'll see to that, Mr. Cork." He nodded and smiled as he jabbed the prisoner in the kidneys.

Yellow Squirrel stood and turned toward the exit. He managed a last grin and a wink over his shoulder as he shuffled through the door, ankle chains jingling against the concrete floor.

"We'll see how wide you grin with a rope around your neck," I called. The door slammed on his laugh.

I rushed from the interview room and leaped up the stairs toward Sheriff O'Neill's office. Once I told him about this conversation he'd have no alternative but to launch a full investigation of Julian's killing. He was, after all, the agent of justice itself.

CHAPTER THREE

I barged into O'Neill's office only to find he was out of town. "For a few days," the secretary said.

I leaned across the counter. "I must see him before the trial."

He dipped his pen in an inkwell, eyes on some document. "What trial is that?"

"Michael Yellow Squirrel, of course."

"Ah, well, yes, the Indian gentleman. I would expect a week or so at the most. Sheriff O'Neill prefers the district attorney to clear the jails of Indians as expeditiously as possible. Creates unrest in the cells."

"Well, if he thinks that creates unrest, make sure he reads this." I scrawled a note demanding the sheriff investigate Yellow Squirrel's threats, printed "Urgent. From Andrew Maxwell" on the envelope, and hurried from the jail. I'd doubtless need O'Neill's assistance eventually, but I had no intention of waiting for his return before I began looking for answers.

* * *

I passed through justice building doors and looked down on the creative chaos of Portsmouth Square. San Francisco was still rebuilding from earthquake and fires of two years before. Hammers pounded. Carpenters, bricklayers, and hod-carriers swarmed the scaffolds. Horse-drawn wagons full of red bricks, raw lumber, and cement jammed the streets. The breeze carried a repellent perfume of pitch, manure, wet lime and clay. South and west, upturned eaves marked Chinatown's meandering boundaries.

I rushed down Clay Street toward The Ferry Building's tower, intent on catching a boat to Berkeley. A full moon had just passed. I had at most a month to thwart whatever Yellow Squirrel and his cohorts had in mind. I wanted to get to my room, my desk. Sit, study, analyze, plan. I figured to attack the problem using all those student skills I'd honed on my way to my degree.

I worked my way through a knot of high-collared, dark-cravated gentlemen, and my heart twisted to think that even if my long-lost lawyer father were among them, we'd not recognize one another. Andrew Stover. His name is about all I knew about him. Had he heard about Julian's death? Would he care? Would this peril to the Maxwells concern him, or had he left us that far behind?

Beyond the homburgs, a tall Indian man, a pair of native women beside him, caught my attention. He was about Yellow Squirrel's age and at least three or four inches taller than my six feet. A blue and red blanket draped his shoulders. Judging by age and resemblance, the women appeared to be mother and daughter. It was not uncommon to see Indians around the Circle M—a diminutive people compared to these, many of the women's chins and cheeks still tattooed in the old way. But Indians of any tribe were unusual on the city's downtown streets, and this group drew stares.

The walkway was too narrow for all of us, so I moved to the outside, expecting them to adjust so we could all pass. Instead, a powerful shove sent me sprawling in the street.

"Out of the way, Maxwell," the Indian said.

My skull banged the pavement, and light burst in my head. I was woozy for a moment, then heard the rumble of an approaching brick wagon, iron-clad wheels headed downhill at a fast clip. I spun out of the way just in time and just short of a pile of urine-soaked horse droppings.

The smell of the ammoniac mess revived me quickly, but by the time I gained my feet, the trio was out of sight. I pursued, pushed and elbowed my way through curses and squeals. Out of the way, Maxwell. He was certainly part of the conspiracy. I jostled an offended matron in a hobble skirt, scrambled around a snorting, kerosene-stinking automobile, and sighted the blue and red blanket in the next block. My first impulse had been to confront the man, but I decided he might lead me to some answers. The little group seemed bound for the jail. Yellow Squirrel's family meeting him to plan some attack? But they headed away from the jail, turned up Montgomery Street toward Telegraph Hill, which they skirted by a tortuous route that took us toward the water. Crowds thinned, and I concealed myself in doorways and behind trees like a comic detective from the dime novels of my boyhood.

My quarry turned away from the bay and into the Barbary Coast labyrinth. After sundown, patrons would swarm the bars and brothels, but it was too early for those crowds, and I was forced to remain nearly a block behind to avoid discovery. They appeared unhurried, and their course became so convoluted I abandoned my speculations about their destination. They headed down Jackson Street, past the very sidewalk where Julian had died. His blood still stained the boards outside the padlocked Fandango Club. I breathed deeply and closed my eyes for a moment. My group had turned the corner a block ahead.

When I arrived at the same corner, I realized we were on Kearny Street, had nearly returned to Portsmouth Square and the jail. They'd known I was behind them all along, had led me in a fool's circle, lured me past Julian's death site. Anger overwhelmed caution, and I broke into a run, threaded my way through a thickening mass of pedestrians, grabbed a handful of blanket and yanked. "Hold on, dammit."

The big man turned, snatched the blanket from my grasp, glowered at me, and pointed a finger at my nose. "Stay clear of us, Maxwell." Behind him, the older woman held the younger in protective embrace.

"What's this about?" I said.

His reply came in a whisper. "Owl Feather." He smiled briefly.

"Is that some kind of riddle?"

A policeman stepped between us then. He pushed us each back a step. "Here, now. What's the trouble?"

"This man deliberately shoved me into the street. I'm lucky I wasn't killed."

He turned to the Indian. "What about it, fella?"

"Accident." His voice and face remained placid.

"No," I said. "It was no accident. And he just now threatened my life."

The cop turned to the crowd. "Did any of you see this incident?" No one spoke.

I stepped behind the officer, pointed over his shoulder toward where I'd fallen. "It was back there, not a half-hour ago. Look." I pointed to my muddy pants.

"Perhaps so, but no one saw it, then, did they? Come back when you collect yourself a witness. For now, both of you best be on your way."

The Indian's face had not changed from the moment the policeman interrupted us. He nodded, turned, and herded his family in their original direction. I began to follow, but the policeman pulled my coattail.

"Let's just let them sleeping dogs lay where they're at, young man. Move along now." He pushed me in the opposite direction.

I held up my hands in surrender, smiled and chuckled. "Maybe you're right, officer. Life's too short to get caught up in such trivia, wouldn't you say?"

"Right you are, my boy."

"Good day to you, then," I said.

My pleasantries didn't erase his suspicion, though, and he followed me for a block, me stealing glances over my shoulder the while. Finally, he turned his back. I circled and resumed the chase. I might as well have chased my tail. For all my trouble I'd gained one short phrase. Owl Feather. A name? If so, who was he? Or she?

I kicked the sea wall, peered across the choppy water, muted green under advancing fog, suddenly amazed at my recklessness. The Indians had known I was trailing them. One of them could have stepped out of sight somewhere along the way and slipped a knife in my ribs. Why hadn't they? Not only wasn't I much of a sleuth, I was lucky to be alive after only a few hours at it.

* * *

Bound for Berkeley, I sat on the ferry deck looking across the salty whitecaps toward the hills of Berkeley. A gull squawked, pinned against the sky by the wind, then tipped and swirled toward the east shore where I'd that morning bid farewell to Mother as she boarded the train with Julian's body, bound for burial on our ranch two hundred miles away. Our farewells had been less than convivial.

Mother and I had renewed the argument we'd had four years ago when I'd come to the university. She insisted I stay off the Circle M until I was prepared to return permanently. She'd helped her parents pioneer their mountain fiefdom and intended her sons to maintain the dynasty. I loved the ranch, but I'd set my sights on a professor's life as well. Not that Mother didn't value education—between her instruction and the academic ministrations of numerous tutors, I'd arrived at the university as prepared as any of my formally educated classmates—but she wouldn't countenance my serving two masters. Despite the family wealth, she'd forced me to finance my education with my own hands, which had turned out to be fine with me. It was fun—or at least satisfying—to make my own way. Now, though Julian was gone, she was in no mood to soften her stance. She did accede, with infuriating condescension, to my "visiting" for the burial service.

However, I now felt that winning that argument was no victory. I'd been acting more out of obligation to Julian's memory and a desire to contradict

Mother than out of any need to witness the burial. In my heart, I'd said my last good-bye at the little funeral we'd held in the Hull Undertaking Parlor in Berkeley. I had no need to watch that box of bones dropped into the earth. I'd serve his memory best by investigating the mystery behind his death.

My first task now was to alert Mother about Yellow Squirrel's threats. By the time the ferry docked, I'd drafted a warning telegram to her, including a query about Owl Feather.

And I'd determined where to begin my search while I waited for her answer.

CHAPTER FOUR

Idashed back to my room, extracted a few bills from the two hundred
dollars or so I'd squirreled away from my coal-shoveling wages. Just
enough for the first steps of my investigation. I hoped the cash would
be enough to finance my inquiries through August 13, the date of the next
full moon. There was no time for the scholarly pondering I'd planned. The
situation required more action than study. I caught a return ferry and headed
back to the Barbary Coast.

My forays with Julian had taught me that bars and brothels harbored
secrets that never saw sunlight. I'd start at The Red Rooster, Madame Gabrielle's
parlor brothel on the Nob Hill slope of Sacramento Street, where Julian and
I had spent a couple of life-changing evenings. Nights which had not only
introduced me to the pleasures of the night, but nearly sunk the ship of my
romance with one Virginia Campbell, the beauty I'd been pursuing like
young Werther for a year.

Mother always said Julian was full of the devil, but I had some devil
in me as well, and I was glad to play Dante to my brother's Virgil for my first
journey to the Barbary Coast underworld. Flush with winnings from a back-
alley crap game, he'd poked a finger in my chest like a drill sergeant. "You're
going to lose your cherry tonight, Big Brother, and I'm paying."

I brought up the matter of diseases.

"Hey, Andy, you're my brother. Nothing for you but clean uptown
whores."

Madame Gabrielle's cry of, "Company, girls," had summoned a parade of six women into the red-draped lounge for what she called her "auction." We instantly chose the voluptuous Chilean twins, Lucita and Liliana, as our guides to the ecstasies of The Rooster, and they led us to delights I had never imagined.

The first evening led to a second, when I'd floated back with Julian on a randy cloud, filled with visions I'd have given gold to realize. In the end, that caper cost me ten dollars, not including champagne—more than a week's wages. And it had, I now feared, cost me Virginia as well.

Virginia's father, a state senator, no less, spotted Julian and me on that second night when we inadvertently walked in on his meant-to-be-private viewing of the evening's merchandise. I was embarrassed, but not he. He'd gone straight to Virginia with the declaration that after what he'd learned "on good authority," no daughter of the eminent James Campbell would henceforth be consorting with the likes of me.

Up to then, she'd been a rebellious child. Suddenly she'd become the compliant daughter. I'd planned to spend this very evening pleading my case to her once more, but as I approached the place Madame Gabrielle had called The Red Cock before the police forced her to change the name, I forced Virginia from my thoughts.

I stepped into the shadows outside the house and dug some cash out of the small purse I'd pinned deep in my underwear to avoid pickpockets. Julian had taught me it was the most secure place. "Even your shoes and socks aren't safe if they blackjack you, but they seldom check down there."

"Come in, come in," Gabrielle said. "And where is your handsome brother, my dear?" She was short, stout, and befeathered.

"He… he couldn't come tonight. Listen, Madame Gabrielle, I must see Lucita and Liliana. Are they free?"

"Both of them? You're feeling like a stallion tonight, are you?" I tried to match her chuckle, but managed only a wan smile. "Of course you know they are not *free*." She giggled and held out her hand, palm up.

I smiled. "If they're *available*, I was hoping I could merely talk to them for a few minutes."

She frowned and looked at me sideways. "Ah, but it is their time that is valuable. What you do or don't do, that's your choice, my friend." She twirled the end of the red boa that draped her breast.

"I understand. Of course I will pay." I handed her two dollars, a tenth of what one regular session with both of them would cost. She took it with her right hand. The boa continued twirling in her left.

"You wish to *talk* for one minute, then."

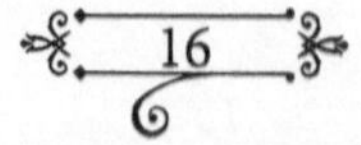

I gave her a five. She frowned again. I longed for Julian's flourish and assurance. I wasn't negotiating so much as begging. "I was hoping for fifteen minutes."

"For two of my most popular girls?" She tossed the boa around her neck and planted hand on hip.

I finally bought five minutes for ten dollars. Twice what I'd hoped would get me fifteen. I'd severely underestimated how much cash this trek would take "The same room you and your brother used previously is vacant, Mr. Maxwell." She tucked the bills into her cleavage.

I sat in a frail wooden chair against the wall. A sweet and tart odor composed of rosewater and lye soap permeated the space. The room was so small my knees nearly touched the iron bedstead. Shredded lace drooped from the curtains, shredded lilacs from the wallpaper, and random nails peppered the wall. A porcelain washbowl draped with wet cloths sat on a bare table across the room. Tawdry. I hadn't recalled it that way.

The twins entered without knocking. They wore identical flowered and filmy robes that left just enough to the imagination to pull the last dime out of customers as hungry as we had been to see the rest. I noticed stained ruffles and bad teeth. I had either not seen them or ignored them before. Still, their generous lips and dark eyes combined with memories of the other evenings to ignite a heat that set me squirming.

Lucita dimmed the gaslight. All the imperfections in the girls and their surroundings began to dissolve. The gift of shadows.

"You will not enjoy a bottle of champagne, señor?" It was the one with the mole on her cheek.

"No time for that, Lucita. I need information only."

They lounged on the mattress, filmy robes half-open. "I've come to ask about the man who killed my brother, Julian. You remember Julian?"

"Ah, the Señor Julian. Yes, of course we remember. He is dead?" They both put their hands to their cheeks.

"Murdered. By an Indian named Yellow Squirrel. He's bent on killing my whole family, and he has a partner, another big Indian. I don't know his name. I thought you might have seen them or heard something."

"He is Indian. He would not come here," Liliana said. "He would have to go to the cribs downtown or perhaps Chinatown," Lucita said.

"But you talk to other girls. Maybe one of them mentioned him?"

Madame Gabrielle knocked on the door once, then opened it. "Time's up, sugar. Come on, girls. Auction time." Lucita and Liliana rose and lolled elegantly into the hallway. I followed. Madame Gabrielle took my hand.

"Let me show you the way out, sweetheart. I have no wish to repeat the interruption with that other gentleman."

"Ah, so the senator is here again, is he? I'd like to say hello."

"Who's here and who's not is none of your business. Now haul yourself out of here pronto. There's the exit."

"Gabrielle… Madame. I'm looking for information." I spoke as fast as I could. "An Indian called Yellow Squirrel murdered my brother. He says my mother and I are going to be killed as well. He's in jail, but I'm trying to track down an accomplice, a big Indian. Or perhaps Yellow Squirrel bragged to some girls somewhere."

"Any Indian came to my door I'd send him down to the nigger houses with the rest of his kind, and we don't talk about our clients and ain't a whore in town would tell you anything with that little bit"—she held her thumb and forefinger an inch apart and wiggled them near her crotch—"of cash you're flashing. Now hit the road, buster, before I call a cop." She laughed and pulled the door open. I jammed my hands in my pockets and hurried down the front steps.

"Oh, hell, wait a minute," Gabrielle called as I reached the sidewalk. "I can't stand to see a little boy pout like that. Try Charley Hung down on China Alley. He knows about every piece of garbage that washes up in this city. But he'll give you nothing for free."

I was plainly out of my element without either Julian's silver tongue, nor enough money to replace it. I kicked myself again for not bringing a bigger bankroll. I started downhill toward the Embarcadero, intending to proceed to the Ferry Building and catch the last boat to the East Bay. But Gabrielle had given me a lead, and I still had a ten-dollar bill and a nickel for boat fare in my purse. Not much, but if I played my cards right, it might buy me an audience with Charley Hung. I turned up Grant Street toward the heart of Chinatown.

CHAPTER FIVE

China Alley teemed like a carnival midway, forcing me to shoulder through the pleasure-seekers sideways. Young Chinese girls wiggled behind the bars of their cribs luring customers with cries of "Nice China girl. Come inside please," granting an occasional peek at the pre-adolescent wares beneath their silk smocks. They wore forlorn smiles that would tempt only the drunk or desperate. There seemed to be ample supplies of both.

I pushed my way through a choking stink of dung, urine, tobacco smoke and sweaty flesh, searched for some indication of a business that belonged to Charley Hung. I found none, but near the end of the alley, a sign reading Silk Road was mounted above steps leading below the sidewalk to a narrow red door. Two red-faced soldiers stumbled up the stairs, brushed past me on their laughing pursuit of more pleasures of the night. I retraced their steps and found myself in a low-ceilinged room lined by booths curtained with beaded strings, black-and-red lacquered cords that barely screened the writhing bodies behind them. A bar, set a couple of feet off the floor, dominated one end of the smoke-hazed room, and a twisting red and green dragon decorated the huge mirror behind it. A bartender dispensed liquor through a window the size of a teller's cage.

Patrons sat at tables, and silk-gowned girls slid around the room fetching drinks, urging men to a session in a booth. I dug the ten-dollar bill from my

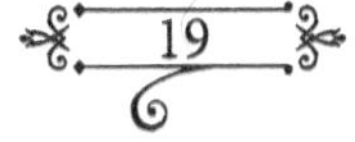

purse and approached the bartender. He waved me away with a skinny hand tipped with long fingernails.

"Table. Go to a table."

"I don't want a table. I want to see Charlie Hung."

"Never hear of him. Now go." He waved me aside and shoved a bottle of whisky and a glass to one of the girls who had come up behind me. Stone-faced, she ferried the booze back to her booth. When she parted the beads, I beheld the brief tableau of a grizzled man with a large grin reaching for the bottle with one hand and her breast with the other.

I stepped back to the window. "I have a proposition for Mr. Hung that could yield him a great deal of money."

He took the skull cap from his head and waved me away. "You want drink, take a table. You don't want drink. Go." He pulled a cord that hung from the ceiling.

"You're a brave man to chance the wrath of Charley Hung," I said. I was about to turn when a hand grabbed my shoulder and spun me around. His clothing was nondescript, but the man who filled it seemed as broad as any bull on the Circle M. He also towered high enough that my eyes came level with his missing left ear. His face was calm, almost bored.

"Boss says you go, you go."

"It would be to Mr. Hung's advantage to meet with me." I waved the bill in the air. "And perhaps to yours as well." I stepped over and laid the bill on the bar. "There's a great deal more where that came from," I said. "The name's Maxwell." And I walked out of the bar and up the steps. I thought it likely that I'd thrown the money down a rathole, but at least I'd escaped uninjured.

Discouraged, disappointed, I plowed back through the alley, ignoring the smells and the grasping fingers. It was well after midnight, and until morning there'd be no boats to take the nickel I'd saved to get home. The sky was overcast, the breeze that had brought in the fog had lost neither intensity nor chill. I decided to walk the streets to keep warm.

As I crossed Grant Street, a small man in dark denim and a red skull cap cut in front of me and beckoned me with a flick of a wrist. I followed his shuffling steps down the street and watched him turn into a narrow space between two brick buildings. It was barely wide enough for me to stand square, too tight even to be called an alley.

Snare or invitation? I stepped into the alley gingerly, waited for my eyes to adjust, then followed him to the end, where we descended steps much like those that led into Silk Road. In this instance, the door he opened was black.

I coughed, and my eyes burned as I peered into the sweet fog of what had to be opium. Inert forms lay on couches and benches, and mute shadows carried bamboo pipes back and forth. My guide shuffled across the floor, opened another door, hurried me into the next room, then closed the door behind me. He remained outside.

Charley Hung's office was draped in yellow silk. The man himself sat behind a lacquered desk carved with figures of men and women engaged in acts and in positions beyond even those with which Liliana and Lucita had regaled us. Ivory statuary in the same theme crowded shelves around the room. Hung was dressed in a green silk robe secured by a red sash. His head was shaved bald, his English impeccable.

"You claim to have something for me, sir?" he said. "Be fairly warned that any deception or treachery will earn you passage on a freighter to my ancestral home in Szechwan."

I had heard a great deal about the Oriental penchant for indirection, had thought to fashion a few somewhat vague remarks while I steered the conversation my way. But this particular Asian individual appeared averse to such tactics.

"Yes, Mr. Hung. I have a situation that we could perhaps turn to our mutual advantage. You see, I'm convinced someone's set out to murder my family. If you could help prevent it, the Maxwells would be grateful and willing to show it." I'd need Mother's consent, of course, but that was a problem for later. Hung nodded. My confidence rose.

"You're Julian's big brother," he said.

I nodded, nonplussed. What did he know of Julian? I waited, hoping he'd give me a clue. He broke the silence.

"Julian was a fairly regular customer when he had money. Which is a matter we'll broach presently. What's this about someone killing your family?"

"Perhaps if I mentioned a certain Indian gentleman named Michael Yellow Squirrel?"

"An unsavory individual. He nearly killed one of my babies. Her usefulness was nearly exhausted or I'd have subjected him to more than a roughing up and banishment from my establishments."

"He butchered Julian and said no Maxwell would survive the full moon."

"That's all?"

"There's another Indian in on this, I believe. A large man. Perhaps wrapped in a red and blue blanket?"

"I can't assist you, I'm afraid." He leaned back in his chair and brushed something from his silk sleeve.

"Allow me to ask about one other name. Owl Feather." Charley Hung brushed the other sleeve, shook his head.

I waited for more, but he sat impassive. It seemed I'd wasted my money and my night on the Coast.

"Well, thank you for your time, Mr. Hung." I rose.

"It's my turn, Mr. Maxwell." He pointed to the chair. The door opened and the huge man from Silk Road entered and stood behind me. He still looked bored. "This ten dollars," Charley Hung pulled my bill from his sleeve and placed it on the desk, "will serve as a down payment on your brother's debt. I assume the rest will be forthcoming presently."

"Julian owed you money? How would that involve me?"

"When Mr. Yellow Squirrel dispatched Mr. Maxwell, the younger, I thought I would be required to dismiss his five hundred dollars as a bad gambling debt. Now that you, Mr. Maxwell, the elder, have so conveniently stepped into the picture, I've changed my mind." Hung smiled.

"Five hundred dollars? How could Julian owe that much?" I stood and leaned across the desk. The one-eared man's hand fell on my shoulder, squeezed hard, and pulled me to my seat. Charley Hung leaned back. His attention seemed drawn to one of the statues above me.

"Do you have any proof? Did he sign anything?"

He chuckled. "Very droll, Mr. Maxwell."

"Mr. Hung. Even if your story is not pure fabrication, it was Julian's debt, not mine. And you can't extort money I don't have." I began to rise again, but stopped myself before the big hand fell.

"And how were you going to obtain the funds to pay me for preventing your family's massacre, Mr. Maxwell?" He was still looking at the statue.

"You'd have a better chance of snatching money from the jaws of a dragon than getting my mother to pay Julian's debts," I said.

Charley Hung turned his eyes from the statue to me. His eyes shone black as lacquered beads. "I have taken the generous measure of freezing the interest on what your brother owes me. Otherwise the amount would be twice five hundred by the time of Mr. Yellow Squirrel's trial, which is when I expect payment."

"But that's only about a week away." I jumped to my feet, dodged the hand that reached for me.

"I remind you that many Orient-bound ships are in need of sailors, Mr. Maxwell." He waved his hand and One-Ear propelled me through a rear door and into a darkness as black as the inside of Jonah's whale.

CHAPTER SIX

I felt my way down the alley, emerging at last on Grant Street and headed out of Chinatown. I searched my mind for ways to secure the five hundred. Short of robbery, the only possible method was to wire Mother. Besides the near-certainty that she'd refuse, the very thought was humiliating. Damn Julian anyway. Even dead, he muddled my existence as much as he had in life.

* * *

I recalled how surprised I'd been to find my brother sitting on the doorstep of my boarding house when I returned from class one day a year ago. It was only midday, but he'd needed the help of the porch railing to stand and greet me.

"Hello, Andy. How about we go get a drink?" He was dressed as if he'd come in directly from the range—riding boots, Levi's, denim shirt, wide-brimmed, high-crowned felt hat adorned with a several sets of rattlesnake rattles on the band.

I shook my head. "It appears you've had a few already."

"You're darn tootin'; and I'm planning to have a few more. Mother and me just had a shootout like you've never seen, and I left home and I ain't going back, so that calls for a toot, don't you think?" He pulled an invisible cord to an imaginary steam whistle. "Toot tooooot."

"Listen, Julian, I have an appointment. Why don't you just take a nap up in my room? We can go out when I return."

"I don't need a nap. Don't you want to hear what happened?"

"Of course, but can't it wait a little?"

"What's so important you can't see your long-lost little brother?" Something on my face must have given a clue. "Oh, a date, isn't it? Well, come on, introduce me. I'll need to approve anyway before things go too far." He laughed and pushed me along the sidewalk.

"You look cute in your little flat hat and tweed coat, Andy. Bet she's head over teakettle for you."

I wasn't sure how Virginia would react to Julian, but I saw no easy way to avoid taking him along to what had become our regular Wednesday afternoon tea date.

The Black Sheep was a combination teashop and ice cream parlor with round marble tables and wrought iron chairs. Crystal bud-vases of fresh pansies or primroses adorned the tabletops. The whole atmosphere was too snobby for my taste, but Virginia loved the gentility. We were a few minutes late, and I could see through the window that she was already seated and waiting, her hands folded primly on the table. A diminutive, flower-bedecked straw hat crowned her pale locks. Her chiffon skirt fell in a classic Greek pattern.

"Now, be a gentleman, Julian," I whispered. "This isn't a barroom."

"You think I don't know how to act?" he said. "I know how to act. Come on."

Virginia's back was to the door, and she didn't turn until I spoke. "I apologize for being late. I've brought a special guest. Allow me to present my brother, Julian. This is Virginia Campbell."

Julian nodded. He and Virginia shared a look of puzzlement, then recognition.

"Mr. Maxwell?"

"Miss Campbell."

"You know each other?" I said. "How?"

"Andy, you know Mother sees that every California bigwig dines at the Circle M at one time or another. She wouldn't neglect a prominent state senator and his beautiful daughter."

Virginia shook a finger at me. "And shame on you, Andy, for not telling me you were one of the Circle M Maxwells."

"Let's be seated," I said. I was attempting to buy some time, wondering how I could help Virginia understand that I'd concealed my background out of humility rather than deceit. A waitress in a black pinafore and a doily-like excuse for an apron took our order. I could feel Virginia's stare. I smiled and sighed.

"If the truth be known, I'm not certain I am one of the Circle M Maxwells any longer. Mother all but disowned me when I entered the university. She said if I couldn't remain on the ranch and behave like a Maxwell, I shouldn't pretend to be one."

"Why, I can't imagine that. She seemed so lovely and gracious."

"She can be," Julian said. "As long as you don't cross her. I'm virtually in the same boat as Andy now, except I banished myself."

The waitress brought a tray bearing a steaming teapot, a plate of assorted sweets, and little flowered cups and saucers. While she poured and Virginia examined the pastry choices, Julian slid a flask from under the table and dumped a generous helping into his tea. I shook my head and pursed my lips in anger. He smiled and offered me a portion. I signaled refusal. Virginia's voice sent the flask back into hiding.

"And how did you raise your mother's ire, Julian? Did you wish to come to school also?"

"School, Ginny?" he said. "Mind if I call you that?"

"No one else does, but if you like."

"Good. 'Virginia' sounds stuffy, and we know each other too well for 'Miss Campbell,' don't you think?"

"Manners, Julian, manners," I said.

"Yes, Mother." He laughed, then stuffed a whole napoleon in his mouth. Virginia smiled. I glared.

"You were speaking of school, Julian," she said.

"Mmm." He held up his hand and swallowed hard. "School isn't the place for Julian, Ginny girl. No, this argument was all about Bridget."

"Bridget Jensen?" I said. "What about her?"

Julian leaned over his cup. "She's beautiful." I remembered Bridget as scrawny and whey-faced, a shy little girl whom I knew primarily from watching her clean up around her mother's café in Sawtooth Wells. "Hey, wipe that smirk off your face, Andy. You haven't seen her for three years."

"I'll take your word for it," I said. "What's the matter? Didn't Mother agree with your assessment of her looks?"

"It had nothing to do with looks. It had to do with—"he tipped his nose in the air and affected a British accent—"Prestige. Class. Rubbish of that sort."

My next comment surprised me. "Perhaps it was more a matter of how young you both are." It was the first time I'd taken this parental tone with him. He and I had always formed a team to oppose the adults—he, the defiant, I, the devious one. Perhaps Virginia's hauteur was influencing me.

"Oh, sure, that came up, too. But it wasn't really the point. Bridget's not good enough for the Circle M, as if it's some sort of holy ground, like Jerusalem or Mecca. Bierstadt painted it. John Muir walked it. Governors eat there. Never mind that Grandfather was a storekeeper or that Grandmother ran off to live with the Indians."

I burst in on his story. "You said that to her?"

"Hell, yes I said that. Told her she could own her ranch but she couldn't own me." Julian pounded the table. Our teacups rattled. Patrons' heads turned. The waitress' hand went to her mouth. Virginia was no longer smiling. She raised her eyebrows at me.

"Andy?" she said.

"So, here I am." Julian drained his cup. "I need another one." This time, the flask was not surreptitious nor was the liquor diluted with tea. I covered his cup with my hand.

"No more, Julian. You promised."

"Promises, promises." He jerked the teacup so hard from under my palm that it flew out of his hand and smashed in a pool on the slate floor. The odor of bourbon floated through the room.

Virginia scooted her chair back. "I think I'd better be going." She scampered toward the door as gracefully as her hobble skirt would allow. I stood and reached toward her.

"Virginia, don't. It'll be all right." But she didn't stop. I turned back toward the table and almost ran into Julian, who had moved up behind me. "Well, Little Brother, happy with the mess you've made?"

"Ah, no harm done, Andy." We were standing in the middle of the restaurant. The waitress was picking up the shards of the cup and eyeing us.

"Here, sweetheart," he said. He tossed two dollars on the table. "That ought to take care of things." He turned back to me. "She'll be back, Andy. She's in love with you. I can tell." I pulled the door open and pointed him toward the sidewalk. Once we were outside, I gripped his arm.

"You don't belong here, Julian. Go back home."

"Don't belong there either. I'll get a job on a ship, sail to the South Seas." He held up his hand. "Never mind. Don't say anything. To hell with you. To hell with her. To hell with all of them." He headed toward the ferry landing at the bottom of University Avenue, crossed to San Francisco, and never returned alive to the east side of the bay.

* * *

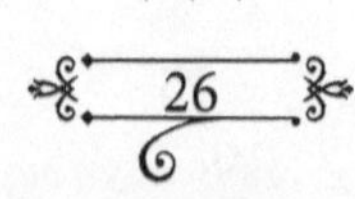

I pulled my grief and anger around me along with my meager jacket. Julian had doubtless spent many nights like this, drifting randomly through neighborhoods, waiting for daylight.

Dawn found me with sad heart and bowed head sitting on the steps of Mission Dolores, first permanent European presence in San Francisco neé Yerba Buena. To protect this mission the Spanish had built a presidio near the Golden Gate. In the battles of the last hundred-plus years, the Mexicans had evicted the Spanish, we Americans had bested the Mexicans, and our military still used the presidio. If anyone knew about Indians it was the army. I turned my steps north and west.

JULY 14

CHAPTER SEVEN

The sun was high by the time I ended my long walk to the Presidio. A surprising amount of earthquake debris remained even this far west of where the army had dynamited blocks of buildings to stop the fires. The Presidio, with its red roofs, green lawns, and white walls looked like a collection of Mediterranean villas overlooking a decaying township. I stated my business to a bored sentinel at the gate, who told me that Colonel Lundren was on an inspection tour and would not return until late afternoon. I didn't fancy waiting or coming this far to return empty-handed.

"Perhaps you can help me," I said

"At your service, sir." The slim, fair-skinned private reminded me of Julian.

"I'm looking for information about Indians. Actually a particular Indian named Owl Feather. Have you heard the name?"

"I apologize, sir. I'm rather new here."

"How about a tall Indian, perhaps with a couple of women?" The private looked blank.

"That's the best description I can give you except perhaps he had a blue and red blanket draped over his shoulders."

"Again, I'm sorry, sir."

"Do you know anyone who might be able to tell me something?"

"Well, there's Sergeant Duffy. He's been through all those Indian wars and such."

"Where can I find him?"

"He tends the stables these days. I'm sure he'll talk to you." He looked quickly around the office and lowered his voice. "If you can sober him up. I saw him headed that way about an hour ago, sir." He gestured toward a group of bars outside the gates.

The bartender in the third saloon I investigated pointed toward a table in the corner. I'd pictured a wizened old geezer with boozy eyes, but Duffy, despite the half-empty glass of spirits before him, appeared soldier perfect—neat mustache, trimmed gray hair. It would have been a good entrée to buy the man another drink, but my nickel would hardly purchase a glass of water. I'd have to accomplish what I could with my powers of persuasion. I strode to his table with what I hoped was a look of upbeat confidence.

"Sergeant Duffy, sir?"

"That's me, youngster." He took a healthy gulp from his glass.

"Mind if I sit down?" He shrugged. I sat.

"The private at the gate said you might be able to give me information about some Indians."

"The cowboy and Indian days are over, young feller. Didn't you know that?" He finished his whisky, slid the glass from hand to hand along the table top.

"Yes, sir, but people seem to think you know a thing or two about them."

"And you don't get to be a 'sir' till you're at least a lieutenant, which I'll never be. Just had to get out of the chill for a spell. Lord, how that wind does blow off the Gate when the fog rolls in." I couldn't tell whether Duffy was evasive, distracted, or just plain drunk.

"Let me explain why I'm here, sir… Sergeant. It's my hope that you can help my family and me out of a difficult situation. Do you know anything about an Indian named Owl Feather?"

"What kind of spot you in anyhow?" He still wasn't looking at me. I slid my chair as subtly as possible to within his line of vision.

"Did you read about that Indian knifing a white man downtown last week?"

"Saw a headline." He nodded, glanced at me, looked away again.

"My brother was the victim." I wished I had a beer to loosen the sudden tightness in my throat. "The murderer's name is Michael Yellow Squirrel."

"Oh?" For a second, I thought I had his attention, but then his eyes wandered.

"They never should have let them Indians off the reservations. Bad for us. Bad for them. Course there ain't never been much in the way of reservations in these parts anyhow. Makes it even worse."

I was getting nowhere and becoming frustrated, struggling to remain calm. Perhaps Duffy was like one of those mules a person has to lead all around the barnyard before persuading them into a stall.

"The private said you've had considerable experience fighting Indians," I said.

"Came within a wink of being with Custer, matter of fact. Got transferred to another outfit a week before. You know, there ain't nothing more grand-looking than one of them warriors on the hunt, but they just don't fit no more. Kinda sad, but there ain't no help for it."

"Just by chance, are you familiar with a tall Indian man, red and blue blanket, two women?" He made eye contact for the first time.

"Drives a little donkey cart?"

"Maybe so."

"It's downright comical the way them redskins overflow that little wagon, like they stole it from some child." He smiled, shook his head and motioned to the bartender to bring him another drink. "Sounds like the one's been coming to the post from time to time wanting the army to kick white people off what he says is Indian land."

"What Indian land?" I leaned forward, my cheeks suddenly warm. Perhaps this was the source of the dispute.

"Up across the Gate a short ways, I guess." His description placed the land in the wrong direction and too close to be Maxwell acreage. My hopes deflated, I settled back in my chair. "I don't doubt he's telling the truth," the sergeant continued. "Them poor devils has been hardly done by many a time. When I was at Fort Bridger, we spent just as much time keeping our own kind off reservations as we did keeping redskins on. But it warn't really no use one way or the other."

"You were stationed at Fort Bridger?"

"Laramie and Bridger both." The bartender brought the whisky.

"On the cuff, sergeant?" the bartender said.

"You don't want a drink, young feller?"

"No thanks." I was lying, but I couldn't afford to be in this man's debt. I should be the one who was buying. "I appreciate the offer, though."

Duffy turned back to the bartender. "Thanks." He sipped from the fresh glass. The bartender seemed about to speak again, but scowled and walked back to the bar. Duffy hadn't answered his question any more than he'd answered mine.

"I guess you wouldn't have run into my grandparents. They came through Bridger with a wagon train in '64."

"Wasn't much left of wagon trains by the time I lighted there in '76."

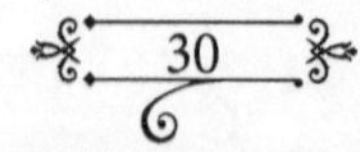

"This big Indian we were talking about, do you know his name, Sergeant Duffy?"

"Calls himself Standing Oak from what I understand. Never talked to him myself." He emptied half the whisky glass in one gulp, looked at it, shook his head. "This'll have to do it for a while. I got to get back on duty."

Feeling I was about to be dismissed, I panicked somewhat. "So you never knew Owl Feather?"

"The name's kinda hazy like. Can't say for sure."

"You have any idea where Standing Oak lives?"

"Nah. Though you might try up around Bodega Bay or thereabouts. Some of them Indians hire out on fishing boats and such. Or they work the farms, too." He took another sip. Made eye contact again. "What do you want with him?"

Now I had to decide how much to reveal. I was fearful that if the word got out I was searching for him, Standing Oak might disappear or retaliate. On the other hand, everyone involved seemed already to know more about me than I did about them. Secrecy was probably impossible.

"I believe Yellow Squirrel's family has something against mine. My name's Andy Maxwell. My brother's name is… was… Julian. I'm attempting to avoid anyone else getting hurt." Duffy's eyes drifted around the room as if he were searching the walls for something. He finally shook his head.

"Like to help you, young fella. These feuds can be an awful thing." He shrugged. "Colonel's going to be back soon." He didn't move, but his eyes drifted away again. This was indeed my dismissal. I thanked him, shook hands, and headed toward the door. I was almost there when he called.

"Maxwell."

"Yes, Sergeant?"

"Your family have a ranch up in the mountains?"

"Yes, the Circle M. You've heard of it?" I returned to the table and stood across from him. He raised his eyes.

"Went up there on a horse buy last year. Pretty country. You know, something's been bothering me about that name, Yellow Squirrel, ever since you said it. Now, I recall a little tyke named Yellow Squirrel used to run in and out of Bridger. Had to shoo him away from the stables many a time. I was afraid he'd get kicked. There were a lot of those little varmints running around the fort. I just remember him cause he kept saying, 'Steal soldier horse. Steal soldier horse.' Kinda cute."

I leaned toward Duffy and held out my hand. "Sergeant, I'm grateful for your help. If I can ever return the favor, you know where the Circle M is." He took my hand, nodded, returned his gaze to the whisky. I left the bartender polishing a spotless glass and the sergeant in command of his table.

I had an urge to jump on a train to Wyoming in search of someone with more than a blurred memory of Owl Feather, a move that would also put me out of Charley Hung's reach. But I couldn't miss testifying at Yellow Squirrel's trial. Besides, it made more sense to keep looking for the man I now knew was Standing Oak or for someone who knew him or knew about him. If I could avoid getting scalped, I might discover what I needed to solve this puzzle. I still had a few days before the trial, so I decided to ferry back to Berkeley for funds and provisions—time I wouldn't have had to waste if I hadn't been so stingy about bringing more cash in the first place—telegraph Mother for help with Julian's gambling debt, then cross the Golden Gate and head for Bodega Bay. A place I'd never been, but going where I'd never been had suddenly become the norm.

CHAPTER EIGHT

I trudged a dusty road up the coast, weary from nearly two days of travel, still angry at the surly farmer who five miles or so earlier had refused me a ride in his empty wagon. My rucksack was heavy, but Mother's answer to my telegram weighed on me even more. She refused to entertain the conspiracy notion, saw it as a ploy to wheedle my way back to the ranch without meeting her conditions. And she saw the idea of paying Julian's debt as capitulating to the criminal enterprises of the Oriental underworld.

I recalled a childhood evening when she was reading Jack and the Beanstalk to me. When she came to the part that described Jack and his mother living alone, I asked about Jack's father.

"I suppose he died, darling," she said.

"Did my papa die too?" This wasn't the first time I had attempted give shape and substance to his shadowy memory.

"No, darling, your papa… went away."

"When is he coming back?"

She kissed the top of my head. "And I'm afraid he won't be back, Andy."

"Doesn't he love us?" I looked up at her. She shook her head slowly, corners of her mouth trembled.

"It isn't that. He just couldn't… Please, Andy, I'll have to explain this to you when you're older. You won't understand now."

But I insisted, and she explained, and she was correct. I didn't understand most of it—how or why Andrew Stover would choose big city lawyering over

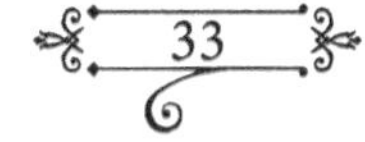

a family and the riches of life on the ranch. But I had a child's fascination with names, and I did understand—and treasure—one remark she made. She pointed to my birthmark, a small, liver-colored figure on my shoulder, shaped not unlike a map of California if one squinted and tipped his head a certain way.

"There's something you should make as much a part of your memory as that birthmark is part of your skin. Your father's name was Andrew, and so is yours. But his name was not Maxwell. And you, Andy, are a Maxwell. Always remember that and honor it."

Honor and remember I had, until I realized that to Mother, honoring the Maxwell name meant subjugating myself to her will. And when I would not submit, she would not yield. And she still wouldn't. Even, apparently, at the risk of all she held important and dear.

* * *

I crested a hill and beheld the shallow cup of Bodega Bay laid out below me. A net-draped sloop pitched fitfully at the dock, and a lone Indian woman stood next to a donkey cart at the base of a sandstone bluff. From the single black braid falling across the ivory shawl that wrapped her shoulders, I knew I'd found Standing Oak, or at least part of his family. I turned my back on the gritty wind, gulped the last tepid drops from my canteen, and rushed down the hill. The woman was, indeed, the younger of the two I had seen with Standing Oak. She stood gazing seaward, her buckskin skirt wet, feet bare, and legs sandy.

She heard me approaching, turned and faced me across the cart. A half-open burlap sack, fresh blue-black mussels spilling from its mouth, rested in the bed. Her cheeks and lips tensed—Fear? Anger? Even wearing this anxious expression, her beauty stopped me for a moment. I guess I'd been focused on Standing Oak so much, I hadn't noticed before. I said nothing, stood captivated by the gentle sienna of her skin and the soft darkness of her eyes, and things went briefly out of kilter, the way they do during a small earthquake. Squaws weren't supposed to be pretty. Virginia was pretty with her pink cheeks and blonde curls, but not Native women. Consuela, maybe in her own way, and Lucita and Lillian. But they belonged in a different category. I was still tongue-tied, trying to force myself to return my concentration to why I was here when she turned away and took several steps toward the ocean. I started after her. "Can we talk for a few minutes?" She stopped and turned back.

"Andrew Maxwell, you'll destroy us and yourself as well. Leave us alone." Like Yellow Squirrel's, the girl's speech was without accent.

"Call me Andy. We can talk better if we know each other's names." I began to circle the cart toward her, palm outstretched. "There's nothing to stop us from being friends, is there?"

She just looked at me. "Or at least friendly. What do you say?"

"We cannot talk." She knelt and lifted a stone, stepped back. The shawl fell from her shoulders. I bent to retrieve it.

"Just a name," I said. I extended the shawl. She drew the rock back, ready to throw. I wasn't afraid, but fighting her would be no way to achieve my purpose. I laid the garment carefully in the wagonbed, stopped and pushed my palms outward.

"All right, but you must know I cannot stand by and wait for Standing Oak and Owl Feather and the Almighty knows who else to destroy my family."

From behind an outcrop appeared the older woman dragging another water-soaked sack. When she saw us, she dropped it and ran across the dunes towards the wagon yelling in panic. Her hair swirled in the breeze as she struggled toward us through the sand. Her eyes were wide and her guttural bellowing, which I supposed was Arapaho but sounded like no language at all, subsided to a whimper when she stopped at the girl's side. The girl lowered the stone, but didn't drop it. Nor did she turn to greet her the woman who from the resemblance had to be her mother. The older woman's dress was drenched. She attempted to grab the rock, but the girl wouldn't relinquish it.

"Please. I mean no harm," I said. I retreated a few steps. "I want only to find Standing Oak."

"My mother's terrified," the girl said. She put her arm around the woman's shoulders. "You must leave now."

"I came all the way from San Francisco to find you. I can't simply leave." Once again the mother began chattering. The girl spoke to her in a comforting voice. She pointed to the bag left behind. The mother began backing toward it.

"Allow me," I said. I worked my way to the dark mound in the gray sand. The mother retreated to her daughter's side. I lugged the briny load, rich with odors of fish and kelp, across the beach and heaved it into the wagon. The women regarded me without expression. The rock remained poised.

"We'll be going now," the daughter said. She urged her mother into the wagon, snatched up her shawl, then climbed to the seat. Neither took her eyes off me. The mother lifted the donkey's reins and slapped the animal into motion. It was a matter of only a few steps to reach the beast's head and grab his halter. The woman cocked her arm, but with the donkey between us, she didn't risk a throw.

"Allow me to come with you," I said. "Or simply arrange for me to meet him."

Mother held to daughter, and the daughter stared past me to the horizon. Both kept silent. They knew by this time I wouldn't attack, but she wouldn't tell me what I wanted to know. Well, they had to live nearby. Someone would know. I stepped aside and motioned for them to pass. She goaded the donkey into a trot, a pace I thought I could sustain for a good while. I jogged after them. Only when they were several yards along the road did the stone finally drop. They soon blended with the tawny grass of the hillside, then disappeared around a point.

I turned to the only other hint of human activity I'd seen in the vicinity—the sloop anchored at the pier. I found a swarthy young man splicing rope on the dilapidated deck. Nets hung from every inch of the gunwales and boom. "Hello, the boat," I called.

He dropped the rope and leaped over the railing to the dock, doffing a blue bandanna, which had covered his head like a scarf. He was not a great deal older than I. "Ah, Signor. You wish to purchase some of my catch. Very fresh." He trailed smells of fish and sweat.

"I'm sorry." I shook my head. "Not today. I wonder if you know those Indian women. The ones who just rode off in the cart?"

"Ah, but Signor. The salmon is excellent. Juicy and mmm." He kissed the tips of his fingers. "People from the ranch they said they would come to buy, but they are not arrived. I make you a very special price."

"Only information, Signor. The name is Maxwell, Andrew Maxwell." I offered my hand.

"Ah, Andrew. My patron saint. A fisherman like me."

He grabbed my hand with both of his and pumped my arm. "I am Giuseppe." It irritated me how people seemed to find a way to talk about themselves no matter what question I asked.

"Yes, Giuseppe. But you have not told me about the women." I disengaged my hand.

"My friend, Andrew, perhaps you know the story of the bread and the fish from the Bible."

"Yes, of course, I know that parable, Giuseppe, but—"

"Then you must know our Lord taught us how many appetites even one fish can feed. And, Andrew, if I could show you my children…" He hung his chin and shook his head.

My cash was precious. I scanned the coastline but saw not another human soul. Giuseppe was my only choice at the moment.

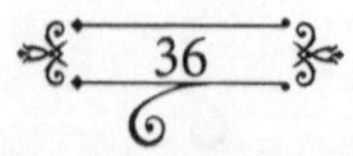

"I may pay you for one salmon. Perhaps not quite so much as you ask since I won't be taking it with me. I can't stop to cook, so I'm making do on bread and jerky. Now, perhaps you recognized those women?" I held two coins in my hand like bait.

"Ah, those two. Thank you, Signor. You will be blessed." He held out his hand. I held on to my money.

"The women, Giuseppe?"

"They come sometimes to gather the mussels."

"And there is a big man, Standing Oak, who comes with them?"

"*Sì.* Sometimes he works on boats, but not so much. He does not like it."

I handed him one coin, palmed the other. His hands were creased and scarred.

"And where do they live?"

"That, Signor, I cannot tell you. They come, they go. I don't follow them. Perhaps you would like the red snapper."

"No snapper. Giuseppe, you have a family. You can understand how a man will do anything to help his family. I must discover all I can about Standing Oak."

"We are both men in need, Andrew. My snapper is a very special price."

And so I paid for two fish I never saw and did not want to learn that Standing Oak sometimes worked on the land of the very farmer who had refused me a lift a few hours earlier.

Bahnhof was his name. I recognized Giuseppe's description of his Van Dyke beard and his wagon lane's intersection with the main road. Giuseppe filled my canteen with water in lieu of the fish I declined, and I tramped back down the road in the direction from which I'd come.

* * *

It was twilight when I began my hike up the track leading to the Bahnhof place. The seaside grasslands gave way to shrubs and then to a mixture of oaks and redwoods. The redwoods spread a canopy that allowed little other vegetation, which gave the place the feel of a gloomy park.

By the time I finally reached it, shadows lay across Bahnhof's ten-acre clearing. A pen of perhaps a dozen bleating goats took up one corner of the plot, where two billies jousted head-to-head. A chicken coop huddled close by. A small cabin with an attached lean-to stable housed the wagon that had passed me by earlier that day. I saw nothing of Bahnhof or Standing Oak.

Daylight was fading. At first I took the faint bleating I heard to be an echo from the penned goats, but as I worked eastward, I could tell it was a separate voice. Something about the situation appeared ominous. Trees—and my protective cover—soon thinned and revealed grasslands and foothills beyond.

I knelt behind a tree, drew the hunting knife our foreman, Shelby Neal, had given me when I was a boy. It was small, more a tool than a weapon, but I'd always loved the dark leather grip framed by brass guard and butt. As a keepsake it was precious to me, and I sharpened it regularly, as he'd taught me. I wondered what might have happened if I'd carried it the night Yellow Squirrel met Julian. Would I have used it? Surely, if I'd had the chance.

I crept toward the sound and presently sighted a young goat tied to a sapling by a short rope. I saw no sign of any other movement or life. Yet, I suspected that Bahnhof was still about. I doubted he'd have ventured far without his team and wagon, and the tethered goat puzzled me mightily. I crouched low and took a few steps toward it. Something jabbed my kidney hard. I gasped at the pain.

CHAPTER NINE

"There is a Henry repeating rifle in your back," the man behind me said. "Caliber of forty-four, and the finger of Horst Bahnhof is on the trigger. If you don't wish the rifle to fire, you will drop your knife." I let it go. "Now, slowly, your rucksack." I complied. "Now," he said, "sit down and wrap your arms and legs around that tree and squeeze as if it was your own dear mother." I began to turn and protest.

He poked hard once more with the rifle. "You must keep your back to me." I sat and embraced the tree trunk. "Next, you will bend your head back toward me." When I obeyed, a loop dropped around my neck. The gun came out of my back. I turned again, but the noose tightened.

"You will not move." Bahnhof flashed in and out of view as he looped and twisted the rope around the tree so that my right cheek jammed against the bark, and both hands and feet were bound on the side of the tree opposite my face. He finished the trussing with a loop through my belt that tightened the noose when I moved. He stepped in front of me, rifle at ready.

"Well, mister, you are the same fellow I saw on the road this afternoon. Something told me you were attempting to trick your way onto my land. I was correct, was I not?"

"I only wish to inquire about an Indian who works for you. Standing Oak." I could move only one side of my jaw freely, and my words sounded distorted, as if I were a man with a toothache.

"It was told to me the government would take my farm for the Indians. And here you are."

"Government? You believe I'm connected with the government? Would a government agent come afoot?"

"Your methods are under the hand. They sent a savage. Why would they not send a boy on foot?" I was suddenly not as worried about Bahnhof's connection with Standing Oak as with proving I wasn't after him or his land.

"Search me. My bag. I have no badge or any other official trappings."

"Of course, you would not be so obvious." He sent the rucksack flying with a kick. "And, of course, this knife in your hand was but a toy." His toe lofted the knife further into the woods. "I could have your life this moment, Mr. Government, and why should I not? A man's land is sacred." He raised his rifle. I struggled against the ropes.

"My name is Andrew Maxwell, from a prominent family. I have papers to prove it."

He shook his head. "And you would know I cannot read English, so you could tell me the papers said anything. No, Mister Government, I am too much the Christian to shoot you in your present helplessness. But you must know that Horst Bahnhof's land is his life and he will not surrender it.

"And now that you are fastened well, Mr. Government. Let us see what dreams you dream tonight about cheating honest men of their property. I will return shortly."

He disappeared behind the cabin for a few minutes, came back carrying a bucket, which he emptied on the knots that bound me. My skinned wrists stung.

"Brine will shrink and tighten the ropes, Mr. Government," he said.

"It'll take some time to dry, Bahnhof. How long do you contemplate keeping me here? And what is the purpose of the goat?"

"Oh, did I neglect to explain? Please forgive me. A mountain lion has taken a liking to my goats. The rain is not so much this year, so he comes for water, finds my animals in the field, returns for more. I cannot for long keep so many in the pen like I have now, but the lion, he has killed three in the field. This goat waits for the lion, while Horst Bahnhof waits also for him and also does the Henry rifle. I will bring his ears to the government for the bounty."

"That lion won't stop with the goat, Mr. Christian Man. You know this is murder."

"Murder? Oh, no. I am too good a Christian to commit such a sin. Let the beast choose, and let the Lord guide his choice. I have constructed a small platform in a tree close by. I will be watching." He disappeared into the darkness.

Leave her to heaven went through my mind. I was, indeed, in a situation similar to Gertrude's—dark humor at my own expense—but Bahnhof's motives were not so noble as Hamlet's, and Shakespeare hadn't figured in a mountain lion.

I waited, the rope and tree bark chafing me the while. I heard only an occasional pawing and whining from the kid. Perhaps Bahnhof had lied about keeping watch, wished to stop me from attempting an escape.

I squeezed the tree with my knees and shifted weight to relieve the cramping. I leaned left and right. Nothing helped much or for very long. A waning three-quarters moon cast eerie shapes around me. If Yellow Squirrel had his way, I wouldn't live to see another moon wane. Bahnhof either. He had virtually nailed me to the tree beside his sacrificial goat. Furthermore, it seemed to me that fear or appetite were more likely than God to determine the cat's selection of a victim.

What would Julian have done? He would likely have walked directly into the cabin and demanded what he wished. But not Andy. What had my innate caution got me? On the other hand, what had Julian's boldness got him?

Wrapped in pain and dripping fog, I pictured the possibilities if the cougar didn't chance by for a meal. Perhaps Bahnhof would decide God wished to spare me as he'd spared Isaac. Or maybe he'd take it as a sign the sacrifice had to proceed. I renewed my tussle with the ropes, leaned forward to create slack, pulled back to loosen the knots. No progress. The goat began bleating again.

I tensed, stilled, peered toward the field. I could discern no sign of danger, but sight was worth little in that world of shadows and dim moonlight. Then I saw movement.

A shadow deeper than the others slid from the grass into the clearing. Stopped. Moved again. Stopped again. The lion bellied slowly toward me. He stopped, waited, probably deciding between me and the goat. I wanted to yell if only to provoke action, end the waiting.

When action came, it was nearly too quick for my eye to catch. The cougar bounded through a patch of light and clamped its jaws on the goat's back. There was no more bleating, but there was a shot. Dust puffed up a few yards on the far side of the lion, and he leaped for cover. A second shot raised a cloud where he'd been. Bahnhof lumbered out of the trees.

"I will finish you now," he yelled.

"Wait," I yelled, "wait for daylight." But he paid no attention. If the lion killed Bahnhof, or they killed each other, I was as good as dead. If not by tooth and claw, then by starvation. The thought sent me into a paroxysm of struggles against my bonds. The ropes didn't loosen, but as I lunged from side to side, I realized what I should have understood earlier—Bahnof had tied me to the tree, but not to the ground. I could shinny.

The tree was a relatively old fir with yards of bare, tapering trunk between the ground and its first branches. I reached as high as I could, gripped the tree with my knees, feet, and arms, then pulled up, gained a few vertical inches. I lifted my knees, gripped again, pushed, and slid back to the ground. Still, the temporary victory encouraged me, and I shoved upward again. After a few more false tries, I raised myself one or two feet, and the tree's diminishing circumference gained me enough slack to begin working myself free from the ropes. And I had to hurry. The lion was unlikely to linger, let alone return, but Bahnhof, dangerous as the cat, might return any second.

The bark ripped at my shirtsleeves, and the rough, wet hemp ripped skin from my forearms as I twisted and pulled the stubborn knots with fingers swollen into what felt like cow's teats. Salt burned the abrasions like hellfire, but I made steady progress. I had slid to earth yet again when I heard a shot and a roar in the distance. Finally I slipped a hand out of the coils. In a few more endless minutes, I freed my feet. I stumbled around the grove, past the goat's mangled remains, until I located my rucksack and knife, then trotted back in the direction of the main road.

"Mr. Government, you will not leave."

I turned expecting to see Bahnof's rifle leveled at my heart. Instead, the rifle hung from his right hand as his bulky, disheveled figure stumbled toward me. His left hand clutched his belly and his breath came in noisy gasps. He dropped the rifle, reached toward me, and staggered a few more steps before he collapsed face-down.

Even after how he'd treated me, there was no question of leaving him here. I knelt beside him and turned him over. His jacket had been flayed from his left arm and I saw a trace of bone in the white light. My first task would be to stop the blood flowing from his arm. I tore a strip from his tattered shirt thinking to fashion a tourniquet, but a snarling from behind stopped me cold. I was willing to attempt saving Bahnhof's life, but not to sacrifice myself for him.

I grabbed the Henry, rolled away from his body, twisted the gun to firing position, and aimed it at a scene I hope never to see again. The lion had gripped Bahnhof's head in his jaws and was jerking his limp body like a drover cracking a bullwhip. I saw no clear target save the hindquarters, but I was forced to shoot at something. I fired.

The animal released Bahnhof and turned back on itself, nipping the flank where the bullet had entered. Then he turned on me. He had to drag his rear with his front claws now, but he was amazingly fast and still dangerous.

I stood, levered in another shell and pulled the trigger. Nothing. The Henry Rifle Bahnhof was so proud of had been a mainstay of Civil War and pioneer life, but it was old-fashioned, its ammunition temperamental—especially when home-reloaded as Bahnhof's cartridges certainly were. The lion was only a rifle's length away by the time I ejected the dud cartridge and fired again. This one did not misfire, laid him in the dirt, still growling, but no longer advancing. I sighted down the barrel to a spot between his eyes, pulled the trigger. Another dud. One advantage to the Henry—it contained twelve shells, and the next one was live. The lion lay, fangs exposed and fearsome even in death. His right ear was bloody and nearly gone, doubtless the victim of Bahnhof's initial shot and most likely the reason he'd attacked the old farmer instead of simply taking to the hills.

I hurried back to Bahnhof and finished my tourniquet. The left side of his face was nearly torn away, and he'd lost so much blood, I thought there was little hope of saving him. But it was my duty to try.

I hurriedly hitched his team to his wagon and led them to their unconscious master. The bloody smells of the dead kid and lion spooked them somewhat, but I was able to position the wagon beside the body. I fashioned a sling from a quilt and the ropes he'd bound me with and hoisted him into the wagon. Blood oozed through the blanket and darkened the floorboards. I checked for pulse and breathing, found a trace of both. Eastern light silhouetted ridgetop trees as I headed the team toward the town of Bodega, a short distance inland from the bay and directly on my route back to San Francisco.

* * *

The morning's overcast was clearing and the temperature warming as I hitched the team outside the general store, where the front door stood open even at that early hour. Bahnof was still breathing, albeit weakly. A meaty woman with sallow face and flat nose scratched at a ledger near the rear of the establishment.

"I have a badly injured man out here," I said. "He needs a doctor quickly."

She laid down her short pencil. "Nearest thing to a doctor around here is vet Michaels, and his place is five miles out. Who is it?"

"Fellow named Bahnhof. Mauled by a cougar."

"Hmph. Crazy old Dutchman. Too bad." She called a raggedly-dressed blond youngster from the back and sent him after the veterinarian. We carried Bahnhof to a cot inside the store and piled on some blankets. The woman's homespun muslin skirt was spotted with blood.

"Might be a mercy if he don't make it," the woman said. She brushed at the red stains on her lap to no effect, shrugged the matter off. "Tore up like he is, his own mother won't recognize him no more." A pot of water was heating on a wood stove, and she pulled some rags from a bin.

I pointed toward the door. "I apologize, ma'am, I can't stay. I have a court appearance in San Francisco and I mustn't be late."

"Little young for a lawyer, ain't you?"

"I'm not a lawyer. I'm a witness against the man who murdered my brother."

She glanced at Bahnhof. "Seems like you kind of attract trouble, don't you?"

"Seems so," I nodded. Not that I was to blame for any of this, but realized how matters must look to her. "At least lately."

The woman bent over the bed, sponging at what remained of Bahnhof's face. She spoke without looking at me. "Well there's no room for your trouble around here. You'd best get on."

"One more question," I said. "Have you by chance heard of an Indian called Standing Oak? Word is he worked for Mr. Bahnhof from time to time."

Now she did look at me. "I said you'd best get on."

I reluctantly obeyed. I mentally apologized to Julian, explained that I didn't know what else I could have done, but whatever it was, I hadn't. I felt somewhat heartened to think that Sheriff O'Neill would have returned to town by now, and I looked forward to laying a substantial list of demands on his desk, to put the wheels of justice finally in motion.

CHAPTER TEN

I lingered at my boarding house only long enough for a nap, a perfunctory wash, and fresh clothes. I intended to storm into O'Neill's office and challenge him to stifle Charley Hung, and expedite Yellow Squirrel's trial. I was hurrying down my front steps when a female voice brought me up short.

"Andy, please wait." I squinted into the morning sun and made out the cherubic, if somewhat distressed, presence of Virginia Campbell, an art history textbook hugged to her bosom, blue eyes shaded by the backlight.

"I haven't seen you since… well, I wanted to express my condolences."

I remained where I was, did my utmost to sound aloof. "I'm surprised. I thought you found both Julian and me despicable beyond your sympathy."

"That's not fair, Andy. Surely you understand, after what father heard, we couldn't—"

"I'm not the only one who needs to understand, Virginia. But pardon me, I have urgent business to attend to."

"I can imagine, especially now that that murderer has escaped. It's all unspeakably horrible."

"Escaped? Who?" I said.

"Why, that Indian, that Squirrel man. Didn't you know?"

"When?"

"Yesterday. It's all in the paper."

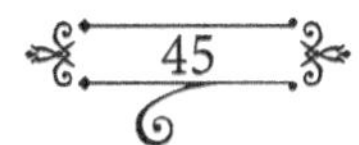

"I'm going to see the sheriff," I said, "and he'd better have some good answers." I turned and ran a few steps toward the ferry, but I realized I hadn't quite finished with Virginia yet. I turned back toward her. She'd remained standing at the foot of the steps clutching her book.

"I haven't told you this, Virginia, because I wanted to protect you. But right now, I believe none of us has much protection from anything. That night in the brothel—your father didn't *hear* about me and Julian. He saw us. Himself." I waited for a few seconds and watched her mouth open to object. "He was there."

"What an awful lie, Andrew Maxwell. You and your brother—you're even lower than I thought. I'm glad you're out of my life." This time it was her turn to run away.

I was too angry to care whether I'd done the right thing or not. I ran down University Avenue, jumped aboard a ferry just as they were pulling in the gangplank, bought myself a *Chronicle*. Even though I knew what it would say, the headline sat me down as if One-Ear had pushed me to the bench—"Indian Killer In Daring Escape." The story itself blurred. All that registered was Yellow Squirrel's name and the fact that this predator was once more going to and fro on the earth and walking up and down in it as Satan puts it in the Bible. I did not intend to end up like Job.

I ignored the clerk who told me Sheriff O'Neill was in conference, yanked open the office door, and threw the newspaper on his desk.

"How the hell could you allow this to happen?"

Two deputies rushed in and grabbed my arms. The sheriff held up his hand.

"I'll see Mr. Maxwell," he said. He turned to the slick-haired dandy he'd been talking to, now backed up against the window. "We'll talk later. Tadich's for lunch?" The man nodded, sidled along the wall, and scurried out the door.

"If you've completed your tantrum, perhaps you'd care to sit down, Andrew."

"This is no tantrum, and it's not over, sir. However, I will sit while you explain how you allowed a cold-blooded killer loose on the streets." O'Neill's office was spare. My chair was unpadded, the wainscoting unornamented. He seated himself on the other side of the narrow oak table he used for a desk. He picked up a paper, turned sideways to me and seemed to be reading as he spoke.

"First of all, Andrew, your brother had a healthy share of the blame for what happened."

"You're not serious, I—"

"Second, no one anticipated that a manacled prisoner would or could jump through—not only from, but through—a second-story window."

"Why was he even outside the cell block?" I edged forward in my chair.

He turned his head, spoke over his shoulder. "Perhaps you've heard of habeas corpus, Andrew? It's in the Constitution. He was on his way to court."

My anger was unabated, but O'Neill's explanation stifled my first argument. "Then you had poor security."

"Perhaps." He sat back, replaced the paper and squared toward me. "But I'll never make that statement to a reporter, and I never made it to you. We'll recapture Yellow Squirrel. Don't worry."

"Very well, sir," I said. "Suppose you do. Did you receive my note?"

"Yes." He folded his hands across his brocade vest, fiddled with his watch chain.

"And have you determined how to plumb the depths of this conspiracy?"

"I talked to Sergeant Calhoun—your infamous badge number six-zero-nine. Yellow Squirrel was toying with you."

"How did he know so much about us?"

"There are newspapers, Andrew. The man can read."

"And how do you explain the Indian who nearly killed me on the street when I left the jail the other day?" I leaned over the table. He dropped his arms, lifted his eyes. I sat back and related my encounter with Standing Oak, my visit to the Presidio, my encounter with Bahnhof.

"That explains those scrapes on your wrists and face. You've had a rough time of it."

"And that's not all. Charley Hung—I see you know the name—has threatened to Shanghai me unless I produce five hundred dollars he claims Julian owes him."

"He has, has he? Well, we'll have a talk with Mr. Hung. And I'm sorry about the other incidents, but of course they're all beyond our jurisdiction."

"Kidnapping? Assault? False imprisonment? Attempted murder? It's surely in someone's jurisdiction. Federal marshals. Someone."

"Except for the business with that Chinaman, all you've told me can be explained in any one of a dozen ways, Andrew. We're after Yellow Squirrel, not a whole tribe of redskins on the warpath. Furthermore, none of it would have happened to you had you not stepped in where you don't belong. I want you out of this until the trial."

"You seem to forget, Sheriff O'Neill, that the Maxwells still have some sway around here. When my mother hears of how I'm being treated—"

He sliced the air with his hand. "If Carrie heard how you've acted—waving the Maxwell name around like a battle flag—she'd be embarrassed to death. I allowed you access to Yellow Squirrel out of respect for your grandfather's memory. A mistake I won't compound by allowing you to interfere with our investigation. Now go on about your business, some of which might include mending fences with your mother."

"I didn't come here to be scolded like a child, sir." I shoved against the desk so hard it moved toward him a couple of inches. He shoved it back, stood.

"No, Andrew, you came here to tell me and every other lawman in the city and county of San Francisco, not to mention the U.S. Army, how to do their jobs."

"I'm only attempting to protect my family," I said.

"Then go protect them. But leave the law to take care of the criminals." He stepped toward the door. I knew I was nearing the edge of O'Neill's tolerance, but I couldn't resist a parting shot.

"I wish I could trust you to do that, sir." He opened the door.

"Good day, Mr. Maxwell. We'll see one another again when it comes time to testify. Give my best to your mother." He laid his arm across my shoulder in what he undoubtedly intended to appear a comradely gesture to the three men in the anteroom. I shrugged it off and left. The wheels of justice stood frozen in place.

* * *

From the jail steps I looked over the heads of the Portsmouth Square throng to a blustery, whitecapped bay. I'd worn out my welcome with San Francisco officialdom, convinced no one else that Yellow Squirrel was pursuing my family, that Standing Oak was the connection to Owl Feather, or that Owl Feather was the key to the conspiracy.

The old moon was waning quickly. Yellow Squirrel would likely head straight for the center of everything Maxwell—the Circle M. And, despite Mother's decree, I decided I belonged there as well. I'd send her a warning telegram, then return to the mountains for the first time in four years.

* * *

A half block down Clay Street, I heard a soft voice at my shoulder and felt a sharp jab in my ribs. "This way, Mr. Maxwell." I turned my head to see the same little Chinese man in the red skull cap who had guided me to Charley Hung's office the week before. "You feel the blade, Mr. Maxwell. You will turn to your right now. Mr. Hung calls for you."

The same policeman who had discounted my story about Standing Oak strolled not ten yards away, but the knife was hidden up a voluminous sleeve, and the warm trickle down my side told me that calling out would be fraught with hazard.

The swarms of pedestrians increased as we neared Chinatown. I attempted to elbow passersby into my antagonist, but he always dodged and stuck to my back like a tick. By the time we were on Grant Street, a block from Hung's office and near the entrance to China Alley, I'd nearly abandoned hopes of escape and had begun to invent tales to explain to Charley Hung why I'd be unable to pay Julian's debt. A dogfight erupted a few feet away and boiled its way across the street in front of us.

I feigned a stumble and pitched myself forward, down, and away from knifepoint. I rolled several times and tripped a few folks to increase the confusion before I jumped to my feet and began running as fast as the multitudes would allow.

I presently realized I'd blundered straight into the dead end of China Alley, but I didn't dare turn back. My instincts took me toward Silk Road. I jumped down the steps and slammed the door open.

The place was as dim and murky at noon as it had been at midnight. I plowed through the tables, setting furniture and bodies flying, hoping to find a back door. From behind a pillar stepped the huge, one-eared bouncer, who grabbed my shirt collar and reached for my belt. An explosion, flash, and screams tore through the melee. A man in teamster's overalls gripped his leg and rolled gasping across the floor, and I saw the bartender preparing to empty his shotgun's second barrel in my direction.

I wondered how he planned to miss the bouncer, who hadn't lost his grip on my shirt and was still intent on grabbing my belt. I grabbed a champagne bottle from the mess on the floor and swung it into the big man's ankle. He crumpled and released me. The floor churned with bodies, liquor, blood, and curses. I crawled for the back, stomach taut with fear of another blast from the shotgun. I dashed down a narrow, dark hallway and tore open a door at the end.

An Oriental woman about my mother's age and dressed in the calico dress of a farmer's wife sat at a desk, grabbed at a Navy Colt revolver. I snatched it away before she could bring it to bear, yanked her to her feet, shoved her into the hallway, closed and barred the door just as One-Ear appeared at the other end of the hall. I headed toward the iron door on the other side of the room, drew the bolts, and stepped outside into a small concrete pit with an iron ladder that led up to daylight. Pistol in hand, I clambered up the ladder, on the verge of escape. Just as I gripped the last rung, a hand on my right tore the revolver from my grasp and two on the left jerked me from the cubbyhole and threw me on my face in a sandy mud puddle.

"Mr. Hung is waiting," said a familiar voice. This time I felt both knife and pistol barrel in my back.

CHAPTER ELEVEN

I faced Charley Hung from the same chair as I had earlier, One-Ear on one side of me, Skull-Cap on the other. The odor of the opium seeped under the closed door.

"You have awakened me early, Mr. Maxwell, an unfortunate occurrence. Now, where is my money?"

I brushed sand from my waistcoat, tried to appear more concerned about preening than breaking away. "You said I had until Yellow Squirrel's trial."

"An unlikely event at this juncture, wouldn't you agree? You've had sufficient time." He nodded, and his two henchmen lifted me to my feet and dug into my pockets. Once again, I'd had the good sense to leave grandfather's watch at home. A few coins, the key to my boarding house, and a pocket handkerchief was all the plunder that lay on Charley Hung's desk when they finished their search. But he nodded again, and they sat me down and pulled off my boots. Again, they found nothing. Nor in my socks. Again Charley Hung nodded. I instinctively grabbed my belt buckle, but the small man tore my hands away while the other unbuckled, unbuttoned, and yanked my pants down to my knees. He tore the buttons from my underwear, jammed his hand inside and groped at my crotch.

"Hey," I yelled and jackknifed my pelvis. But One-Ear didn't interrupt the search. Charley Hung laughed.

"I'll wager you prefer the way they do it at The Red Rooster, don't you, Mr. Maxwell?"

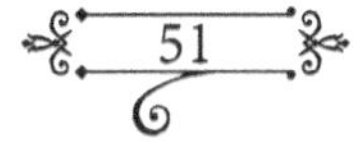

One-Ear soon tore loose the small reticule I'd safety-pinned to my underwear.

"Ten dollars," Charley Hung said. "And four bits. Counting the other ten, just four hundred and seventy-nine fifty remaining."

"Sheriff O'Neill and I discussed all this only this morning. You're digging yourself a deep hole." He laughed. Mother's name carried no influence with O'Neill. O'Neill's name carried no influence with Charley Hung. I was on my own.

"He'll not find you where you're bound," Hung said. He gestured toward the door and Skull-Cap grasped the knob.

"Very well," I said. "I do have some money, but it's all I had saved for school. I suppose I'd rather surrender that than become shark bait. I'll deliver it to you this afternoon." I stood to go, but One-Ear swatted me into the chair.

"Mr. Maxwell, experience has taught us the sad lesson that we cannot trust you." Skull Cap had returned to my side now. "You wounded Hector's pride with your brief escape." He gestured toward Skull-Cap with one hand, then to One-Ear with the other. "And Ulysses is liable to carry a grudge about his sore ankle for some time. They look for the solace of success, Mr. Maxwell, and will therefore accompany you to your hoard of cash. And I trust the matter will reach resolution before the sun descends. Agreed?"

I pulled my pants over my torn undergarments. "Does it matter whether I agree or not?"

"And in case you have another escapade in mind, I should point out that there are worse things than a sail to the Orient." He nodded again. I saw a flicker of movement on my left and felt a dart of pain in my ear. I slapped a hand to my head and brought away a palm covered with blood from the gash Skull Cap's blade had sliced in the lobe.

"You might wish to use this." Charley Hung handed my handkerchief to me. I pressed it to the side of my head. "Now go."

* * *

It was a calm, warm day on the ferry, completely at odds with my mood and situation. I wondered how I must appear to the other passengers with a bloody handkerchief to my ear and a Chinaman on either side. Certainly someone would call the law or intervene. But no one did. Mother wouldn't refuse the money if she could see me now. But she couldn't.

As we tramped up University Avenue toward campus, I sifted through my mind for a solution. I'd thought of going to Mother's lawyer in the city, but knew he'd not release money without her authorization. Perhaps I could buy time with the small cache of dollars I had in my room, but the prospect was slim. My one narrow chance required taking advantage of my landlady's hatred and fear of Orientals.

We climbed the boarding house steps, and I twisted the bell handle, praying that Mrs. Krebs was at home. No answer.

"Use key," One-Ear said.

"It's only for my room," I lied. "Someone's always available unless one returns after hours." I turned the handle again. Finally the door opened and the tiny and gray Mrs. Krebs stood before us in a long dress that matched her complexion.

"Why, Andy, why—" I inched forward so that the doorjamb held One-Ear and Skull Cap slightly behind rather than beside me. I pursed my lips and rolled my eyes upward in attempt to indicate trouble at my back.

"Who are these men? What happened to your ear?" She whispered as if they wouldn't be able to hear. I answered in a normal tone.

"Everything's in order." I opened my eyes wide to indicate that things were very much out of order. "They're with me."

"Well, that's fine, Andy, but they must use the back door like all the other... people like them." I turned to One-Ear.

"You heard the lady. I'll meet you at the back door."

"We come with you," said Skull Cap, who prodded me surreptitiously with the knife tip. I leaped sideways away from the knife through the half-open door, slammed it shut as I went, and threw the deadbolt. One-Ear's pistol sounded and a bullet tore a hole in the door and through the leather umbrella stand in the corner. Mrs. Krebs stumbled backwards, and I caught her at the base of the staircase just before she fell.

"Lock yourself in the cellar, ma'am. That shot should summon the police. I'm sorry for the trouble, but I must get out of here."

I bounded up the stairs, seized the rest of my cash, my watch, knife, and rucksack and looked out my window. As I'd anticipated, One-Ear was running through the yard to cover the rear. Skull-Cap would either circle around the other side or keep watch on the front.

Mrs. Krebs' rhododendrons were her pride and joy. I blessed her for them and mentally apologized as I jumped from the window, crashed through their cushion, and made for the hedge that fenced us from the neighboring yard.

I sprinted toward the covering banks and bushes of Cordinices Creek, ran and crawled and stumbled my way down the stream and underneath a stone bridge. I heard police whistles and shouts in both English and Chinese. One-Ear suddenly appeared in mid-stream, his pistol leveled at me. I dived behind an abutment. Two shots followed, each from a different gun by the sound. One ricocheted off the stone near my head.

Someone yelled, "Get back here, you yellow devil."

Now that the police had arrived to distract my captors, I worked my way unmolested through culverts all the way to town center, praying Mrs. Krebs hadn't been hurt.

It was nearing twilight when I arrived at the railroad depot just in time to catch the last eastbound train of the day. I set my flat cap at an angle to hide the slashed ear and took a seat in the last seat of the last car. I was headed home for the first time in four years.

CHAPTER TWELVE

An early-morning local brought me to Placerville, where I hired a mount that brought me the last ten miles to the Circle M late the following afternoon. Memories crowded in as I crossed our rangeland on my way to the house.

When I was about fourteen, Julian and I were riding roundup. We separated to encircle a small clump of heifers milling about in a juniper patch. I headed downslope at a steep angle, hazing the cattle toward Julian, who was to drive them to a clearing. I rode west, and the sun was setting. A line from a sonnet crossed my mind—"When I consider everything that grows/ Holds in perfection but a little moment." I remember smiling, feeling smug about bringing Shakespeare to the range where I so often felt out of place. A rattlesnake whirred in the rocks beside me. My horse lurched and whinnied, and in my poetic fog, my equestrian skills—usually more than adequate to such a task—deserted me. I flew from the saddle and bellyflopped on the gravelly slope of a ravine. I plummeted down the steep bank, managed a brief grip on a shrub, spun a hundred and eighty degrees, and stopped only when my private parts fetched up against a pine sapling. I collapsed in breathless pain, heard several pistol shots.

"You all right, Andy?" Julian called from above. I could utter not a sound, but I waved. Julian tossed a loop around my shoulders and hauled me up the bank. His bullets had turned the rattler into a rope of bloody scales. I feigned a brave stride and retrieved my fallen hat.

"Many thanks, Julian."

He snapped the tail from the snake. "Twelve whole rattles plus the button. They'll look grand on my hat."

From then on, no matter who was older, there was no doubt which of us was top dog on the range. I'd settled, contentedly, for being top dog in the classroom. Now the snake-killing fell to me.

* * *

I stopped my horse on a high point of the road overlooking the Ranch. I looked up through fading light at Sawtooth Peaks, which stood like a trio of praying monks over the Circle M's burial plot. Even from this distance, the soil on Julian's grave looked fresh. Granite Creek sparkled into the late-afternoon sun and across the valley toward the hamlet of Sawtooth Wells five miles behind me.

I watched my mother and the foreman, Shelby, emerge from the ranchhouse and stand talking at the bottom of the steps that led off the gallery of the multi-gabled log-and-stone house Grandfather had designed and built. The layout of the yard and its surrounding buildings and corrals mirrored Carter Maxwell's creative and orderly mind. It was squared with nearly military precision, not scattered with the higgledy-piggledy randomness that characterized so many spreads. Grandfather had reveled in innovation, set most of the structures on stone and concrete piers instead of traditional foundations, an echo of the southern-style underpinnings he had seen in Mississippi during the Civil War. This technique, he maintained, kept the structures cooler in summer, warmer in winter, and safer from floods. He'd even built a little sawmill powered by a Chicago-imported Pelton water wheel so the Circle M could mill a large portion of its own lumber.

Mother wore her typical working clothes—pants, boots, shirt, western hat—that had shocked so many visitors to the ranch. Her dark hair hung loosely to her shoulders. She could pretty herself up in grand fashion when she chose, but her role as a rancher came first. A wide black armband signaled her mourning for Julian.

She and Shelby were crossing to the barn by the time I rode my horse across the bridge and under the archway—a replica of the ranch's brand, ax-hewn from a single cedar log by Grandfather Maxwell—into the ranch's main yard. Two half-breed Border Collies I didn't know dashed across the yard and circled my horse in a roil of yelps and dust. Shelby whistled them off, then he and Mother froze as they realized I was the rider. Mother broke the tableau, stepped toward me. The corners of her lips tilted in the beginning of a smile.

"So, Andy, you've decided to return to us after all."

"Hello, Mother. Hello, Shelby. It's a pleasure to see you." Shelby nodded and smiled. His 'Hello, Andy,' was soft and warm.

"Didn't you receive my telegram?" I said. Mother never completed her smile.

"Andrew—It was 'Andrew' when she was irritated.—Your ridiculous theory—"

"About the jailbreak."

"You know the conditions, Andrew. You don't return unless you intend to stay."

"May we please go inside?" Silence. "Ten minutes." The same amount of time I'd requested with Yellow Squirrel. She finally turned to Shelby and issued a few instructions. She seemed compelled to demonstrate that ranch business took priority.

"Very well, Andrew. You'll have your ten minutes."

She swept across the yard and up the gallery steps. I was expected to follow. She waited at the door until I could overtake her and open it. She led me through the living room with its high bare-log beams, oversized furniture, and fireplace tall enough for a man to stand in. My grandfather had built as big as he lived. We settled in the office at last.

She reached high to lay her hat atop Grandfather's rolltop desk, sat stiffly on the edge of a wheeled oak chair, and finger-combed her hair from her face. She motioned me toward a maroon leather wingback. I laid my cap beside her hat and perched on the edge of the padded seat. There was no offer of refreshment.

"Michael Yellow Squirrel is certain to pursue us," I said.

"Your ear—"

"Only a scratch. I won't waste time explaining."

She smiled and shook her head. "Sheriff O'Neill telegraphed. We're not to be concerned about Mr. Squirrel. Apparently the sheriff is rather put out with you."

Much as I desired to defend myself against O'Neill, I focused on my errand. "About Owl Feather," I said. She stiffened.

"Where did you hear that name?" I sensed an opening, moved to exploit it.

"Mother, you must listen to me for once in our lives. Yellow Squirrel killed Julian and threatened me, us… the family. Another Indian, Standing Oak by name, I found out later.

"Standing Oak."

Her tone revealed nothing. The fact that she'd repeated the name revealed a great deal.

"He pushed me off the sidewalk nearly into a freight wagon. He knew who I was, declared it payment for someone called Owl Feather. Now Yellow Squirrel has escaped. Don't attempt to convince me this all means nothing."

"What did Yellow Squirrel say, exactly, when he made these threats?"

"He said Julian wasn't the first Maxwell to die, that he wouldn't be the last." Mother paced across the room to the row of decanters on the library table. "And he said it would be soon. By the next full moon. Three weeks, Mother."

She poured two whiskies and took a healthy swallow of hers before handing me the other.

"When the Arapahos kidnapped your grandmother and me from the wagon train, it was 1864. I was only three, so of course I remember almost nothing, and Mother and Father never wanted to speak of it…."

"But you know about Owl Feather."

"He was their chief."

So there was a direct link between Owl Feather and the Maxwells. "What happened to him?"

"I don't know."

I took a sip of whisky, stared at the floor a moment. Then, without raising my eyes, asked, "Mother, who else in our family was murdered?"

A knock at the door prevented her reply.

"Yes? Come in," she said. Our long-time cook stepped timidly into the room. "What is it, Ling Chu?"

"Miss Carrie… oh, Mr. Andy, I did not know you were here. Welcome. One more place for dinner. Very good. Sorry to interrupt, Madame. Someone ate the blackberries I was saving for supper. Need more or no dessert."

"Ah, a true Circle M crisis, Andrew. Ling, need we look further than the front corral for the blackberry culprit?"

"It is not my place, Miss Carrie…"

"Never mind. You know Shelby's weakness as well as I do. Andy"—I was suddenly Andy again—"you remember how to fill a berry bucket don't you?"

"Mother—"

"Of course you do. Don't worry, Ling. It's taken care of." She swept out of the room. If I wanted my answers, I'd have to follow.

CHAPTER THIRTEEN

The nearest berry bushes were a hundred yards or so up the fenceline behind the house. She spoke as we walked.

"No Maxwells were murdered, Andy."

"You're certain? Not Grandfather?"

"His killer was his own prize bull, as you well know. Perhaps you think Owl Feather transformed himself into Jerome III?"

"Grandmother?"

"There have been no murders here, Andy, believe me." We reached the brambles. She began picking, as did I. "Now, I'm not ignoring your speculation entirely, Andy. I went so far as to wire the Army at Fort Washakie about Owl Feather."

"Why couldn't you just say you didn't think my theory was so ridiculous?"

"I knew if I opened the door a crack you'd attempt pushing all the way into the room."

"I belong in the room," I said. I jabbed my finger into a thorn, jerked it back, tugged out the protruding barb, licked away a drop of blood. A telegram to the fort in Wyoming in charge of the Arapaho reservation where the abduction had originally happened. Such a simple step. I should have thought of it myself.

"Have they answered?"

She smiled. "Now don't stop your picking, Andy, or no desert." I smiled back, resumed tossing berries in my pail. "Not yet," she said. "I understand the Bureau of Indian Affairs is about to assume control of Fort Washakie and the Wind River Reservation from the Army. I imagine matters are in some confusion there."

"Well, we have to get ready here in any case. Yellow Squirrel's probably on his way. Perhaps he and Standing Oak together. Now that you mention Wyoming, though, I wonder if he might go there first for reinforcements. No matter. We must protect this place. And now."

"I suspect he's more worried about saving his own neck than about coming after us. Every lawman and army post from San Francisco to Wyoming is searching for him."

"We can't afford to assume they'll get him. O'Neill said he'd protect me from Charley Hung, and I'm fortunate I'm here to tell the tale."

"Charley Hung? That gangster?"

"I had to crawl through half the storm drains in Berkeley to escape his henchmen. But leave Charley Hung out of this for the time being." I stepped in front of her, forced her to look at me. "Yellow Squirrel doesn't have to come after you and me directly. What about the stock, the buildings?"

She held her pail still and looked at me. "You're relentless and wearing, Andrew. Rather like water dripping on granite. Very well, I'll call in the hands from fencing and haying, hire extra roundup men early, post sentinels around the ranch until this Yellow Squirrel is recaptured."

She attempted to step away, but I pressed my advantage. "And if the government won't respond, we must take matters in our own hands and head to Wyoming. We can find records there, people who remember. Yellow Squirrel is only part of this picture. An attack could come from anywhere, from someone we wouldn't suspect. Perhaps they'd pose as ranch hands. Or what about those Indian vagrants you're always feeding?"

She fairly jumped past me and began yanking berries from the vine, firing them into the bucket. "We are in no danger from our natives, Andrew." Her tone was sharp.

"How can you know that?"

She ceased her picking and looked at me hard. "I know." She commandeered my pail, emptied it into hers. I'd picked half the amount she had. She stepped toward the house. I hurried after her.

"Perhaps we'd find a clue in that trunk of Grandma and Grandpa's belongings." She turned back.

"That trunk remains locked, Andrew, and there'll be no trips to Wyoming for either of us. We'll not presume to interfere with the law." I called after her.

"It's my family, too, Mother. You seem to forget I'm a Maxwell."

"I'm not the one who's forgotten." She tossed the last remark over her shoulder. In this mood, I knew it was futile to continue, yet I followed again. "Very well," I said. "At least you're doing something. Now, I'm going to visit Julian's grave. If I'm allowed."

She reached the porch and turned. "Shelby should be in the yard somewhere," she said. "Tell him I wish to see him."

The kitchen door slammed behind her. Julian and I had both received our share of ultimatums from Mother over the years. I usually bit my lip and dodged confrontation, but he preferred defiance. In the end, neither of us seemed to get what he wanted.

* * *

The peaks had shaded the entire yard by the time I reached the front porch. Shelby was in a corral examining the hoof of a sorrel colt. I rinsed the berry juice from my hands in a watering trough, then assumed a familiar perch on the top board of the fence.

"Looks a great deal like Sailor," I said.

"She should. Going on twenty-five and the old boy still keeps them mares pregnant." Shelby smiled, doffed his hat, and wiped the sweat from his face and neck. In most respects, his countenance, with its blue eyes and freckles, reflected the heritage of his Irish father. However, the lady he called his 'high yaller maman from New Orleans' had bequeathed him nose and lips which labeled him forever black, even though his skin had the caramel tan of new leather and his hair was no more tightly curled than half the Italians I knew. He walked toward me and opened his arms.

"How are you, mon fils? Does these old buffalo soldier eyes good to see you again."

I dropped to the corral floor and we embraced.

"I graduated, I assume you know." He nodded.

I paused. I didn't need to explain my conflict with Mother. Not to Shelby.

"I simply don't know how to cope with her sometimes, Shelby."

"A mother's love is a precious thing, boy. Not to be squandered," he said.

And I didn't know what to say to that, so I changed the subject. "She's asked to see you. She's at least taking me seriously enough to hire extra protection for the ranch."

He reached out and touched my shoulder. "You see there? She ain't a dragon, boy." I heard a rifle shot, and Shelby fell. His body draped itself over the lower rail of the corral. I dived behind the watering trough and crawled toward him. I found myself face to face with a dead man.

CHAPTER FOURTEEN

"Shelby. Shelby," I said. I knew it was futile to place my hand over the hole in his throat, but I did it nonetheless. His life flowed around my fingers, pooled muddy in the dust.

"Andy. Shelby." My mother shrieked from the porch. I'd never heard her voice so uncontrolled.

"Down," I yelled. "Down." I surveyed the yard, saw nothing, then heard whinnying and stomping from the barn. Another shot. A buckskin stallion burst from the barn and galloped up the trail behind it. The rider on his back was Yellow Squirrel, and his devilish shrieks cut through all other sounds on earth.

Mother ignored my warning and raced to Shelby's side.

"Get Ling Chu," she said.

"It's too late, even for his medicine, Mother. I'm going after Yellow Squirrel."

"That was him?"

"I knew he'd come."

"Don't go alone, Andy. Combat is not your strong suit."

"Everyone else is out on the range or buried or about to be. I'll grab myself a rifle. Send word to Sheriff Halstad." I didn't wait for more argument.

Another gruesome surprise awaited me inside the stable. The place smelled warm and salty, like the ground under Shelby's head. Not only had

Yellow Squirrel taken the best mount, he'd placed a bullet between the eyes of the only horse remaining in the barn. That left only old Sailor in the far corral.

"You're older and wiser than I am," I said to Sailor. "Show me the way."

I made no attempt to hurry him up the steep and rocky stretch of trail above the springs we called Sawtooth Wells. We'd both crossed it hundreds of times and knew how treacherous it could be. I saw many places where Yellow Squirrel and his mount had slipped and faltered in the loose scree. It didn't look as if they'd fallen, but I doubted they'd made much better time than Sailor despite their haste. I wondered if he'd shot Shelby by accident or design, wondered if he'd been aiming at me, wondered—then was certain— he'd known Shelby was nearly part of the family, perhaps counted him as a Maxwell.

We reached the point where the trail leveled and entered a stand of heavy timber. Ideal for an ambush. Yellow Squirrel may have been set on escape, but he was also set on revenge. I took an untraveled uphill route around them and above the timberline where my view would remain clear.

I discovered no sign of Yellow Squirrel on that route, and by the time I rejoined the main path, darkness was nearly complete. The trail climbed from here to its highest point, a boulder-littered ridgetop more than a mile farther on. Another fine place for an ambush. But Yellow Squirrel didn't know this country like I did. I tied Sailor to a log, and, rifle in hand, began climbing on foot.

If Yellow Squirrel were waiting to shoot me as I rode up the trail toward those boulders, I had a good chance of sneaking up on him. I crept to the rocks overlooking my side of the ridge, hoping to surprise the killer who waited to surprise me.

But Yellow Squirrel had chosen none of the rocks I expected. Perhaps he was on the other side, downhill from the summit, thinking to gun me down the moment I skylined myself atop the ridge. The cover thinned rapidly as the trail descended, and hiding places were scarce. Perhaps he hadn't planned an ambush at all, but had concentrated on escape. I scanned the slope a last time before heading back to Sailor and continuing the pursuit on horseback. That last look paid off.

His boot looked nearly like part of the small log that screened the rest of his body. Yellow Squirrel had chosen his spot shrewdly. Anyone working his way down to him would likely loose a noisy shower of gravel. I called on Julian's spirit.

Step by careful step I worked my way down and across until I was parallel with and perhaps two body lengths away from my quarry. His attention was fixed uphill, his rifle flat on the ground behind the log. My position was perfect. The Indian had managed to shed both his shackles and his prison clothes. He was dressed like a common ranch hand. His normalcy enraged me. I raised my rifle. My heel inadvertently found a soft spot in the gravel. A few stones dribbled down the hill, ample warning for Yellow Squirrel, and he rolled as I fired. Dust puffed under his arm. He yelled, grabbed his elbow, kept rolling downhill into the shadows, leaving his rifle behind.

I scrambled toward him, my gun ready for another shot. A heavy blow slammed into my thigh and pain rocketed through my body. A fist-sized rock bounced down the slope behind me. I yanked myself around and saw Yellow Squirrel with a second rock lifted in his left hand. His right dangled at his side. I snapped off a shot, but dodging the rock spoiled my aim, and I hit nothing. He dove to the side and skidded down the embankment into darkness. I fired again from my knees, but I had only noise for a target. Silence returned. I was alone with the moonlight, the shadows, and a fist of pain in my thigh.

No use pursuing. My right leg would bear almost no weight. I retrieved Yellow Squirrel's rifle and inched my way to the top of the ridge by hopping from boulder to supporting boulder. With his arm injured and knowing I had both rifles, it seemed unlikely Yellow Squirrel would pursue me. Had I been unhurt myself, I would have found his horse and put him afoot. As it was, I'd be lucky to make it back to Sailor. Perhaps my leg was broken, perhaps not. It seemed hardly to matter at this point since I couldn't walk on it. I improvised a crutch and hopped and skipped my way down the moonlit trail.

But Sailor wasn't where I'd left him. Had I tied him securely? Of course. Yellow Squirrel? He'd not had time to get there. Besides, why bother with my horse when he was after me? I crawled and limped and hopped down the trail. My mouth grew dry. I chewed my tongue for moisture. I couldn't think. Simply getting to the next rock, the next tree, the next bush consumed me.

When I finally saw the ranch below me, I took a boyhood shortcut and slid off the trail, down the bank, and straight through the springs to the yard. Dawn was crowning the eastern hills, and I was a hurting, muddy mess when I dragged myself up on the ranch house steps like a grizzly-smacked hound, Yellow Squirrel's demonic ululations echoing through my brain.

CHAPTER FIFTEEN

T**he day of Shelby's funeral, Mother opened the front door for me and I hobbled from house to porch on my cane. I tried to absorb the strange sight of armed guards stationed around the perimeter of the Circle M yard. More, I knew, rode the fencelines out on the range. Doc Robinson said my leg wasn't broken, but the bruise was deep. The back of my thigh had the color of the mussels Standing Oak's women harvested. The wound on my ear, however, had diminished to a small scab.

My city clothes were both battleworn and out of place, so I'd dug some ranch clothes from my old wardrobe—pearl buttons, pointed pocket flaps, twill pants. I did stick with the comfort of my everyday flat-heeled, blunt-toed boots, which had cleaned up tolerably even after the skirmish with Yellow Squirrel.

Mother's hair was gathered in a bun crowned with veil and combs in a manner suggestive of a mantilla. Her black silk dress, somewhat old-fashioned but still elegant, dropped nearly to the ground. The sleeves puffed slightly at the shoulder then clung to her arms till they reached a lace cuff at the wrist. Her appearance harked back to a California that had disappeared long since, and I felt strangely proud to be the son of this *doña grande*.

We watched Sheriff Halstad ride across the yard and dismount. He used his low-crowned hat to beat dust from his black frock coat, then climbed the stairs, holding the hat to his chest, a hand gripping each side of the brim.

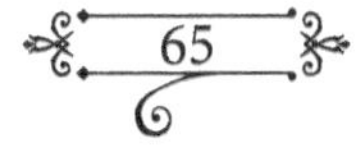

"Shelby was as fine a man of any race as I ever knew," he said. "I'm truly sorry about this."

Mother and I chorused our thanks. "Any progress on Yellow Squirrel?" I said.

"Yes and no. Looks like there were three horses came down the ridge and across Circle M land to the main road, but there was too big a mix of tracks to trail them any further."

"Three horses?" Mother said.

"Standing Oak," I said.

Halstad sounded puzzled. "Standing Oak?"

"It had to be. He followed Yellow Squirrel and me, then took Sailor with him."

"He's the feller you say shoved you in San Francisco?"

"Exactly. I just wonder why he passed up another chance to finish me."

"I'll add him to the notices I sent out this morning. Don't worry. We'll have those killers before long."

"People keep telling me that." My Mother's eyes snapped toward me, but she said nothing. I knew my remarks would carry even less credibility if I spoke of my other suspicions—that the Indians had an accomplice on the crew, someone who helped Yellow Squirrel to his sniper's post, showed him the back trail, directed Standing Oak to Sailor.

We watched a procession of black-clad funeralgoers pass through the Circle M's entry arch under the scrutiny of a mounted rifleman. I recognized several neighboring ranchers, Hale Gentry, the owner of Sawtooth Wells' only saloon. What was he doing here? On foot were Shelby's sister, Amelia, and her husband, Cooper, the only other colored folks in the area. Shelby had told me Amelia, complexion velvet as melted chocolate, was not the offspring of his father, but of his mother's '*amour de Coeur.*' Shelby had once lost track of her, but had discovered her whereabouts when I was twelve, and he'd returned to Mississippi to join her. At the time, I'd feared he was gone forever, but he'd come back, brought Amelia and her husband to California and settled them on an abandoned homestead across the valley. Both Mother and I had lost, then refound, Shelby at one time in our lives. Now we'd both lost him forever.

Shelby's grave lay beside Julian's, and four headstones stood in the Maxwell plot now, silent echoes of the peaks that overlooked them. It had been scarcely forty years since my mother had crossed the plains with her family, and already a sizeable number of them lay in the California earth they had fought to get and keep. My grandfather Carter gored. My grandmother Julia, gone mad and native, killed in a fall wandering the night hills. Julian, torn asunder for reasons none of us understood. And now Shelby.

We clustered around the mound of earth that would soon cover Shelby's coffin. "The good men do lives after them," the headstone read. Had Mother misquoted the Bard? No. Her mother had filled her with a love of literature. Her father had forced her to spend two years at Stephens College for women in Missouri—her own little exile—and she still read insatiably. Mother would presume to bend even Shakespeare to suit her. Still, I had to confess the words fit.

The service was brief, doubtless at Mother's instruction. When the time arrived for remembrances, I chose to relate the story of a day on the range with Shelby when I was perhaps nine or ten. No incident I knew more exemplified his gentle toughness.

* * *

Cletis Harvey, one of the ranch hands, had been with Shelby and me that day. An unrepentant southern rebel still angry about losing the war, he was a wiry little man with red hair and a belly that ballooned incongruously from his otherwise bony frame. Cletis had thrown a loop over the horns of a cow and hauled her out of a swampy bog. She lay exhausted. He drew his knife and prepared to cut the taut rope. I reined in behind Shelby, who had been waiting and watching, lasso in hand.

"Ride in and shake off your loop, Cletis," Shelby said.

"Like hell I will. I ain't goin' near that crazy beast."

"It's Circle M rope, and you ain't cutting it." Shelby remained calm.

"Ain't no shit-colored son of a bitch gonna tell me what to do." Cletis poised his blade under the line.

"Cletis, I warned you."

Cletis looked at Shelby for a moment. "All right, all right," he said. He moved as if to resheath the knife, but instead dropped it and drew his pistol. Shelby had anticipated the move. He flicked his rope, and slapped the pistol to the ground.

"Nigger bastard." Cletis spat in Shelby's direction.

"Dismount." Shelby's voice was calm as if he'd asked the potatoes to be passed.

"The hell you say." Shelby threw a quick loop and jerked. Cletis was sitting in his saddle one moment, in the dust the next. Shelby rode in and flipped the lasso free before Cletis could find his bearings.

"Sawtooth Wells is a four- or five-hour walk due north," Shelby said. "You can make it before dark if you start now and step lively. We'll send your horse and gun and pay to the sheriff's office soon as we get around to it."

Cletis pointed his finger. "You black—"

"I'm starting to get offended at your manner of addressing me, Cletis."

The little man dropped his hand, turned his back, and began walking. Shelby watched him over the crest of a ridge, then freed the cow, retrieved the pistol and knife, and handed me the reins of Cletis' horse.

I pointed in the direction Cletis had gone. "Why didn't you shoot him, Shelby?"

"Now what good would that do?"

"Well, it would teach him not to be insubordinate."

"Insubordinate. Andy, I swear you know more words than a dictionary."

"But you can't just let people run over you, can you?"

"Do you think he ran over me?"

"Well, not exactly, it just doesn't seem right for him to walk away scot free. Besides you're not shit-colored."

"Now that's a word you shouldn't be using and you know it."

"Sorry," I said. "but—"

"Andy, I could have shot Cletis. And around here, I probably could have got away with it, even though most places, a man my color can't shoot a white man for any reason and expect to live out the week. But so what? Shooting Cletis's is like shooting rats. Every one you kill, a hundred more are waiting to take his place. Just keep yourself ready. There's almost always another way."

Another way. A way I had only a couple of weeks left to discover.

* * *

The parson said a closing prayer. Mother announced that Ling Chu had prepared a repast in the dining room.

"Plenty of good food," said Ling Chu. "No one go home hungry. Big insult to me."

On the way back to the house, Ling Chu walked beside me, doing his best to adjust to my halting gait. "After you eat, I will help you again with the healing needles, Mr. Andy."

"I don't know whether I should, Ling Chu. Doc Robinson says that kind of treatment is heathen and unhealthy."

"Mr. Andy, do you hurt more when you have the needles or when you don't?"

"I was teasing, Ling Chu. Needles it is. And welcome. This leg is beginning to throb again." Ling smiled. Almost. And hurried ahead.

I felt a tug at my sleeve, heard a soft drawl.

"Mr. Andrew. If you please, just for a moment." I turned to find Shelby's sister standing behind me. She held a small package in her right hand, wrapped in weathered brown paper. She pointed over her shoulder. "This is my husband, Cooper, I think you know?"

"Of course. Good to see you both." I shook Cooper's hand. "Even in such sadness."

"Yes," Amelia said. "I won't keep you. It's just Shelby wanted that you have this." She handed me the paper, carefully folded, but not tied. I unfurled the wings to find a gold military medal engraved with fighting men and a Latin motto—a reference to iron and freedom that my Latin was insufficient to fully translate—attached to a red, white, and blue ribbon.

"General Butler pinned that on Shelby hisself. After the battle of New Market Heights, when the colored troops won the day. He was more proud of that than… " The rest of her sentence caught in her throat.

"Why me? Something this important shouldn't it be yours or—"

Amelia closed my hands over the medal. "My brother had a powerful affection for you, Mr. Andrew. Believe me, it's yours." I embraced her, shook Cooper's hand again. Cooper put an arm around her shoulders as they walked away. I refolded the paper around the medal and slid it carefully into my pocket.

Mother waited on the porch, greeting and thanking guests as they filed into the house. I watched Hale Gentry deliver his blond-haired, white-toothed condolences.

"I've always said you were a gypsy queen, Carrie." He lifted her hand to his lips. "In mourning, you look more like one than ever."

"And your flattery knows no bounds, Mr. Gentry, but I thank you for the kind words." She dipped her chin in a mock curtsey, made to withdraw her hand, but he held her fingers.

"You know, the ranch will need a man's hand even more now." Mother lifted her eyes and met his gaze squarely.

"We will sorely miss Shelby's gentle authority."

Gentry glanced in my direction, nodded to me. "Condolences, son," he said. He released her hand and stepped into the house with the other guests. Mother and I were alone.

"He's not aiming to take up with you, is he, Mother?"

"Who?"

"Him. Fancy pants Gentry."

"A mosquito." She flicked a hand across her face. "Nothing."

I chose to believe her, let it drop. "Shelby's gone, Mother."

"Yes. Gone. Yet here just the same." She turned to me and held out her hand. I clasped it, and our eyes met.

"Two Maxwell deaths in two weeks," I said

"I can't afford to lose anyone else, Andy."

"You haven't lost me, Mother. And you won't."

"I wish—"

"Not now, please." I broke eye contact.

"Let's join the others," she said and started toward the dining room. I held back, unready to socialize.

"You know, I believe I need a few minutes with Julian. I'll return soon."

* * *

Shelby's casket already lay under fresh soil. I breathed deeply and knelt at the foot of Julian's. "Flights of angels sing thee to thy rest," his headstone said. Julian would have trekked forty days through the wilderness rather than read Shakespeare for ten minutes.

A faint keening drifted down from the hillside.

An old Indian woman dressed in buckskin appeared above the gravesites, shifting and shuffling from foot to foot, wailing and chanting in harmony with the still shadows. Crazy Lou had been a fixture in the valley my entire life. A solitary native who wandered by her own idiosyncratic path through the valley, everyone knew of her, but few actually saw her. She seemed to gravitate more toward the Circle M than any other ranch, so I was one of those who recognized her on sight, though many would have known her immediately just by the legend. This song, I knew somehow, was her prayer for Shelby. I bowed my head and let the ritual music weave its way through my meditation. I dug my fingers into the fresh soil, clasped thus in my hand the spirit of duty to my brother, my family, my own name. Lou was still chanting when I departed, her voice flowing down the slope into some ancient well darker than an amalgamation of all the nights since creation.

CHAPTER SIXTEEN

Later that evening I lay on the living room sofa with a dozen or so of Ling Chu's healing needles sticking out of me here and there. Two even sprouted from the top of my head. The connection between them and the pain in my thigh was a mystery to me, but they stopped the throbbing. Owl Feather was on my mind. Owl Feather and Wyoming and getting to the bottom of this plot and how to persuade Mother to help.

She entered, dressed in a simple shift, her hair tied back with a black ribbon, her only visible sign of mourning. She sat in a rocking chair facing the fireplace and giggled as she looked at me.

"We don't usually allow porcupines in the living room."

I laughed. Needles stabbed here and there. "Whoa. That hurt," I said. "Please no more jokes for a while."

"But you're better, Andy?"

"I should be completely mobile before long."

"Have I told you yet today how glad I am you came back alive?"

"Once or twice. It's always nice to hear."

Her face grew serious. "Andy, when this is over, when Yellow Squirrel is captured or killed—"

"I don't think it will be over then, Mother. Even if he is captured."

"And why not?" Her tone was challenging.

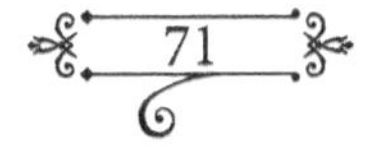

"You've forgotten about Standing Oak already? And Owl Feather? And the next full moon? Which is only a couple weeks away?" My persuasion campaign stalled before it began.

"Beware the Ides of August, Andrew? And Owl Feather doesn't enter into this any longer. I received a telegram from Fort Washakie today. Owl Feather is old and dying."

"He can still give orders, can't he? He probably wants to get his revenge before he goes to the happy hunting grounds. Shelby died because everyone ignored me. There will be more deaths unless we stop Owl Feather."

"As I was saying—" she stopped, her eyes fastened on a window that looked out on a side porch.

"What's the matter?" I said.

"Excuse me for a moment." She rose and walked down the small hallway past the office and out the back door. There'd been no alarm in her voice, but that didn't quell my apprehensions.

I hesitated, then followed her, plucking out the bone needles as I went. I peered off the back step, saw only dark specters of house and fence and bushes. Then I heard Mother's voice and that of another female around corner of the house. She was making a target of herself, not only for Yellow Squirrel, but for the newly-hired guards, who might mistake her for an intruder. I hurried toward her. "Mother."

The voices stopped. Mother, or a vague silhouette of her, appeared. Then another silhouette, this one behind a bull's eye lantern. A man with a rifle slanted in our direction. "Who's there?"

"Just me, Jasper, Mrs. Maxwell."

"Thanks for being alert," she said.

"I thought I heard voices." Jasper was close now, his red beard glowed in the lanternlight.

"No trouble this time," Mother said. "But you were right to investigate."

"Evening, Ma'am. You too, Mr. Maxwell," Jasper said. I nodded. He put two fingers to his hat brim and withdrew.

"What brought you out here? Or who?" I said.

"Nothing. Nothing at all. Just one of those Indian beggars you were complaining about." She took my arm and ushered me back into the house. I sat on the large couch, worked on extracting the rest of the needles.

"A bit late for the begging natives, isn't it?"

"Not usual," she said, "but not unheard of." Something was askew here, but nothing in her voice or demeanor betrayed whatever it was. My thigh pain began to creep back from incipient to manifest. She went on. "Now, as I was saying, *when* this is over, when Yellow Squirrel is captured or killed,

I'm thinking of changing my conditions about you and your place here on the Circle M. What do you say to returning here part time, say every other month, to learn the skills you'll need to manage the ranch eventually."

I pointed a handful of needles at her. "Mother, it was your idea to banish me just because I wished to go to school. And wasn't it you? Yes, I think it was, who said quite recently, that ranching is not my strong suit."

"I said combat."

"In any case, I wouldn't want to disappoint you."

"I'll be forty-seven next month. I want to prepare for that distant day when I'm incapable of performing every task that needs doing. The Circle M must remain in Maxwell hands, and I'm wagering that one day you'll find the will and the way to head it up."

"Now that I'm the only one left?" Her eyes flashed, then moistened.

"I'm going to ignore that," she said.

I wanted to apologize, wondered what stopped me. Again, I changed the subject instead. "I think you should go to Wyoming, Mother. You can't investigate everything by telegram. If Owl Feather is so ill, you can talk to him. He'll remember you, maybe repent. I'll be fine a in a day or so. I can hold the fort here."

"I refuse to chase your wild geese for you," she said, "and you are not yet prepared to take over this ranch, especially with roundup approaching."

"If he sees you in person, surely he'll want to put matters right before he dies."

"Owl Feather wouldn't know me from Adam, and I think the telegram makes it clear that our presence is not required. We'll discuss the other matter soon." She rose and strode across the room, back straight, chin high. She turned at the foot of the stairs. "I'm happy you're feeling better," she said. And climbed toward her room. The nonpareil of beauty—and of authority. Her intractability left me with no other choice but to defy and—surprised I had the power—hurt her again.

CHAPTER SEVENTEEN

The next day. I'd always respected Mother's wishes to stay out of my grandparents' trunk despite my curiosity about what family secrets it held. No longer. I climbed the stairs to the loft room, glad to find I required my cane only every third step or so. The door was padlocked. The universal skeleton key I'd taken from the office was useless. So, she'd known I'd attempt this. Well, she didn't know everything.

Julian and I had often played a little game in which we'd lock each other out of the house and attempt to break in without a trace. I knew how to defeat the locks on the windows. For that, though, I'd need to make a risky trek across the steep roof. With the sentinels about, that was a job for the dark, and I was still too lame to chance it. Another twenty-four hours of rest should give me the mobility I needed.

* * *

Mother decided to begin my managerial training by assigning me to reconcile a few Circle M accounts. The complexity of the ranch's finances amazed me. Wages, wire, groceries, riding gear, wagon parts, office supplies and hundreds of other items drew on the bank accounts all year, even when there was little or no income from cattle or crops. I'd have to develop enough business sense to juggle it all. An hour or two into the task, my confidence waxed, but my interest waned. Curiosity about my grandfather's death overcame me. Shelves of ledgers lined the room, each spine labeled with its year—a thin volume marked "1865" was the first—up to the present.

Perhaps a Wyoming trip was unnecessary. Perhaps the key to it all was here. I pulled down the three-volume set from 1883—the year Grandfather was killed—and turned page by page until I found the names of three men Mother had fired—Moses Giles, Kenneth Split Rock, Billy Summers. Three other Indian names appeared on the crew list, but nothing suggested more trouble than usual, let alone a plot. It appeared I was headed for Wyoming after all. I couldn't wait to delve into the trunk upstairs.

A chorus of shouts and barking dogs arose in the yard. Then voices at the front door.

"Why, Senator Campbell. And Virginia. What a nice surprise," Mother said. I would hardly have been more surprised to hear Julian and Shelby. I wanted to flee. I also wanted to run to Virginia like a lap dog.

"More for dinner, Mr. Andy," said Ling Chu. "Now even more important for you to go to town."

I must have answered him, but I don't recall what I said.

"Andy," Mother called, "where are you? There's someone I'd like you to meet."

I attempted an air of composure and stepped into the living room. Virginia had just doffed her wide-brimmed straw bonnet and duster coat and was handing them to Mother. She looked exceedingly fetching in a pink and yellow calico dress that showed to great effect both her hourglass figure and her blonde ringlets. Mother added the Senator's bowler and duster to the pile of garments in her arms and stepped toward the hat tree Grandfather had fashioned from elk antlers. She still wore the mourning ribbon in her hair and a black blouse along with her customary range attire.

"Well, Andrew, this is indeed a surprise." Campbell held out his hand and smiled. He was a big man with unnaturally small hands. His nose was hooked, his thin lips pale, and his cheeks perpetually flushed. I conjectured that Virginia's angelic looks had come entirely from her long-deceased mother. "I understood you were residing in Berkeley." His smile appeared strained, and I was glad to discomfit him.

"Yes, sir." I took his hand after a moment's hesitation, wished it were his daughter's instead. I turned to Mother. "Miss Campbell and I met at the university. I'm pleased to see you again, Virginia." Desire and resentment stirred beneath the polite nods and smiles we exchanged.

"I see," Mother said. "Well, why don't we all sit down. I'll ask Ling Chu to serve our dinner here, and we can enjoy a nice chat."

She saw to the seating and absented herself to give Ling his new instructions.

"I was just telling your mother, Andrew," Campbell said, "that we meant to be here for the funeral yesterday, but I was delayed on business. Nevertheless, we thought it important to deliver our condolences in person, however belated."

"I didn't know you were acquainted with Shelby, sir."

"Oh, not well-acquainted, of course, but I met him once or twice, and he seemed a fine, fine fellow."

I suspected Campbell's visit had more to do with politics than with compassion. Virginia busied herself gazing around at the ranch house architecture and smoothing her skirt.

"I understand you chased the killer, did you?" Campbell went on.

"Andrew was rather badly hurt," Mother returned from the kitchen. "We're quite fortunate to have him still with us." She conferred a gentle smile, which I returned. I thought I saw a shadow of concern pass over Virginia's face. I hoped so.

"The truth is, sir, that Mother and I and the Circle M are all in danger as long as Yellow Squirrel and his fellow conspirators are at large," I said.

"Conspirators?" Campbell leaned back and looked at me out of the corner of his eye.

"Jim," Mother said. "I believe you must have some business to discuss. Why don't we take a ride? I've been cooped up for so long I feel a bout of cabin fever coming on."

I stood. "Mother, please. It's too dangerous."

"I will not be held prisoner in my own land," she said. "Besides we've fortified this ranch so well that Crazy Horse and the whole Sioux nation wouldn't dare attack us." She stood and started toward the door, obviously expecting Campbell to follow, but he approached his daughter instead.

"Won't you accompany us, Virginia?"

"No thank you, Father. I have my sketch pad in the carriage." She moved past him toward the big window overlooking the yard. "I've been looking to draw these peaks."

"I'd prefer you joined Mrs. Maxwell and me." He glanced in my direction.

"I'll be perfectly all right, Father."

"I have some bookkeeping waiting," I said. One blatant lie deserved another.

I limped back to the office, sans cane now, and fortified myself with a glass of whisky while I waited for Mother and her politician friend to leave. At last, I heard their horses drum across the bridge.

I found Virginia on the front porch, leaning against the rail where her sketch pad rested. My eye lingered for a moment on the small of her back. Her weight was shifted to the right, her left heel slightly raised, allowing the skirt's ruffle to drape over the back of her white-stockinged ankle. I peered over her shoulder to watch her charcoal stroke quickly across the pad. She kept to her task as if I weren't present. Her spare, stylized rendering of the mountains had a distinct Oriental tone.

"Bamboo?" I said. "I doubt there's a twig of bamboo in the entire Sierra."

"A mountain's spirituality is unbounded." A few more lines, and her page reflected the peaks as clearly as would a still lake."

I remembered one of our previous conversations, ostensibly about religion and philosophy, but actually, I'd thought—still thought—small talk designed to keep my words—and hands—from straying where they longed to go. "I recall you once told me you didn't believe in God."

"I believe I said most of the time. Stop being so boorishly literal and concrete."

I held my peace for a while longer. Despite the exotic touches in her work, anyone who had seen Sawtooth Peaks would recognize them in her drawing, which is more than I could say for the unidentifiable crests of the treasured Bierstadt sketch that hung in our living room.

"I want to explain something about your father."

"We won't talk about that." She pointed the charcoal at me. I snatched both the stick and the pad from her hand, flipped to a clean page. She attempted to grab it back, but I turned beyond her reach and stabbed some quick, dark lines across the paper, shoved it front of her.

"I apologize for my poor technique," I said, "but I presume you can guess what this is."

"Give that back to me, Andrew." Her tone sharpened, and I took pleasure at the crack in her veneer. She reached again. I pulled it away.

"As soon as you guess."

She folded her arms. "This is stupid."

"Do you want it back or not?"

"Very well. A ladder."

"Guess again."

"Railroad tracks."

"Precisely. And that's why he's here. He wants something from the big men at Southern Pacific, and he believes my mother can help him get it. This visit had nothing to do with Shelby. Perhaps that gives you some pause about accepting his word for other things as well?"

"Hand me the pad, Andy." I acquiesced. She returned to her drawing.

"You have nothing to say?"

She slapped the porch railing with the pad. "I told you we will absolutely not discuss this. Especially when you have spirits on your breath. And I recall you mentioned something about bookkeeping." She picked up the sketch pad and held it between us. "Leave, Andy."

"For now, Virginia. For now. You're too intelligent to ignore the truth forever." I executed as powerful an exit as my injured leg would allow. I knew Virginia would spend the night here—it was too late for them to return now—and I knew which room mother would give her. Its window was to the immediate the right of the room that harbored my grandparents' trunk. I went back inside to await the blessings of shadows.

CHAPTER EIGHTEEN

It was a long wait through supper—the Senator's babbling, the tension between Virginia and me, the phony skirmishing over whether the visitors would spend the night—until a quiet slumber finally settled over the house. I was confident I could still operate the wire loop Julian and I had used to manipulate the window latches. My leg had healed sufficiently for me to creep over the roof with little pain or risk of falling.

I donned dark clothes and a pair of moccasins, slipped a rucksack on my back, and crept from my window into the nearly-moonless night. The watchman in the yard below, one of the new hands I didn't know, paced the area with his bull's eye lantern, but he seemed never to look up. The lanterns cast a weak beam for two feet or so, but beyond that, they were useless, more useful as targets for snipers than at detecting intruders. How simple for Yellow Squirrel to do precisely what I was doing.

The roof was pitched precipitously, the shakes slick and uneven, and my journey seemed more precarious than I recalled from my boyhood. I planned and tested each step before I committed my weight, as if I were crossing a streambed of mossy stones, lunged for grips on gables and chimneys, felt always on the edge of a plunge into the yard. I had to squeeze close to the glass to gain purchase on the sill while I threaded the wire between the upper and lower sash. This south side of the house received the brunt of sun and storm, so the lock lever, stiff from years of exposure and disuse, refused to move. Pulling too hard would throw me off balance and off the roof. I delicately jerked and yanked till inch by fraction of an inch, the lever began to yield. Finally the sash seemed free to rise—had it not been warped in place.

I pried with Shelby's knife, broke the sash's grip on the casement, resheathed the knife, hooked my fingers under the frame and worked it back and forth and up. I was in the midst of what I hoped would be the last pull when the window squawked like a blue jay. I caught my breath and crouched low. The watchman stopped, turned. I realized he wasn't any more acquainted with me than I with him, would likely shoot before asking my name.

He lifted his lantern in the general direction of the roof, and the beam traveled toward me. I was suddenly not willing to trust to the limitations of the lantern, but jammed myself and my rucksack through a gap I was moments ago certain would never accommodate me, pushed my way past the curtains, and shut the window. I watched for the beam to crawl across the pane, but it never came.

I had brought only wooden matches for light. Even had there been a kerosene lamp in the room, it would have been too risky to ignite it. Heavy wool draped the downstairs windows, but thin cotton prevailed upstairs. I closed the curtains to take advantage of what little masking they provided and kept my body and my cupped hand between the match flare and the window. The low glimmer revealed the steamer trunk against the opposite wall. I carefully lifted and turned the chest—pausing and planning after each move to avoid the slightest noisy scrape—so its lifted top would shield from the window the brief flare of the matches as I combed through the store of papers and mementoes. The lock was ornate, but simple to force.

I had to travel light, and it was difficult to decide which items would most likely make the best evidence. I considered taking my grandfather's Civil War service revolver for protection, but decided it was too ancient to be reliable. I'd lift one from the office gun cabinet. I resisted the impulse to open what I surmised was a picture frame or book wrapped in brown paper, tied with a string, and labeled "Mother and Father. Wedding day. November 15, 1859, Valparaiso, Indiana." No time for souvenirs, I decided, only clues. I finally settled on my grandmother's journal—three slim, ribbon-bound volumes—and my grandfather's trail log. Somewhere in their pages must lie hints about what had precipitated the vendetta and about why Mother so adamantly guarded this trunk.

Before I left, I placed Shelby's medal among the mementoes, still wrapped in the brown paper just as Amelia had given it to me. I thought it as honorable a piece of Maxwell history as any of the others. In the midst of lowering the trunk lid it struck me as odd that my grandparents' wedding package was concealed here, not displayed or honored somewhere in the house. It was, after all, rather small and weighed little. I climbed back on the roof.

Relocking the window was even harder than unlocking it, but I persevered and succeeded. Mother would guess what I'd done. I delighted to think she'd perhaps admire me even in her anger as she tried to determine how I'd accomplished it. The watchman stood at the far end of the yard, pointing his lantern toward distant shadows. I was virtually home free. And I was also one dormer away from Virginia's room. Was it worth the chance? The mind may calculate and ponder, but heart and body have decided long before.

I crept to her sill and sounded the pigeon-cooing signal we'd used for our midnight rendezvous at her boarding house window. Three calls evoked no response, and I was about to use my wire loop when the curtains parted. Rembrandt couldn't have shaped her face more beautifully than the light from the candle she held.

I pressed close to the glass, waved and motioned her to raise the sash. She waved me away. I held my hands in a praying posture, crossed my lips and my heart, and held my thumb and forefinger close together. A silly, serious game of charades.

She shook her head and reached up to close the curtains. I mouthed "please" and repeated the prayer gesture. Finally she relented and raised the window.

"What do you want, Andy?"

"Are you going to leave me out here on the roof?"

"Please have your say, then leave. I'm quite exhausted." She folded her arms and pursed her lips in a pout.

"It'll be difficult to say it from out here."

"You'll just have to try." She turned her back, presenting me with a blonde cascade of curls unfettered by ribbons or combs. My chance. I thrust myself into the room. She turned.

"Andy." A fierce whisper. Two steps backward.

"Just a moment. That's all." I held my palms outward. I want to apologize. For everything. Before Julian came to San Francisco, I never could have imagined myself in those… situations. And your anger is… I deserve it."

She turned her back again. "Don't attempt to pass blame to your brother. Or my father."

"All I did, I own to. I'm saying only that I did it all with him and wouldn't have without him."

"Is that all?" She turned around as she spoke, and ringlets bouncing.

"I'm leaving tomorrow. No one knows, and it's better I don't reveal where I'm going, but it concerns Julian's killing. I simply hoped you'd forgive me, or at least promise to see me again when—if—I get back." I leaned toward her. Her lips were nearly close enough to kiss.

"If?" She drew back.

"They mean to kill us, Virginia. There's no guarantee they won't succeed." I leaned farther. She stepped back.

"Andy, listen. If it makes you feel any better, I know you weren't lying about… about that night… and my father."

"Then why—"

"I'm not completely ignorant about men, and I'm certain anyone who courts me will leave parts of his past unspoken. But now… everything between us is spoiled. Don't you see?" She stepped toward me, maddeningly close.

A knock and a call from the hallway interrupted us.

"Virginia? I thought I heard voices. Are you all right?" Her father.

CHAPTER NINETEEN

I dived behind the bed, huddled out of sight and scarcely breathing.

"Come in, Father. Yes. I'm fine." I heard the door open. Footsteps crossed the room.

"I was star-gazing," she said. "The air is so clear up here, it seems as if one is closer to heaven. If I believed in heaven."

"Of course you believe in heaven, my love. This agnostic business you've been spouting lately is only schoolgirl rebellion."

"Ah, Father dear, how little you know your darling daughter."

"I'm certain that's true," he said, "but I know enough to protect her, and it's not a good idea to stand here at an open window with all kinds of scoundrels creeping around."

"Don't be silly. Who'd be foolish enough to climb around up here? Why it's so steep they'd slide off in a second unless they had wore hobnail boots or something, which would be way too noisy for a sneak attack. I'd hear him before he got within ten feet of the window, or the door, for that mattter."

"Nevertheless." The window slammed shut and I heard the latch slide in place.

"Now, once again, good night." Footsteps retreated. The door closed. I crawled out of hiding.

"What did you mean—"

She crossed to the window, flung it open. "Go." Another intense whisper.

"Not until—"

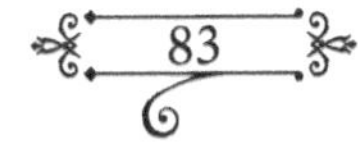

"Out."

So I slipped over the sill, clenched myself to blend with the gable wall, my feelings in as tight a knot as my body.

I'd been positive that exposing her father for a liar and hypocrite would bring Virginia to my side. But she already knew, and somehow that knowledge had spoiled our relationship. Spoiled. Like a bruised peach? I made my way past the loft where the trunk lay, on toward my own bedroom.

It was no more than three steps from the loft room gable to the next chimney, but my toe caught a shingle and I suddenly sat on the roof and started sliding down feet first. I scrabbled for the chimney, missed. I now knew a bit about how Lucifer felt on his way down from heaven.

CHAPTER TWENTY

White light washed the darkness as I dropped off the edge of the house toward the roof of the porch a few feet below, where I managed to alight almost standing. I sat quickly, and broke the slide by planting my feet against gingerbread scrolling that jutted above the roofline. The watchman's lantern blazed full in my eyes.

"Hands up, mister."

"Easy, there. It's only me, Andy." I swung down and dropped the six feet or so to the porch.

"Andy don't mean nothing to me." It wasn't Jasper, but a wiry man I didn't know, lantern in one hand, pistol twitching in the other. "You stay right there and keep your hands high."

At least he hadn't fired. Lucky. Had hiring all these strangers made us more safe or less so? He backed up the steps, set down the lantern, and yanked the rawhide string that rocked the dinner bell. Five or six other hands answered the alarm, running from their stations at corrals and barns. Jasper wasn't there. Worst of all, my berobed and sleepy-eyed mother stepped through the front door followed closely by the senator in a velvet-lapelled smoking jacket. As appropriate as a tuxedo at a square dance.

"Caught this scallywag red-handed." The watchman jabbed toward me with his gun. "Heard someone crawlin' around up there and yelled at him so fierce he got scared and slid right down to me."

I let Tom's exaggeration of his prowess pass without comment.

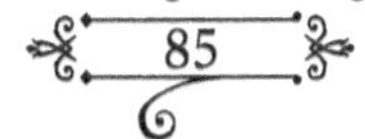

"Good work, Tom," Mother said, "but embarrassed as I am to say it, this is my son. Go on about your duties, now, all of you."

We watched men disappear into the darkness, then Mother flung the door open and pointed me toward the living room, her chin set, back arched. I walked into the house and stood by the fireplace. Mother and Campbell marched toward me.

"Andrew?" was all she said. Then waited.

To hell with all the intrigue, I decided. "I wanted to talk to Virginia, but he's forbidden her to see me." I caught a movement in my peripheral vision. Virginia crouched in the shadows above the stairway.

"And for good reason," the senator declaimed. He lifted shoulders, chin, and voice into an affectation of regal bearing. "I'm sorry to reveal this, Carrie, but your sons, rest poor Julian's soul, were seen in a most compromising situation in a place which delicacy prevents me from naming. I acted to protect my precious darling's virtue."

"I'm not quite so delicate, Jim. Name it, please."

It was a treat to see the senator flush even more than usual. "Respectable citizens term it a… house of ill-repute."

"You and Julian in a brothel, Andy? My, my." A hint of a smile?

"It's not the whole story." I watched Campbell. The left side of his mouth curled into an incipient smirk, as if he were daring me to tell everything. I hesitated to humiliate him while Virginia watched. "But yes, it's true."

"I heard voices and looked in on Virginia not fifteen minutes ago," Campbell said. "Obviously, I need a word with her. I'll leave you to deal with your son, Carrie." Virginia's shadow disappeared. The Senator climbed the stairs, still in his version of royal posture.

"I apologize, Mother," I said. I started to follow him up the stairs.

"Not yet, Andrew. Not quite yet." I turned to face her. She waited until the senator was out of sight.

"I'm still waiting for an explanation, Andrew."

"It was Julian's idea—"

"I don't care about the brothel. What were you doing on the roof at two A.M? And few gentlemen I know go courting with a rucksack on their back. What do you have in there?"

"Just some books and things." She narrowed her eyes and pulled her head back. "You don't trust me?" I said. "Would you care to look for yourself?" I jerked the rucksack from my shoulders and held it toward her. I hoped audacity would substitute for honesty.

"I most certainly would," she said. She took the pack, reached into the bag, lifted the items out one by one and laid them on the mantle.

"I underestimated your determination." The sack empty, she handed it back to me. "And I overestimated your honesty. What were you planning to do with these?"

I threw down the rucksack. Its wood frame thumped on the floor. "I want to save our lives. And the ranch." I spread my arms. "Is that wrong?"

"Noble motives, perhaps, but you've broken my trust."

"If you trusted me so, why did you padlock the loft?"

She twisted her hands together, and her eyes glistened. I tightened my lips to mask my confusion and surprise at her distress. But her voice neither whined nor trembled.

"Andrew, please sit down." I perched on the edge of the couch. She gathered books and package from the mantle and held them before me. She did not sit.

"There are matters in here so precious to the Maxwell heritage that they must not become known until it's absolutely necessary—probably not in my lifetime. This information would harm many, and it can help no one. Believe me, none of it can possibly bear on Yellow Squirrel or any of his gang, if there is one. Do you understand, Andrew? Tell me you do."

"Perfectly."

"Now then, please, your solemn promise that you will never again while I am alive disturb anything in that trunk." Her eyes fixed me as if I were a hide nailed to a wall.

"I'm all the heritage the Maxwells have remaining, Mother, and I'm old enough to come to grips with a family scandal. Suppose we look together. We might discover something about this conspiracy you haven't suspected. And you can help soften the blow of whatever horrors you're hiding."

"Once more," she said. "Your pledge."

"No peeking till you're dead? What if you're sick? Injured? Kidnapped?" I rose. "Sorry, Mother, but I can't promise that I won't try to save you. Us. The ranch." Her features softened, mouth trembled, eyes reddened, but her voice remained steady.

"I'm so sorry to hear that, Andrew. I'm going to ask you the same question in the morning. If you hope to set foot on the Circle M while I live, I hope you'll reconsider. For now, I'm going to lock these away and retire."

She tucked books and picture under her arm, grabbed the skirt of her robe, and strode toward the office. I heard the safe open and close. She reemerged and climbed the stairs without another word.

I snatched up my rucksack and followed, shuffled my way to my room, and sat on my bed in the dark. So Mother put keeping her secrets above survival itself. No secret was worth dying for. I needed what she had locked in that safe, but I didn't know the combination or where to find it. The grandfather clock in the living room chimed three. Only a couple of hours until daylight.

I crept downstairs, gathered more matches from beside the fireplace, and tiptoed to the office. The combination had to be somewhere other than Mother's memory. She was too careful for that. It could be locked in a bank or a lawyer's office somewhere. But she liked keeping matters within her control. She might tell a lawyer where to find the combination if something happened to her, but she was unlikely to give it to him.

I stepped into the office, drew the drapes tight, and lighted the kerosene lamp atop the desk. Ledgers I'd pored over earlier were still stacked there. Rolled pieces of paper poked from cubbyholes. A gun cabinet held racks for several rifles and pistols. The key for that, I knew, lay on its top. The skeleton key I'd taken from the office earlier and then used upstairs had escaped Mother's detection. I used that key to close and lock the office door. I'd take a pistol for my Wyoming trip before I left, but first the combination.

I didn't know how much Grandfather had paid for the the six-foot tall, two-ton, black Mosler, with its gilt lettering, but I knew he was proud of the bargain he'd struck for it after the Old Solon Hotel in Sacramento burned down.

It would have been unlike either Grandfather or Mother to use an obvious hiding place, but I had to start there—cubbyholes, the underside of the rolltop's drawers and the safe itself. No results.

I turned to the account books on the shelves. I was lifting the 1880 ledgers from the shelf when I noticed light spilling from under the office door into the hallway. I stripped off my shirt, plugged the gap, and sat down to examine the ledgers. The clock chimed the half-hour—3:30 A.M.

Page by number-filled page I worked through seven volumes all the way until 1883, the year Grandfather died. I attempted to enter my grandfather's mind and spirit, but I saw nothing I recognized as a combination. Even if I found a combination from those years, Mother might have changed it.

The clock struck 4:30. I peeked out of the drapes. Still dark, but I knew I had only a half-hour or so before the ranch began to awaken. Where else could I turn? I'd have pounded the desk if I hadn't feared the noise. I would almost rather have set out for Wyoming without a gun than without the information in that safe.

I forced myself to scan the shelves again, touched each volume one-by-one on the chance my hand would find something my eyes had missed. And they did. Hidden in the shadows toward the rear of the shelf, beside the slim 1865 book which recorded the sums of the Circle M's first year, I touched a smaller volume, pulled it out. No date marked its spine.

Bold block lettering on the frontispiece declared the book contained Circle M Historical Landmarks. The opening entry read "June, 1865—founding of ranch and registering of brand." Beside those words, a drawing of the capital M—a nearly-perfect freehand circle surrounding it. Commemorative entries followed for the completion of the house, barn, and other buildings. Other entries announced significant stock purchases including the famous Jerome III, who had gored Grandfather. It was all fascinating, but seemed irrelevant. I traced each numeral with my index finger. I eventually noticed faint pencil lines under parts of some of the dates—the "65" in "1865," the "18" in "1880," the "87" in "1874," and the "1" and the "9" in "1879." I grabbed a sheet of paper from the desk drawer and copied the underlined numbers. Standing alone, they looked as if they could be a combination—65, 18, 87, 19. But if they were, it wasn't enough information to open the safe. What was the sequence? Which way and how many times must the dial turn? I calmed myself and resumed tracing with my finger.

I found my answer in the prize bulls. Each animal's name was followed by a single pedigree number—except for Jerome I. He had two such numbers, and the second read "4L3R2L."

I rushed to the safe and turned the dial four times left to "65," three right to "18," twice left to "87," then back to "19." I didn't hear the click I was listening for but turned the handle anyway. It didn't move. I wrote the failed combination down so I wouldn't repeat it. How many possible sequences were there? The mathematics eluded me. I raised my eyes to the ceiling searching for a logical next step, and my eyes lighted on the ledgers, their dates in perfect reverse order. Then, I understood. Mother had talked of Grandfather's seeing himself as a left-handed man in a right-handed world. The backwards shelving order was more than an inconsequential non-conformity—it reflected the essence of Grandfather's thinking. The clock struck 5:00.

I returned to the dial and reversed the order of the numbers. Still the handle didn't move. I again recorded the failed sequence. I could hear Ling Chu in the kitchen now. Mother would be down shortly. She'd head straight for the office to retrieve the order of the day's work. But I was now certain I was on the right course. I reversed both the numbers and the order of the turns to right and left. I heard the tumblers fall and rejoiced as the handle moved easily. I wrote down the winning sequence, swung the door open and retrieved my treasure. The doorknob rattled.

"Why is this door locked? Who's in there?" Mother called.

CHAPTER TWENTY-ONE

"Just a moment." It took what seemed like an age to stuff my treasures back in the safe and restore the room and myself to their original condition so I could let Mother in.

"I couldn't sleep," I said. "Thought I'd come in here and try to finish those accounts."

"No need to lock the door for that, Andrew." She stalked past me to the safe, confidently spun the dial, and opened the door. Everything she'd put in the night before remained in place—with the unfortunate addition of the Landmarks book I had shoved in with everything else. I slumped to the desk chair as she closed the safe. When she turned, I saw something I'd never seen before, even at Shelby's funeral, even beside Julian's coffin—tears wet her cheeks.

She fetched a small chair, sat opposite me, and held out her hands, palms on her knees. I remained still.

"I suppose I would have done the same. Now, I'm pleading. Please accept my solemn vow that only sorrow will come of what you find there."

"If it's so dreadful, why don't you simply destroy it?"

"I can't bring myself to obliterate the last traces of my parents, Andy." Her words came in whispers, sobs behind them. "Will you promise?"

I leaned forward, laid a hand on hers. "I can't, Mother." She slowly withdrew her hands and dropped her gaze.

"I'm afraid I can't have you here, then, Andrew. You're too stubborn and too… smart." She gestured toward the safe.

"And where would you have me go? Charley Hung's waiting for me in one direction, Yellow Squirrel in the other."

"Very well," she said. She wiped her face dry with her sleeve. "I suppose I have to accept that school is your natural environment. I'll clear Julian's debt and call off the Oriental gangsters. I trust that will be satisfactory?" She raised her hand when I started to speak. "We can defend ourselves against Yellow Squirrel without you, Andy." She opened her arms and smiled. I stepped into her embrace, heard her whisper, "Godspeed," and clasped her in my arms. A soft and salty aroma surrounded us.

"Come back if you change your mind, if you're ready to… join me," she whispered.

"I'm ready now."

"Perhaps I'm the one who's not ready, Andy." She stepped back and grasped my arms.

"Just one thing, Mother."

"Yes?"

"All the enemies may not come from outside. There are many new men here. Some of them could be after more than Circle M wages."

"Ling Chu will pack you some food. I'd have Tom saddle a horse, but with all these extra hands we've no stock to spare. You may hire one at the livery stable in town and lay the charge on the ranch account." She motioned for me to precede her out of the office, then locked the door behind us. I headed to my room to pack. I was halfway up the stairs when she called.

"Andy." I turned. "Godspeed," she said again, then walked toward the kitchen. Mother had not shown me such tenderness since I was a child, yet she had also turned me out. Cuddled with one hand, slapped with the other. And she probably knew I was headed for Wyoming, not Berkeley.

* * *

It didn't take me long to pack. Ling Chu fixed me some food. While in the kitchen, I grabbed a handful of matches and filched an oilskin tablecloth. July 25. Less than three weeks till the August 13 full moon. Looking at the calendar was like watching a burning fuse.

I didn't head straight out of the yard, but doubled back behind the bunkhouse. Mother had ordered horses and mules confined to the barn and its adjoining corral, and they were closely guarded. But only one man was assigned to the bunkhouse and nearby pigpen. I bellied up and opened the gate. A few well-thrown stones got the pigs moving toward their exit. As soon as someone saw the roaming hogs and sows and called for all hands to help round them up, I scampered to the office window, shoved it open, and dived inside. First, the package and books. Then a pedestrian .44 revolver no one was likely to miss for a time. There was no holster, but I found a twenty-five cartridge box of ammunition in the gun cabinet drawer. I slung my leg out the window and closed the sash, then turned around to find Ling Chu watching from the porch.

I walked toward him, struggling to formulate an explanation. As I drew closer, I saw that his cheeks were as wet as Mother's had been earlier.

"Ling Chu, we could all die if I don't do this. Please don't say anything." He turned his back and walked into the house.

I wrapped the books in oilskin, burning for the moment on trail or train when I'd find time to delve into them, including the matches in what I hoped was a waterproof package. Armed now with knowledge and a bit of Julian's bravado, I would come at my problem from the past—the diaries—and the present—my journey to Wyoming—and the two would meet and consummate in a grand victory—West-to-East and East-to-West—like the 1869 joining of the Central and Union Pacific. Thus run the grandiose scripts we write for ourselves. If we're made in His image, as the preachers claim, why do the scripts we actually live out so seldom match the ones we create?

CHAPTER TWENTY-TWO

My injured leg was pulsing after the three-hour hike to town. I nodded and chatted with feigned airiness when I ran into people I hadn't seen for years, full of compliments and good wishes for Mother, less extravagant greetings for me. I worked my smiling way to the livery stable, traitor and scoundrel, as I was about to become.

"Ain't got no horses," said Jesse the stable hand. How old was he now? Eighteen? Mother had hired him—a favor to his father—to help load hay the summer before I left for school. He'd spent more time avoiding work than doing it, and when she caught him tossing her cat into a watering trough, she'd fired him. Now he leaned against the stable wall. A hand-rolled cigarette dangled from his lipless mouth. Dusty hair hung over his eyes and dripped down his neck.

"I see two behind that fence," I said.

He shook his head. "Reserved."

"Is your father available?"

"Gone for a few days." He lurched away from the wall and stood with his feet planted wide and his thumbs hooked in his belt loops. "I'm in charge." I held my ground, smiled.

"And when will he return?"

"Tomorrow, supposed to."

"I'm headed to Placerville in a hurry."

He grinned and twisted the cigarette butt under the ball of his foot. "You own the Circle M and don't know where to find you a horse?"

"Perhaps that mule?" I pointed to a stall behind the horses. Jesse turned and laughed.

"Old Stephen? He ain't broke to saddle or nothin'."

"But is he rented?" I moved past him to the fence.

"You want him, he's yours." He waved me toward the animal in mocking imitation of a doorman ushering an honored guest into a hotel. A neophyte Yellow Squirrel.

"I'll require a saddle," I said. "And you can put the charges to the Circle M."

I approached the animal, saddle in hand, hoped I displayed more confidence than I felt. One of the rites of passage on the Circle M was to stay aboard Sailor, who always bucked like a clipper ship in a storm the first time anyone tried to ride him. I'd done well with him, so the mule shouldn't be much of a challenge.

Stephen stood amazingly still for saddle and bridle, but he objected strenuously to a rider. I managed to avoid thumping my bad leg both times he threw me, and on the third mounting I stayed aboard. When Jesse fetched my rucksack and canteen, he was no longer smirking.

I headed west past the canoe-shaped patch of dried grass and needles where a large pine splits Sawtooth Wells' main street. Though Stephen tolerated my presence on his back, he didn't take at all well to being told where to go and when. Riding-horse bridle signals meant nothing, seemed to irritate him in fact.

Even on a saddle horse, the nearest railroad station in Placerville was an all-night ride. On Stephen, I wondered if I'd make it at all, let alone have a chance to get started reading the diaries as I'd hoped to do. If it weren't for my leg, I'd have tried walking.

* * *

Aroound midnight Stephen simply stopped. I kicked, swore, pleaded, and urged. I dismounted and pulled on the reins. Stephen lay down in the road. Mules are generally hardier and stronger than horses, but I'd come face-to-face with the reason they are not folks' first choice to ride. I had seen muleskinners kick and beat recalcitrant animals till they bled without moving them an inch. I'd also seen gentler measures fail.

I decided to appeal to his need for both companionship and water and began walking. I kept looking back as I went. Before long, he appeared to be no more than a black mound in the night, then blended into the darkness altogether.

The night was clear and starry, and at this lower altitude the road cut through chaparral instead of timber. It would have been a pleasant stroll if I hadn't been limping and hurried. At the bottom of the hill, I tried to outwait Stephen for another half hour before I tramped back up the grade to find him as prone as before. I fashioned myself a cushion of leaves, used my rucksack as a pillow, and lay back for a few minutes rest.

* * *

I don't know whether dawn or Stephen awakened me. It was half-light, and the mule stood in the road a few yards away. A horse might have nuzzled me, but the mule had to make it seem as if he and I simply happened to be in the same neighborhood. I limped to his side, my leg stiff, but less painful. He waited for me to climb aboard, then repeated his bucking routine of the previous day—a few stiff-legged jumps to the side followed by a rolling rear-end kick. I'd learned enough about his habits not to repeat my tumbles.

I munched a piece of Ling Chu's sausage as Stephen bumped and wandered down the road with his jarring gait. I calculated we'd reach Placerville about noon. I didn't know the locomotive schedule from there, but I vowed to climb aboard anything that moved on tracks—from a maintenance cart to Ambrose Bierce's private car.

* * *

Placerville had been named Hangtown until some merchants decided the name was bad for business, changed it, and felled the vigilantes' hanging tree. The new name still hadn't taken with many folks, though, and Hangtown signs proliferated on saloons and stores.

The station agent said if I just took the Sacramento bound train out of Hang… er, Placerville, the next day, I could catch the eastbound two days from now because they ran every other day, don't you know. Of course, there was a logging train due to come through that evening, which might get me there in time to catch tomorrow's eastbound, but you didn't want to get caught trying to ride it. The railroad bulls were a pretty rough lot, most of them crooks and thugs themselves, so, no, he wouldn't advise anyone to do that, no one at all.

With time so precious, though, I'd have to risk it. I bid Stephen farewell at the livery stable, and headed for the far side of the yard. An empty boxcar would make a fine place to await my luxury coach.

I soon found a car whose sliding door was open barely enough to allow me in. I settled down, thinking to hazard a peek at the diaries.

"This ain't your car, buddy." The voice came from a far, dark corner. "Get out."

TWENTY-THREE

S o much for my reading. "There's room enough for us both, isn't there?" I said. "My name's Andy. I won't be here long." I offered my hand.

"Damn right you won't." A second voice said. "About ten more seconds would be my guess." Both men moved my way. I dropped my hand to my knife hilt, regretted leaving the pistol inside the rucksack.

"Very well. I see you want no company," I said. "I'll be on my way."

"Wait a minute, Jim," said the first man. He sidled into the arm of light from the doorway. Pitted red cheeks puffed from his dark beard. "We're being kind of inhospitable. He don't take up much room." He smiled at Jim, looked him in the eye.

"Well, sure, I guess so, sure. Beg pardon." Jim had shaved sometime in the last two weeks. His large mouth was a slice of white in brown stubble. "We get kind of testy with the bulls running around banging heads and all. I'm Jim, like he said. This here's Ezra." I shook hands with both men.

"Pleased to make your acquaintance. I appreciate your offer, but I'll find another car." I backed toward the door.

"Ah, no," Ezra said. "We'd feel like our bad manners drove you away." Jim was edging to cut me off. I lunged toward the opening. Jim managed to grab enough of my ankle to trip me and send me headfirst into the cinder and creosote of the track bed, and he maintained his grip on my trousers. My hat flew off. I flopped like a fish on a riverbank while he tried to haul me back into the car. Then we heard a shout and a whistle.

"Hey, you men. Hold it right there."

Jim released me, and I landed on my back athwart a rail. A huge figure in a dark uniform about fifty yards away brandished a truncheon and lumbered towards us. I snatched my hat, rolled under the car and scrambled down the tracks on my hands and knees, hoping Jim and Ezra would draw his attention, and from the clamor of shouting and scuffling I heard it seemed that had happened. When I finally reached a position to peek, I saw the railroad man lying unconscious, and Jim and Ezra disappearing into the gloom. A whistle announced the approach of other lawmen. My ear was to the ground, and I heard the rumble of an approaching train.

I crept toward the main track, as the train approached. It slowed and slowed, and I thought it would stop to fill its water tank, but the engine rolled past the water tower, which meant that for this engine Placerville was a mere hesitation. The agent had said the train would come through, but I guess he'd never said it would stop. Only two flatbed cars loaded with logs remained between me and the caboose, which I had to assume was occupied.

I executed a poor imitation of a sprint and grabbed the chain binding logs to car. My boots dragged a good ten yards through the cinders as the train gathered speed, but I finally swung myself aboard.

Even inside a passenger coach, a train in motion is noisy as thunder. Out here, the cacophony of shrieks and bangs was painful. I was sticky with pitch from clambering over the logs, and the smell of butchered pine was heavy as kerosene. Apparently, criminality and hostility were to be my daily bill of fare now.

I gazed skyward and considered climbing to the top of the load where I could enjoy my ride through the warm night, decided it was smarter to remain hidden. I snuggled into a splintery crevice, jammed against logs and suspended about two feet above the hitch.

The train slowed to a crawl well before it had traveled long enough to reach Sacramento. Perhaps we'd hit a long grade or had switched to a siding to allow another train to pass. I peeked out, saw piles of logs and a millpond. We hadn't been bound for Sacramento at all. Footsteps crunched the cinders and a red lantern approached my car.

I pulled my head back in and cowered into my nook as tightly as I could. The footsteps stopped very near me. I heard more tramping from the other direction.

"You there, Ralph?" A voice on my right.

"Right here." The new voice came from the left. They were talking across the hitch between my car and the one behind it.

"Well, I don't see anyone, Mike," the first voice said.

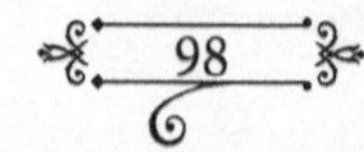

"I couldn't exactly tell from the caboose, but he jumped on right in here someplace. Has to be around."

"Probably drunk and fell off. Or maybe we'll find him in the pond when we unload. Come on. We got enough to do without worrying about some worthless tramp."

"I don't like it, Ralph. This here's supposed to be a logger, not a passenger train."

"It is a logger and we got logs to take care of. Forget it."

"I swear he's right around here somewhere." The man called Mike poked his lantern between the two cars and swung it back and forth almost in my face. I hadn't thought it was possible to freeze myself more solid than I already had, but I did.

"Mike, there's no one here."

"Hate to have these deadbeats get away, but all right. We do got to get out of the way for the noon load." Mike withdrew his light, and I heard the footsteps recede toward the front of the train.

I jumped off the car and hobbled my way back up the tracks, thankful for the dark moon. There was little cover beyond the train, so I stayed low in the trackside shadows. No time to hide. I had to keep moving.

Twenty-four hours ago, it was a balky mule, now it was an errant train. Not a good start to this journey. I'd have to follow the tracks into Sacramento and the noon train I must not miss since it would cost me two days of the eighteen remaining until Yellow Squirrel's deadline. I broke into a brief and painful jog.

The sun rose at my back, and my shadow stretched before me like the answers I was chasing but seemed never to catch. When the sun reached its zenith and the shadow disappeared, the train would leave the Sacramento station. I must look repulsive and frightening with a two-day beard and filthy as a tramp.

About mid-morning, I trudged toward a thicket of willows and blackberries that towered above my head and crowded the tracks. The tracks curved into a thicket. When I rounded the curve, I did something I'd been warned against all my life—I surprised a bear.

CHAPTER TWENTY-FOUR

He was on all fours, back toward me, happily munching berries. He hadn't caught my scent, so I eased backwards, but like the gravel on the mountainside with Yellow Squirrel, the crunch of cinders betrayed me. He turned, reared, and bellowed.

For one of those insane moments that can happen in the midst of danger, my mind took time to note that he was male, young and small for a black bear, and capable of slapping me the twenty yards to the river in one swipe. I'd heard somewhere that a bear will lose interest if one lies down and plays possum, but the sight of that red mouth and white dagger-teeth picked up my feet and sent them scrambling.

Thorns and canes tore at my clothes and rucksack, and I stumbled and rolled and for the first time in weeks, thought of neither Yellow Squirrel nor Julian nor Virginia nor anything but survival. His claws tore like scythes through the brambles. A cloud of stench from his fur and breath engulfed us. and he cast a putrid spray when he swung his head in frustration each time I dodged out of reach. I wondered if I'd feel the blow that finished me.

I dived under and over the brambles like a salmon leaping upstream, cursing the dense underbrush, which I'm now certain was all that kept the beast confused and encumbered enough to allow me to reach water. I plunged into the river, shoved for the main channel and the chance to swim with the current, hoping he'd quit at the shoreline even though he could swim like few other animals if he chose to. I heard a roar and splash behind me. He hadn't stopped. I turned to see him powering toward me, coming on at a speed I'd never outpace. I dived.

The river had been leveed into a narrow channel to protect property and crops from flooding, and it was deep and muddy this close to town even in late summer low-water. I sought a solid rock on the bottom, thinking to launch myself upstream and escape to the bank while the bear searched in the opposite direction.

My lungs were aching by the time I finally found purchase and kicked, but the foothold turned out to be sunken log, which rolled away and turned my launch into a desperate, flailing struggle for the surface. I finally made it, sucked in air, jerked my head to clear hair and water from my eyes, and caught sight of the bear a few yards downstream churning in my direction. I managed a second breath and dived again, this time with the current. I slid downstream, passed just under the floundering claws. Any more of this dive-and-surface routine would finish me. I had to finish him first.

I expected the bear to reverse direction toward me any moment, so I kicked toward the bottom, following the current, and freed my knife from its sheath on the way. I held hard to what little breath I had and planted a foot on what I hoped this time would be something solid. The bear's foaming shadow surged a yard or so above me, and, having chosen my footing well this time, hurled myself toward the center of the massive body, looking to bypass those ripping claws.

My head collided with a thrashing leg, but I managed to grab a handful of wiry fur and pull myself close enough to plunge the knife into his torso. My first thrust hit only bone and cartilage. The front legs surrounded me. I was seconds from being crushed. I aimed my second thrust lower and hit soft tissue, twisted and jerked and twisted some more. The squeezing eased, and the water turned opaque with foam and blood. I screwed the knife into the warm slime of his gut, shoved upward under his rib cage, worried the handle until I could hold my breath no longer, and pushed away.

A blow to my chest, a blow that would have crushed my rib cage without the water to cushion it, turned the world into starry blackness for a few moments. I sucked in a lungful of water, coughed and spit my way to consciousness amid a red froth, floating downstream, face-to-face and scant yards from the wounded beast, who roared and swiped as fearsomely as ever.

The current slammed us both into a deadfall. I grabbed a limb, struggled my way onto the rotting trunk and crawled to the bank. The bear, floating farther out in the stream, had to work his way through a tangle of smaller branches, but he was close behind me and gaining when I clutched an overhanging branch and hauled myself into the limbs of a huge valley oak. Talons raked my leg as I laddered up the trunk, every moment expecting a second clawing to drag me to earth. Fear and panic trumped pain, and I hoisted myself to smaller branches where I hoped the bear would be too heavy to follow, then I risked a glance toward the ground.

My adversary had stopped climbing a yard or so up the tree. His roaring and growling had turned to a soft, slobbery whine. He attempted once more to push himself higher, but fell backward and thumped to the ground. He shuddered and crawled back toward the tree. He'd lost a great deal of blood and strength, but not a scintilla of determination.

My right trouser leg was shredded, and bloody furrows ran down my leg from thigh to ankle. I'd lost my knife somehow, but I had the revolver in my rucksack.

The bear regripped the tree and pulled himself up to the first branch. Intestines dripped from the bloody gap I'd torn from his belly as he climbed. I couldn't find a clear shot at his head, so emptied the gun at his torso. He shrieked and swatted at his pain, and dropped to the ground on his back. He rolled over to all fours and stumbled back to the river where he splayed out on his belly lapping water in the shallows.

I wanted to remain in the tree until all signs of threat disappeared, but there was no time. I worked my tentative way down through the branches, amazed how high I'd climbed, baffled by how I'd done it.

When I reached the lowest limb, the bear had quit drinking and lay still at the water's edge, but he was still breathing. He'd smelled bad before, but with his guts exposed, he reeked like something only the vultures could love, which they presently would.

Reloaded pistol at ready, I yelled twice, then again. He lifted his head and looked at me, but his eyes were dull and he made no move to rise, so I dropped to the ground.

The struggle had carried us to the far bank from the railway, and the bear lay between me and the river I had to cross. I sidestepped my way around him until I got a good aim at his head. My third shot opened a red dot over his eye and dropped his head to the beach. Finally. According to some tradition or another, I was supposed to honor the animal for his courage. But I didn't feel that way.

"Serves you right, you son-of-a-bitch," was my only reaction. "Should have left me alone." We are tested. Sometimes we pass.

I was about to wade into the river when I glimpsed my knife inside the bear's gut. Prudence and press of time dictated that I leave it where it was, but Shelby had given me that knife.

I circled behind the carcass and poked my gun barrel in his spine. No response. I poked the head. Still nothing. I bellied over his back and reached for the knife, deep inside the body cavity. Just out of reach. I held my breath against the smell and stretched. My fingers touched the handle, but it was too slimy to grip. I squirmed closer, grabbed, pulled, tumbled over and landed squarely between the paws.

I've since named the bear Lazarus. He suddenly heaved and flailed with a strangled growl. Pain streaked my back, and I crabbed away from the smothering mass, emptied my gun blindly into it. Finally, the bear fell still. Twelve of my twenty-five bullets gone, but I was alive.

I knelt before the inert pile of guts spilling out of the tub that had once been a body. "You're not only a son-of-a-bitch, you're a double son-of-a-bitch. In fact, you can double that again and add a double bastard to it. Who sent you, anyway? I retrieved my knife, wiped it clean, kissed the blade before I resheathed it.

My leg was a mess. The claw wounds could have used stitches in places. Their pain, combined with that of the bruise from Yellow Squirrel's rock, would keep me limping for a while longer. Rivulets of blood trickling down my right hip into the ragged pants leg signaled some damage on my back. My chest was sore and the rest of my skin and clothes were a mess of rips and scratches. I'd packed no change of clothes, intending to rinse soiled garments in lakes and rivers from time to time.

I washed as well as I could, used strips of shirt and trousers to improvise bandages and tie down sleeves and legs to keep them from flapping in the breeze. I presented a sad picture, but the injuries weren't disabling.

The sun was high. My watch had frozen at ten-fourteen, probably about the time I'd jumped in the river, which meant I had at most an hour, probably much less, before the train headed out. I dogpaddled my way across the stream, found my hat in the torn blackberry vines and climbed back up to the rails.

The two days I'd lose if I missed the train would put me in Wyoming on July thirtieth, give me only a flat two weeks to take care of matters that I could only guess at and return home. I executed a hurried limp down the tracks for what I supposed was a half-hour or so when the depot came in sight and I broke into the semblance of a run.

CHAPTER TWENTY-FIVE

y throbbing jog turned into a sprint when I rounded the depot corner and saw my train getting underway. A porter grabbed at me and yelled as I dashed across the platform, leaped to the tracks, and began chasing the caboose.

The train was moving through the yard at a snail's pace, but even a slow train was too fast for me to overtake on foot. I panicked. Then I grinned.

My life as a swashbuckling savior of all that was Maxwell had hardly begun, and already I'd suffered more perils than any dime novel hero runs into in a whole book. Snipers, malevolent hoboes, railroad bulls, savage beasts, and now a runaway train. So this is what a derring-do existence was like. Why not have fun at it?

I waved and whooped and dashed toward a horse tied near the front of the station. I leaped into a saddle. I banged the ribs of what turned out to be an old plug, slapped his neck with the reins and headed down the tracks. A brakeman looked up from a switch lever he'd just thrown and stepped nearly in front the horse, who had worked herself into a slow lope.

"Coming through," I yelled. The horse had more gumption than I'd thought. He barreled on as if the man weren't there, forcing him to jump aside and sprawl on his rear. I at last pulled parallel to the caboose's rear platform, but began falling back immediately as the train gained speed.

"Here we go," I said to my mount, then grabbed with both hands the rail of the ladder which climbed from the platform's center to the top of the caboose. My left boot caught in the stirrup. The train pulled me in one direction, the horse in the other. I reminded myself what fun I was having, gave three mule-like kicks and freed my foot.

I was hanging in space now, trying to swing onto the rear platform. Just like the circus. My ankle banged against the platform railing and my hands slipped off the ladder. My feet dragged through the cinders and bumped over the ties, and every jolt threatened to break my grip. I was down to my fingertips. I flashed on the memory of Julian's joyous "toot-toooot" which gave me a surge of strength sufficient to pull myself toward, then atop, the railing and fight my way aboard.

* * *

No one was in the caboose. I collapsed on a bench next to the potbellied stove, cold in the heat of summer. I closed my eyes, exhausted, but triumphant. A petty triumph, perhaps. but I was truly on my way.

By now Mother had discovered virtually all I'd done. Had I staked my birthright on a fantasy? Become a bit of an outlaw? It still seemed wiser than staking our lives on the likes of Sheriff O'Neil.

"You the one damn near killed yourself getting yourself aboard?" The wheezy, high-pitched voice belonged to a porcine conductor whose cheeks bulged until they nearly hid his eyes.

"It was a near thing, yes, sir." I said.

He jammed his fists against his hips. "If we didn't have a schedule to keep, I'd toss you off right here. Only reason I'm glad you didn't break your fool neck is we'd've had to stop and make a report."

"I'm in no mood for a scolding," I said. "And I've beaten tougher than you today."

"Looks to me like you're the one got whipped. Anyhow, we ain't gonna be arguing. We'll be putting you off at Roseville. I don't allow bums on my train."

I stood. "I'll have a ticket, if you please. To Lander, Wyoming."

"And you're not riding in this caboose even the short distance to Roseville. It's for the crew. Get on to a forward car." He pointed me toward the exit.

"Soon as I get my ticket, I'll be out of your hair."

"Won't get it from me. None left. Have to get it at the station. Besides, like I said, I don't allow bums on the train." He put a hand on my shoulder, pressured me toward the door. I pushed his arm down.

"Then I'll purchase it at Roseville."

He began shoving again. "No agent on duty at Roseville today. We're only picking up the mail. And letting you off."

I shook him free once more. "Hands off, friend. Relax. I have money, which makes me a customer, which makes me always right. No tickets at Roseville? Then I'll buy one at Auburn, or perhaps Truckee, or perhaps Reno. In the meantime, you will please leave me in peace. Understand?"

His jowls flushed and trembled. His round, undersized blue and red hat perched on his bald head like the stem on a melon.

"You get up with the other passengers like I said before I telegraph the Roseville sheriff."

I walked in the direction he pointed. He watched, hands on hips, while I made my way to the next car and took the sole empty seat in the back. Blood-tinged lymph seeped from the scratches on my leg, and it was painful to lean the right side of my back against the seat. But there seemed to be little bleeding. It should all scab over and heal soon, provided I kept it clean.

My watch still read ten fourteen, as it doubtless ever would. Still, I couldn't discard it. The inscription read, "To Carter from Julia. 1874." Mother had entrusted me with the keepsake when I first went away to school. Another betrayal.

But guilt and regret were worth about as much as a drunk's promise to quit as soon as he finished the bottle in front of him. I pulled the oilskin packet from my rucksack and held my breath, wondering what might have been destroyed. I unwrapped first the slicker, then the tablecloth. The covers of the diaries and the trail log were wet, as were many of the page edges. Water had turned words, sections, even whole pages to streaks and blots. But the damage seemed minimal considering the soaking they'd had.

The matches had dropped to the bottom of the package, and their heads had nearly dissolved. The paper containing the combination to the safe was mush. I closed my eyes and tried to burn the numbers into my memory. I wasn't certain I'd succeeded.

I opened the books carefully and fanned the leaves, delicately separated those stuck together. My bandanna had dried on the walk from the river, so I used it to towel as much moisture as I could from the books, then placed them open, spines up, on the seat to let them dry. Except for the 1859 date, the wedding day inscription on the outside cover of the paper-wrapped package had blurred to near-illegibility, and I feared for the condition of whatever was inside. I untied the string and unfolded three layers of wrapping. The third was only damp. Inside, I saw that the glass of a simple wooden frame protected a fine tintype. Droplets of water spotted the glass, but the picture seemed undamaged.

The train stopped. Roseville was a short ride. The conductor appeared at the front of the car and waddled down the aisle, followed by lean man in a dark suit sporting a tin star on the lapel. The conductor's head was turned toward the lawman as he moved, but his finger pointed directly at me.

CHAPTER TWENTY-SIX

I laid my treasures aside and stepped into the aisle. I looked a sorry character, but I reminded myself of my mission, determined not to be stopped by this officious oaf and his badged minion. I proffered some damp bills.

"Yes, officer?" I smiled. "Thanks for your trouble. Must be you've been able to arrange for me to buy a ticket."

The sheriff had pushed past the conductor to confront me. Now, though he looked at me, his words were for the man behind him.

"The gentleman offered to purchase a ticket?"

I said, "Yes, sir. The conductor there had apparently sold his last one. However, as you see, I'm prepared to pay as soon as one becomes available."

The lawman turned his back to me and spoke quietly to the conductor, whose response was unintelligible except for the whiny and exasperated tone. At last, the sheriff turned in my direction.

"May I inquire as to your identity, sir?"

"I'm Andrew Maxwell. Of the Circle M Ranch."

"An outfit of some reputation. You seem a little dishabille to be sporting a name like that."

"I'm not sure I'd trust a man in my condition either, Sheriff, if I were you. I've had some unfortunate encounters in the last day or so, and I've had no time to clean up. Nevertheless, Maxwell is my name, and I'm prepared to pay my way."

"Well," he said, "during the sotto voce conversation you witnessed between Harry and me a moment ago, he recalled that he had a few more blank tickets he'd forgotten about. He'll sell you one as long as you put cash on the barrelhead."

"Thank you, sir." I waved my bills. He shoved them aside.

"And I've another caveat. I'm riding the train as far as Reno, and I'll wire ahead for my colleagues to be looking for you down the line after that. No trouble. Understood?"

"Perfectly. There'll be no trouble from this quarter," I said.

"See to it," he said. The train lurched and I took the opportunity to resume my seat. The lawman worked his way hand over hand down the aisle and exited the car. The conductor sidled after him as fast as his bulk would allow.

Once we were underway, I cradled the tintype in my hands and gazed for the first time on an image of my pioneer grandparents, the ancestors who had founded the Circle M. Why had this remained hidden all these years?

I'd heard descriptions of them—Grandfather a big man, sandy hair, Grandmother small and dark. It was hard to tell coloring from the black and silver tintype, but the other details were clear and true to the stories, even though the picture was little larger than a calling card. My mother's face is a more delicate version of her own mother's—aquiline nose, full mouth, round cheeks. My heavy jawline comes straight from Carter, Julian's pointed chin from our grandmother. Her lips have an incipient smile, unusual for those days when subjects were required to remain stiff for long periods—sometimes even braced at the back and neck—waiting for the photographer's plate to be exposed. I imagined her gazing into an optimistic future. Carter appears stolid, resolute, peering ahead at some near goal. The tips of his moustache are waxed and pointed up and back toward his ears. He looks surprisingly stylish, a little like a dandy with a knack for turning a sharp deal.

I was folding the driest of the paper to rewrap the picture when the conductor returned with my ticket. I kept him waiting while I finished the wrapping and knotted the string. He filled the silence with a toe-tapping, then a warning.

"Now remember, any monkey business at all and you're off and no refund."

I smiled my reassurance. "No trouble from you, no trouble from me. Agreed?" I handed over thirty-three dollars with one hand and held out my other for a handshake. He took the bills, but ignored the hand.

"I'll hold you to your promise," he said, "and so will every lawman between here and Landry."

"I'd expect no less, sir, from such a fierce guardian of public order."

His fists clenched. I smiled, nodded. He turned and pushed his way into the next coach. Apparently people found it hard to argue with a smiling man. And more fun for the smiler.

I put aside enough cash for my return fare and examined the remains. A hundred and twenty-two dollars. With this, I'd have to eat, hire horses, meet contingencies. I returned to my research. I untied the diary's ribbon and turned to Julia's story. My grandmother had recorded her thoughts in an ornamented hand as wonderful to look on as to read.

* * *

June 12, 1859

By the calendar I am nearly 16, and I have suddenly become a new person entirely. How often have I read of love and passion overwhelming heroines in poems and novels, and how often have I longed to be swept up by those same emotions and carried away like a leaf on the wind. And how often have I feared I would waste away here on the Indiana plains, "A flower born to blush unseen," never to know or understand the noble thoughts of those great characters of history and literature. Yet today I am certain that they could feel nothing more grand than the sensation that fills my heart. I burn to transform those thoughts to deeds, but first I must record everything I can about this, the most momentous day of my life. A day of happiness, destruction, death, and, finally, love.

The happiness came when I woke up to begin my 16th year. The destruction came with the fire that consumed the house of the dreadful and pitiable Barlow family. The death was that of the infant I failed to save. The love bloomed the moment I cast my eyes on Carter Maxwell.

What possessed me to enter that burning house alone instead of seeking help? Doubtless some primal instinct warned me a human life was in danger even though the dwelling seemed deserted. When I opened the door, I felt I was standing at the very gates of hell boiling with flame and smoke. Yet it was surely Providence, not the devil that guided my foot to set rocking that little cradle on the floor. Ah, the thrill of fear when I knelt and lifted the baby and crawled with him into fresh sunlight. And, ah, the grief that stabbed me when I found I'd been too late.

And it was surely Providence that turned Carter from battling the fire to heed my tearful cries. And, ah, the love that overwhelmed my soul when he enfolded me and I buried my tears in the roughness of his shirt. I will recall forever the comfort in his eyes when I finally dared to look up to him. his face dusted with charcoal, his light hair and moustaches stained with soot. And I will also recall forever how he defended me against that horrible Mathilda Barlow.

How dare she accuse us of burning her family's house to drive the family from Valparaiso? I have never called the Barlows "trash" or "looked down my nose" at them. It was she and her drunken husband who took their children to the tavern and left their infant grandchild alone next to a burning cookfire. Her outrageous explanation? If the older children had remained to watch the mutton, they'd have eaten it all.

Such a pitiable scene to see Missy Barlow, younger even than I, attempting to nurse her dead baby. Yet, Mathilda made no attempt to comfort her grieving daughter, turning her energy instead to spewing invective on Carter and me. "You'll pay for this, Carter Maxwell, you and your hussy." She was fearsome as a witch on All Hallows Eve, and I trembled at the hateful look on her face. But I treasure the moment when Carter stepped between us and swore she would pay for her negligence, then sent her packing.

The Lord must have blinded Carter to the soiled and singed state of my skin and clothes, for the bond we formed in the moments that followed will, I know, endure all our days. I herein give thanks to the Almighty for all my blessings and pray for the strength to be worthy of them.

* * *

My train labored up the Sierra foothills, and my mind lingered on the tintype, taken fifty years before, the subjects my age—younger—and committed to each other for life. And me—committed only to a dubious undertaking in which no one else believed.

I had found in my family history a love story tinged with threats of revenge. Perhaps this was what I'd been searching for—the source of the plot. Julia's narrative carried me through the afternoon and into twilight.

* * *

August 15, 1859
How will I ever survive interrogation on the witness stand with the whole town and those horrid Barlows staring at me? I do want them punished for that poor baby's death, and I am sure it is God's will that they pay for what they did. Yet, without Carter and his love and valor, I doubt I could find the courage. Surely he was sent to help me bear all this. The cherubic face of the child I failed to save haunts me, yet it will take all the prayer and strength I have to do my duty.

I am afraid I will never again possess "a heart whose love is innocent."

* * *

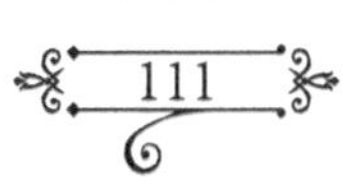

August 30, 1859

Benjamin Maxwell. Mary Maxwell. Burned. Dead. I stare at the words I just wrote and cannot believe what I am reading. How could the Lord take Carter's parents, their store, their house, their lives? I know this is not the all-consuming fire scriptures speak of, but it must be a harbinger of it. Had Judge Wasley only sent Mathilda Barlow to prison with her husband this never would have happened. "Lamentable," he said, "but worse to leave the other children orphaned. The state can't afford to pay for their keep." A family sacrificed on the altar of Mammon. As it was, had Missy not confessed her mother's arson, we might never have proved the source of the fire.

I shudder to recall poor Missy's whimpering as she crawled to us, barely able to speak, and the left side of her face purple from the blow the vicious hag had laid on to prevent her warning us. The poor girl was terrified to come to us, but, praise be, her conscience would allow nothing less than to reveal her mother's perfidy. Carter is so filled with wrath I fear for his very soul. I am almost glad the evil mother fled before he could find her. Pray God the law captures her before she does more harm in this world. As for us, all we can do is attempt to live the Christian virtues and let his will be done.

* * *

OCTOBER 15, 1859

Much as I miss my family, I know moving to Chicago was right. Valparaiso had become haunted for both of us. Carter's store is doing even better here than in Valparaiso. Not only is it a fresh start for us, but for Missy, whom I finally convinced Carter to offer refuge with us. She has proved a virtuous soul and a hard worker. Mathilda Barlow's wicked spirit will follow us always, but oh, please do not let her appear in body to blacken our new life. I can think of no measures beyond our flight from Valparaiso and prayer to prevent that. "'Tis too strong a knot for me to untie."

* * *

I'd never heard this story of what happened to my great-grandparents. Perhaps it was simply too painful for my grandmother to tell. Even to Mother? But surely Mother knew of these events, had read this, even if she hadn't been told. Why had she withheld them from me? From anyone? Whatever the reason, I saw nothing here to justify her Cerebus-like guarding of the trunk.

Unless, perhaps, Mathilda Barlow was the beginning of all this vengeance. Could Yellow Squirrel and Standing Oak form part of a scheme

112

hatched in Indiana probably before they were even born? One wouldn't think so. But who would think Owl Feather would emerge to threaten Mother's life and mine more than forty years after she'd been rescued? "Redeemed" as they termed the liberation of white women from the clutches of savages? Or Satan. As if life with natives endangered not only the female's physical self, but her very soul as well.

There was enough room on the bench seat to curl up, and while the train made its way down the eastern side of the mountains, I drifted into slumber amid thoughts of my grandmother, Indians, the resurrection of the dead and the life of the world—or at least the morning—to come.

JULY 29

CHAPTER TWENTY-SEVEN

Dawn in the great basin of Nevada. The train sped us in comfort and safety over the same wastes my forebears had plodded across on foot with wagon, livestock and families, though in the opposite direction. The emigrants' route had been dictated, as was ours, by the only source of water in the basin—the Humboldt River—which ran near and parallel to the tracks. It was a trickster river, the Humboldt, a tease which sank into the sands forty searing miles short of the desert's western end. My train's window framed immense stretches of sage and thistle interspersed with barren salt flats, like recumbent tombstones.

My belongings had dried nicely in the arid environment, and I carefully repacked my rucksack, then turned once again to the diary. I skimmed over the story of Julia and Carter's years in Chicago, Mother's birth, Grandfather's ride to war, Grandmother's loneliness during his absence, traced the lines with a finger, alert for any mention of Mathilda Barlow. I was convinced she was the clue I'd been seeking. But Julia seemed to have forgotten her.

Through one beautifully penned page after another, I followed my grandparents through the tumult of Carter's return from war—his spinning of extravagant tales he'd heard about California, his insistence that they stake everything on the uncertain bounty of a mythical land, and Grandmother's reluctant acquiescence to his dreams. Then came their trudging progress beside the broad, yellow Platte, over the treeless path tens of thousands had worn during the previous twenty-odd years. And there, in the middle of the third week out from St. Joseph, Missouri, I finally came upon Mathilda Barlow again.

* * *

June 30, 1864

 A terrible ruckus erupted from the wagon train next door, and several of us ran over to see the trouble. There she was, throwing a ladle at a fat man who was drunk as a lord, stumbling around and cursing in Beelzebub's own tongue. I was so startled to see her I confess I did not remember to cover Carrie's ears until they had endured a vile onslaught. The wretches traded insults a while longer, then she ran off into the night with her drunken adversary in hot pursuit.

 Missy is beside herself with fear. Carter is beside himself with rage. I am at sixes and sevens trying to perform my household duties in these primitive conditions and protecting our precious slumbering one from all the evil that surrounds us.

* * *

July 1, 1864

 They buried Mathilda Barlow this morning. She was found a mile from the wagons, her throat cut and her dress set afire. The deed is laid at the head of her "husband," who is nowhere to be found. May God have mercy on her soul, and on mine, for I confess I am not sorry she is dead. But of us all, Missy is in greatest need of prayer. She grieves for her mother, yet counts herself fortunate to be rid of her, and even yet is guilt-ridden at her desire to embrace her good fortune.

* * *

With Mathilda's death, it seemed I'd followed to her grave what I'd thought was my lead to the genesis of the conspiracy. Now, though, I had new questions. Suspicions. Had Grandfather been the instrument of the Barlow woman's doom? Julia offers not a hint of it, but given Carter's anger and the fiery manner of Mathilda's death, it was difficult to dismiss the idea. Not that I could blame him.

But even if he had killed her, who would care enough to avenge Mathilda Barlow? I thought perhaps my grandfather's trail logs would reveal more. The book was larger than Julia's diary, more the size of the ledgers he was doubtless accustomed to in his father's business. I had just laid it across my lap and lifted the cover when a gray man with a few brown teeth and a scraggly moustache stomped into the car.

"Where's that damned conductor? I tell you if I don't find him, I'll throw them off myself."

A well-dressed man in the front stood and blocked the aisle. "Pipe down, there, mister. And watch your language. There's ladies in this car."

"I haven't seen the conductor this morning," I said. "What's the problem?"

"Redskins. That's the problem. Went to sleep nice and easy last night and woke up this morning with a couple of squaws next to me. I don't ride the same train with no Indians."

"I'm sure we'll be at the next stop before long," I said.

"Been too long already. Never should have let them on in the first place. Country's going straight to hell. They'll let niggers on next. Beg your pardon, ma'am." He stomped up the aisle and out of the car.

The dozen or so passengers in the car traded glances and murmurs. We soon rolled to a stop, and I lifted my window to look forward. The conductor stumbled down to trackside carrying a burlap sack which he threw as far as he could into the desert. He began yelling, and motioning frenetically until a young Indian woman jumped down from the car. There was no mistaking her dark braid and ivory shawl.

My disappointment over the diaries' scant yield evaporated. Finding Standing Oak's women here must mean they, too, were bound for Wyoming, for Owl Feather. I'd go to their car where they couldn't slip away so easily, where I'd have hours to gain their sympathy and friendship.

I gave brief thanks that the Humboldt provided the only route across this barrenness, shouldered my rucksack—too precious to leave unattended for even a moment—and leaped off the train. The warm morning air tasted sharply alkaline and chalk dry. In the distance, naked hills thrust up from the plain like the spines of primordial beasts.

I arrived at the scene just as the young woman was helping her mother from the train. The little gray man stood at the top of the steps supervising the operation with his arms folded and a satisfied smile on his face.

I turned to the conductor. "Surely you're not about to abandon these women out here in the middle of nowhere."

"We got a schedule to keep, mister. I warned them when they got on at Elko last night. They could stay unless there was trouble."

"What trouble did they cause?" I said.

"White man complained. That's trouble. And that bag of theirs smells like an outhouse. Don't worry about them. Diggers know their way around these parts."

"Listen," I said, "we can take them to the next town, can't we?"

"I warned you about making trouble, too, if I recall. Now, get yourself back on the train before their menfolks come along and massacre us all."

"Haven't you heard? Those cowboy and Indian days are over." I smiled. He glowered. Apparently I'd met the limits of my new tactic of amiability.

"I refuse to reboard unless they're allowed to as well," I said.

"Suit yourself, mister," he said. "I can't risk the whole train for one idiot." I looked past his florid cheeks, saw no warmth and no hesitation in his colorless eyes. He signaled to the engineer and climbed back aboard. The train clattered and clanked into motion.

I watched the locomotive race along the rails into the distance. Its bulk soon shrank to a dot, a perfect illustration of the vanishing point principle I'd learned in the art course I'd taken with Virginia. I was a long way from Virginia now. Fifteen days left in the most important journey of my life, and I'd voluntarily traded wheels for feet. I was short on food, money, and far—how far?—from town or help. Inexplicably, I was happy to be here.

"Andrew Maxwell," said the younger woman, "I didn't recognize you with your beard. What are you doing here?"

CHAPTER TWENTY-EIGHT

"Looks like a nice day for a walk. Care to join me?" I said. She started to smile, then squelched it. "You can call me Andy, by the way."

"No thank you. You go your way. We'll go ours." She hurried to her mother, who was limping badly as she made her way toward the burlap sack the conductor had thrown. The two retrieved the bag and, the older woman leaning on the younger, they began to inch their way east along the tracks.

I knew we were west of Wells, where the Humboldt began. We needed only to follow the river and the railroad. How far I had no notion. I judged the temperature to be at least eighty. It would soon climb beyond a hundred. They each carried a small waterskin, but they wouldn't get far on their own. Besides, if Owl Feather's illness drew these women toward Wyoming, I might simultaneously help them and gain entrée to the old chief. I trotted after them.

"Since we're going the same way. . ."

The mother waved her hand, shook her head, and made the same sort of guttural noises I'd heard at Bodega Bay. They kept walking for a ways, then stopped. I hurried to catch up, moved to support the older woman's arm on the side her daughter wasn't holding. The woman jerked away, stumbled a couple of feet and fell to her knees. The daughter regarded me angrily, dropped the sack, and stepped over to help her mother. I picked up their sack and approached them. I hated to admit the conductor had been right about the smell. How could anything so rank be so important to them? The daughter's face stiffened when she saw me.

"You're being ridiculous," I said. "You can't carry your mother and this bag through the desert alone. What's in here anyway?"

She extended her arms. "Give it."

I handed it over. "I'm only trying to help," I said. "What happened to your mother?"

"You would help most by leaving us alone."

She drew a small knife and waved it in my direction. I stepped back and raised my hands. They tottered toward the river, maintaining an excruciating slog through the sand, weaved among the clumps of sage and greasewood which spiced the scorching air, their buckskin dresses and dark hair seemingly part and parcel of the gray-brown landscape. Something in the younger one insisted on keeping the ivory shawl around her shoulders despite the heat. I followed at a discreet distance.

The river had scarcely enough water to merit the name, sometimes dwindling to a series of stagnant pools. Even where the water worked itself into a visible current, it glided silently through sand without gurgle or splash. The only sounds were our panting and grunting, the brushing of our feet against the sand, and the scraping of our clothing against the bushes, nearly all of which seemed to be thorned, built to jab and tear.

Hours passed. I doubted we'd made as much as five miles. The sand became hot enough to blister a bare foot. I couldn't imagine how the women bore the heat, shod only in moccasins, for even in my thick-soled boots I felt as if I were walking on Ling Chu's suppertime stove. Finally—I judged it to be somewhat past noon—the sun became too scorching even for them.

The bank was steep at the point where they began searching for a resting place beside the river, but its height afforded a scrap of shade at the bottom. The daughter set the bag down, stood behind her mother, and cupped hands under her shoulders to ease her down the bank.

The older woman's weight shifted, the daughter lost her hold, and her mother tumbled over the edge into a mossy puddle. The daughter executed a controlled slide to her mother's side. I followed as quickly as I could.

The daughter shot me a poison look from narrowed eyes, but she allowed me to help turn her mother on her back and pillow her head with my rucksack. The mother was dripping with algae and appeared dazed, though she bore no visible injuries from the fall. I toweled off the slime with my bandanna, flinched when I gained a closer look at her right ankle. It was swollen to twice its normal size, colored the same as my thigh had been a few days earlier. Above the ankle was a yellow mound, circled in red with a black spot deep in the center.

"She was riding our burro when he collapsed and died. She fell into a thistle." The daughter rose, walked a few steps to a scraggly willow and cut some wands.

"None of our herbs grow here except this." She handed a branch to her mother and spoke softly. Her mother began chewing. "It helps a little with the pain, but it is not enough."

"Let's at least get her in the shade," I said.

We moved the mother as gently as we could. She objected the whole time. I sensed the objection was not the pain, but my involvement. She tightened her lips when I tried to give her water. Her skin was hot and dry as much from fever as from the desert sun. She finally accepted a drink from her daughter, who sat next to her mother's head, her legs drawn up under her. She placed her shawl over her mother like a coverlet. I squatted beside the woman's foot and began probing the area around the wound.

"Many Clouds," she said.

"What?"

"You asked my name, Andrew Maxwell. I am Theresa Many Clouds. You should call me Many Clouds."

Why now? One more instance of her confusing behavior. The inflamed skin was taut, but my fingertip left a cup wherever I probed.

"Well, Many Clouds," I said. "I'm no doctor, but I've no doubt your mother will lose her leg or her life unless we treat that infection immediately."

"Treat her how?" There was a challenge in her voice.

"We must drain that infection, and the only way I know is to lance it."

"Cut her open?" Many Clouds said. The mother waved her hands weakly and moaned. "Have you decided to kill us, Andrew Maxwell?"

"I could have done that many times."

"You want to find Owl Feather. That's the only use you have for us."

"Not true, but If that's what you think, you know I'll do my best to keep her alive." She hesitated. "She has a fever. The infection must come out." She closed her eyes, her fingertips on her mother's brow, nodded curtly.

"Then we need a fire," I said.

Gathering leaves and sticks was a slow job under enervating sun. I'd wet my hair and beard in the river, but they baked dry in minutes. By the time we'd scraped together a skimpy pile of kindling, the horizon far to the east began to darken and blur. Thunderheads floated above the remote peaks, then dark curtains descended and hid the mountains entirely. We'd have welcomed their cooling shade, but they were far away. Lightning flashed, but we heard no thunder.

What we collected formed a mound a few inches high and covered an area not a great deal larger than my two hands. Was it enough? It would have to be.

I wet my bandanna, gave it to Many Clouds, who laid it across her mother's forehead. The older woman was barely conscious. I didn't know how much bleeding to expect, so I removed my belt and wrapped it around her leg in case I needed a tourniquet. I had Many Clouds lift her mother's head for a moment while I reached into the rucksack. Her eyes widened and she pulled backward when she saw the forty-four I pulled out.

"Don't worry. This isn't for shooting. At least not at the moment." I removed the cylinder and entwined the barrel into the twists of the belt. "Just tighten this if I tell you. I hope we won't have to use it."

I lifted the mother's head again and rummaged through my rucksack for the ruined watch. My knife was the wrong tool for the job, but I had no other, and I scratched and gouged the surface below Grandmother's inscription as I pried off the back and removed the works to reach the crystal. I spread the watch's machinery carefully on my rucksack, hoping that I'd be able to make it whole again.

Shelby had introduced Julian and me to the trick of focusing the sun's rays to start a fire. A summer blaze had charred a thousand acres or so of brush and timber above Sawtooth Valley one summer. Shelby had checked the damage and held up a broken bottle.

"Here's the culprit," he'd said. Julian and I shared a puzzled look, so Shelby dismounted and scraped together a pile of dead grass. He held the bottle between the grass and the sun and soon had it ablaze. He immediately recognized the potential mischief in our eyes. "This is for survival, not for play, boys. Look around you. We got no worse enemy than fire."

At first, my best efforts here produced smoke, but no fire. Many Clouds was apparently more experienced. She cupped her hands around the smoldering leaves and breathed the embers into a tiny blaze. I carefully fed the fire twigs and grass, and it grew fitfully.

I laid the knife blade on the fire, turned it back and forth. The parched fuel blackened quickly.

"These sticks are burning too fast," I said. "We have nothing to use for stitches, and if there's a great deal of bleeding, I may have to heat the blade again to cauterize the wound."

"The bag," Many Clouds said. She drew her own knife, ran to the burlap sack, cut it open, dumped its contents on the ground, and ran back.

The dark mound she left behind quivered a moment, then lay still as a rock. We worked together, pushing the bag, little by little, into the blaze. It seemed the burlap would do the job.

I knelt at the woman's foot with my back to her head and to Many Clouds. I poked tentatively at the swollen area, unsure where to cut or how much force to use. I was afraid of slicing muscles or tendons, or, worse, an artery or large vein. Should I pierce the cut directly or begin at the edge? I decided to plunge to the heart of the infection, held my breath, thrust the knifepoint in, and drew the blade toward me.

CHAPTER TWENTY-NINE

The leg stiffened, kicked, and Many Clouds' mother screamed—weak, but piercing—while her tearful daughter spoke in soothing tones. I pushed the leg back down and examined my work. I was a little amazed that it looked like I'd done things right so far. Bloody pus oozed from the incision, but there was no hemorrhage. I gently pressed above and below the cut, forced putrid spoonsful of lumpy yellow pudding from the wound. Deep inside, I caught sight of the dark spike that had caused the trouble, but I couldn't reach it with my fingers.

"Hang on, Many Clouds," I said. "This may hurt even more than the first time."

I waved my knife through the flames, then dug its point into the blister-red flesh. I finally retrieved the hooked thorn and held it high for Many Clouds and her mother to see before I tossed it to the flames. They nodded tear-soaked faces. I smiled. Suddenly, I realized I hadn't thought about a bandage.

"The shawl," Many Clouds said without hesitation.

"It seems so precious to you," I said. "We could use my bandanna."

"You sacrificed your watch, Andrew Maxwell. We will use the shawl."

"We must wash it first," I said. I stepped to a small current of clear water in the center of the streambed, rinsed my bandanna, and sponged in and around the wound while Many Clouds tore her treasured garment into strips and dipped them in the river. "I'm worried that we have no way to boil this water," I said. "Perhaps it would help stop the infection if we cauterized the wound after all. I don't believe it will do any harm."

"Do what you think best," Many Clouds said.

The sticks were nearly burned, but I added burlap to the fire until it was hot as I thought it would get, then snatched the blade from the coals and jammed it briefly into the incision. Again, the leg jerked and the woman screamed and Many Clouds' voice assumed its reassuring quality. The wound sizzled and steamed. I'd expected something like the odor of branded calf's flesh, but absent the musk of burning fur, the faint mist around my blade smelled like frying pork. I pulled the knife back. I'd raised a blister at the edge of the incision, but otherwise the wound looked as it had before. Many Clouds wrapped strips from the shawl around the leg. The mother lay still, her breathing steady.

I tidied up, put my belt back on and reloaded the pistol, jammed it into my waistband instead of returning it to the rucksack. I noticed Many Clouds watching me. "We might see a snake or something," I said. I managed to piece the watch together, then climbed to the top of the riverbank to plan our next move.

The sun was still high and hot, and I calculated that it was perhaps three or four o'clock. Feathery veins draped the eastern horizon from sky to earth. To watch rain pour down afar despite the heat on the back of my neck was disorienting for someone accustomed to a womb of mountains and hills.

We had at least two hours before the air would cool enough to continue. It seemed doubtful Many Clouds' mother would be able to travel tonight. I had so little time, yet I couldn't leave them out here. I dropped back down to the river. Many Clouds still knelt by her mother, encouraging her to drink water and gnaw on the willow bark.

"Perhaps you should lie down," I said.

"No."

"We should at least eat something. I have some jerky in my rucksack." She drew her knife, walked to the dark lump she had cast from the gunny sack, sawed at it for a few minutes and returned with two amorphous hunks of dark and dry meat.

"We carried as much of our burro as we could," she said. "Most of it is no good now, but this is from deep inside. It won't sicken us."

For taste and texture, I might as well have eaten my belt, but I supposed the burro was somewhat more nourishing. While I chewed, Many Clouds worked away at the decaying meat until she'd created a few consumable strips, which she draped across a willow bush at the water's edge. She attempted to force a small piece between her mother's lips with no success.

"In Wells, we can find her a doctor," I said.

"You know doctors won't treat us." She gave up trying to feed her mother and returned to her seat on a hillock of sand beside me.

"Do you know how far it is?"

"About one day's walk. The river will disappear before we get there." She worried another bite from her strip of meat, but didn't answer. I shoved my last bite into my mouth and spoke around it while I chewed.

"The place I come from is called Wells, also. Sawtooth Wells. In the Sierra."

"Yes, Andrew Maxwell. We know about your Sawtooth Wells and your Circle M. We know about your family. We know about your… crusade." The hostility had returned to her voice. How to defuse it?

"How long have you lived in California?" Silence. Many Clouds' mother still slept, and her fever seemed unchanged. Perhaps the fact that she was no worse was a good sign. I stripped a leaf from one of her willow branches and tossed it in the water.

"Leaves have to go wherever the current carries them," I said. "We have the gift to take our own direction."

"We sometimes believe so," she said.

"Without that power, we aren't completely human are we?"

"Perhaps not." We watched the green leaf bob and drift, like a toy canoe.

I lay down, curled up, folded my hands and put the rucksack under my head.

"We'd better rest if we're going to be walking most of the night," I said. There was, again, no answer. I didn't think there would be.

CHAPTER THIRTY

Sleep was impossible, of course. The gritty sand was no mattress. At last, the heat diminished enough to start out again. We shared another piece of burro meat when the sun perched above the horizon. Canteen and waterskins full, we raised Many Clouds' mother to a sitting position, speaking softly to her until the older woman's eyelids fluttered open. She waved away food, accepted a swallow of water and a piece of willow bark. I hitched my rucksack to my shoulders, knelt, and hooked an arm under her left armpit. Many Clouds did the same on the right.

"One, two, three," I said. We lifted together, operated like a pair of crutches. The mother could put no weight at all on the wounded leg. She rested on her daughter and me, swung her good leg forward a foot or so. We caught up with her, then we repeated the procedure. After five minutes, we'd crossed only the few yards to the four-foot bank we had to scale to emerge from the river bed. At this rate, a normal half-day's walk would require a week.

"This is impossible," I said. "I suggest we go ahead and return with a doctor. I won't mention her race. He won't refuse to treat her once he's here."

"He will help like your friend the conductor helped. You go on with our thanks. You've helped us a great deal."

"You want me to go, don't you?"

"I wish I'd never heard the name Maxwell," she said. "But I'm not what you call completely human, so I couldn't decide my own fate." She turned her back, moved toward the stream. I stepped to her side.

"Those are my words, but not how I meant them. I could bring someone from your own people from Wells."

"You'll find people of my race in Wells, Andrew Maxwell, but they are not my people. And they wouldn't come on your word even if they were."

"But if I were to come with them—"

"They would think it was a trick." She turned and looked at me. "We have the river for water and enough meat to keep us until we reach town. You may leave with a clear conscience."

"My conscience would never be clear if I did that." I extended a tentative hand toward her arm, didn't quite touch her. "I'll remain with you until I know you're safe."

She glanced at my hand, turned her back. "Or until you find out what you want to know." I shook my head. "Don't pretend, Andrew Maxwell. You are kind, but you are not smart."

All my attempts to build rapport, and Many Clouds might as well have brandished her knife in my face again. I sat in the awkward silence and watched the last glints of light the receding sun sprinkled across the river's surface.

Many Clouds squinted her eyes into slanted lines to shield against the glitters, which played across the gingery satin of her skin, highlighting her high cheekbones and the graceful arch of her nose. She pulled her braid in front of her, untied the rawhide string that bound it and began to loosen the plaits. She stopped, turned to me.

"You're staring, Andrew Maxwell." I looked away. When I sneaked another glance, she had retied the braid and sat still and expressionless as a rock.

I heard thunder and lifted my head. Without a cloud in the twilit sky, the sound made no sense. The ground began to tremble.

"Flash flood," Many Clouds yelled. She and her mother began a frenzied scramble up the bank.

An avalanche of muddy froth hurtled around the upstream bend. The eastern storm I'd watched all afternoon had reached us after all. Many Clouds and I could escape in the few moments remaining, but saving her mother would be another matter. I leaped to the top of the bank, yanked Many Clouds up with me, then we each grabbed one of her mother's wrists and pulled with all the strength we could muster. It wasn't enough. The careening water slammed into her and tore her from our grip. In an instant she disappeared.

CHAPTER THIRTY-ONE

ven on high ground, water swirled thigh-deep around us, roared like storm-driven surf. Many Clouds shrieked and hurled herself at the torrent in an attempt to pursue her mother. I caught her feet in mid-dive, fought her struggles and a stubborn current till we'd reached relative safety on a slight rise fifty yards or so from the center of the stream. Many Clouds sat amidst the muddy pools surrounding our little knoll and keened, her chin lifted like a coyote's toward the flaming western horizon.

"We'll find her," I said, placed an arm around her shoulders. She didn't reject my embrace, but whether she accepted it or was simply unaware of it, I couldn't tell. Her wail soared over the flood.

It was dark by the time the water began to recede, and as if a train had just passed by, the desert resumed its silence. The newest of moons showed like a lopsided grin above the western peaks. Many Clouds hugged her knees and stared at the ground.

"We should begin searching," I said. I tightened my embrace. She stiffened.

"It's no use. We won't find her. It wouldn't matter if we did."

"We'll find her," I repeated. I rose and extended my hand to help her stand. She stood unassisted. The moon offered little help. Difficult as the desert was to cross in daylight, it seemed impossible in darkness, full of gullies, sinkholes, mounds, thistles. The river had subsided, but was still higher than it had been during the day. I expected a long trek to find Many Clouds' mother.

There were no logs or snags to catch her body. We walked for what I judged to be well over an hour with no success. Then Many Clouds saw the coyotes.

Two of them lay on the far bank, shades against the dark sand, bellies down, heads up, like porch dog silhouettes. Their eyes were fixed on a dark heap a few feet in front of them. Many Clouds screamed at them, but they turned their heads toward us only briefly, then began circling their anticipated meal. I pulled my revolver and aimed. It was too far for accuracy, but I had no need to hit a bull's eye. Two shots sent one yipping and limping into the sagebrush and brought the other to attention. My third bullet missed, but frightened him into the shadows. Five cartridges left.

We hurried across the stream. Many Clouds whimpered and sobbed all the way. Her mother lay draped face-down on one of the stream's infrequent gravel bars. I surmised that the current had torn into the bank, then left her when it receded. Many Clouds stood by and watched as I turned her mother over. I'd never seen a dead body before Julian's. Now I'd gazed into three pair of lifeless eyes in as many weeks, but I was not becoming inured.

"The animals must not have her," Many Clouds said. I nodded.

"We can take her to higher ground and cover her with rocks," I said.

"It is not our way, but it will have to do," she said.

"Not our way either," I said. "But, yes, it will have to do."

Internment took most of the night. We found few large stones in the gravel bar. It seemed that we had carried thousands of rocks from the streambed up the bank, laying each on her mother's corpse. I tried to imagine Virginia laboring this way. I'd never seen her in any garb except skirts and petticoats, although I supposed she wore other attire during summers on her father's Napa Valley farm. She couldn't have been a total stranger to life outside the parlor and classroom. Still, I couldn't picture her in Many Clouds' place.

Dawn was oozing pink and yellow light in the east by the time Many Clouds and I stood over the cairn we'd constructed.

"I don't know your customs, Many Clouds, but it seems we should say a few words of blessing or good-bye."

"You must step back," she said.

I retreated a few feet, then a few yards, under her insistent stare. She I watched and listened as she chanted and danced over her mother, repeating her ritual in all four directions of the compass, much as Crazy Lu had over Shelby. I was filled with admiration for her ability to conduct such a thorough and energetic ritual in the face of her loss. The sun had lifted above dawn and into daylight proper by the time she finished, on her knees, facing the west. After a pause, I approached her.

"Would you mind if I took a turn?" She shook her head.

"What was her name?"

"Sarah Rushing Creek. But she refused to wear the white name."

I decided to risk an inquiry. "Like her husband?" Her eyebrows raised in puzzlement.

"Standing Oak doesn't use a Christian name either."

"My father's been dead for some time." Many Clouds looked at me with tight lips and a challenge in her eyes and I asked no more questions, but bowed my head.

"Lord, receive the body of your servant Rushing Creek," I said. Then I murmured what I remembered of the Twenty-third Psalm. Still waters. He restoreth my soil. I could have used more of the former, and as for the latter, I felt as if it was going to take more than a prayer to put my shredded spirit to rights. All my vaunted joie de vivre seemed to have dissolved in the Humboldt's torrent. I went on to the Lord's Prayer. Many Clouds' voice joined mine for the last lines.

"For thine is the kingdom and the power and the glory forever. Amen." I looked at her in surprise.

"The missionaries," she said.

I nodded. Adversity, supposedly, brings people together. Or does it simply prompt hatred to don a mask? I handed her a piece of jerky. "We should go," I said. We topped a small rise and turned to look back at the stony mound. A coyote pawed the boulders. A vulture stained the pale sky.

JULY 30

CHAPTER THIRTY-TWO

We retraced much of the ground we'd covered the day before, though the landscape looked considerably different since the flood had washed and flattened it. The Humboldt had fallen nearly to its previous level. The thunderheads to the east had given way to thin white brushstrokes.

We tramped hour after hour, mile after mile. Cinder cones appeared to the north, their peaks tipped black, like snuffed candles. The sun passed the zenith, and it became clear that Many Clouds had underestimated our distance from Wells. Breathing the midday air became like inhaling inside a furnace, but I was determined not to stop until she did. I never heard a more welcome sound in my life than the first words she spoke in hours.

"I can't continue, Andrew Maxwell. We must find shelter or be food for vultures."

"If you insist," I said. We again found shade under a high bank and drank. The river had become such a meander now that it was difficult to identify the main channel. We'd apparently reached the springs or seeps that were the genesis of the Humboldt. Even in the glare, the silence between us had grown dark.

I thought of time lost, how to recover it. July 30. The day I should have arrived in Wyoming. Two days behind a schedule that never had room for error. If we reached Wells tonight, perhaps there'd be a train. If not a passenger train, perhaps I could board another freight. Would Many Clouds board one with me? Then I realized we had seen no trains since the one that had abandoned us. I had no explanation for that. I split my last piece of jerky and handed her half.

"Why don't you get some sleep?" I said. "We'll need it."

"Not now," she said. "Perhaps you."

"I'm too nervous," I said.

"And what makes you nervous?" It was the first real question she'd asked me. I wasn't sure whether to be honest with her. Her head was cocked to the side, her expression serious.

"My train, my family." I paused. "You." She smiled.

"I make you nervous? How can that be?"

"I don't know what you'll say or do any moment. I'd prefer more… predictability."

"You've chosen a strange life for someone who wants the predictable—running from place to place, fighting, intruding."

I thought for a moment. Nothing she said described the life I'd led before Julian's death. "At the moment, this life seems to have chosen me."

"You could not take your own way?"

"Touché. In a way, I chose what I did, but in another way my choice was made for me as much as the river chooses a way for the leaf. I had to act. My brother's murder, Shelby's murder…" I waited. She displayed no reaction. Since she didn't ask about Shelby, she must have known about him, which meant she'd seen Yellow Squirrel since his escape. Or had at least heard about him.

"I'm having a hard time getting cooperation. I seem to be the only one in my family who understands the nature of this threat."

"And what do you understand?"

"Not as much as you do, Many Clouds." I was suddenly leery of her questions. "I know some names, and I know what's occurred, but I don't know why. I also don't know why you and your mother are—were—so afraid of me."

"My mother could speak once," she said. "Though I never heard from her any sounds but the kind you heard."

"Not Arapaho?"

She shook her head. "One afternoon a trooper from Fort Bridger filled himself with whisky and decided to ride through our village and practice his roping. He threw a loop at what he considered the first animal he saw—my pregnant mother—and he caught her around the neck and dragged her through the teepees. My father tried to stop him and received a bullet in the heart for his trouble."

"That's ugly beyond words, Many Clouds." She nodded. "What happened to the soldier?"

"By law, Indians could not testify against him. They called the roping an accident and my father's death the natural result of a native fighting the U.S. Army. So, you see, Andrew Maxwell, we have the same fear of you we have of every white man."

I leaned toward her, placed a hand on her arm. "Every white man doesn't jump from the train to help you out of trouble. I'd like you to trust me."

"Whether we trust you or not, Andrew Maxwell, makes no difference." She emphasized the "you." "You do not control others." I had no ready answer.

"You are silent for once," Many Clouds said. "You do not trust these others either or you would not be here. Is that not so?"

"Do you trust Yellow Squirrel?" I said. She looked toward the eastern mountains.

"Every white man wants something from us and won't rest until he has it." She moved her arm away.

I wanted to continue, but her head was turned. She'd shut me out again. I lay back on my pack and closed my eyes.

* * *

My second desert sunset was a welcome sight. Encouraged by the thought that we would surely reach Wells this evening, we took a last muddy drink, filled our water containers and set out once again across the dusky sands. I'd done my best to rinse off the dust, and I'd finger-combed my hair, but with my untrimmed beard and ragged pantsleg, I was sure I looked the model of disreputability.

Once again we followed the tracks, still inexplicably devoid of trains and followed them until twilight dimmed to dark and stars dotted the firmament. The monotonous tramping combined with two days of intense action and virtually no sleep leadened my legs and fogged my mind. A faint glow seemed to crown a hill before us, but I didn't allow myself to think it more than another desert illusion until we found ourselves looking down into a small basin speckled with lights and buildings.

My first thought was that Many Clouds and I would share the first real meal either of us had eaten in days, but I immediately dismissed that as a fantasy. A white man's town was to Many Clouds not a haven but a new set of dangers. In addition to the normal perils of rapacious and lecherous drunks, she was wanted by the law, though she probably didn't know it. I'd given hers and Rushing Creek's descriptions to Sheriff O'Neill along with those of Yellow Squirrel and Standing Oak.

"Suppose I fetch some food. We can meet someplace and eat together." The expression on her face was hidden in shadows, but the slump in her shoulders bespoke exhaustion.

"That would be kind of you, Andrew." She nodded. I didn't miss her use of my first name without my last. Maybe we were halfway to "Andy."

"You've been here before. Do you know of a place?" I said.

"Perhaps when we get closer we'll see."

I nodded and stepped forward, new energy in my step, but our progress over the last stretch into Wells was slow. Twice we had to step aside to allow riders to pass us. Twice I stopped to let the faltering Many Clouds catch up. The third time I sensed she had fallen back I turned to find that she was not there at all.

CHAPTER THIRTY-THREE

Had she fainted? Fallen? I rushed back along the road calling to her. There was no answer and no sign of her. I searched both sides of the road for prints leading in another direction. Nothing. She'd simply walked away from me.

I stood and allowed pain and resentment to wash through me. I'd saved her, helped her. A person doesn't simply desert someone who does all that without a word of gratitude. Her vaunted fear of whites was no excuse. I wasn't a fearsome man, and she knew it. What's more, my idea of tracking her to Owl Feather was no more than mist and vapor now. I kicked sand ahead of me as I set off toward town.

* * *

Wells was a dusty collection of saloons whose lights still burned at the late hour. Despite the fact that it was named for the headwaters, the "wells" of the Humboldt, it was a considerable distance from those springs and was apparently the center of very little. Not surprisingly, no one was on duty at the train station and no schedule was posted. The alternatives to rail? I might beg a ride on a freight wagon. Notoriously slow. A horse would be faster, but it would need food, water, and rest. I'd find a locomotive somehow.

The Silver Crown, the closest saloon, seemed as good a place to find a meal as any, so I pushed through the doors. The room held four shabby round tables, a faro setup, and, incongruously, a hand-carved walnut bar. A single cowboy slept in his chair, half-empty bottle of whisky before him. A shaky staircase to the bar's right led to a glass-beaded curtain doorway above. The faro dealer was playing solitaire when I entered, but scooped up the deck and smiled a greeting when he saw me.

"Care for a game, partner?"

"Not now, but I'd certainly appreciate a bite to eat."

"Sure thing. Hey, Rosie," he yelled. "Get on out here and take care of your customers."

"Hold on, hold on," called a voice from a room behind the bar. I took a stool and waited. Despite the name, I thought the voice I'd heard belonged to a man, but the low-cut neckline which barely covered a plump bosom showed Rosie was definitely female. She looked years older than Mother, but the flouncy pink satin dress she overflowed was the attire of a much younger woman.

"Well, partner, you look like you been through it all and back again. What can I do for you—Bath? Drink? Girl? Name's Rosie, from my hair, in case you hadn't guessed."

"How do you do. My name's Andy. To tell the truth, Rosie, what would please me most right now is a couple of steaks."

"Two steaks? Not the size we have, Andy. You'll never get 'em down."

"If I don't, I'll save it for tomorrow," I said. "But I wager I will."

"You really want to bet? How about double or nothing?" I shook my head. "Come on, take a chance."

"I regret I've nothing to take a chance with, ma'am. The steaks and potatoes will be fine."

"Shoot, partner, you're no fun at all. All right, have a seat at a table. We'll bring it out pronto. Want a shot while you're waiting?"

"Just the food, I guess."

"All right, all right. I always did have a soft spot for someone down on his luck. It's on the house." She poured a water glass half full of whisky from an unlabeled bottle. "Don't turn your nose up," she said. "It's free. Steak's coming right up."

"Don't mind if I do, Rosie," said the dealer. His brocade vest and patent leather hair framed a swarthy face that would require two shaves a day to keep the whiskers in check. He left his table and took the stool next to mine. His vest swelled slightly over a shoulder holster. From the small size of the bulge, I guessed he was concealing a derringer.

"Yours ain't free, Luke," Rosie said.

"My table sells more booze than I drink in a month, and you know it. You can afford to tip me once in a while." He smiled and beckoned with his index finger.

"Ah, hell's bells. But no more." She poured and left.

"Mud in your eye," Luke said. He tossed his drink down. I sipped and nearly gagged. The whisky tasted like the kind of rotgut I'd heard Shelby describe from the old days—grain alcohol cut with water, red pepper, molasses, and tobacco or some such combination. I'd have to find a way to empty the glass without drinking its contents.

"Ain't much of a drinking man, I see," Luke said. He smirked.

"Perhaps I'll grow into it some day."

"Well, in the meantime, suppose I help you out some." He grabbed my glass and poured half my measure into his, tossed half that down as well. "Now we can sip and get sociable," he said. He pointed a thumb in the direction of his table. "A couple of the right cards, you could double your cash. Travel in style." He smiled and wiggled his eyebrows.

"Speaking of traveling," I said, "do you know the when next train east is due to arrive?"

"Should have been one today," he said. "But I reckon there won't be another for a good while. Not till they fix them bridges got washed out a couple of days ago."

So. Stranded. I swallowed more whisky. It suddenly didn't taste so bad. Rosie entered with two huge plates, one stacked with potatoes, the other with two steaks that spilled over the edges the same way as Rosie spilled out of her dress. When she set the food in front of me, Luke pulled a watch from his vest.

"Two o'clock, Rosie. Andy is the only fish swum in here since midnight, and he ain't biting, so I'll see you tomorrow."

"Night, Luke. You better come in early and earn that drink," she said. "Both of them." Luke said nothing, but winked at me and ambled out the door.

"Eat hearty, friend," Rosie said, and she headed up the stairs "Call if you need anything else," she added as she parted the glass beads at the top. Then she disappeared behind the glitter.

The meat was tough—probably from an old bull—but tasty. I surprised myself by finishing the whisky and liking it. I'd consumed all but the second steak when Rosie descended the stairs. Two women—one appeared to be no more than sixteen, my grandmother's diary-writing age—followed her. Their clothes were better fitting than Rosie's, but every bit as tawdry. They struck awkwardly seductive poses, bodies leaned backward against the railing in profile, smiles turned in my direction. With a bit of practice, they might be ready for Madame Gabrielle and the Red Rooster, but they'd have to practice with someone else than me.

"Well, you going to finish that or not, Andy?" Rosie said. She continued down the staircase. The girls remained halfway up.

"I'm glad I didn't bet you, Rosie. My eyes were bigger than my stomach, I guess."

"Didn't I tell you?"

"You did, indeed. This will have to wait. Have you something to wrap it in?" I tried not to look toward the stairs. Rosie didn't respond to my request, but picked up my plates, glasses and money. I removed my bandanna and managed to cover most of the meat before I stowed it in my rucksack.

"You need a room, Andy?" Rosie said. How about another drink? Celia and Maggie there'll be glad to set you up. One or both of them."

"Oh, I'm sorry. I'm so short of cash I can't even afford a room. I'm camping out by the cottonwood grove on the other side of the tracks. Oh, I could use a few matches if that wouldn't be too much trouble."

Rosie turned on her heel and clomped toward the kitchen. I smiled up briefly at the girls. They held their silent poses. Rosie returned, thumped a dozen or so loose matches on the table.

"Two bits," she said.

"Uh…"

She smiled. "That was a joke, son. You really ain't no fun."

"Thanks for the hospitality," I said as I scooped up the matches. "Perhaps I'll see you all for breakfast." I picked up my rucksack and waved as I backed out the door. The three watched me all the way, smiles fading as I exited.

* * *

I curled up in the cottonwood grove, grateful in the chill desert night for the small fire Rosie's matches furnished. Perhaps sleep and a new dawn would inspire a notion on how to get on my way to Owl Feather. Despite my exhaustion, I soon gave up on sleeping and began walking. I had no destination, intended merely to keep moving, stay near town, keep the blood flowing.

Only a barking dog kept me from walking directly into the Indian village, whose dark huts blended into the dunes. I retreated quickly and knelt behind a stand of sage. I waited until the stillness was absolute, then circled the village in a crouch. All I could make out were a dozen or so dwellings and a small herd of horses and burros. Perhaps those animals could substitute for the train after all. I could take two, alternately ride one and lead the other. My thoughts buoyed me, and exhaustion dissipated—or so I thought.

* * *

It was probably the same dog whose barking had challenged me in the dark that challenged the rising sun and woke me at the same time. I pushed down a spurt of fear as I scanned the village for signs that I'd been discovered, but the only mark of human activity was an older woman spreading her skirts and squatting to make water near a gully behind one of the lean-tos. Soon after, a man appeared, a woman following. None other than Standing Oak and Many Clouds. They walked purposefully toward the most substantial house in the village—a shack of scrap lumber with a tin roof. Standing Oak knocked loudly, then pushed the door open and stepped inside.

CHAPTER THIRTY-FOUR

Many Clouds remained outside. Where was Yellow Squirrel? Perhaps close by. I felt once again fortunate that I'd jumped off the train. Trailing Standing Oak and Many Clouds to their destination—undoubtedly Owl Feather—would be the most efficient way to the heart of this whole matter. Or perhaps I could put one of my adversaries out of the picture immediately.

I looked—first with longing, then with anger—at the remuda which stood hobbled only a few yards away. Sailor stood a hand or two higher than the two paints that flanked him. My own horse was tethered immediately in front of me, yet completely inaccessible. I entertained, then dismissed as foolhardy, the idea of stealing him. Not here, not in broad daylight. I looked again at Many Clouds, who seemed to be gazing in my direction. I dug both fists into the sand and gripped hard to subdue my fury.

Standing Oak reappeared with a squat man dressed in Levi's, hat, and boots. His bare gut hung well over his three-inch-wide belt. Many Clouds watched the men stroll among the animals, finally settling on one of the paints beside Sailor. Standing Oak rigged bridles, but no saddles, and led Sailor and the paint away from the other horses.

Behind my sagebrush screen, I pulled the pistol from my rucksack and loaded it. If they remained close enough to my eastward-running gully when they left, I could surprise them. I stooped and ran up the ditch. I ran till I was winded and my legs felt like water, then found a place to spring my ambush where the ditch took a sudden turn north. I threw myself against the bank and crept to the top.

The Indian village was out of sight over a rise which the riders now crested, slogging toward me through the sand, a half-mile or so distant. Though they paralleled the gully, they were a couple of hundred yards south of it. Too far for my pistol, too far for surprise. Perhaps I could lure them to me.

I shed my rucksack, held my breath and climbed out of the gully. I pretended not to see them, stumbled across the dunes far enough that I could be sure they'd see me, then dropped flat on my face.

I couldn't know right away whether my ruse was working because I dared not move or look up. In truth, lying in the warm sand was a welcome rest. I clutched the pistol to my belly. I stayed still, and stayed and stayed and stayed. Moments ago, I'd run farther than I thought I could run. Now I was lying still longer than I thought possible in a waking state. Every muscle taut, listening for footsteps.

It wasn't foossteps, but voices murmuring in Arapaho that finally signaled that my plan was succeeding. Surely Many Clouds would recognize my clothes. Would that be an advantage or not? Finally I heard sand grind under heavy feet. I fought the impulse to tense even more. I must appear completely inert. I felt light blows to my head, to my shoulder. Prodding. I didn't react. A toe dug into my ribs, shoved hard, lifted, rolled me to my back.

I opened my eyes to find Standing Oak, backlit and menacing as the deepest shade of hell, hovering over me. A perfect target. I raised my pistol. What I didn't see was Many Clouds on my gun arm side. She screamed and knocked the barrel aside at the same instant I pulled the trigger. I rolled clear of them both and gained my knees to see Standing Oak leveling his rifle. I panicked and fired a second shot before I'd fully raised the pistol, all at the same time that Many Clouds sent Standing Oak's shot awry by grabbing his arm. She hung on to the big man for a few seconds, but when he shook her off, I had a clear shot and fired. He dropped his rifle, staggered back, sat down, and clutched a shoulder. I ran forward, gun ready, but Many Clouds scooped up the rifle, stood between me and Standing Oak, and aimed it straight at my chest.

"No one dies here if you stop right now, Andrew."

"That man belongs dead or in jail, Many Clouds, and that horse has the Maxwell brand. You're protecting a horse thief and a killer."

"If you want him, you must shoot me first, Andrew." Standing Oak had struggled to his knees. How I had failed to kill him at such short range baffled me. Despite myself, I was a little glad that I hadn't. That baffled me too. He was everything I was fighting, yet I was happy he lived.

"Remember all I've done. Your mother. You won't shoot me, Many Clouds."

"You know better," she said. I stepped toward her. She sighted down the barrel. I lowered my pistol and watched while she and Standing Oak backed toward the horses and mounted. Many Clouds carried on a running conversation with Standing Oak, in Arapaho, kept her body and her paint horse between him, me, and Sailor while they mounted. Both of them hauled themselves to their horses' bare backs with one arm. I had no chance for another shot. I hoped for an opportunity once they resumed their ride, but Many Clouds screened him until they were well out of range.

What had stopped me? She was just as much a part of this as anyone. I supposed the idea of shooting a woman accounted for part of my hesitation. Then, even if our little sojourn on the desert had meant nothing to her, it seemed to have touched a soft place inside me. Maybe inside her also, or she might have pulled her trigger. In sum, I wasn't yet the warrior I needed to be to do this job.

July thirty-first. Even on fast horses, I didn't see how I could cover the distance to Wind River in less than three or four days. After that, I'd have only a little more than a week to end all this and return home. And I had only one cylinderful of bullets remaining.

Yet, I still had money, and once I acquired some horses I should have no trouble tracking my quarry, at least till we reached the mountains where the trails became rocky. If the weather held. Finding horses and supplies would cost a few hours, but a half-day's delay could give me the distance between us I needed to keep them from knowing they were being followed.

* * *

I found a wrangler distributing hay and oats to a half-dozen horses in a corral near the train depot. The bandy-legged cowboy, dressed in denim and a stained brown hat, had finished with the feed and was hauling buckets of water from a hand pump to a trough. I watched him fill the second of the two buckets, then stooped to lift one of them.

"No thanks," he said. "I like to carry 'em both. Keeps me balanced." I followed him as he sloshed his way across the ten yards to the corral, then I emptied one of them into the trough while he dumped the other. Two of the horses stuck their noses into the fresh water.

"Kinda determined to help out, are ya?" he said. "Must want something."

"Helping's in my nature," I said. "My name's Andy."

"Ira," the man said. We shook hands.

"Nice bunch of mustangs you got here," I said.

"All broke, too or the next thing to it," Ira said. "Got a fella up in Montana all ready for 'em, but I'm losing money waiting for that train."

"Perhaps I could help you reduce your losses," I said.

"Suspicioned you wasn't all just helpful-natured," Ira said.

"Well I am that as well." I smiled down at him. "However, I'm stranded by the same train you're waiting for and I thought I'd try getting to Wyoming on horseback instead. I'm willing to rent or buy, whichever you prefer."

"Renting don't do me no good less'n you're going to take these all the way to Montana, and I sure as hell ain't gonna to trust someone I don't know to do that. Don't matter how good-natured he is."

"Very well, then," I said. "Suppose I purchase two at fifty dollars each. You needn't include a saddle. A bridle will suffice." It was nearly the whole of my cash, but Ira looked at me with a smile, dropped his cigarette in the dirt and ground it under the ball of his foot.

"You can't buy a goat for that, Andy."

"You said yourself they're scarcely broke," I said. "They're certainly not trained to handle stock. And how much are you paying for this feed and corral?"

"Got to admire your gumption, Andy, but you're gonna stay afoot if you can't offer no more than that." He walked away toward the saloons.

"I'll offer a hundred and forty for the pair," I called to his back. That would include most of my return train fare. He stopped and turned back to me.

"Two hundred and twenty five and no tack is as low as I'll go," he said. "Train's bound to come through soon."

I considered. While I was thinking, Ira gave up on me and resumed his hike toward town.

"Very well," I called. "A hundred and seventy-five. It's my last offer."

"Sorry, Andy. But until you show me two hundred, we're wasting each other's time. And no bridles either."

"You've struck a deal, Ira. I'll expect to ride out of here before lunch time today. I'll meet you right here about eleven o'clock?"

Ira waved a dismissive hand and walked down the street toward a saloon around the corner from The Silver Crown on Wells' only other street. The Gold Crown. Folks around here seemed short on imagination when it came to naming their establishments. I stepped behind the railway station and transferred a silver dollar to my pocket and a ten-dollar bill to my boot. I hoped Luke had taken seriously Rosie's order to come in early. Now my horses, my life, depended on my eyes moving faster than a gambler's hand.

CHAPTER THIRTY-FIVE

Even in my drinking days with Julian, I'd never gambled. Success at faro and blackjack required remembering which cards had been played. Julian found it easy, but I could never do it. Poker was full of odds and tactics I hadn't mastered. Three card monte, however, was simple, and I had an aptitude for following the crucial card. I'd never valued the talent, never dreamed I'd need it the way I needed it now.

Luke was alone in the saloon devouring a plate of steak and eggs when I entered. "Andy. Good to see you. Join me." He pointed to a chair with his fork.

I took the chair. "You're up with the chickens. Rosie's word must be law."

"Ah, she knows I don't sleep in. She just had to say something to make herself think she's got me under her thumb. Hey, Rosie," he yelled. "Get in here and take care of your customers."

"Hold on, hold on," the husky voice from the back room answered. It seemed this banter didn't change from one day to the next.

"Well, well, well," Rosie smiled when she saw me. "Didn't expect you back, Andy. What'll you have?" This morning's dress was lavender, but the cut and fabric were identical.

"Coffee only, thanks." I said. "I filled myself this morning on last night's steak."

"Young man, I think you're undernourished. But, okay. Back in a minute."

"You know, Luke," I said. "I decided I might take you up on your suggestion from last night."

"What suggestion was that?"

I leaned across the table. "I'd like to increase my bankroll a little."

"Well, well," he said. "Let's get to it, then." He shoved the half-finished plate away and stepped behind the semi-circular table that was his dais. He picked up a deck, executed some fancy shuffles, dealt three cards face up in front of me, stacked the rest to the side.

"Do you have a notion what the time it is, Luke?" I said. He pulled a slim gold watch from his vest pocket. I had a pang of nostalgia for my own disabled timepiece.

"In a hurry to lose your money, Andy? I got three minutes after ten. What say we get to dealing? Name your poison," His smile disappeared. His casual posture gave way to squared shoulders and straight spine.

He shook his head when I told him what I wanted to play. "Not a good choice for a man down on his luck. My best game."

But I insisted, and he shrugged his shoulders and I chose a deuce of hearts.

I laid a silver dollar on the table, and said, "Do your best."

"Whole dollar, huh?" he said. "You're rolling high, Andy." He carefully displayed the other two cards—a five of spades and jack of clubs—then laid all three down and began to slide them around the table. When he stopped, I placed my finger on the center card. Luke turned over the deuce.

"Okay, Andy, you just doubled your money." He replaced my dollar with two chips.

"Let it ride," I said. Twice more I won. Seven dollars ahead. I needed to win at least a hundred to buy the horses and keep my return fare intact.

"Perhaps we could up the ante, Luke?" I made a show of reaching into my boot for the ten-dollar bill.

"I don't know, Andy. I'd hate to get cleaned out so early in the day." He broke his tough-gambler demeanor with a slight smile. Two cowhands had entered the Silver Crown. They carried a bottle and glasses to one of the tables. Rosie kept herself busy behind the bar.

I turned the ten into twenty. Luke's hands moved faster, blurred. Losses followed. Then more gains. By ten-thirty I was fifty dollars ahead, considering whether I should take my winnings and attempt to negotiate Ira's price down with a show of cash. I decided there was little chance. I pondered a while longer. Luke broke the tension.

"Rosie," he said. "Andy here needs a drink. On me."

"Thanks, Rosie," I said. "I'll have a victory drink later. Proceed, Luke." He did. And my fifty turned into thirty, then into sixty. The two cowhands had wandered over and begun watching.

"Care to place a side bet, gents?" Luke asked. They both shook their heads. Luke made the cards dance, stopped. I chose the one to my right. Luke turned the Jack instead of the deuce. Again. The jack again. Twice more, and I was suddenly down to my original ten. I couldn't understand how I had lost my instinct. Then I thought maybe I hadn't. The ten disappeared. All I had left outside my underwear was a silver dollar. I turned it over and over. The audience had grown to four.

"Well, Andy," Luke said. "You going to put it down or not? I have customers waiting." I placed the bet. Luke began moving the cards. Slowly at first, then with increasing speed. I reached out and grabbed one of his wrists with my left hand and drew my knife with the other. He reached for the shoulder holster. Under the table I jabbed his knee with my knifepoint. He winced.

"Leave the gun alone, Luke. I'll bury this knife in your gut before you clear the holster."

CHAPTER THIRTY-SIX

I was running a bluff, of course. I had almost no skill at throwing a knife, and I'd need a saber to span the two feet between my hand and Luke's belly. But he stopped. The four men behind me retreated. I'd have to trust they didn't want to get involved.

"Now, Luke, perhaps you'd care to turn over those three cards. One at a time."

"Don't take it out on me just because your luck turned, Andy." He tried to pull loose, but shuffling cards wasn't much of a muscle builder compared to shoveling coal.

"Turn them."

"I been running an honest game here for a long time. You men can tell him," he said. I couldn't see their response, but I heard nothing.

"If you please, sir," I said.

"Oh, for Pete's sake, let me do it." Rosie appeared at Luke's side. "We can't have this kind of trouble in my bar." She reached a pudgy hand across the table and turned over a five of spades and two jacks of clubs. She looked at Luke and shook her head. No deuce.

"Thought I'd finally found an honest dealer. Get out of town now, you two-bit hustler, before I call the marshal."

"Don't play innocent, Rosie," he said.

"And don't try to lay your cheatin' at my door, Luke. I said you're done, and you're done."

I kept my grip on Luke's wrist. I wasn't interested in parsing the dispute between him and his boss. "My life depends on obtaining two horses, sir. You may leave Wells when I receive the hundred dollars I need."

"Here it is," Rosie said. She reached under the table, pulled out a pouch thick with greenbacks, and counted out the money.

"And you deserve an extra twenty for the aggravation." She slapped down the bills and slid them toward me. I sheathed my knife, gripped the money as tightly in my left fist as I gripped Luke's wrist in my right. "And an extra helping for the house." She lifted a handful of bills from the pouch without counting, then threw the pouch, considerably thinner, back on the table.

"The gun, Rosie, if you please," I said. "At least until I'm out of Wells."

"My pleasure, Andy," she said. She reached into his vest and removed a handsome Remington four-shot pepperbox. A twenty-two caliber. I had another thought.

"How about the leg?" She cocked her head at me, eyes large with surprise.

"Not quite the greenhorn you seem, are you?" She knelt.

"Son of a bitch," Luke growled to me through closed teeth. When she stood, Rosie held another derringer, a perfect mate for the first. Luke had names for her, too. "Stinking, traitorous whore."

"Thank you both," I said. "It's been a pleasure, sir. Madame." I released my grip on Luke's arm. He jumped to his feet and grabbed the pouch. He looked, apparently for support, at the surrounding crowd. Finding none, he slouched toward the front door. When he was halfway there, I followed and watched him down the sidewalk.

"Thanks to all," I said. "I have an appointment."

"Hold it a minute," said Rosie. "Girls," she called up the stairs. "Celia, Maggie, come out here a minute." The younger of the two appeared shortly, puffy-eyed and barely wrapped in a dowdy robe. "Toss down a couple of pair of them trousers we got up there," Rosie said. The girl shook her head in disgust and disappeared.

"We got an occasional hombre leaves in hurry," Rosie said. "Some of these ought to fit. Anything'd fit better than them torn up rags you're wearing. Am I right?"

I didn't trust Rosie any more than I did Luke, but I was in no position to turn down her offer providing it came without strings. "I suppose," I said.

The girl tossed the pants down the stairs, then stomped off, presumably to bed. There were three pair—a black serge with embossed leather suspenders still attached, and a couple of manure-stained denims.

"Thanks, Rosie. I'm sure one of them will be perfect."

"Come back when you've had a bath, Andy. I bet you clean up real good." She laughed. I hurried out the door toward the corral across the tracks.

Horses dozed in the hot sun, yet Ira was nowhere to be seen. Neither was Luke, but he might not be far. By the sun I reckoned it close to noon. Ira might have already decided I wasn't coming. More likely, he hadn't taken me seriously in the first place. I retraced my steps from the corral to the bar into which Ira had disappeared earlier.

The horseman occupied a seat at one of the Golden Crown's two card tables. I approached, watched the dealer rake in Ira's faro bet. The wrangler emptied a whisky glass and refilled it from a bottle at his left elbow.

I covered the glass with my hand. "I apologize for the interruption, but I've come for my horses."

"Andy, my friend," he said. "Good to see you. How about a round of cards?" He tried to pull the glass from under my hand, but I held firmly.

"I've no time, Ira. Let's go settle up."

"I'd love to, Andy, but you see, those horses belong to this gentleman here. Just for the time being, you understand." He indicated the dealer, a stoop-shouldered blond with a pink mole on the left side of his nose. "I'll win them back soon as I get me up a stake. Don't worry about that."

"Place your bets or step aside, gents," the dealer said. His bass voice came from deep in his chest.

I pulled Ira off the stool and hustled him out the door. There was a good deal of liquor in his step, but he managed to remain upright.

"Stay away from my mustangs, now, cowboy." The dealer waved a bill of sale at us.

"Won't be yours for long." Ira slurred the sentence into a string of mushy consonants.

"Come, Ira," I whispered. "We're about to do some horse trading." I ignored his objections, pushed and pulled him, staggering, down the sidewalk. I looked left and right to make sure Luke wasn't visible, then turned toward the corral. A few steps later, I felt a yank on my arm. I retained my hold on Ira, and we both stumbled backwards into the narrow alley between the bar and whatever adobe building stood next to it. We found ourselves backed against a wall looking into the barrel of a large pistol. Behind the pistol stood Rosie's former card sharp.

CHAPTER THIRTY-SEVEN

"Believe you have some money that belongs to me," Luke said.

"Cheating money's not precisely yours," I said.

"What's happening?" Ira said.

Luke pointed the gun at Ira's nose. "I'll get to you in a minute." Ira slid down the wall and sat in the dust. Luke turned the gun on me. "Turn around." I started to refuse. He motioned with his gun, and I decided this wasn't the time to resist. A lady under a parasol crossed the sidewalk near the alley. She didn't look our way.

Luke pulled the bills from my pocket. I cursed myself for not taking the time to secrete them in my purse, but his next words made my self-scolding irrelevant.

"And now that little cache in your underwear."

"Underwear? What do you want with my underwear?"

"You need to be more careful about who's watching when you open your purse, friend Andy."

"You won't shoot me here, Luke. It would be suicide with so many people in the neighborhood. I lowered my arms and turned toward the street. I actually turned my back to Luke. What a fool's ploy is bravado. A blow to the back of my head sent me to my hands and knees. A kick in the back sent me to my belly. A toe in the ribs turned me on my back.

"You're right about the shooting, Andy." Luke's voice was faint, and I was barely aware of his tossing the empty purse in my face. "I got what I want from you, and I don't like using more violence than necessary. Now it's that double-crossing Rosie's turn. See you gentlemen later."

I regained my senses when Ira, apparently attempting to help me up, fell across my chest. I pushed him off, jerked him to his feet, and pushed him toward the corral. Heat waves swam through the air. Consciousness swam back into my brain. We stumbled like a pair of drunks to the compound that held the mustangs. Ira was starting to walk more steadily but I still had to throw his arms across the top rail of the corral to keep him standing.

"Now. We made a deal this morning and I'm holding you to it."

"He stepped back from the corral, stumbled, clutched again at the rail for support. "I told you these ain't my horses no more. And you ain't got no money nohow."

"Your gamblin's not my affair," I said.

I scratched an i.o.u. into the board of the corral with my knife, pointed Ira's head at the writing. "Two hundred dollars, bridles included. Present that at the Circle M ranch, Sawtooth Wells, California. You'll find it's as good as money in the bank." I strode to an adjoining fence where the gear hung.

"Hey, I said no bridles."

"That was before. And I'm including a sack of oats." He started toward me, realized he had no supporting fence, and grabbed the board again.

The mustangs were skittish, but the sun was hot, and they weren't in the mood to run around much. I chose two, led them out the gate, hitched them to the rail. I roped two sacks of feed together, threw them and my canteen across the stallion's withers.

I suspected Ira had been stretching the truth about how well-broken these mustangs were, so I was ready when the mare did a twist and a few stiff-legged hops when I mounted. I managed to stay aboard, though I'd have earned no points for style at a rodeo. I unhitched the stallion and started out of town. Ira sat in the dirt, leaning against the corral.

"You ain't nothin' but a damned horse thief."

I rode past without looking down. "Add it to my record."

I was out of food and money, but I was out of Wells. I decided the Indian Village was my best bet for finding provisions and advice on a route to Wind River. I'd then take shelter and await the blessing of cool shadows.

CHAPTER THIRTY-EIGHT

I sat out the heat of July's last day in the uncertain shade of the dry wash near where I'd attempted my ambush. I'd traded the fancy pants and suspenders Rosie had given me for some pemmican and sketchy directions to Wyoming. The two pair of Levi's were droopy, but wearable and intact. I was amazed how much confidence I gained from donning whole pants, even worn out as these were. I'd been about to examine Grandfather's trail log when I'd left the train. I turned back to it now.

Carter Maxwell's text was as different from Julia's journal as his build and coloring were from hers.

* * *

Camped today at Grand Island, Platte River, after traveling 19 miles in good weather. General Fremont stopped here 1843 and recorded his position as Longitude 99°37'45", Latitude 40°39'32." I am gratified to find my readings nearly identical to his, the only variation being that my reading shows 38" Longitude, 34" Latitude.

* * *

As to Mathilda Barlow, Carter's entry on the day of her death is as enigmatic as his wife's:

Buried M. B. today. Justice done at last.

If Carter had exacted vengeance by killing the Barlow woman, no one remained to tell it. And I supposed it didn't matter any longer. Still, a murder is a murder, and Grandfather left a revered legacy of pride and service and land. Surely it did matter if the hero of good works was also a killer who stepped outside the laws of heaven and earth to satisfy his blood lust. And if Julia had known?

But I had present murders to deal with, future killings to prevent. I plodded through more of Carter's other notes about trail business and navigation but found no doorways to the mystery.

* * *

At dusk, I pulled out of the dry wash and fastened on the hoofprints of the horses—one shod, the other not—that carried Standing Oak and Many Clouds across the desert. The sand was stirred up where we'd fought. I shivered as I rode across the site. A quarter mile farther, Standing Oak's rifle lay on the sand.

I wondered at their carelessness, but I welcomed the gift of another weapon. The abandoned rifle, however, proved to be no windfall. My bullet had ripped open the magazine below the forearm and jammed the action. I'd been smug about bluffing Luke, but Many Clouds had bluffed me with a useless rifle. Nevertheless, I was on their trail, and it seemed they were now without a firearm.

* * *

I lost the trail the next morning. Even in the dark, the tracks remained visible in the sand, and by switching horses I'd been able to ride virtually non-stop for over twelve hours. But the way had become steep and rocky now, and my quarry's direction, even the existence of a path, became less and less evident. I gave up the effort after the third time I'd ridden in widening spirals around a rocky saddle, looking for where the two horses had stepped off into softer ground. I was wasting time.

Now the confusing verbal sketches of peaks and trees that the Indians at Wells had given me were all the directions I had to go on. That and one old man's remark that trails followed water. "Not much water, very few trails," he'd said of the way across the hills.

I followed a brook to a hillside spring and stopped to water, rest the horses, and nibble some pemmican. Beside the spring, I found a distinct trail.

I'd somehow deviated by a few degrees, but, true to the old man's words, the stream had led me back to the main path.

As I filled my canteen, I noticed my reflection in the pool was beginning to appear rather gaunt, despite the beard. I imagined waxing and grooming my moustache in the old-fashioned style of my grandfather. Perhaps I'd play with that idea when I got through all this. First of August. Exactly two weeks left, and I was still days away from the reservation.

I fed each horse a handful of oats, then climbed aboard and set my mental compass—foolish not to bring a real one—at northeast. In another hour, the way up the hill we climbed became so steep and narrow I dismounted and led both horses over and between the boulders and roots that blocked our way. We walked a veritable shelf on a forty-five-degree cliff. Had I been able to turn the horses around, I'd have gone back to lower ground and searched out a gentler grade, but now the only way was up.

I didn't understand the import of the first warning—a head-sized rock that bounced off the boulder above and missed me by scant feet as it shot into the canyon. Then the earth began shaking like a bridge under a freight wagon. I dived beneath a boulder's overhang while rubble and dust clouded the air until I could barely breathe or tell up from down. The lead horse tore his reins from my hand. I heard a whinny, then both animals disappeared behind a curtain of dust. A ululating cry sounded through the roar, and shadows and crashes rained past me. I pressed my face to the bank. Something slammed like a piledriver into my rear then there was only thundering weight, pressing me farther and deeper into a world which knew no light.

CHAPTER THIRTY-NINE

Waking was like banging my head against a bank vault door. My mouth was dry, and darkness deep as the inside of midnight surrounded me. I began to recall what had happened, remembered the war cry mixed with the thundering avalanche. I'd lost Standing Oak's trail, but he hadn't lost mine. How long had I been unconscious? My canteen was with the stallion, wherever he was. I yelled a few times. No response. Perhaps I would have been unhappy about who answered my call in any case.

I ran my tongue around my teeth to generate saliva, extended an exploring hand. As nearly as I could tell, I lay on my back in a small chamber, the keystone of which was the boulder I'd leaped under when the slide began. I had about an arm's length of space above me and on either side, but my lower body seemed trapped, and I couldn't roll over even enough to reach the rucksack behind me. I scrabbled around, trying to loosen something, admit some light, discern how far underground I lay buried. At first, I accomplished little more than scraping my fingertips on the gritty surface of the rocks. Eventually, however, I managed to loosen a melon-sized boulder below my waist, drag it up over my head, and drop it behind my left shoulder, where it rolled gently down and rested itself between my shoulder blades. I held my breath and listened for a shift in the pile that might signal a cave-in, but all seemed stable.

The rock at my back propped me up somewhat, and I now could shift my right hip a couple of inches. The progress encouraged me despite the headache ballooning inside my skull. By wiggling and scraping my shoulders through a space they weren't designed to fit, I reached forward and cleared a jagged fragment jammed against my right shin. I found I could move the toe of my boot in a small circle. That was good news, of course, but one end of what felt like a hog-sized boulder still pinned both thighs securely and nearly immobilized my hips as well. I sagged for a moment. Three deep breaths and the thought of Mother dead and the Circle M in flames dispelled the panic. I returned to work.

I leaned up and forward as far as my pinioned legs would allow and carefully removed rocks one at a time and dropped them behind me. I tested each rock carefully before I removed it, counted to ten after each shift, afraid that every gap I created would be the one that brought down the whole pile. I eventually cleared a space in front and nearly filled the little pocket behind me, expecting to see light any second. Then the entire cavern collapsed.

Only the rocks that pinned my lower body prevented the impact from crushing me. My predicament was worse now. I had space to breathe, and I could still move my shoulders and head, but I was effectively buried from the waist down with nowhere to place any rocks I might move. I leaned back, rested my hurting head, closed my eyes. It was too dark to see anyway.

* * *

I was sure I hadn't slept. Almost sure. Just drifted off for a few minutes. It seemed as if it might all end here. Yellow Squirrel, Standing Oak, Owl Feather—they'd have their revenge after all.

I indulged my self-pity for a few minutes, then began to grope for a new solution. I'd been concentrating on the space in front of me, but now my hand came up against a sandy wall a foot to the right. Perhaps I could open up something in that direction. I drew my knife from the sheath at my hip and began digging. Gravel sifted into the little tunnel, but I spooned it with my hand into crevices between the larger rocks that surrounded the rest of my body. And I encountered no boulders. Perhaps the mass of the slide had remained fairly central, then graveled out at the edges. Even if my theory about the slide's configuration was correct, I had no idea how much earth I'd have to move to find daylight, and another two feet would be the limit of my reach.

In time—how much?—my wrist aching from the awkward angle, the passageway's diameter and depth grew to a foot, then to a foot-and-a-half. My legs ached and throbbed as the big rock's pressure played havoc with my circulation

I cleared another six inches, then jammed against something. Something wooden, round, scaly, sticky, perhaps four inches in diameter. A root? It wouldn't budge, and whittling through it would take hours. Dig around it, then. Again, process was laborious and slow, but fruitful. I cleared a space above and below the root and stretched to dig beyond it. Something prickled my wrist. Needles. This wasn't a root, but a tree, or at least a branch. If I could simply push it aside I might clear a pile of rubble along with it. But it still wouldn't move. Not yet.

I leaned and stretched to what seemed my limit, then pushed beyond. When I found a pocket of sand through which I could maneuver my hand with little resistance. I knew I was nearing the edge of the slide, but I couldn't reach far enough to break through. I settled back and breathed and thought. Gnawing my tongue had ceased to alleviate my thirst. What now? Was it day, night? Which day, night?

Nature's call, which I had been staving off for some time, became urgent. Wherever we go, we carry our needs with us. No putting some things aside even in a crisis like this. I managed to relieve myself in a rocky downhill corner that wouldn't foul my nest, then returned to my tree.

I began digging along its length instead of around it. A short distance downhill, it had broken off in ragged splinters. A few feet uphill, it simply ended. Uprooted or snapped off. I pushed, pulled. Nothing moved. I reached high, gripped the uphill end and tugged that my way. It shifted at last.

I poked and rotated the shaft through the downhill rocks, in essence drilling a passageway. At last fresh air diluted the gritty atmosphere I'd been breathing. A weak pencil of what seemed to be daylight followed soon after. Dusk or dawn?

I could see only a narrow strip of downhill scree. But I had a path out now, and I began rolling my imprisoning rocks out the new tunnel and down the hill.

My headache was intermittent now. The light seemed to grow stronger. Perhaps it was morning—the morning of August second, if I was lucky. Less than two weeks short of the full moon. Less time than I'd counted on, but perhaps enough. But perhaps it was August third or even fourth. Then what? I worked faster.

Finally, I'd cleared everything in range of my grasp. Until I removed the boulder from my hips, I was no better off than when I had the rest of the mountainside atop me. I lay back again, exhausted and hurting. I tried to move my legs, but I couldn't tell whether I'd succeeded because I couldn't feel them. The sapling had been the key to everything else. It would have to open this door also.

I jammed it under the slab that pinned me. I shifted several rocks underneath for a fulcrum, pulled downward. The boulder raised a couple of inches, and I pulled my leg toward me. Then the tree broke, the rock hammered my thigh.

"Damnation, you bastard," I yelled. And of course, the break in the sapling was not clean. Limp, resinous ropes attached the broken end to the main branch so I couldn't get a strong edge back under the rock. I hauled the damaged section back up to my chest, chopped and scraped at the tough spaghetti of wood with my knife until the broken end detached, then I jammed it back in and yanked down just as the fulcrum collapsed and the big rock scraped a couple of feet downhill. I managed to slide my hips out from under. Free.

CHAPTER FORTY

I crawled from my little tomb into the late morning sun. A fiery tingling filled my legs and feet as blood returned. I massaged them into aching life and looked upward. Two switchbacks along the trail, a large rip in the earth marked where the boulder that had triggered the landslide had torn from the side of the mountain and plowed a ditch down the hill. Ax blade marks on the sapling's trunk showed where the tree had been felled and used as a prybar to loose the avalanche. I pictured Standing Oak flinging it into the slide as he launched his war cry, remembered I'd been somehow glad my bullet hadn't killed him earlier. My feelings hadn't been reciprocated. This meek one had inherited a lot more earth than he bargained for.

The corpse of my mare lay below. Two vultures circled just above the treetops. I walk-slid down the slope to her. Wolves had gnawed on the haunches. They'd return to finish her tonight, but she hadn't begun to stink, so it seemed I'd been buried no more than a night. I saw no sign of the stallion, which meant my canteen was gone. But I had some food in the rucksack.

I'd forge on to the Wind River reservation, where I could probably locate Standing Oak's tracks once more. He and Many Clouds wouldn't be watching for me now. I climbed back up to the trail.

My body was an aching, tender jumble of bruises. My left leg threw me into a limp, but I was still mobile, if halting. I inched my way over the landslide and resumed my trek up the mountainside. I'd detected no trail sign as I climbed, but found a great deal at the spot where Standing Oak had started the slide. Sailor's iron shoes had scarred the rocks in several places, telltale marks I'd now be able to read. I found few of Many Clouds' prints. Had she objected? Tried to stop her uncle? Stood silently and watched?

I was about to resume my journey when I heard singing. I at first attributed the sounds to concussion-induced hallucinations. Yet, the more I listened, the more real became the soprano voice rising from below and keening an Indian chant, interspersed with an occasional "Hey, nonny, nonny, come hither, come hither."

I crouched behind a tree and saw a squaw come into view leading the missing stallion. She seemed vaguely familiar, but I couldn't imagine that I knew her. Her hair was double-braided, each braid entwined with ribbons. And I couldn't understand why she spoke in this mixture of Indian and English.

She stopped singing, approached the pile of rocks that had nearly become my tomb, gazed down at the dead mare, up in my direction. She carefully led the horse down the slope and around the slide, then regained the trail and continued toward me. Whatever and whyever she was singing and whoever she was didn't matter now. She was returning my horse, giving me a fighting chance at beating the full moon.

She approached my hiding place, stopped at the site of the landslide's beginnings, and I realized she was the Circle M's own Crazy Lu, the deranged Indian woman I'd seen only a few times, only from a distance, the last time keening on the hillside above Shelby's grave. I waited until she was opposite me, then sprang to the trail and grabbed the stallion's bridle. "I'll take my horse now, Lu."

She smiled and released the reins without a struggle. "Here you are, Andrew."

I stared for a long moment. Aristotle calls such moments of revelation anagnorisis, sudden transitions from ignorance to knowledge. And so it was for me when I knew that Crazy Lu's features were a latter-day version of those on the tintype in my rucksack.

"My God in heaven, Grandmother Julia," I said. "Are you really alive?"

CHAPTER FORTY-ONE

"I'm going to see an old friend in Wyoming," she said. Her tone was conversational. "I understand he's very ill."

"But your grave, the tombstone, everyone said… " No more words came to me. I looked at the knife in my hand, resheathed it. The tintype must have been what Mother had been hiding, fearing that Grandmother would be revealed as crazy, gone native, a family disgrace. She and Grandfather had literally tried to bury the secret. But did Mother have a hand in the plot? She'd have been a young girl when her mother had purportedly died. What other secrets lay waiting in the diaries?

"Perhaps we can travel together," Grandmother said.

"Grandmother, do you know what this is all about?"

Her eyes wandered. She set about untying my canteen. "You must be thirsty. You fashioned a good rig. The horse was running hard, very frightened, but everything stayed fast." She handed me the canteen. "Drink now. We have no time to waste."

"What is the date, Grandmother?"

"My friend is very sick," was all she said.

We resumed our way up the trail, leading the horse. I was bewildered at meeting this apparition, dismayed that only one of us could ride at a time. Still, it was possible—probable, the more I thought about it—that her "old friend" was Owl Feather. She'd perhaps save me time in the long run. Whether she'd been to Wind River before, she knew the trail, had probably come this far on her own. But she was a Maxwell. If Owl Feather, Yellow Squirrel and the rest knew who she was, she'd be walking straight into a trap. I now had family to protect here as well as in California. Strangely enough, I welcomed the idea. After all, I now had a grandmother.

"Are you hungry?" I offered her a piece of pemmican.

"We can share," she said. She took the piece and broke it in two, handed me one as we walked.

Why had Mother allowed the Crazy Lu charade to continue? Only one conclusion: She'd been unable to change the mind of her strong-willed mother. I knew how that felt.

We reached the top of the hill before noon, only to find ourselves facing a steep downslope and more hills beyond. I thought we should be headed north and east, but it seemed our quarry was heading south. We sat on a log to rest before continuing down the hill.

"All these years, Grandmother," I said. "Why did they let us think you had passed away?"

"I did pass away, Andrew."

"But now we're sitting here, talking, just as if we've always known one another."

"Well of course we have," she said. My mind and heart boiled with questions, but I decided to turn to the present.

"There's a plot to kill me, Grandmother. To murder all of us Maxwells. The man who shot Shelby—Yellow Squirrel—he's part of it. The one who tried to bury me back there—Standing Oak—he's part of it." She watched me intently. Her gaze so steady and penetrating, I looked to the ground for a moment to relieve the tension. When I lifted my eyes again, hers had not moved.

"I believe Owl Feather is the key to the matter." She shook her head slowly. I stopped, lifted my chin and squinted.

"Am I mistaken?" She only continued watching me. "If you know something about this, Grandmother, please. If I know why, maybe I can stop it." She made no move.

"If it isn't Owl Feather, is it connected somehow with Mathilda Barlow, with her… the way she died?" Grandmother rose slowly. She looked past the mountains into something beyond physical distance.

"I wish you could have seen your mother in those days," she said. "Every day it was 'ride daddy horse.' I couldn't keep her beside me on the wagon seat even then. So young, but she wanted to ride in front with her father, the captain of the wagon train. She and Carter made such a glorious picture loping over the prairie. If only there'd been a camera that could capture it." I stood beside Grandmother and looked in the direction of her gaze, as if following her vision hard enough and far enough would allow me to see beyond the mysteries that seemed to cloak my every step.

"But then there was Mathilda Barlow," I said. "And the Indians kidnapped you."

"Mathilda Barlow. She changes shapes like the devil." She turned to me and laid a hand on my arm. "You be careful of her."

"But she's dead," I said. Grandmother smiled and removed her hand from my arm.

"The slope is gentle on the east side," she said. "You're limping. You ride first. I'll lead the horse." Suddenly, she'd returned to the present world, present time. I argued briefly, but was glad for the opportunity to take weight off my painful legs.

As I mounted, I said, "I'm certain Many Clouds and Standing Oak are on their way to Owl Feather, but their trail leads south, and the Wind River reservation where Owl Feather is lies to the north. What do you make of that?"

"By indirection find direction out," she said. "We'll go south also." Indirection seemed to be all I would get from Grandmother, but she was leading the way.

CHAPTER FORTY-TWO

I gripped the stallion's mane, watched her slim, buckskinned figure glide down the mountain, brightly colored braids bouncing like a girl's. It felt like the day Shelby returned from Mississippi, when I'd thought he was gone forever. I'd not been born yet when Grandmother first died. First died? Then I'd touched her through the pages of her diary. And now she was here in the flesh.

I recalled the first time I lost Shelby. After the rope-cutting incident with Cletis Harvey, Shelby and I talked often. He became the first man who engaged me in serious conversation, answered with care my infantile questions about life. For his part, I suppose I was a safe audience for his thoughts and reminiscences, not an employee, not a boss. He became like a friend, an older brother, even a father. Then, one warm summer's day we'd spent forking hay, he called me aside. We stood behind the wagon, just inside the barn. Late afternoon sun wandered through the stall windows, floated on hay motes through the rafters. The air was warm, pungent with the smell of cut grass and manure.

"Andy, I got a letter the other day. I think I should tell this to you before anyone else. You remember I said I lost track of my two little sisters after the war. "This came from the younger one." He pulled a battered and disintegrating envelope from his back pocket. "Amelia's her name. Look here at the postmark. Took almost a year to get here."

"It's a wonder it made it at all. It's not even addressed to us."

"Ain't that something? All she knew was I was in the Army. But this letter found me anyhow. I take it as a sign. Here, read it. No, better let me. Writing's kind of faded. His chocolate bass echoed softly through the gauzy light.

Dear Shelby,

I don't know if this will ever get to you because the man Corporal Bonners who told me about you doesn't know if your even still in the army but I got to try. After Mama died all those years ago I come up to Natchez to work for this white lady Mrs. Stanton then I got married to Mr. Duprée who cut wood around here and owned him a house outside of town. We opened us up a boarding house and do pretty good. He is good to me but we never had any children and I am lonesome for some family since I never did find out where sister Etta went to. So Corporal Bonners came and stayed with us on his way to Alabama and said he was in the army with you and said you talked about us some time and might like to hear a word or two. I was so happy to think I might see you again. Me and Mr. Duprée wrote this right away. If you get this please let me lay my eyes on you before I die.

Your Loving Sister,
Amelia

I must admit to a lump in my throat when Shelby finished, and I think his eye was gleaming too. He opened his mouth, closed it, seemed as if he couldn't speak, so I said it for him.

"So you'll leave us and go on back to Mississippi and I'll never see you again, is that it?"

"Well, the first part's right. I reckon we will see each other again, though that's only partly up to us. Anyways, I wanted you to know first cause it seemed like we got along good and if I somehow don't get back, of all the folks here, I'll probably miss you the most."

My arms ached to hug him, but embracing was simply not part of our relationship then, so I extended my hand. He gripped it without shaking it, then reached around and patted my back. "Good luck to you, mon fils. I know you gonna do some good in the world."

It was while Mother and I watched Shelby ride away through the Circle M arch that I realized how well she understood me. Better than I'd ever given her credit for.

"I know you miss your father, Andy, and I'm sad for you that he couldn't be here. But you know, in many ways, you couldn't have asked for better than Shelby."

Of course, Shelby did return to California and brought Amelia and Mr. Duprée—Cooper—with him, so I did get him back again. For a time. And now I had Grandmother back. For how long? A long time and a good time if I could.

* * *

By sundown, I was leading the stallion, Grandmother on his back, up a trail nearly as steep and narrow as the one where the mountainside had come crashing down on me. She'd begun singing again, and Standing Oak's trail had withered to invisibility. We might be following him and Many Clouds. Might not. The trail had turned north again at the bottom of the canyon, and Grandmother seemed sure of herself, optimistic about the direction. I couldn't tell whether she knew the way or was off in her own world.

She'd walked with amazing speed and endurance. I could outpace her easily if I were healthy, but in my present condition she nearly matched me. How old was she? I thought sixty-five a minimal estimate. I couldn't recall the dates on her tombstone, only the epitaph, "She should have died hereafter." The sentence was in the wrong tense, it seemed. She would die hereafter, and she was no Lady Macbeth. But her death would not come, I hoped, on my watch.

* * *

Two days of wearying ups and downs brought us to the top of a hill where we beheld a cluster of huts and teepees on the far side of a dry wash. Surely the beginnings of the reservation. Two women sat on the ground in front of a brushwood shack working at a rude loom. A lone horseman rode from behind one of the shacks and angled off to our right. Our stallion plodded like a draught horse and both Grandmother and I felt bone tired from endless climbing and lack of sleep. Was it August third, fourth?

"I must go on alone, now, Andrew," Grandmother said as she slid off the horse.

"You can't. If they find out you're a Maxwell, they'll kill you."

"It's true the Barlows are everywhere," she said.

She smiled and opened her arms. We embraced as if she were a conventional grandmother whom I saw every day and would see again tomorrow.

"We'll meet again soon," she said. She turned and began singing and walking down the hill.

"Grandmother," I yelled and trotted after her. She ignored me, so I grabbed her shoulder and turned her toward me. "You can't just walk away." She pushed my hand from her shoulder, and her eyes flashed in a manner that put me in mind of Mother.

"I will go where I must, and you will not oppose me, no matter who you are." I was speechless. She fixed her eyes on mine for a long moment then turned and resumed her singing descent.

"At least take the horse," I called. But she didn't turn or even acknowledge she'd heard me. I wouldn't give up protecting Grandmother so easily. Besides, she appeared to be on her way to Owl Feather. If I followed from a distance, she'd surely give up her objections before long.

The rider below had stopped now and turned in our direction. The distance was so great I could determine little more about him than the buckskin color of his horse, the black hair flowing down his bare back, and the bandana circling his right bicep. He soon resumed his route and disappeared into the gully.

She was stepping down the slope between boulders and mesquite trees, a distant figure, soon to cross the wash and enter the village. Perhaps Owl Feather was there. She descended a path into the gully and was soon out of sight. I waited for her to emerge and continue toward the rude lodgings. Time passed. More than seemed necessary.

I waited a bit longer, then mounted the stallion and trotted down the hill. The wash ran north and south, a good thirty feet deep as far as I could see to where it curved west to the south and east to the north. I rode south along the edge, followed the narrow ledge Grandmother had used to drop into the gully. Her moccasins made only occasional and slight impressions in the hard soil, and I lost her trail. Another path ascended the gully's other side about a quarter-mile south. If she'd planned to climb out and continue north toward the village, she'd do so there. A few yards later, it became clear she'd never reached the path.

CHAPTER FORTY-THREE

The signs were easy to read. The soil was churned up in a six-foot circle. Large, deep moccasin prints led down the gully to the south. There'd been a struggle and someone had carried Grandmother away. The rider? Probably. Standing Oak? Not with his wounded shoulder. Owl Feather? He'd be Grandmother's age. Yellow Squirrel. The bandanna on the rider's arm probably covered what remained of the wound I'd inflicted in our skirmish at the Circle M. How had he known? It didn't matter. I had to move while the trail was fresh.

Both my horse and I needed rest, but we'd get none. They were two people aboard one horse, so I should be able to gain on them, even on my weary stallion. The gully turned east about a mile from where I'd entered it, then grew more and more shallow as it approached a mesa in the near distance. The shallower the gully, the rockier the ground, the fainter the tracks. Soon I had to dismount to follow, then I couldn't follow at all. Perhaps I could get help at Fort Washakie. No. Grandmother was probably doomed if Yellow Squirrel saw the army coming. But perhaps they could point me in Owl Feather's direction. And I could find out the date.

* * *

It took what I estimated to be two hours of hard riding through dusty hills, suspicious looks, and reluctant answers to find my way to the military headquarters of the Wind River Indian reservation—the United States' designated home for various divisions of the Shoshone and Arapaho peoples. The place appeared neglected, half-deserted. Tufts of brown grass sprang from the parade ground. My first question to the private in the fort commander's office was the date. August fourth. It had taken me a week to reach here, now I had only ten days to solve the whole mystery and return home.

A private escorted me immediately to Colonel Hough, who stood atop one of the fort's rude lookout towers, binoculars to his eyes. I climbed the ladder and introduced myself.

"So, Mr. Maxwell," he said. He didn't lower his binoculars. "Got a little hitch in your getalong, it seems."

"It's nearly healed, sir."

"And you're a few days late."

"Late?" I said. "So you knew I was coming." Mother.

The Colonel brought down the binoculars and looked straight at me. "I received a telegram. 'If my son Andrew comes seeking information about Yellow Squirrel and Owl Feather request no cooperation. Stop.' Rather cryptic, Mister Maxwell. Would you care to explain?"

"You do know about Yellow Squirrel, don't you, sir?"

"He's wanted for jailbreak and a couple of murders. Yes, I know about him."

"He killed my brother and our ranch foreman."

"My sincere condolences, Mr. Maxwell. This must be a terrible time for you and your mother. It still doesn't quite explain what brings you and this message to my desk." He started scanning the hills with his binoculars again, as if the answer might be out in the mesas somewhere.

I outlined the conspiracy, but didn't mention Grandmother's abduction. Colonel Hough looked me up and down. I wondered whether he was sympathetic or planning a way to be rid of me.

I said, "I think if we can talk to Owl Feather, we can discover what triggered this whole thing and find a way to stop it before my whole family is destroyed."

"And your mother?"

"She believes Yellow Squirrel is the beginning and end of the matter and that I should allow the law and the army deal with him."

"I can't comment on the conspiracy, but she's absolutely correct on the last two counts. In either case, you'd best head back to California, and let us take care of Yellow Squirrel and Standing Oak—if they show up."

"What about Owl Feather? Is he still alive, sir?"

"He's still alive—as far as we know. But we don't know where he is."

"Don't know? He's one of your charges. A sick old man. How could you not know?" Hough's tone sharpened. He pointed his binoculars like an admonishing finger.

"There are well over a million acres on this reservation, young man. Fort Washakie won't even be a military post by this time next year, and while bureaucrats are squabbling over how much the Department of Interior is going to take over from the military, I'm so short of men, I have to serve my own lookout duty. Show me another colonel in the entire U.S. Army who has to do that and I will eat that man's boots. So you see, Mister Maxwell, Indians who decide to disappear don't have much trouble doing so."

Apparently my worries about the army getting involved in Grandmother's abduction or in anything else related to the Maxwell murders were fantasies at best. "So even if Yellow Squirrel and Standing Oak returned to Wind River, the Army wouldn't be able to do anything about it?"

"We have our ways of keeping an ear to the ground and picking up what's important," he said.

"But neither your ears nor your eyes have any news of Owl Feather."

"Asked and answered." It seemed I had provoked the colonel into obeying my mother's instructions.

"Well," I said, "it looks as if I came a long way for nothing." I held out my hand. "I appreciate your help, Colonel. I hope your transition goes more smoothly." I held my hand in the air some time before he deigned to grasp it. I started toward the ladder, then had a thought.

"Do you suppose I might have a look at some dusty old records on the off-chance I turn up something that might help find Owl Feather?"

"Part of your conspiracy idea, Mr. Maxwell? No, most of our records have already been transferred, and if they were still here, they'd be confidential. Can't help you there."

"Or with Owl Feather."

"His eyes fixed on mine, and his lips compressed. His low voice turned his conventionally pleasant words into a threat. "Have a good trip, Mr. Maxwell. A speedy trip. Back to California." He lifted the binoculars to his eyes and turned them west toward the afternoon sun.

CHAPTER FORTY-FOUR

Lander, Wyoming, the nearest town to the reservation, was somewhat livelier than Wells. Buildings lined both sides of the single main street for well over a quarter mile. The post office and schoolhouse were stone and brick, and a trio of automobiles joined the parade of horses and wagons up and down the byway. Though selling liquor to Indians was illegal, a number of them had found enough firewater to incapacitate themselves and collapse in alleyways. Indian women sat near a small wagon with a display of baskets and blankets for sale. I thought I might learn something at a church, but a sign on the school stated that Father Kennedy offered mass every third Sunday, nearly a week away. An itinerant priest would probably not be a rich mine of information anyway. That left the Black Jack Saloon or the sheriff's office. The saloon was closer.

An Indian man and an eight- or ten-year-old boy sat on the edge of the low sidewalk near the bar's entrance. The man was in his forties. The boy had a book—an old McGuffey reader—on his lap, and the man was indicating words with his finger. I paused to watch the tutorial for a moment. A grimy sergeant stumbled from the saloon. He was a man, it seemed, troubled by none of the ambivalence toward Indians that had bothered Sergeant Duffy of the Presidio. One look at the reading lesson enraged him. He kicked the book with a manured boot and sent it plowing into the dusty street.

"Might as well teach a nigger to read as an Indian," he said. "Can't learn nohow and spoils 'em if they do." He spat on the book and stomped it with his boot.

"I can't allow you to treat a book like that," I said. "Or a human being either." I retrieved the book and held it out to him. "I'd suggest you hand it back to these people and apologize." He looked at me as if I'd proposed marriage.

"Well I'd suggest you shove that book up your interfering arsehole," he said. He smacked the volume skyward with one hand and delivered a punch to my gut with the other. I stumbled backward against a pole.

The trooper advanced on me, fist cocked. I readied a kick, realized I'd chosen the wrong leg when the knot in my injured thigh protested. I still managed a bang on the shins and a dodge of my head that avoided the trooper's looping right. Booze had slowed and clumsied him somewhat, so the momentum of his swing turned him crossways to me and bent him over. I locked my hands in a double fist and clubbed him in the back of the neck. He went down to the boards on his hands and knees. This time I used my left foot and kicked him hard in his downturned face.

I thought that would finish him, but I suppose he was a veteran of too many bar fights, drunk and awkward though he was, to give up so soon. He charged into my knees, locked his hands around my ankles and yanked my feet off the ground. In a flash, he leaped on top of me, one knee in my stomach, and walloped my ear. Red bloomed in my head. I felt his weight shift with the blow and realized the punch had unbalanced him once more. I rolled to the left, shoved upward with all the force I could muster, and found myself looking down at his face, his lower body stretched at a diagonal to the street. With a twist of savagery I didn't know I possessed, I jammed a knee into his throat, shoved a thumb into each eye and bore down hard with both. His body jumped like calf on a rope, but I didn't let up an ounce. Whether I'd have killed him or not, I don't know, but he rendered the question moot when he hooked a heel into my gut and rocked me backward. Suddenly I was on the bottom again.

Before he could plant his full weight, I rolled over, a move which sent his right fist glancing off the back of my head instead of smashing me squarely in the face. His knuckles hit the slivery board and evoked a "stinking bastard." A splatter of tobacco-laden saliva smacked against my ear. He clawed at my face with his left hand and raked his nails across my cheek, but I rolled out from under, jumped to my feet, and dropped both knees into his back. His wind exploded. I leaned forward and grabbed his wrists, looking to pin them behind his back, but I got too close to his face, and he had enough fight left to clamp his teeth into my left index finger.

I yowled and pounded on his right ear, but couldn't dislodge him. I grabbed his hair and started pounding his head into the boards. He finally went slack and released my finger, but I didn't trust I'd subdued him, so I jumped to my feet and was about to launch another kick to his head when I felt a hand on my shoulder.

"We'll take over from here, young fella."

CHAPTER FORTY-FIVE

The voice behind me was deep and smooth as an operatic baritone. I looked up to see a small man about the color of the weathered buildings along the Lander main street. He wore a badge. The sergeant was on his knees, rubbing his throat and coughing. Two other troopers stood behind the sheriff along with a small group of spectators. The Indian man and boy stood next to the saloon door. I didn't see the book.

"Collins here gets feisty when he's had a few," the sheriff said. "These soldiers'll take him to the brig to cool down."

"Thank you, Sheriff. Let me introduce myself. My name's Andrew Maxwell."

"Yes, Mr. Maxwell. Your reputation precedes you. I'm Sheriff Ferguson." Like the colonel, he didn't offer to shake hands. He motioned for the two soldiers to take custody of the fallen man. They lifted their comrade to his feet and escorted him away.

"All right, folks," said Sheriff Ferguson, "fun's over. Back off, now." He made scooting motions with his hands. The crowd complied, but I did hear a muttered "Damned Indian lover" as they dispersed. Ferguson turned to me.

"My understanding was you were on your way home, Mr. Maxwell."

"You and the colonel must have a telephone out here."

"Hardly that. But the colonel did send me a message."

"I'd be honored to buy you a beer, Sheriff. In thanks for your assistance." My gratitude and hunger for information had overcome my memory. I had no money, wondered what I'd do if the sheriff accepted.

"Just doing my job. Besides, you'd be wasting your money and your breath, considering I'm a temperance man. Also, I don't know any more about Yellow Squirrel than Colonel Hough does. And I understand you'll be on your way soon?"

"In the morning, I suppose." I understood why the San Francisco people had wanted to be rid of me, but why the colonel and the sheriff? Perhaps I was gathering such a reputation as a troublemaker that everyone saw me as a threat, which maybe meant I was getting somewhere.

"Good, good. In the meantime, you could use some doctoring on the side of your face. Looks like it's starting to color up. Finger don't look good neither."

"I'm obliged, sheriff." I watched him saunter down the street. More bruises and lacerations. A shrugging matter. And I'd won the fight. I couldn't help thinking that if I'd done as well with Yellow Squirrel on the Barbary Coast, Julian might still be alive.

"Mr. Maxwell, we would like to thank you." The words came from the alley beside the saloon building. The Indian boy wore only a pair of ragged broadcloth pants. His companion—his father?—was dressed in a denim shirt and a pair of threadbare army trousers. He wore a dark leather hat with a simple horsehair band. The man approached me, pushing the boy in front of him.

"This is William," he said. His was the speech of a cultivated man.

I crouched and extended my hand. "Hello, William. My name is Andy." The boy lifted his hand to a forty-five degree angle, and I grasped his limp palm. "I see you're learning to read."

The father lifted his denim shirt to show the book stuck in his waistband. "I should have known better than to tutor him in public, but William is so hungry to learn I didn't want to pass up any opportunity."

"And your name?" I said.

"Earnest. Earnest Flowers in your world. I've discovered my native name is a little tricky for your people."

"And William?" I said.

"William Hawk."

"Not precisely his given name either?"

"I believe our people must adapt to this new world or be extinguished."

"Quite an interesting philosophy," I said. "I'd like to discuss it further."

He hesitated. "We shouldn't be seen together, Mr. Maxwell." He gave me directions to a location outside of town. I refilled my canteen and took a free pickled egg from the saloon. Hostile stares followed me out the door.

* * *

I found Earnest and William waiting under a cottonwood tree beside another of the dry washes that cut through so much of the surrounding territory. They were engrossed in the book again. I welcomed the shade. We shared greetings and a drink from my canteen.

"It seems you've had a good education, Mr. Flowers," I said.

"The missions. I work with as many of my people as I can. When I meet a student like William, here, I seize the moment."

"So he's not your son?" I said.

"No. Though I'd be proud to call him mine. William's parents died in an influenza epidemic. I help his aunt and uncle take care of him."

"They don't want me." They were the first words I had heard the boy speak. Earnest placed an arm around him.

"You know it's not that, William." He turned to me. "They have seven children of their own. You can imagine a two-room house with that many."

"I want to live with you. I want to be able to read and write like you," William said.

This discussion was too personal for me. "Earnest and William," I said. "I came to Wind River because of my own family situation." I recounted once more my story of the killings and the vendetta. I supposed a time would come when the pain would lessen with the retelling, but that time had not yet arrived. I held back on Grandmother's kidnapping.

I finished at last, lowered my head and took a deep breath. When I raised my eyes, Earnest was standing with his back to me, gazing up the wash. William squatted, watching his mentor. I could barely hear Earnest when he finally spoke.

"You have helped us, so we have both an obligation and a desire to help you. On the other hand, Mr. Maxwell, you bring with you the white man's so-called law."

"How does hiding bad men help your people?" I said.

"Even well-intentioned whites mean trouble for us. Chief Washakie in his time helped us live with less bloodshed than most other tribes, but we surrendered a great deal of land and pride." He turned back toward me.

"The sheriff wants you to leave. If you have no objection, you may stay tonight in my teepee. I will think and we will talk more. If I can find a way to help you without hurting my people, I will do it. Come."

I followed Earnest and William to a village on the banks of the Wind River. Thunderheads drifted, gathered, put us in sun one minute, shade the next. A breeze twisted dust across the plain and among the few shacks and even fewer teepees scattered among the mesquite bushes. The mountain range I'd just crossed rose to the west. We collected stares as we walked. Earnest waved and greeted people, but received only grunted acknowledgements and minimal gestures in return. Was I the cause for the meager response, or was Earnest a bit of an outcast himself?

"This is it." Earnest gestured toward a teepee which, unlike the others—predominantly plain, predominantly canvas—was constructed of highly decorated animal skins sewn together with sinew, its seams sealed with pitch. I circled it, examining the drawings—scenes of Indians and soldiers in combat, of hunting and fishing expeditions, of cosmological figures. I tethered my stallion beside two paint horses a few yards from the teepee.

"I'm doing my best to live in the ways of our ancestors," Earnest said. "We must adapt, but we can't afford to forget our history. We must live in the past and the future at the same time."

I nodded, but sadly. His speech might have gone well in a college classroom, but I doubted it had much of an audience here.

"How do Yellow Squirrel and his kind fit into your dream?"

"They don't," said Earnest. "I'll start the fire. We'll eat before we talk." He spoke in Arapaho to William, who fetched a leather bag from inside the tent. He drew out a flint and steel and began striking it over a pile of dry moss.

"Of course, our true ancestors would not have had steel, but you folks brought it to us a couple of hundred years ago, so I allow it. Even we stone age folks had progress. We'll let William finish building the fire. Follow me."

He untied the horses and led them to the river. While they drank, he waded out to a small willow structure near the bank. He reached in through the top, yanked a good sized trout up by the gills and carried it to the shore. Thunder sounded in the west. "A weir," he said. It traps your fish and keeps it fresh till you're ready for it."

The meal of spit-roasted fish, wild onions, and acorn mush was simple and tasty. Supper finished, he sent William, over the boy's objections, to visit his cousins. We sat on logs before the tent, faced each other over the campfire. Finally, it seemed, we were to have our talk.

"I must have a promise from you," he said.

"If I can."

"Whatever I divulge, you can't bring in the army or the sheriff or anyone else. If you want to continue with your quest after what I tell you, you'll do it on your own."

"Can you lead me to Owl Feather?"

"Your word."

"Can you at least tell me where he is?"

"Your promise first."

"I can promise that only the guilty will pay," I said.

"If you were speaking for yourself, Andy, I would trust you. But you know there are others who do not care who pays as long their skin is dark."

"Very well, Earnest. I'll promise, but only while I'm on Wind River. Outside the reservation, I can promise nothing."

He hesitated. "Those who come to hunt us won't care about boundaries," he said.

"I can't promise to sacrifice my family." I said. "What you won't tell me, I'll seek on my own."

Earnest turned his back and, as he had done earlier, walked a few steps away from me. Lightning flashed near the horizon. The wind picked up. I waited and watched. Finally he turned to face me. The setting sun fanned light through a cloud break behind him.

"I am like the bull trying to turn a stampeding herd away from the cliff, Andy. If I fail, we will all be crushed. You understand."

"I'm disappointed, Earnest. Shielding a murderer."

"I've shared the fruits of my lodge, Andrew. It is all I can do." I watched the sun disappear.

"If you won't tell me everything, maybe you could answer a question or two." He said nothing.

"Can you point in the direction where I might find Owl Feather. Not a location. Only a direction."

He hesitated, then pointed west. "An empty lodge," he said. My throat clenched.

"Owl Feather is dead, then?" Earnest said nothing. His face was unreadable.

"Or he may have preferred not to die here in the white man's shadow," I said. "Where would he have gone?" I was speaking a monologue. Earnest was no more responsive than the log on which he sat. The air stilled. The fire was an orange bubble in the dark, its flames at rest in the glowing coals. A swelling moon floated above the hills.

"Somewhere on his old hunting grounds, perhaps?" I said. "A place he went before the treaty that created Wind River?"

Earnest rose. "You'll no doubt be headed south and west now, back toward your home," he said. "Perhaps there's one more favor between us before we part."

"Favor between us?"

"Your stallion is a good horse, but he's weary. To ride one of my mares would help you. To have a stallion to breed my mare would help me. "Keep the north star behind you." He held out his hand.

I shook his hand. I picked up my rucksack, switched the mare's hackamore for my bridle and bit, led her back to the campfire. "Thank you, Earnest. Good luck to you and to William."

He nodded, handed me a small bag of pemmican, but said nothing. I turned my back on the big dipper and headed into the darkness.

AUGUST 6

CHAPTER FORTY-SIX

Aday and a half later I stood, I was nearly certain, on the site of my mother and grandmother's 1864 kidnapping. I'd pored over more of Julia's diary and Carter's logs on my ride from the reservation. The log placed the Maxwell Wagon Train's camp northwest of Fort Bridger, and a teamster I'd passed on the main road told me I was about twenty-five miles north of the fort. The small glade at the bottom of the slope precisely matched my grandparents' written descriptions.

Julia, without her diary or the opportunity to write during her ordeal with the Indians, had poured the story into a twenty-page narrative in the first hours or days after her return. When I'd first opened the diaries on the train, I'd felt I was communing with her spirit. During my journey from Wind River, her voice had spoken from the page.

* * *

We womenfolk were together a short distance from the train, well-guarded as is our custom, but all our precautions proved no defense against the sudden attack of the hidden Indians, who grabbed me, Carrie, and poor Missy Barlow and carried us away in an instant.

* * *

Why had Grandmother been so far from the train? She, her precious child who would be my mother, and Missy, the unfortunate daughter of the woman she to this day considered the incarnation of evil? Perhaps it was modesty in bathroom matters which prompted them to seek the concealment of the bushes, bushes which also hid her captors. Carter's logged response was typically terse, factual.

* * *

Indians took Julia, Carrie, and Missy, headed northwest. Army too slow. Taking out with two men. Will leave sign on the trail and notes on these pages for others to follow.

* * *

I staked everything on my theory that not only did Owl Feather wish to return to the scene of his last battle to die, but that Yellow Squirrel now carried Grandmother to him. It must have taken a storekeeper's faith in recordkeeping for Carter to cram log, pen, and inkwell into his saddlebags in such an emergency. As it was, the notes were scanty and sprawled across the page, probably written while riding, or in the dark.

Trails in the arid west don't fade much with time, but remain like scars on a weathered cheek. Three led from the glade where I stood. Two appeared recently traveled, one nearly untrod. The one that led the most nearly northwest led also to a grove of aspens. The Indians would have depended on speed and camouflage. It was one of the more frequented trails, but there was no reason to assume that the way to Owl Feather's hideaway wouldn't be well-traveled, at least near its beginning.

There had been three in the marauding band, each carrying a captive on his horse. I imagined my grandmother snatched from her feet, galloping toward the nearby trees, then repeating that experience now, forty years later. I looked down the trail into the shadows, felt her horror as I recalled her description of the abduction.

* * *

His strength was astonishing. I was unable to budge even the smallest of the fingers that clutched at my hip no matter how I tore at them. He seemed not even to notice the blows I rained on his legs and back. Behind me, I could see Carrie and Missy gone limp, their bonnets askew and hair undone. Missy's constant wailing carried even over the sound of the hooves. Carrie yelled for me. I answered, "I'm here, sweet pea."

Would my precious one be killed? Or worse, enslaved and raised as a savage? The thought of my delicate and sensitive child spending her days in a teepee, filthy as a dog in a swamp, surviving on bugs and roots, subject to the heathen whims of whatever cur might take a fancy to her terrified me even more than the rancid stink of the savage who gripped me.

* * *

I was an hour down my chosen trail before I topped a rise and saw that it dead-ended at a corral and a line shack. I returned to the meadow and began following a second trail. It was faint, but plain, led up the slope through juniper and rocks. The hillside was warm, and the sun in my eyes as I picked my way through the bushes. The route seemed too bare. Why would fugitives have remained exposed for so long? I stopped and looked back toward the meadow. My answer was in the tree stumps I had passed almost without noting them, so intent had I been on keeping to the trace. The slope had been logged. When the kidnapping took place, this must have been a forested hillside. The culprits had been undercover within a hundred yards from their crime.

Shadows lengthened, and the trail climbed into rocks and disappeared. There was no timber here, apparently never had been. I dismounted and walked in circles, hoping to recover the path. Nothing. I checked the trail log. No mention of this site. Another trail lost.

Finally, I climbed a boulder. Perhaps I'd sight softer ground farther along, someplace with trail sign, but rocks blocked my view. It was becoming too dark to travel. The next day was August seventh. Three days to finish my business here, if I hoped to return to the Circle M by the thirteenth.

I knelt to ease myself down the boulder's side when I saw a pile of small rocks near my hand. They'd been scattered somewhat by weather and animals, but they were definitely placed there by human hands. A trail marker. Carter's? I needed another if I were to find my bearings. I headed downhill from the boulder on my hands and knees. I thought at first it was wishful thinking that lent significance to a rough circle of shale near the bottom of a small slope. But no, it had once been a pile of crumbling granite stones. The earth softened a few yards farther on where I thought I'd find a trail. But I saw only a plot of bushes and bunch grass.

Once again, I circled, ran up against high brush. Nothing remained but to kneel and crawl into the thicket. Finally, muddy and scratched, I spotted a narrow trench of packed earth leading into and out of the shallow pool at the base of the spring. Perhaps the spring had appeared since 1864. Perhaps it had been dry that year. In either case, the grass and bushes hadn't covered the trail when Carter was on his chase. And his markers pointed clearly to this path down the slope.

My pony was glad for a drink and a brief meal. The tiny slice of moon I had seen on the desert with Many Clouds was visibly swollen now, ready to give birth to a host of demons unless I could abort the process.

It became too dark to ride and keep my course, so I led my horse through the short bushes and down the hill.

I lost the way again in the next grove of trees. The ground was soft and dark, hidden under the duff. I had to admit I was finished for this night. I tied my horse, curled up on the ground, knew I needed rest, even if sleep was impossible.

CHAPTER FORTY-SEVEN

Thunder awoke me. The air was wet, and lightning webbed the sky. I was in for a drenching. A sudden wind hissed around us, and the mare snorted and whinnied. I made doubly sure she was secure, found a rotting log and snuggled as far beneath it as I could. The heavens alternated cracks of lightning and thunder for another half-hour, then deluged. I had witnessed many of these storms, but had never been caught outside in one. Ten minutes after the rain started, I realized my shelter lay at the foot of a ditch. A sudden brook soaked me as thoroughly as if I'd stood in an open field.

I huddled close to my horse. We took comfort and warmth from one another as we watched the water and flashes of light whirl and tear around us. I thought of Sawtooth Peaks, their solidity amid the dynamic power of storms that warred around them.

It all stopped before sunrise. The moon gave some light, but there was yet not enough to find a trail. When first light poked above the hills, I led the pony through the grove, looking again for the track. No luck. Nothing in Carter's log to help. He'd have found nothing permanent here with which to make a sign. He might have broken branches or left fabric, but that would all be gone by now. I began circling again, spiraling out from my starting point. It was tedious, and the sun was well over the peaks when I finally came on a faint trace.

My stomach was a fist from the danger, the waiting, the nearing deadline, the wishing for something—even something dangerous—to happen. I felt like a miner who'd dug for weeks and found nothing but mud and sandstone.

I followed the trace through the woods, a hundred false turns, more circling. The wet Levi's chafed the inside of my thighs. I judged it was near noon when I finally dropped out of the woods into a clearing where I could see the trail snaking toward a creek below.

Downhill to creek, read the log. *Stopped here. Women prints with the moccasin ones. Seems they're alive. Crossed south.*

Julia had also mentioned this place.

* * *

He dropped me on my face in the mud. I jumped up spitting and wiping muck from my eyes, looking for Carrie. He pushed me down again, dragged me to the stream and shoved my face in. He said something in Indian. I could hear Carrie and Missy crying. Another voice spoke in English. "Drink. Hurry."

He yanked me to my feet and tore at my bodice. The other voice stopped him. I could see them both now as they argued. The tall one who had carried me, the shorter, stockier one, who had carried Missy. The youngest one held Carrie, who was sobbing for me. I tried to run to her, but the tall one slapped me aside, continuing the argument with his cohort all the while. Soon the shorter one said, "You're coming with me, Mrs. Maxwell. The other girl will go with Running Deer."

The one called Running Deer was still very angry. He grabbed Missy and yanked her up on his horse. I do believe Missy had mercifully lost all sense of who or where she was by this time. Her sobbing was continuous and incoherent. I was scarcely better myself, consumed with concern for Carrie. "Come, we must hurry," came the command as I was pulled to horseback. And we plunged once again into the night.

* * *

The trail edged back up through rocks and brush. It wasn't difficult to follow, but slow going. It had taken Carter a full day from the creek to his first meeting with the Indians. I was a day ahead of Grandfather's schedule. Time to expect trouble, to seek cover, slow down to live instead of hurry to get ambushed. Bushes paralleled the trail on the lower slope, so I moved down, close to cover, but still in sight of the trace. Finally I recognized another landmark from the log.

A swamp downhill. Can't see into it, but must pursue.

My horse slipped and stumbled down the muddy hillside and into the shadows of the jack pines. The water slowed under the boughs, and spread until it became more of a bog than a defined stream. The water oozed into a clump of aspens where the ground was spongy, laced with roots and pools of stagnant water. Insects buzzed and whirled around my head. I dismounted again. The roots posed too great a threat to the horse's legs.

After another hour of threading my way through a swampy gloom, light began to grow and the vegetation to change. The swamp waters trickled out into another creek which flowed toward a broad meadow. Carter had found the Indians here. Or they had found him? The log was unclear on the point.

Two Indians. Owl Feather, Running Deer. Message to cavalry. Grant hunting lands, and the captives will be freed. Otherwise our women will be killed. Three days.

Carter's trail log ended here. Julia's diary carried no clues about their route, only her sketchy portrait of the camp at the end of the journey.

I crouched behind a stand of willows, pistol drawn. The Indians' camp where Julia had awakened the morning after the kidnapping couldn't have been far from here. If I was right, I would find Owl Feather there. Perhaps today.

Finally satisfied I was alone, I mounted up and headed into the meadow. What I thought was a humming insect turned out to be a spinning rope. I flew off my horse, hit the ground, and looked up to see Yellow Squirrel—striped in red and yellow paint and dressed only in a breechclout—smiling at me from atop the Circle M buckskin he'd ridden out of the barn after killing Shelby.

CHAPTER FORTY-EIGHT

"Hello, Big Brother. Surprised to be alive?" I said nothing, concentrated on catching my breath. The suspense was over. I felt excited to be fighting my elusive foe at last. Yellow Squirrel went on.

"I could have used a rifle instead of a rope, you know. But we thought it'd be fun for the Maxwells to gather together and watch each other die when the moon fills out."

Yellow Squirrel had thrown a good loop, pinned my arms between shoulders and elbows, and I'd dropped my pistol during the fall. I struggled for a moment, but the buckskin was cutting-horse-trained to keep the line taut. My heart filled with fear, anger, and determination. My hand was free enough to pull my knife, masked from Yellow Squirrel, out of its sheath on the front of my hip. I began furtively cutting the line around my chest. I heard movement behind me, sawed harder at the rope.

A poke in the back reminded me of Bahnhof and his old Henry. "Hands behind you, Maxwell." The rope parted, went slack. The horse snorted and shuffled. I felt the gun barrel pull away from my spine. Although I couldn't see Yellow Squirrel, I took a risk that the animal's movement had distracted him, rolled from under the rifle and stabbed toward his bare legs. The blade scratched a red line on his shin—a shallow cut, but enough to evoke a yell and a jump backward. I scanned the ground for my pistol, didn't see it.

I leapt to my feet. Yellow Squirrel was attempting to bring his rifle into play. I threw myself toward the gun, slashed at his arm, but my knifepoint glanced harmlessly off his gunstock. I launched a kick at his knee, connected, and sent him to the ground. I raised my knife and jumped, but he rolled away from my thrust, and I plunged the blade into dirt. He came to his knees, back turned to me, more than a body's length away, rifle rising to his shoulder. He'd be able to turn and fire before I could reach him, so I ran the other way, toward the trees at the meadow's edge. I twisted an ankle on a slick root, and flopped into a pod of aspen as he fired and missed. I bellied my way deeper into the swampy ground, lay still, listened. Sometimes we're the hunter, sometimes the hunted. I preferred hunting.

I heard only silence for a long space. Between the slim white trunks, I caught a hint of silver in the far grass and knew I'd found my pistol. My mood brightened at the sight, but it lay seemingly miles away. Then came Yellow Squirrel's voice.

"So you've learned how to fight a little, Andrew Maxwell. Now I'll have to kill you early." I smiled slightly. I supposed he'd meant to lure me into answering so he could locate me. I slowly turned my head toward his voice, glimpsed movement. He was in a moving squat, back to me, about twenty yards away. Had I the pistol in hand, I could have finished him.

I crept backwards on my stomach toward the meadow so I could watch him while I worked toward my pistol. I'd crawled only a few yards when he disappeared behind a tree trunk. Now he could change direction or speed at will and trap me in the open. I imagined I had a bull's eye on my spine as I jumped up and ran for the gun.

The buckskin had remained moored to the severed rope. Earnest's mare had disappeared. I grabbed my pistol as I dived and rolled toward a shallow ditch. The shot I'd been expecting sounded while I rolled, and something pounded my foot just before I came to rest in the depression. It felt good to have my hand around the grip of a fully-loaded firearm, and I resheathed my knife. I had become the hunter again. The meadow lay silent and empty. The buckskin had finally shied after the last shot and dragged the rope to the end of the field like a boat trailing a painter.

I was surprised to feel no pain in the foot I thought had been struck, so I glanced behind me to find that half the heel was missing from my right boot. The same glance showed me a clump of willows that would afford more cover than the six-inch bunch-grass around me, but could give Yellow Squirrel a place to steal up on me. I inched backwards, pistol at ready, alert for movement in the trees or near the horse. When I reached the bushes, I rose to my knees and turned to part the branches and creep into cover. The window I opened brought me face to face with a crouching Yellow Squirrel. We both froze, and he seemed as surprised and frightened as I.

He held his rifle across his chest, unprepared to shoot, so he clubbed me in the ribs with the stock. I fired, but missed high. I sprawled on my side into screening branches and hugged the ground. Yellow Squirrel fired, and the bullet clipped twigs high and to my right. I jumped from the thicket to my left and leveled my weapon at his head, but he swung the rifle against my arm, and I not only wasted another bullet, but watched the pistol arc from my hand into the bushes. He chopped the rifle barrel down toward my stomach. I grabbed it, jammed it toward the ground as he fired. The move saved me a bullet in the gut, but the inside of my left thigh burned. I hung onto the rifle and worked my way hand over hand up the barrel until I was face to face to painted face with him, precisely as we had been in the San Francisco jail. I slammed my forehead into his nose. He grunted and jerked back. Blood smeared the paint across his mouth and chin, and his grip loosened. I had the rifle now, but the sudden loss of resistance sent me backward on my rear, and I found time only to lever out the old shell casing before Yellow Squirrel dropped toward me once more.

His knees were doubled, aimed at my midsection. I lifted my legs up to deflect him, and his momentum hurtled him part way past me and to the right. He seized the rifle stock with one hand as he fell, and we rolled and grappled until he sat atop of me, the rifle wedged across my neck and choking me. I kicked and pounded to no avail, then my right hand found the knife again.

I aimed low to avoid deflecting ribs. He sensed my movement, released the pressure on my neck, snatched the rifle toward my knife arm. I'd have buried the weapon as deep in him as I had in the bear, but the rifle stock grazed my forearm and sent my thrust into his hip. He yelled and turned, and I twisted and jabbed. He released the rifle, reached for my knife arm and clamped it with a powerful fist, but his blood had slicked my wrist. I tore loose and drew the knife back to stab again.

Suddenly the space above me emptied. I panicked to recall that the rifle was near and turned to see the big Indian on his belly reaching for it just beyond his fingertips. Just as it had the day Julian rescued me from the snake, a line of poetry nonsensically popped into my head, and I recalled Browning's declaration that a man's reach should exceed his grasp. I was heartily glad to see it played out for Yellow Squirrel at that moment. Blood streamed from the raw cut on his left hip. I flipped over and jumped for his back, knife high. But he rolled away, and my knees hit the ground he'd just vacated.

I jumped back into the thicket to avoid creating a target for the rifle he'd now recovered. Two quick shots, then a third, ripped the foliage around me. Once again there was silence. I lay still, my thigh afire, my throat bruised and aching, but somehow confident.

I heard tramping in the willows for a time, then hooves in the distance. I raised my head cautiously as the hoofbeats receded, stepped back into the empty meadow—empty of Yellow Squirrel and the buckskin. And empty of my own horse as well.

Where had he gone and why? I hadn't hurt him badly enough to defeat him. It dawned on me that perhaps Yellow Squirrel liked to fight only when he had the advantage. Julian. Shelby. The night on the Circle M trail. Perhaps he'd decided to set a new trap for me. He'd probably intended to truss me up and deliver me like a Christmas turkey to Owl Feather. He'd count on me to track him as far and as fast as I could, and I had no other choice. He'd be waiting. So would Standing Oak. Owl Feather. Many Clouds. So would Grandmother. I could only hope to avoid his next snare more successfully than I'd avoided his lasso.

I spent the better part of an hour on hands and knees looking for my pistol. I'd begun to fear Yellow Squirrel had absconded with it when I finally spotted one chamber poking from the mud under a snarl of branches and vines.

The weapon was fouled, inoperable. I disassembled it and did my best with sticks and rags to restore it to useable condition. With only six shells remaining, I didn't dare risk a test firing, but the action worked, so I reloaded and prayed it would answer the call the next time I needed it.

My thigh wound was painful, as bad as the claw wounds I'd received from the bear. The ankle I'd twisted in the aspens was throbbing, but walkable. I kept swallowing to relieve the ache in my Adam's apple. The consequences of tramping around on a pair of one-heeled boots remained to be seen.

Yellow Squirrel's trail followed the water down the hillside and into timber where the thick mat of needles obscured hoofprints. Light was failing, but I had the creek as a marker. I'd follow it until I found them.

The moon emitted enough light to shadow the trees, but barely. Several times I slipped, stepped into what appeared to be solid ground but proved to be empty shadows. Finally, it became more foolish than courageous to continue. I burrowed into some pine needles and pillowed my head on the rucksack.

The throb in my ankle shot up and down my leg, and I slept little. The odd way the uneven boots shifted my weight had generated a new pain in my knee. Finally, a promise of light appeared above the trees. I began moving, cautiously. August eighth. Five days left. Perhaps at home events had played out already. Standing Oak could have returned to the Circle M, killed Mother and burned the ranch. Or perhaps they'd sent an agent, someone none of us knew, let alone suspected.

Before long, I stumbled into what I took at first for a stump, but soon realized was a fence post. I pulled back and crouched down. I made out a few rails stretching into the trees on either side of the post, but no one had maintained this fence in some time, and there was no sign of human activity around the rough boundaries of a manmade clearing which nature had nearly reclaimed. Scattered hunks of charcoal and a stone chimney poking above the weeds told the fate of the cabin that once stood here. An old apple tree huddled among a knot of pine seedlings like a defeated soldier. Anyone tracking me would find this a first-rate site for a bushwhacking.

Squirrels and chickadees darted through the ruins. Julia and Carter had started the Circle M with less, but someone else's aspirations had died here. The apples were few and small, but made a welcome variation from pemmican.

The creek was sizeable at this point—three or four feet across—and had descended into a fairly steep-walled canyon. Pain had become simply a part of my being by now, but the ankle remained functional, though swollen. I used branches and rocks to pull myself up to a point where the canyon leveled off a bit and I could slide along the bank. A faint game trail followed the canyon wall, but I didn't trust myself, in my lame state, to maintain my footing. I angled off into a side gully, planning to come back to the creek when the slope gentled off.

Soon, I lost even the sound of the water, and thought better of my detour, feared I'd lose my way entirely. I zig-zagged up the steep bank to the top of the ridge and prepared to drop down the other side when I saw the teepee resting on a small plateau below. *The lodges were clustered beside a creek in a clearing at the bottom of a hill.* The place was exactly as Grandmother had described it.

CHAPTER FORTY-NINE

The creek flowed across the flat, and the teepee stood beside the water on the near side, a stone-rimmed fire pit in front. To the right of the teepee rose a rude cross eight or ten feet high. An object I couldn't make out sat on its top. Sailor and four other horses grazed, hobbled, in a rope corral in the middle of the plateau. The other horses included the Circle M buckskin and the mare I'd acquired from Earnest. It appeared I'd found the whole clan.

The teepee flap opened, and Many Clouds emerged carrying a small basket in one hand. She walked downslope, filled it with water from the creek, and reentered.

I drew my pistol and sidled down the ridgetop to get a closer look. A rustle in the dry leaves below froze me. Standing Oak, rifle in hand, stood sentinel over the trail I'd have taken had I kept to my original course. Presently, he stepped from behind his oak-tree cover and began sauntering down the hill toward the teepee. I lifted my pistol, but he was about forty yards away, and I trusted neither my marksmanship nor the accuracy of my revolver. And I had no shots to waste. Where was Grandmother? Perhaps she wasn't even here. Wasn't even alive. What about Yellow Squirrel? On lookout duty somewhere else?

I inched down the hill and took up vigil behind Standing Oak's tree. Below, he called in the direction of the lodge, waited, then called again. Many Clouds appeared, handed him a bowl. He sat on a rock and began a two-fingered spooning of the bowl's porridge-like contents into his mouth. Many Clouds turned toward the lodge, then Yellow Squirrel emerged, a bowl of the same mush in his hand. He wore no paint, was dressed in the same ranch-hand clothes he'd worn on the night of our encounter on the Circle M. He limped somewhat, and the left rear side of his pants bulged from what I supposed was a dressing on his hip. He and Many Clouds exchanged words. Their conversation grew loud, and Yellow Squirrel finally flung the bowl toward the creek. He advanced on Many Clouds and raised his hand, but she pointed her finger at his face and his arm dropped.

It was exasperating to see both my adversaries in plain sight, unaware of my presence, and to be so powerless. Had I a rifle, I could perhaps end everything right here. But I had only my pistol. Besides, I still suspected that killing these two wouldn't kill the problem. The drama below me escalated.

Yellow Squirrel raised his fist at his brother and yelled. Standing Oak answered him, gestured toward the teepee, toward the cross, toward the hillside. Yellow Squirrel gave a dismissive wave and reentered the tent.

After Yellow Squirrel left, Standing Oak gazed for several moments toward where I sat. Then he picked up his rifle and jogged off in the opposite direction. Gone, at least for the moment. Owl Feather was probably with Yellow Squirrel and Many Clouds in the teepee. Perhaps Grandmother also. No one on guard. They must know I could be close. Did they fear me so little? Or was their dissension intense enough to diminish their caution. I took heart at that thought. This could be my opportunity to create the situation I needed.

I dipped into a low crouch, retraced my steps up the ridge, then dropped down the hillside and approached the tent from below, where the cover was better and the footing more certain. The last few yards between the creek and the teepee were bare ground, so I took a deep breath, pulled myself with elbows and knees up the grade, and curled as close to the tent as I could. To my right, the canvas bulged with the impression of a large form. I peered around the other side of the tent where the cross stood, topped by what I could now see was the bony remnant of a buffalo's head. What they meant I couldn't guess.

I heard Many Clouds pleading in Arapaho and a man's faint response. After all these weeks, could I be hearing Owl Feather's voice? Yellow Squirrel spoke. The bulge next to me was his.

"Please, Owl Feather, you're too weak with those wounds to refuse food." English. Grandmother's voice. Yellow Squirrel barked in Arapaho. Owl Feather answered in English.

"I told you she is not to be harmed, my son. I did not ask you to bring her here, and I will not tolerate any injury to her."

"Thank you for protecting me once again," Grandmother said, "but your commands will mean nothing to your sons and your granddaughter if you die. Please eat."

"My commands mean little enough to my sons while I live, I'm sorry to say. I thank you, but take away the food. My sun dance was at the wrong time, done in the wrong way. It didn't please the Great Spirit. Until he sends a vision to take me to the next world, I must eat nothing."

Sun dance. Of course. The cross and skull were connected with a ritual that generated such fervor among the natives that the government had outlawed the ceremony years earlier. They tied rawhide thongs to each end of pegs stabbed through a warrior's skin, then fastened the thongs to the cross. In pursuit of a revelation, a long ceremony of dancing and fasting ensued, and the warrior leaned back and danced till the pegs tore through his flesh. I'd thought it was a spring rite. Perhaps it was, the reason behind Owl Feather's "wrong time" comment.

But the rebuke of Yellow Squirrel. Perhaps the elder was not the source of the vendetta. Perhaps his sons had taken up arms against his wishes. Another exchange in Arapaho. Then silence.

I had just decided to storm into the tent, rescue Grandmother, and demand answers when a distant shot changed my mind. I scooted back down the slope, intending to circle up the ridge to my previous vantage point. I'd reached cover in the willows and was moving upstream when Yellow Squirrel crawled from the teepee, rifle in hand and headed toward me in a crouching walk.

I was trapped. Shooting him would leave me with two women and a sick old man waiting for a forewarned Standing Oak. I feared what Many Clouds would do here on her home ground if I killed her uncle. Even with all the conflicts among the family, they'd unite against an outsider. Especially me.

Yellow Squirrel stole down the hill. I was prepared to fight him, but not with Standing Oak in the offing. He began to angle to my left. I shrank back, my breath held, taking care not to drag feet and dislodge rocks or raise dust. He passed so close to the bushes I could hear his breathing, imagined I could feel the heat of his body. The limp from his bad hip sent him into a stumble, and he slid toward me. I tightened the grip on the pistol, lifted the barrel, but I held fire. He regained his balance and moved out of sight around the other side of the teepee, apparently satisfied that no intruders lurked in the immediate area. I was certain now that my best position would be above the scene, where I could see all and wait for the right moment to intervene.

I assumed my old place just as Yellow Squirrel hobbled out from a cluster of manzanita and headed in my direction. I froze once again as he climbed toward me and took up a position just below mine.

How long my secret standoff lasted, I don't know. Perhaps ten minutes, perhaps thirty. A muscle in my calf knotted, began to quiver. I couldn't remain still much longer. Yellow Squirrel put his rifle to his shoulder. I raised my pistol, but the rifle remained pointed downhill and I let my gaze slide cautiously in that direction. A solitary humpbacked figure appeared over the rise, trudging toward the tent. Yellow Squirrel relaxed, rose, and headed down toward the camp.

The plodding form soon took shape as Standing Oak, the body of a small doe draped across his shoulders. He stood his rifle against the teepee, strung the carcass up by its hind feet from a small fir, and called loudly toward the dwelling. He walked to the creek, and rinsed his hands. Many Clouds came out of the tent with a knife and began gutting the animal. I squirmed to imagine that they'd love to have me in the same position as the deer. Yellow Squirrel picked up his rifle and resumed his lookout post. Standing Oak disappeared into the tent.

Shadows seeped into the canyon. The evening of August eighth. The moon would show three-quarters full tonight. I wished I could reach up and arrest its swelling. If an opportunity didn't present itself soon, I'd have to manufacture one. Many Clouds started a fire, sliced hunks of meat from the flayed carcass and laid them on stones near the flames. I felt my own hunger, remembered our sharing the burro meat in the desert. Suddenly all three heads turned toward the teepee. Grandmother crawled through the flap supporting the arm of a feeble man who could only have been Owl Feather.

CHAPTER FIFTY

S tocky and powerful were the words Julia had used to describe him in her diary. Even using an old woman for a crutch, the words fit. He was bare-chested, his hair—still black—poured over his bare shoulders and chest. For all his big frame, he was gaunt and wasted. Skin hung from his jaws and ribs like crinkled drapery. His chest was patched with bandages—doubtless to cover wounds from the sun dance pegs—and he wore an incongruous pair of cavalry pants. Once standing, he removed Grandmother's hand from his arm. She appeared unhurt. Her hair was unbraided, hung straight down her back. Owl Feather walked to the cross, lifted the buffalo skull from its perch and began chanting and turning with a slow rhythm. The other Indians took up the chant, dancing shoulder to shoulder in a circle until the sun had nearly disappeared, and I could barely discern their forms near the firelight. Grandmother stood silently to the side, shifting her weight with the dancers, yearning, it seemed to me, to join them.

Owl Feather stopped at last, stepped toward the fire, the buffalo skull in his hands, uplifted like an offering to the heavens. Standing Oak and Yellow Squirrel came forward, each standing behind one of his shoulders. The old man turned with the skull first toward Yellow Squirrel, who lifted his hands to receive it, but Owl Feather turned instead to the setting sun. Then he turned toward Standing Oak, who lifted his hands, but again Owl Feather drew it back. Finally, the old man knelt, laid the skull before the fire, and began another chant. At this move, Yellow Squirrel yelled and drove a fist into Standing Oak's face.

I jumped to my feet and scrambled downhill toward the sudden chaos, my gait rendered awkward by my injuries and my asymmetrical bootheels. Standing Oak fell backwards. Yellow Squirrel grabbed a rifle, pointed it toward his brother, and Many Clouds threw herself across the fallen man's chest. I triggered a running, off-balance shot. My bullet kicked up dust between Yellow Squirrel's feet just before he fired. Many Clouds screamed. Standing Oak twitched once, then lay still.

"Stop, Andrew," Grandmother yelled.

I continued my downhill stumble, shot again, missed again. Owl Feather advanced on Yellow Squirrel, yelling and waving a fist. The younger man bounded toward the horses, no sign of a limp, leaped aboard the buckskin, and tore away in full gallop and full cry. I stopped and steadied my weapon at the fleeing Indian. He was in my sights and in range and I squeezed the trigger. And the gun froze, suddenly became a sculpture of a pistol with a cocked hammer and a useless trigger. I heard a metallic snap behind me and turned to find myself staring into the barrel of Owl Feather's Winchester.

"Drop your gun," he said.

I held the pistol where he could see it. "It's jammed."

He sighted down the rifle barrel. "Out of respect for your grandmother, I have not shot you. Yet." I laid what had been my gun carefully on one of the rocks beside the fire.

Many Clouds sat beside Standing Oak, grasped her left hand with her right, blood seeping between her fingers. A dark hole gaped above the big Indian's left hip. Puddling blood stained the earth beside him.

Many Clouds said, "Grandfather, don't—"

"He tried to kill my son."

"A son who shoots his own brother and sets the white law on our trail."

The old man lowered the rifle to his hip, but the barrel still pointed at me. Red blossoms spread on his chest bandages. "You will not move."

Grandmother dropped to Many Clouds' side and examined the rip the bullet had torn in the webbing between her thumb and forefinger. Standing Oak moaned, rolled up on his right elbow, examined his bleeding side.

Grandmother took Many Clouds' hand. "I think it's not so serious, Many Clouds," she said. "I'll wrap it."

"Look to my Uncle," said Many Clouds, "I can wait."

Grandmother prodded the hole in Standing Oak's side. "It went completely through. He will heal, but we must tend to it immediately." She helped him sit up.

The big man looked at me, shook his head, and he smiled briefly. "You must be like your man-god, Andrew Maxwell, to rise from underground." I could barely hear his words.

"We must leave, Grandmother," I said. "Yellow Squirrel's off to kill Mother if she isn't dead already."

Owl Feather raised the carbine again. "You will stay."

"We mustn't allow the Barlows to keep us from our Christian duty, Andrew. Help me."

"My first duty is to protect our family from them." I pointed to Owl Feather. Then to Standing Oak. " Let them destroy one other if they wish."

"Please, Andrew. What you do unto the least of these… Carrie understands that." Her eyes turned up to me. Her lips were firm with command, the rest of her soft with pleading. "Plant the seed of righteousness and righteousness will grow from it."

I closed my eyes, swallowed my anger, turned to Owl Feather, and gestured toward Grandmother. "May I?" He nodded sharply, then settled by the fire. His rifle barrel followed me while Grandmother and I boiled water and herbs, prepared bandages. I tore into strips the spare pants Rosie had given me. Many Clouds rested her hand on my lap while I wrapped the gash. Despite her life outdoors, her skin was soft as a debutante's.

Grandmother cleansed Standing Oak's wound. The big man's eyes were closed, his breath shallow. I found myself wanting his smile again, the smile of a man who'd tried to kill me twice. I turned my focus to Owl Feather.

"Why did you set your sons against the Maxwells?" I said. He tightened his wide mouth.

After a short silence, Many Clouds spoke for him. "He didn't."

Grandmother displayed no reaction to the conversation. "They came in your name," I said.

Owl Feather growled something in Arapaho. Many Clouds shook her head and tightened her own lips. "They came against his wishes," she said.

"Then why turn your rifle on me?"

"All of us—" Her eyes turned to Standing Oak for a moment, then back to me "—do what we must to protect one another, but Grandfather—" Owl Feather's reproach was louder this time, but Many Clouds continued. "Grandfather stopped blaming the Maxwells long ago. Even before—"

This time Owl Feather wasn't satisfied with a simple reprimand. He leaped to his feet, loudly berating Many Clouds. Then he stopped, stumbled back toward the fire. I grasped his arm with one hand to prevent his falling into the flames and pulled the rifle from his loosened grip with the other. He slumped to the rocks bordering the coals, would have tipped backward without my support. Even weakened as he was, the muscle under my hand was firm. Many Clouds hurried to his side, knelt and embraced him. Blood dribbled from her wound, meandered down her grandfather's neck and bare chest. Then the old man looked to the sky and nearly chanted his next words.

"An eagle lives with his family in a nest. They all feed on a great fish. No matter how much they eat, the fish is never consumed. One day, the eagle tires of fish and wants other food, so he flies off hunting. He swoops down on a rabbit, but the moment the rabbit is in his claws, it becomes a wolf, who turns on the eagle and devours him. The wolf then disguises himself as an eagle, flies to the nest, and devours the family as well." He murmured something to Many Clouds in Arapaho. His chin dropped to his chest.

"You have found your conspiracy now, Andy. You should go." She finished wrapping her own hand.

"That little parable? That's no explanation at all."

"It is his vision." She began sponging her blood off her grandfather's chest. "At last it has come."

"That provoked Yellow Squirrel into shooting his brother?"

Many Clouds said something else in Arapaho, but nothing else in English. I examined my pistol, but found the action too damaged even to retrieve the four precious unfired cartridges.

"Will you go now, Grandmother?"

"We haven't finished," she said. I felt a flash of the same anger I so often felt toward Mother. She held forth a handful of herbs. "Drop these in the water then soak the bandages in them." It seemed as useless to argue with her as with Mother, and I seemed powerless to disobey, so I followed her instructions. First, though, I levered the rest of the shells from Owl Feather's rifle and stood it against the tent well out of his reach.

"What was Many Clouds about to tell me that made you so angry, Owl Feather?" The old man rose and shuffled past all of us into the tent.

"Please let my grandfather pass to the Great Spirit in peace."

"But that story," I said. "Who is the eagle, who the fish or the rabbit or the wolf?"

"What you came to learn is in that tale, Andrew. I can tell you nothing else."

Owl Feather's vision was murky as a Delphic Oracle, but whatever it meant, neither he nor Standing Oak had the power to marshal a vendetta now and the conspiracy had become a conspiracy of one.

I helped Grandmother tie the last knots in Standing Oak's bandages, then picked up the Winchester and began reloading it. "Do you have another weapon here, Many Clouds?" She nodded toward the teepee. "Then you won't be defenseless. Now we'll go, Grandmother."

"No, Andrew," She moved to the fire pit and gazed into flames.

"I can't leave you," I said. "Not after what happened last time."

"You should have seen us," she said, "after the warriors left to fight the army and the women had to flee. Poor Carrie's dysentery was so bad I couldn't let her wear underwear. And when that was over the fever came." She drifted off into a chanting and singing, rocking back and forth, the shadows of the fire snaking across her face. Many Clouds and I shared a look, then she dropped her eyes. Sadness burned my own.

"I must go and I can't take her like this. But I swear, if anything happens to her…"

Many Clouds laid her hand on Grandmother's arm. "She will be as safe as we can make her, Andrew. Grandfather understands, believe me, about devotion to the grandmother. She held out her uninjured hand. "Thank you." I reached to take her hand, then clasped it in both of mine. She retrieved it slowly, adjusted the sling Grandmother had made for her.

"Many Clouds," I said, "when you had the drop on me back there. Would you have pulled the trigger?"

"It wouldn't have mattered if I had, Andrew," she said. "The gun was broken."

"Yes. But if it weren't." She said nothing, only cocked her head to the side and pursed her lips into a smirk. My hand wanted to touch her cheek, soft in the shadow, but I stopped the half-finished gesture and turned to Grandmother, who had sat down, fallen silent, and was staring at the coals.

"I'll return soon to take you home, Grandmother." She shook her head.

"You can't stop the Barlows with killing," she said. "You must find another way." She began humming and rocking again. I turned back to Many Clouds.

"I can wait no longer, but matters won't be settled until Grandmother's back home and the violence stops."

"You brought a great deal of trouble, Andrew. I tried to warn you."

"The trouble was here long before I came," I said. "Take care of her." I fashioned a sling for the rifle out of the few remaining scraps of my spare trousers and strapped it across my back. I then sliced a few pieces of venison from the hanging deer, stuffed them in my rucksack, walked toward the horses.

"One moment, Andrew," she said, and disappeared into the teepee. In a short while, she emerged carrying a pair of moccasins. "Your white man's boots serve you badly."

I didn't ask for whom the new shoes had been made, but they fit tolerably well.

"Thank you." She nodded. "Take care of Grandmother," I said. She nodded again. I stepped toward her, lowered my voice. "And of yourself as well," I trotted to Sailor, mounted, and headed west into the faint glow of a nearly full moon, a warrior with only five days remaining to save his tribe.

* * *

I'd never ridden Sailor bareback and was surprised how good it felt not to have a saddle between me and him, how much I'd learned from my time between Wells and Wyoming about how to use knees and balance to communicate with a horse. Perhaps the communication with Sailor helped awaken the mystical side of me. A solution to Owl Feather's conundrum dawned on me. I was the eagle, unwilling to remain in the Circle M nest, destined to be devoured for leaving it by Yellow Squirrel-become-wolf. Unless Yellow Squirrel was the eagle, I the rabbit. Yes. That was the version I liked. No wonder they were all afraid of me.

I presumed that Yellow Squirrel would head directly for the ranch. Unless he found a way to board a train or acquired another horse, he'd be hard-put to reach the Circle M before the moon filled out. Still, he was volatile and unpredictable, and I couldn't rule out his taking time to ambush me. He might even circle back and attempt to hurt Grandmother. However, I felt I could rely on Many Clouds and Owl Feather to shield her.

I rode steadily, just below the ridgetops, alert for blinds where Yellow Squirrel might lie in wait. I could travel faster without Grandmother, but that wasn't why she'd stayed behind. Why then? My body at alert, my mind turned to what I recalled of Grandmother's description of her redemption.

* * *

Always, we have been afraid of the Indians, but until our flight, I had no idea what terror we ourselves held for them. The calm and organized village where we were first taken turned to panicked chaos. They broke camp in great haste. Old and kindly Lolo, Owl Feather's own grandmother, smeared us with mud lest someone identify our race from afar. There was almost no pretense to cover our trail. They sought only to flee as quickly as possible. And a pathetic group they were, wretched and disorganized. Mistreated though I was by many, I found many others kind of heart. And I now see these people as human beings fighting against injustice, injustice inflicted by my own people. And yet I was also their victim. I suppose I should call them enemies, but my heart will not allow me to hate them. Misguided though their methods were, all they sought was to treat for land where they could live their lives in peace. They thought my people would trade us—Carrie, Missy, and me—for that dream.

The bedlam gave me the opportunity to sneak about and find Missy, but I wish I hadn't. She was in Running Deer's tent, wrapped bare as a newborn in a buffalo robe, bruised and nearly unconscious. She barely knew I was there. I understood then the fate from which Owl Feather had saved me that night on the creek. However, Owl Feather was not strong enough to protect us both, and neither was Carter.

Carter thought the army was not moving fast enough, so he came after us himself with two men from the wagon train. They found what they thought would be reinforcements in a pair of horse traders running a herd through the hills. Carter had no intimation of their savagery. He said when they came upon us the light in those men's eyes put him in mind of demons looking to feast on human souls.

They ignored Carter's calls for caution and plunged after us. We heard their yells before we saw them. We were all exhausted from running and fear. Women dropped bundles, abandoned horses, and dived for cover down the ravine, anywhere they could hope for refuge. I grabbed Carrie and ran for a thicket of manzanita. There was a shot, and poor Lolo, running beside me went down. Done up like squaws as we were, I was certain we'd meet the same fate.

From our hiding place, I saw Missy dashing down a hill. She tripped over a rock and fell, face up. A huge red-haired man galloped toward her, pistol drawn. Carter was behind him, yelling, "That's Missy, you fool." But the man shot anyway, and she lay still. Carter made quick justice of the matter, but it was too late for that poor, wretched girl who was sacrificed for Carrie and me. I only hope her time with us Maxwells made her short and awful journey on earth a bit brighter.

And so we redeemed. Such an odd expression. As if retrieving captive females was a religious act instead of a violent and often bloody one, however courageous. Missy and poor, kindly Lolo, harmless grandmother of the man who at once kidnapped and protected us, came to bloody ends along with many others whose murders I did not witness.

And yet, amid the horror how extraordinary to think I would learn great truths from the lips of an Indian brave in a teepee. In the end, Owl Feather was unable to protect either us or his own people, and he certainly went about his chosen mission in the wrong way. But in those few days, we shared time when we were neither Indian nor white, man nor woman, captor nor captive, but simple human beings united in our devotion to human truth and justice. I set down his story here, not to excuse his deeds but to honor his spirit.

Owl Feather, son of a chief, was captured as a child and carried away by Sioux. Apparently, this is a common practice among the Indians, though it seems barbaric to us. But then, I wonder what could be more barbaric than the slavery so-called civilized Christians have practiced for so long?

While Owl Feather was still a boy, the Sioux moved to a reservation, and a childless missionary couple adopted him. Kind people.

But then came an uprising against a corrupt Indian Agent. Owl Feather's parents and several other missionaries were killed. Suddenly, he found himself without a people. Having lived in both the white and native worlds, he thought he could help everyone find a peaceful and dignified coexistence. And so he planned to return us—Missy, Carrie, and me— to our people in exchange for his people's being allowed to do the same. But men like Running Deer and the white barbarian who shot poor Missy and Lolo destroyed the plan. The dream.

Despite our reunion with Carter, the return to Fort Bridger was joyless, as Missy's bruised and battered corpse followed us like a specter. I could almost imagine the ghost of Mathilda Barlow hovering over the procession.

* * *

Carter recorded nothing of his feelings. His log began again when the wagon train resumed its California trek and stuck to the concrete details. Perhaps Owl Feather and his sons held Grandfather Carter responsible for Lolo's death. He hadn't fired the deadly shot, had apparently executed the man who had. But he'd led the charge. Perhaps they blamed him—and Grandmother and Julian and Mother and me—for spoiling their impossible notion of a permanent Arapaho homeland. Yet it appeared Owl Feather had harbored no rancor. It had been Standing Oak and Yellow Squirrel who had launched this frontier version of the Oresteia.

Brief images drifted through my mind—Julian's wide, amazed eyes and mouth as he fell to the sidewalk. The lifeless face of what looked like Shelby but suddenly wasn't. Standing Oak's smile—why did both of us seem pleased the other was alive? Perhaps at his core he had no more taste for all the bloodshed than I did. The rage of the furies had come down to Yellow Squirrel, and to me fell the role of the Orestes. Somewhere, perhaps, there were gods voting on which of us should win.

CHAPTER FIFTY-ONE

Nearly twilight the next day, I rounded the knob of a small hill and spotted the distant roofs of Evanston, Wyoming. Since there had been no ambush by now, it was certain Yellow Squirrel had headed straight for the ranch.

Railroad tracks stretched across the plain on both sides of the town, and occasional wagons and riders moved along the road that paralleled them. I needed about thirty dollars train fare to travel as far as Auburn, thirty miles from Sacramento and sixty miles from the ranch. I figured I'd be close enough to home then to use Circle M credit to complete the journey. I figured to use Sailor to raise money for the fare from Evanston to Auburn.

* * *

I saw no one in or near the livery stable, called, but received no reply. The stable inside was larger than Gilligan's in Sawtooth Wells, but it was in poor condition. The stalls hadn't seen a shovel for some time, and saddles and bridles—many of them in need of oiling and mending—hung here and there on random nails. I called and poked around for a few minutes when I heard grunting and scraping from above. I approached the ladder that led to the hole-in-the-floor opening to the loft.

"Anyone up there?" I said.

"Yeah, yeah. I hear you," called a male voice. Presently, a man with a darkly-bearded face, big eyes and a small mouth that lent his head the appearance of a triangle appeared at the entrance. He was fastening the shoulder straps on his overalls.

"What do you want?" he said.

"I'd like to help you make some money, if you're interested," I said. "Perhaps you'd care to come down and talk about it. I'm in a bit of a hurry." He turned his head over his shoulder and grunted something I couldn't understand, then turned back to me. He didn't begin descending the ladder.

"Talk fast. I'm pretty busy." His speech was slurred.

"My name's Andrew Maxwell, sir. I'm from the Circle M ranch in California. It's a fairly large outfit. Perhaps you've heard of it?"

"Nope."

"Well, sir," I said, "You're fortunate to find me at an awkward moment. I'm in need of money for a train ticket and my train leaves in a half hour."

"If you're from such an almighty big outfit why do you have to scrounge up train fare?"

"I don't have time to explain fully, but I can show you a way to turn thirty dollars into sixty without even getting out of bed."

"Sounds like snake oil to me," he said.

"You'll have to come down here to find out."

"Talk to me from there or no dice."

"Very well. I'll find someone else." I led Sailor toward the barn door. We were halfway into the street before I heard the voice pursuing me.

"Hey. Hey. Hold it." He climbed slowly down the ladder, wrapped bony hands around his overall straps. "But make it quick." The man smelled like a jug of moonshine.

"As I said, Maxwell's my name. Andrew Maxwell." I held out my hand. He hesitated.

Finally, he took my hand and muttered, "Jones. Hannibal's the first name."

"Well, Mr. Jones, let me introduce you to Sailor. Prize sire of the Circle M."

"Appears to be short a saddle, don't he?"

"I need thirty dollars to get home, Mr. Jones. I can see you have a practiced eye. Sailor's worth twice that amount, wouldn't you agree?"

"Don't know." He drew back Sailor's lips for a look at his teeth. "This animal's getting on."

"Here's my proposition, Mr. Jones. You give me thirty dollars. I'll give you a bill of sale. In two or three weeks, I'll return with twice the cash and take him off your hands."

"Don't know you. I could get stuck." His puckered lips showed pink in the thicket of his beard.

"If I don't return by September fifteenth, you're free to sell him, and double your money." He wandered away from me and leaned against a wall.

"I'd have to board him all that time, clean up after him." I resisted the temptation to remark on the stable's lack of maintenance.

"The extra money should compensate for that."

"Tell you what." He slid down the wall and squatted, arms crossed in his lap. "Maybe you throw in that Winchester you're carrying, I'll take the deal."

"The Winchester remains with me," I said.

"Then the thirty dollars remains with me," he said. "Now git." He turned back toward the ladder.

It was useless to argue more with this hardheaded drunk. It seemed the saloon was my only other alternative. On my way out the door, though, I heard muted scuffles and incoherent vocalizing from above. A faint steam whistle sounded. I crossed to the bottom of the ladder.

"Mr. Jones," I said. "Is something wrong?" Silence. "Jones?" I called. Still silence. I'm not certain why I decided to climb that ladder, still not certain it was the right thing to do, but I'm certain I was right to take my rifle with me.

The one small window at the east end of the loft admitted virtually no light, and it took a few seconds for my eyes to adjust to the darkness. Straw scraps littered the boards near me. A wall of stacked hay loomed at the far end. I made out a faint heap of color at the base of the wall.

"Mr. Jones?" I said once more. The heap moved, took form. Jones sat up. His coveralls and underwear hobbled him at the ankles. A boy, maybe ten or twelve years old stood up, not a stitch to cover what God gave him.

CHAPTER FIFTY-TWO

Jones stumbled to his knees, reached to pull his tangled clothes up, tripped himself and fell to his side.

"What the hell you doing up here?" His speech was growing more slurred by the second.

"Come with me," I said to the boy.

"Can't," The boy said. "He'll kill me." He covered his privates with his hands. His eyes darted around. I stepped across to the boy, kept the gun on Jones, who had planted one foot and was struggling to stabilize the other. I retrieved a pair of overalls. "What's your name, son?" I said.

"T-T- Theodore."

"You get below, put these on."

"That's my nephew," Jones said. "Family. You ain't taking him anywhere." He was looking to sober up now, trying to stand and pull on his underwear, but he was still very unsteady on his feet.

"Toss me your clothes," I said.

"Like hell," he said. I waved the rifle at him. He toed the overalls toward me a short distance, but they still lay close enough to him to allow an attack were I to reach for them.

"Farther," I said. He grunted, but did as he was told.

"Now drop the underwear."

"You interested in looking at something, are you?"

"Only your money," I said. Rat's nests of black hair littered Jones' pale scrawniness. I never had understood why one man would want another, but it was beyond my farthest imagination why anyone would want a boy like Theodore, who had no more hair on his body than the day he was born.

I found no money. He couldn't have paid me if he'd wanted to. "I'm leaving now, Jones, but I'll be back. And if either that horse or that boy is not healthy and happy, you're going to lose a lot more than your clothes." I dropped his overalls through the loft door and climbed down. Near the bottom of the ladder, I saw Theodore already dressed. Outside, I heard the train pull into the station.

"Watch out, mister, he'll shoot us." I leaped from the ladder, grabbed Theodore, and headed toward the front door where I'd dropped my rucksack. A gunshot followed us. I shoved Theodore into a corner and took cover behind a hay bale. Jones slipped and stumbled down the ladder. He hit the ground with both feet and started in our direction, revolver raised and ready, ignoring his own nakedness.

"Ain't nobody gonna get away with stealing from me," he yelled.

"Drop the gun, Jones," I said. He fired in my direction. I fired back, attempting to shoot low. I had no wish to be held here for a killing, however justified. He fell, lost the gun and grabbed his leg. I ran from my hiding place and kicked his pistol aside. I looked back to see Theodore with his face to the wall.

"It's okay, son," I said. "Come on." I picked up Jones' pistol, stuffed it into my trousers, gripped Theodore's hand and headed toward the train station. We left Jones groaning on the floor of his barn.

The nearly-full moon, a looming reminder of my deadline, cast a low light on the dirt street. A few yards from the stable, I saw the sheriff running toward us, gun drawn.

"Hands up," he said. The lawman appeared to be about my age, a head taller, straight and skinny as a telegraph pole. Furry sideburns puffed out his sunken cheeks. I didn't put my hands in the air, but gestured toward the barn.

"You'll find Hannibal Jones in there with a bullet in his leg. I must catch that train."

"Not so fast." He pointed the pistol at my heart. "Who the hell are you and what are you doing with Theodore, here?"

"I'm Andrew Maxwell of the Circle M ranch in California. Theodore's uncle's been using him the way a cowboy uses a saloon girl."

The train whistle blew. Steam nearly engulfed the engine. "Take good care of him." I patted the boy on the back and sprinted toward the station.

"Hey, hold on," the sheriff called, "you can't just leave." His pistol was raised, but he didn't fire.

"Sheriff." The weak voice belonged to Hannibal Jones, who had crawled into view between me and the train and was waving feebly from his knees, overalls draped over his arm and held in front of his crotch. I stopped momentarily. The sight of his uncle, even so disabled, sent Theodore careening to me, and he hung on tight as an infant to its mother.

"I can't stay now, Theodore. The sheriff will protect you." The train began to move. Theodore still clung. It took all my strength to peel his arms off me. The sheriff in the meantime had knelt beside Jones, looked back and forth between him and me. I wanted to cuddle Theodore, but I pushed him away, hard enough to send him sprawling in the dirt. "Sorry. I'll be back." I ran toward the train once more. I dared not look back.

It seemed I was making a habit of leaping aboard moving trains. This one had already gathered nearly as much speed as the logging train I had intercepted in Placerville. But this time I had a better start. I caught the rear ladder on the side of the baggage car, dragged and stumbled my way to a perch on the lower rung. I looked around to see whether anyone had detected me, glanced rearward just in time to see Theodore leap toward the caboose ladder. His jump carried him to the platform steps, but he didn't catch hold. He collided with the speeding car and flew back into the dusty street where he lay still.

I saw the sheriff and another man approach the little form, but never saw it move. An emergency cord or an alarm to the conductor might have stopped the train, but I never seriously considered either. If Theodore was dead, I couldn't help him. If he was alive, there were others who could.

I thought of my father's desertion. The hours I'd spent pitying myself now seemed a shameful self-indulgence. He'd left me in loving, if somewhat stern, arms. I'd never been consigned to the brutal hell Theodore—and Missy Barlow before him—had endured.

CHAPTER FIFTY-THREE

I worked my way to a roost inches above the coupling between the baggage car and the passenger car behind it. I tried the baggage car door. Locked, of course. I leaned out and surveyed my chances of climbing underneath the moving car, decided I had better odds of surviving a leap off one of the Sawtooth Peaks. Where was the next station? Ogden, probably. How far? A hundred miles? Two hundred? I didn't know. I did know I had to remain hidden until then and be prepared to deal with a large, well-patrolled railyard.

Passengers and conductor would soon be milling in the car behind me, and my roost was visible from the door window. I huddled as low and as small as I could. The cars rocked, knocked, and rumbled over the roadbed, nearly dislodged me. My situation would become more precarious as the train snaked and tilted its way up and down the impending mountain grades.

The train climbed a hill, slowed nearly to a walk. Perhaps I could dodge underneath to the rods at this slower speed. I worked my way out to the ladder and leaned over. Although the big cars were moving slowly, the wheels spun a dizzying silver in the moonlight. We hit a rough patch of rail, and I had to hug the ladder to avoid falling. I worked my way back to my original perch, wondered if I'd ever again see the full moon as romantic instead of threatening.

"What a dull world you live in, Andy," Virginia had told me once when I'd asserted that moonlight was no more than the reflection of sunlight off a large rock. "The whole universe is poetry if you let it be." Her delicate modesty somehow quaint to me after the gauntlet I'd run.

The train plunged downhill at a pace that seemed destined to derail it and dislodge me. I grasped the platform frame with one hand, the rifle with the other, and the coupling frame with both feet. I told Julian if he was in a position to help me, now would be a good time. The general clatter covered the noise of the baggage car door opening, and it nearly knocked me aside as it slid past, immediately above my head.

"Too damn hot in there for a cigar," growled a voice above me "If you're gonna smoke, do it out here." I couldn't understand the answer, but presently two pair of legs appeared in the corner of my eye. If the men they belonged to looked down and to their left, they'd see me, even in the half-dark of the moon.

One pair of shoes disappeared, the other, expensive black boots, remained at the door.

The boots paced back and forth twice, thrice, stood in place. A comet of sparks arced toward me, and a burning cigar butt landed in my lap. The boots disappeared, so it seemed I was alone, but the train was on a banked curve, and I didn't feel safe letting go. I bucked my pelvis twice, but succeeded only in rolling the coal a few inches down to cradle in a fold of my pants. I reached over my head with one hand and twisted up, hoping to straighten my body and loose the cigar. The move dislodged one foot, and I lost hold of the rifle as I lunged for another handhold. The weapon bounced off the platform, then the coupling, then fell under the train. Had my fingertips not found a piece of strap iron, I'd have followed it. I had no time to lament the Winchester's loss, for the lurch had not freed the cigar, and my pants were beginning to smolder, my leg to blister. I thought my hold firm enough now to attempt another kick, but before I could, the door slid away and my right hand lost its grip entirely. The sliding door carried me to the side, put my body at right angles to the coupling, and I dropped belly first toward the cinders below.

CHAPTER FIFTY-FOUR

I lost my wind when I hit the coupling, but managed to hang over it like a rag on a clothesline for a few seconds, tipped headfirst toward the blur of ties and rails. I squirmed until I returned to a balance point. At least I was no longer in danger of catching fire. Jones' pistol in my waistband stabbed into my belly and thigh. Beneath me, the coupling flexed and pitched like a mechanical beast. I had no handholds, could only rock and twist my weight, felt always as if I were about to plummet beneath the racketing wheels. In a state of constant fear, I finally worked myself prone and lengthwise on the coupling. I raised myself to a shaky kneel and crawled back to where I now felt curiously secure.

* * *

Ogden's railyard wasn't as large as I'd expected. It must have been at least midnight, and the place looked deserted. I stood and tested my legs. They felt rubbery and numb, but a little massaging restored my circulation.

I peeked around one side of the car, saw no one. Peeked around the other side. The brakeman was near the locomotive, red lantern at his feet. He puffed a cigarette and talked to a railroad guard who swung the bull's eye lantern in his hand back and forth in a nervous arc. The passengers and other crew remained inside. The lack of activity could mean everyone was asleep, but it could also mean that this was a short stop.

I shifted to the other side of the car, dropped to the ground, and worked my way under the baggage car. Darkness hid most of the undercarriage, and by touch I could find nothing that would hold me for the ride across the desert. I wondered if all the tales of hoboes riding the rods were mythical.

I crawled toward the passenger cars, away from the locomotive and the guard. Under the next car, I did find rods that tied the rectangular iron frame. They were an inch or so thick, and held well when I yanked down on them. I hauled myself up and found a position where I could lay out full length and remain secure, but it was no feather bed. The rods supported only my back and thighs. My chest and legs were jammed into a foot or less of space between the shafts and the car's undercarriage. The rest of me hung down between the rods. I wondered how I'd support my head.

Footsteps crunched the cinders, and a beam of light licked its way under the cars ahead. It appeared that my car was next in line as the bulls searched for hoboes. There would be no way to escape the probing light, so I dropped down to the ties, rolled back out from under the car, and leaped to the rungs of the boxcar ladder on the opposite side. Light flashed under the car I'd just vacated. I climbed up higher and squeezed closer. Someone blew his whistle. Two other lanterns bobbed toward our train from fifty yards away. Other whistles sounded. I swung around the end of the car and straddled the coupler once again.

"I heard something around this car here," called a reedy voice. "Can't see nothing now. You two take that side and we can trap him."

Perhaps they wouldn't try the roofs. I braced arms and legs against adjoining cars, stepped my way to the top, and attempted to merge with the tarred top. Below me, the three guards worked their way to the rear of the train. I scrambled forward on hands and knees, hoping for refuge near the front. I stopped on the last car and looked back. One of the lanterns was ascending the caboose. They were going to search the top after all. In front of me was the tender, which carried the coal and water to fuel the steam engine that propelled the locomotive. The cab appeared empty. Perhaps the engineer had joined the search. The water tank was closed, but the coal bin was exposed. I jumped.

I'd had plenty of experience with this oily, sooty stone, but I'd never before wallowed in it. The tender was nearly half-empty now, and the level would continue to drop as we steamed over the desert and the fireman fed the hungry monster in front. Still, I knew I was lucky to find a coal tender. Train companies were in the process of switching their boiler fuel to oil, and if there'd been an oil tank in this one, I'd have had no room to hide. Not that all was necessarily well. If the coal level became too low, I'd find it difficult to escape the twelve-foot bin. If they stopped to refuel from one of the Central Pacific's over-the-rail hoppers, I could be crushed under more weight than the landslide Standing Oak had sent down on me.

"Well, looks like he got away this time, but we sure as shootin' scared him off," said the thin voice. "I thank you boys for the help."

"One more of these wild goose chases and you can blow that whistle till kingdom come and I ain't a-coming," said another man. "You're spookier'n a goose in a wheat field."

"Now, Max," a third man said, "we got to help each other. You had a false alarm or two in your time."

"Not like him. He allus interrupts me in the middle of one of Maggie's roast beef sandwiches." Crunching footsteps faded away. I crouched and listened to scuffing, questions, commands, clatter as the engineer and fireman climbed back into the cab and prepared to depart. Clouds of steam wafted above my haven, and the train inched forward. Clanking and scraping echoed through the tender, and coal lumps jiggled under me when the fireman pulled shovelsful from the bottom of the pile. As he stoked the boiler, he was digging his way to my last hiding place. I sharpened the edge of Shelby's knife against the railcar steel.

CHAPTER FIFTY-FIVE

I woke to a sky so pale blue it was nearly white. The train moved smoothly. Level ground. I chinned myself on the edge of the car, saw eastern peaks behind us, the desert before us. The morning of August tenth.

The coal supply had diminished alarmingly. They'd have to refill somewhere near—perhaps Wells, perhaps Elko. We would pull into whichever town in broad daylight and someone was certain to see me crawling from the tender. Maybe the caboose offered better cover. The entire top of the train was visible from its cupola, and perhaps no one would check there for stowaways.

I heaved myself out of the bin and crawled toward the rear of the train. Even on smooth ground, my progress was slow and shaky. Handholds were few and footing scarce. I kept in mind the tales I'd heard of men who made a life of this sort of thing and kept reminding myself that they were no smarter, no stronger, than I. Certainly no more desperate. I soon stretched out diagonally, face-down on the roof, hands around a grab rail. My griminess worked as protective coloration against the black roof, so if I pressed myself close down, I might remain undiscovered. Before long, Wells manifested as a distant blob.

I thought perhaps we'd sail through, but we did stop, and it appeared to be a major delay. A coal car waited on a siding, three men leaning on their shovels atop its load. A water tower, its spout extended over the track, stood by to refill the tank. Prospective passengers stood beside their trunks. A small collection of other citizens, for whom the train's arrival was the major event of the day, smoked or played checkers in the station shade. Moving now would assure my discovery, but even if I remained still, someone was certain to see me before long.

Crew and passengers began to step from their confines, stretching and yawning. I fixed my attention on the platform and the locomotive cab, but the assault I feared came from the other side of the train. A hand-sized rock bounced off the cupola roof, and a young voice cried, "Hobo. There's a hobo up there."

Two nine-or-ten-year-old boys opposite the station sent forth two more rocks and a series of yells. To run toward the station would have meant certain capture, so I slid down the ladder toward the boys, yelling at the top of my lungs. They took me for a monster and fled behind the train, which screened me from the mass of spectators on the platform, but to run north and out of town meant revealing myself. I sprinted across the street, past a confused and startled couple who were descending from their buckboard, and through the alley where Luke had robbed me. I flung myself on my belly next to the back porch of a dry goods store and caught my breath.

In the distance, voices speculated on my whereabouts. Footsteps crossed boards above me. I heard a swishing, and puffs of dust drifted off the porch as someone swept the boards. The footsteps recrossed the porch and a door slammed.

I was safe only for a moment, and I'd run away from the train I needed to reach home. Beyond the rear of the building was open desert. A clump of greasewood and sage grew twenty or thirty yards away. Not good for cover, but should do to create a distraction. I dashed toward the skimpy vegetation and dived on my belly. My pockets and moccasins were filled with coal pebbles, and I fashioned a small mound at the base of a greasewood bush. Rosie's matches, still in my rucksack, lighted up immediately, as did the coal. In less than two minutes, black smoke plumed around me.

Nothing in this dry climate frightens people like fire, not even a runaway hobo. I dashed away from the smoke and circled back toward the train. Behind me, someone blew a whistle, someone else answered with another. People began running toward the smoke. I mentally congratulated Wells on its makeshift fire alarm system. And thanked the people for drawing attention away from me.

The train had pulled down the line, and the two men were shoveling coal into the tender. Chugging sounds told me the crew was firing the boiler and that my lifeline to the Circle M would depart any minute. They'd apparently decided the fire was a local matter, not on their schedule. I sneaked behind the station and into the corrals where Ira's horses had stood. The big corral was empty, but the small adjacent pen housed the same pigs and goats that had been there a week ago. The pen's improvised gate was a three-or-four inch diameter pole of pinion pine. Bent nails stapled a few strands of wire to it, and wire loops top and bottom made for a rude gate.

I nicked Shelby's knife blade prying the nails loose, wrapped the loose ends of the wire around the fenceposts, and took the gate pole with me as I slithered along the side of the station building. I watched the conductor climb to the caboose cupola and survey the top of the train, then wave to the brakeman, who made a cursory inspection of the undersides of the cars. Apparently satisfied that they carried no unwelcome patrons, the brakeman waved to the engineer, then climbed aboard. Steam ballooned from the front of the train, and wheels began turning. I dived under the train, flung my little pole to bridge the space between two of the undergirding's trusses, then climbed belly down on my makeshift bed. I clung to the rods with my hands, squeezed as tight as I could with my feet to minimize the weight on the gnarled stick that would be my mattress. Ties blurred, rails and wheels flashed as the train gathered speed. I'd at last secured a ride home.

* * *

As the hours passed, heat ripples faded along with the sunlight. Shade enveloped the plains. We began to climb the eastern slope, and the vegetation changed from sagebrush and greasewood to manazanita. I even detected an occasional conifer.

Sometime well after dark, the train began to slow and labor, and we commenced our climb up the east side of Donner Pass. I shifted my weight to restore circulation to my tingling feet, heard a crack, and felt my body sag at the waist. My slender pine bed was splintering beneath me.

CHAPTER FIFTY-SIX

I stiffened my back and gripped the rods, but my efforts were futile, and I finally dropped to the railbed and let the cars pass over me. Even with the train moving slowly up the steep grade, the fall battered and skinned me anew. I raised myself to my knees and watched the cars disappear into a snowshed. I felt the way a man tossed overboard on the ocean must feel watching his ship disappear across the waves. Suddenly too weak to stand, I raised my eyes to the moon, which seemed complete, though I knew its official fullness wouldn't occur until three evenings hence. I judged myself at least a two-or-even-three-day walk from the Circle M.

It was some combination of fear, pride, and determination that lifted me to my feet and begin my trek. I slid down the cinder bank and jumped five feet from one boulder to another, slid down that one to a little trail. Gravel crunched under my feet as I shoved myself toward the summit.

I knew nothing of this country except by tale and reputation. Donner Lake was a dark pearl in the moonlight below, and I imagined the dread spirits of that unfortunate party as I walked some of the same ground where they must have camped some sixty years earlier. If I continued southwest, I'd surely see Sawtooth Peaks, and then I could make a beeline for home. I might have been better advised to sit by the tracks and await another train. It wouldn't be difficult to board one as it crawled up the slope. However, the thought of sitting still and hoping rather than acting seemed palatable as arsenic. If I kept my eyes open and my wits about me, I'd find a way to recover the lost time.

* * *

I was hurrying down the spine of a hogback when I emerged from a stand of sugar pines and saw one of those mountain meadows that occasionally shelve out from cliffsides and catch springwater spilling from the high peaks. Two hundred head or so of sheep clustered in the near corner on the uphill side, a tent pitched hard by, dead campfire before it. Sheepherders loved to poach government fodder in the high country when summer scorched valley rangelands. I wasn't interested in sheep, though. What caught my eye were the two horses hobbled in the pasture some distance from both the sheep and the tent.

I had no time to approach this politely or even legally. Rosie had said that some in Wells regarded me as a common horse thief. I now determined to become one in earnest. Ragged and penniless as I was I had no hope of persuading the herder to lend his animals to me. I'd circle the clearing until I was on the downhill side of the meadow, downwind from the horses, then crawl back uphill from there. Hannibal Jones' pistol had but four shots remaining. I wasn't prepared to kill for these horses, but I wouldn't hesitate to brandish my weapon or to fire a warning.

I sidled down the hillside slowly, learned the true meaning of the word "tenderfoot" as my moccasined soles, which had been protected by thick boots for so long, jabbed against rocks and roots. I dropped to hands and knees, then to belly to enter the clearing. The meadow was lush, replete with bogs and mosquitoes. My forearms smeared with blood each time I wiped off the constantly-renewing coat of insects, and the high-pitched buzz of the swarm around my head and face deafened me. I tightened eyes, lips and nostrils against invasion.

Opposite the tent, I counted to five between each move. I had nearly cleared the shelter and fixed my eyes on the horses when I froze at a rustling of canvas. The tent flap, then a drape of mosquito netting, flew open, and a shadow stood arm's length away. He wore only his long underwear and a dark Stetson. I pressed myself to earth. The four-or-five inch grass seemed at that moment short as a trimmed lawn. He turned in all directions and slapped at bugs with his hat. He stepped a few feet away from the tent, fumbled at his crotch, and poured a stream into the bed of his dead campfire. Once finished, his hat waving at the insects, he lifted a kettle near the fire and ladled himself a drink of water. Then he crawled quickly under the netting and into the tent.

I counted to five hundred this time—every piece of exposed skin alive with crawling, sucking, buzzing—before I resumed my crawl toward the horses. They stood head-to-tail, apparently asleep, but one of them sensed my presence a few yards from him and snorted. I stood slowly, crossed the remaining distance, and calmed both animals with low voice and gentle hands. I improvised a lead with my belt before I removed the hobbles from one, used those hobbles to fashion a halter for the other, then led both animals toward the far end of the meadow.

I had nearly reached the cover of the trees when the shouting began. I ran without looking back. A rifle banged, sheep bleated, and my horses skittered and balked as I pulled them down the hillside through trees, bushes, and fallen logs. I fired once in the air, hoping the shot would send my pursuer into cover and buy me some time.

My ruse apparently worked, for when I reached the bottom of the hill, I heard no more sounds of pursuit. The shepherd would spread the news before long, but I doubted there were settlements nearby. Moreover, he was afoot, and he'd hesitate to leave his sheep. But bad news rides a fast horse, as Shelby used to say, and I'd be a known fugitive in no time.

I dropped to the bottom of a canyon and began to follow a stream shortly before dawn etched the forest against the eastern sky. Mounted again, I still had a chance to intercept Yellow Squirrel—provided I could locate home from where I was.

CHAPTER FIFTY-SEVEN

I squinted at the sunrise through eyes swollen nearly shut with mosquito bites. My left eye was virtually useless, my right clouded with seepage. The mud I'd smeared on my skin soothed the irritation only slightly. My arms, hands, and feet also were covered with welts, but they didn't throb. They itched. I'd never reacted seriously to mosquito bites before, but I'd never been subjected to an onslaught of this magnitude.

I continued southwest, scanned the hills for some sign of my peaks. They were grand enough to stand higher than anything else around them, but at certain angles and distances they'd be hidden even by smaller hills. It was difficult to determine whether the day or my eyes were misty. My feet were still sore, and I'd punched several holes in the moccasins in my scramble down the hillside. I surely cut a fine figure with my muddy, bloated skin and shredded footwear.

I kept to concealing side trails. My limited vision sent me into many dead ends. The purloined geldings, obedient and sturdy animals, carried a Rocking LR brand, one I didn't recognize. However, the brand would surely be part of the telegraphed description that must be circulating by now. Their colors—one bay, the other black—made them even more recognizable.

Near midday, I rode over the crest of a hill and thought I glimpsed the high tip of one of the peaks far to the northwest. I dabbed and cleansed my good eye to confirm the sighting. I'd come too far south. I knew that a considerable canyon now lay between me and the peaks. I'd have to loop south and approach the ranch from that direction. Two more days and nights remaining. Even with these horses, it would take considerable good fortune to reach home on time.

The canyon was hundreds of feet deep in places, the stream at its bottom a shining thread, visible only occasionally between the sheer banks. I knew the chasm twisted back west somewhere and ran itself out against a cliff where I could ride around it and head back north, but by sundown it still stretched south as far as I could see. I saw no more hints of my peaks before sunset. The moon seemed to wear a mocking face as the horses picked their way through rocks and trees.

Had I been able to stay with the train, I'd have nearly reached Placerville by now. I'd have reached home a day before the full moon, marshaled the hands to defend the assault of the thirteenth. I was sluggish with lack of food and sleep, throbbing with the pain of my bites. I half-slumbered through the moonlight ride, changed horses at intervals. When the sun pulled itself up I nearly wailed in frustration to see that the canyon still blocked my way west.

That discouragement was the last thing I remembered before I awoke to find both horses stopped and grazing. I could not have been dozing long, or I'd have fallen off the bay and hit the ground, but my lapse angered and puzzled me. Even with the lack of sleep, I couldn't understand my drowsiness. Maybe the insects had poisoned me somehow. Whatever the case, chagrin faded when I surveyed my surroundings and discovered that the way west was clear at last.

By mid-morning on this eve of the full moon's eve, I turned north, rested the horses, and rinsed the clay and coal dust from my face. I trekked through the mountains, worked up one hill, down the next. My spirits lifted as I crested each hill, plummeted each time I weaved down the other side without sighting my home mountains. Finally, as the afternoon waned, I topped a rise and saw the misty outline of the tallest Sawtooth Peak due north. What hills or valleys might lie in the way I wasn't sure, but I allowed myself the hope that a concerted ride would get me home by the next night. I'd remained under cover along the ridge, but saw a wagon road winding through the little canyon below me. Perhaps the hour had come to gain some speed, even at the chance of capture.

The wagon road helped increase my pace considerably. I saw only distant field hands as I moved through the little valley. Then, as I emerged from a shallow draw, I found myself approaching the rear of a slow-moving wagon so loaded with hay I couldn't see the driver. I judged it was headed for the barn a half mile or so distant. I overtook it easily, began to pass it. I was a bit surprised to see a woman driving, but I'd grown up watching mother do everything she required of her employees, so I found the sight anything but astonishing. I never expected good manners to undo me, but I committed a grave misstep when I said, "Howdy, ma'am" as I attempted to slink past without attracting undue attention.

"Good afternoon," she said pleasantly. Then her eyes narrowed and she pulled a revolver from somewhere under her skirts. "Hold it right there, mister, or I'll blow your thieving brains out."

CHAPTER FIFTY-EIGHT

I raised my hands. "I'm not a thief. You're mistaken."

"Only mistake is you coming back down this road bold as brass to the scene of the crime. Now get down off that horse."

"I've never been in these parts before," I said. She stood in the wagon box, one hand still gripping the reins of her aged pair of plowhorses.

"Down," she said.

I quickly slid off the black's left side, used the horse as a screen, then dived under the wagon. She held her fire, and I was safe for the moment. But I'd lost contact with both my horses and she surely wouldn't let matters drop.

"Where are you, Bill Kingsmith? I want that gold back."

"I know no one named Kingsmith," I said. She fired toward my voice, and the bullet tore the boards above my head. I thought to misdirect her fire while I worked my way to a more advantageous position. I crept to the back of the wagon and yelled to the rear.

"I'll prove it to you," I yelled, then scurried to the front like a cornered squirrel. Another shot. A hole appeared in a rear sideboard. "Allow me one minute," I called from the left side of the wagon, then scurried to the right. Another hole. I gambled that she would continue facing the direction where she'd last heard me, sprang up on the right side of the wagon, leaped into the wagon box, grabbed her gun arm with both hands, and wrenched the pistol from her hand. Losing the revolver subdued her little. She kicked and swung furiously.

"Damn you, Bill, you son of a seacook, you never were no good." I emptied the cartridges from her forty-five, pocketed the ammunition and threw the gun in the ditch. I now had reloads for Jones' pistol.

"You can retrieve it later," I said. "Now I must recapture my horses."

I poised to jump from the wagon when I heard galloping hoofbeats from behind. I turned to find myself once more staring down the barrel of a Winchester.

"Hold it up, sir, if you will," said the man behind the rifle. His voice was soft and low, and his full, gray beard nearly hid the badge on his vest. I stopped, but I didn't raise my hands.

"What's the matter, Flora?" he said.

"Can't you see, Zeke? We finally got Billy Kingsmith. Make him tell you what he did with that gold."

"I'm not Billy Kingsmith, and I know nothing about any gold, Sheriff."

"Hop down from there, friend," he said, "and grab on to that wagon wheel." I hesitated, but he wagged his rifle barrel, and I obeyed. He rode his horse beside me. "Now, you keep one hand on a spoke all the time you're taking off that rucksack."

Separation from the rucksack meant separation from my pistol, so I was more than reluctant to follow his instructions. But my choices were limited. Soon it lay at my feet like Tantalus' grapes.

"Now kick it off the road."

I lifted it gently with my toe and lofted it a minimal distance.

"Now that knife." His voice was as calm as if he were asking me to pass the mashed potatoes. I lifted the blade from the sheath and tossed it atop the rucksack. Zeke pitched me a pair of open handcuffs. "Now cuff yourself to one of them spokes.

"You can't arrest me," I said. "I didn't do anything."

"You shut your lying mouth. We been waiting ten years for this," the old lady said.

"We'll sort things out in due time," Zeke said with a wink. His wink may have been conspiratorial, but that hope was a slim reed to hang on. I closed one cuff around my wrist, the other around the spoke of the wheel. "All the way," Zeke said. "I want to hear them ratchets click." My attempt to feign the locking of the cuffs had failed, so I was forced to clamp it closed.

"False arrest is a crime even for someone wearing a star," I said. Zeke ignored my remark and sidled his mount up beside the wagon seat.

"Climb on beside me, now, Flora. I'll take you up to the house, then come back and deal with him."

"No, Zeke, I want to watch." She sat down and closed her arms.

"You know I can't allow you to be present when I interrogate prisoners, Flora. Now the sooner you climb on the sooner I'll find out what we need to know."

Slowly, looking back and forth between Zeke and me, Flora edged toward the far side of the wagon box, then accepted Zeke's hand to assist her to a seat behind the saddle.

"What if this team decides to follow you?" I said. "I'll be crushed."

"You keep still. They'll keep still," Zeke said. "I'll be back directly." I soon lost sight of them behind the wagon and team. I yanked and kicked at the wooden spoke a few times, hoping it was rotten and breakable, but I succeeded only in making the team nervous.

My right hand was cuffed to the wagon's right front wheel. However, I'd used one of the lower spokes to secure the handcuffs, so after stretching my joints as if I were on a torture rack of my own making, I managed to touch my rucksack with my toes. I leaned out to glimpse my two stolen horses, grazing peacefully, a hundred yards or so down the road. Probably only fatigue and distance from home had prevented their fleeing the area. Even if I could extricate myself from the shackles, recapturing them wouldn't be easy. Was this some sort of ironic divine intervention? Zeke and Flora surrogates for the shepherd, punishing me for my thievery?

I twisted on my belly and managed to slowly drag the rucksack toward me, praying every moment for Flora to delay Zeke somehow. Finally, I had my rucksack and my pistol.

I was still manacled to the wheel, but I was armed. I held the barrel inches from the chain and as far from my hands as possible, turned my head to protect my eyes, and fired. And missed. The horses shied and nearly jerked my arm from my shoulder. A second shot parted the chain. I was free, though I still had a cuff on my wrist.

I knew the shots would draw Zeke, but I hoped to gather my mounts and be gone before he returned. The horses would shy from a man on foot, but not normally from a team and wagon. I shoved the pistol in my waistband, resheathed my knife, grabbed the reins and jumped to the box, ready to guide the team to my wayward pair of horses. Then I saw Zeke trotting my way, rifle at ready.

I jumped back to the ground. I had only two bullets remaining, and no time to shove in any of the five shells I'd pulled from Flora's gun. I crouched behind the wagon and waited. Zeke stopped a few yards away, dismounted, and approached the team. He stood with his back to the horses and sidestepped around them, using them as a shield. He soon came in view of the wheel to which I'd been cuffed. In the meantime, I'd circled behind the horses and approached him from the rear.

"The rifle, sheriff. Drop it, please." His shoulders drooped. Then he tossed the gun a few feet away. "The key now, sir," I said. He pulled it from his pocket and held it toward me. I reached, but he stepped away.

"Now, sheriff," I said. "I've urgent business on the far side of Sawtooth Peaks." I held out my hand. He tossed the key over his shoulder and behind him a few feet. To retrieve it would require shooting and stepping over him or circling behind him. I circled. He followed.

"My wife gets some crazy notions sometimes," he said. "Sorry you got caught in the middle." I said nothing, kept edging toward the key.

"Still and all, it does strike me a bit strange that a young feller like you—moccasins instead of boots, all swole up, dirty as a hog in a waller— would be traipsing around the country with two horses that ain't equipped with so much as a proper hackamore."

I finally located the key, inserted it in the lock, dropped both cuff and key on the ground.

"Please climb on the wagon with those reins in your hand," I said. He slowly walked to the wagon box. I followed.

"I can't leave Flora alone and I can't take her to town with me to check the wanted bulletins, so I can't fuss with you whatever you done, so you're wasting your precious time holding that gun on me."

"Simply drive slowly down the road," I said. "I'll collect my horses."

"Your horses," he said, snorted, and clucked the team into motion. The team plodded. The horses continued grazing peacefully. We soon pulled opposite them.

"Ease over, sheriff," I said. I directed Zeke to pull close to the black, the leader of the two. I reached out slowly to grasp his lead, but he whipped it aside and trotted a few steps away, stood eyeing us. My attempt at the bay ended the same way. The western hills were in shade, and a twilight haze rose from the fields of the little valley. Zeke's mount stood patiently where he'd dropped its reins near the wagon's previous location.

"Call your horse, sheriff."

"That's the only saddle mount on my place, boy, and he ain't much."

"I'll return him."

"I ain't gonna do it, and you ain't gonna shoot me, neither."

"I suppose you've known that from the beginning. And I'd be loath to shoot one of your team, but I'd do so if necessary."

"We need them horses to survive."

I kept an eye on him while I pointed the pistol toward the left-hand draft horse.

"He won't come. Have to go get him."

"Any horse trained to ground hitch is trained to come when he's called." My statement was not necessarily true, but I thought Zeke a man who'd take pride in a thoroughly-trained mount. We remained at stalemate for some time. The longer he leveled his eyes on me, the more determined I grew to pull the trigger if necessary. He finally whistled sharply between his teeth. The horse walked to the wagon, and I climbed into the saddle.

"Two horses for one, Zeke. You've made a profit."

"Them horses ain't no more mine than they are yours."

"I'll balance our books one day soon, sheriff. That's a promise." I was leaving a number of unsettled accounts in my wake. I hoped I'd live to clear them. "You can get on home to your wife now."

I pushed my new horse to a canter and headed toward the peaks, now swallowed by the night. How far away were they? A day's ride? Two? Only twenty-four hours remained until Yellow Squirrel's deadline, and I must cover the distance on a single horse.

AUGUST 13

CHAPTER FIFTY-NINE

I returned to the dark side-trails, climbing out of one valley, dropping into the next like a ship sliding up and down the waves of a moonlit sea. I normally loved riding these forests, but the scents of cedar and pine, the sight of a gently sailing owl, the splash of a brook did not seem attractions, but obstructions. None of them were Circle M trees, birds, waters.

Zeke had told the truth about his horse. The animal tired easily, demanded frequent rests and a great deal of water. Finally, well before sunrise, he stopped entirely partway up a steep switchback. I dismounted and led him to the top of the ridge, but when he saw the pitch of the descending trail he refused to move. I couldn't stay with him, but I didn't wish to leave him as prey for cougars. I watered him, stripped his saddle, and walked on in my thinning moccasins. Perhaps he'd follow, perhaps he'd return home. I hoped he'd survive.

The warmth of dawn presaged a hot day, even in the high altitudes I was traveling. I saw the Peaks only when I topped the highest hills, and they seemed no closer than they had the evening before.

I'd fastened on the notion that Yellow Squirrel would attack tonight, but I realized nothing prevented him from a daytime raid. He might wait for me, but perhaps he'd discarded his fantasy of arranging a Maxwell gathering for some gruesome finale. I prayed that he hadn't returned to Owl Feather's camp for Grandmother, somehow ferried her back to the Circle M. I prayed that my apprehensions about Mother's ignoring the threat were unfounded. I prayed for the right order of everything beyond my control.

About noon, my burning feet forced me to a cooling stream. I waded up a small creek for a ways without removing my tattered footwear, cooling the blisters and cuts, but the brook soon diminished to a rivulet and disappeared in a rocky hillside. I rinsed my face, less swollen, but still sore and sticky with oozing welts. I unwrapped the oilskin and slicker from the diaries and cut sections from them to insert in the soles of the moccasins. I hurried on. "Hurry" being a bit of hyperbole.

* * *

A gauzy full moon appeared while the western sky was still full of sunshine, and I was still well south of home. Though I could see all three peaks now, I'd never approached the Circle M from this direction.

I cursed the bad fortune that had stripped me of money, horses, weapons, that had abandoned me in the wilderness. But was it fortune? "The fault is not in our stars" was a mere shibboleth. I had not brought this on myself any more than Julian had invited Yellow Squirrel's knife into his belly. But had my insistent drive for the truth beneath the truth only spawned more violence and death? Perhaps Mother had been right after all to conceal it all in her trunk.

The sun set. The moon rose, plump and ripe. I clawed and scrabbled my way along game trails, along no trails at all. Strength flagging. I'd begun to believe I'd see sunrise before I saw the ranch when I stumbled into the first sign that I was near home—the familiar shaft of an abandoned gold mine. Looking back down my trail, I noticed a huge fallen pine where Julian and I had dodged and jumped and laughed, a knoll where a colony of ground squirrels lived. I'd passed them all in the dark without recognizing them. A mile or so farther on, I reached Cedar Spring, a Circle M overlook beside a granite-lined pool named for the fragrant trees that surrounded it. I'd finally arrived.

* * *

The ranch appeared peaceful. The moon created a chiaroscuro much in the spirit of the picture Virginia had sketched on the porch. The extra guards were still on duty. The buildings were standing, secure. I saw no signs of violence—imminent or recent. But knowing how Yellow Squirrel loved ambushes, I wasn't satisfied all was well.

I loaded Flora's bullets into Jones' pistol, unwrapped my feet, laid the rucksack aside, and approached the yard. Tom swept the area with his lantern, careful to scan the roof. I decided to investigate farther, took an uphill route above the wells and the ranch yard, vigilant for any indication of intruders. I circled wide around the yard, kept clear of the buildings and the watchmen, found nothing. It occurred to me what a fine tactic it would be for Yellow Squirrel to hold hostages inside the darkened house, ready to entrap me when I entered.

I crouched behind the bunkhouse, planned a route to the back of the house, made ready to sprint to the corral and thence to the ditch I had taken earlier to reach the office. The watchman turned his back and started toward the opposite end of his area. When I tensed to run, two shadows emerged from behind the four-hole outhouse at the rear of the bunkhouse and stepped in front of me.

"Ah, Mr. Maxwell," whispered One Ear. "Mr. Hung said we would find you here when the moon was full."

CHAPTER SIXTY

One-Ear stuck a pistol in my stomach, while he snatched my own weapon and stuffed into his waistband. He backed me out of sight behind the bunkhouse while Skull Cap stepped behind me and jabbed a knifepoint to my spine.

"You will cause no alarm," Skull Cap said.

"Mr. Ulysses, Mr. Hector," I whispered. "I apologize for that little trick I played on you in Berkeley. But I'm in a much better position to pay now."

"You will deliver us one thousand dollars. Then we will deliver you to Mr. Hung," One-Ear said. The knife-point pulled away from my skin, but a loop of twine encircled my wrist, tightened, and pulled my arm behind me.

"The debt was only five hundred," I said. The dagger jabbed again.

"You dishonored us," One-Ear said. "And there has been interest."

The dagger pulled away, and the little man pulled my other arm behind me and began wrapping it.

"Didn't my mother take care of—?"

Skull-Cap poked his knife through my shirt and moved it across my skin, raising a thin pain. Blood dribbled warmly down my back. He lifted the pistol from my belt, the knife from its sheath. I couldn't see what he did with them. "You will take us to the money," he said.

There was seldom that much cash on the ranch, and the only place it might be was in the safe. Getting to that depended on finding the office open and the combination unchanged.

I thought to feign cooperation, then put some distance between me and my captors so I could raise an uproar. "Follow me," I said.

I stooped low and dashed toward the corral, nearly fell on my face with my hands tied behind me, but they stayed on me like yellow jackets on a steak.

We reached the back door without being discovered, but found it locked. We'd never locked the doors before. Was Yellow Squirrel inside? No, he'd want us to come right in.

I crept to the window that opened above office desk, my captors following as if we were choreographed. I signaled with my head for them to open the window. One-Ear pushed up without success. I crooked and jabbed my elbow toward the window to indicate they could break the glass and reach the latch, but they shook their heads in the negative without even consulting each other. I shrugged. I understood they feared the noise, but I had no other suggestions. One-Ear shoved the gun in my ear. I shrugged again. He cocked the hammer.

Once again, fear spawned creativity. I twisted my bound hands far enough to point to the empty knife sheath at my side, made prying motions with my hand, pointed with my head to the window. He didn't understand my charade until I'd tried it twice more and waggled my fingers in a "gimme" motion.

One-Ear motioned to Skull-Cap who cut the twine and handed over my knife slowly and with angry looks at his partner. They both crowded around me, nudged me with their weapons as I stepped up on a foundation pier and lifted the knife to a window pane whose putty was chipped and cracked. I scraped and pried until the glass tipped into my hand. I'd planned to smash the glass, slash out with the knife, break for the kitchen door, and create enough noise and confusion to escape and bring the guards running. But I lost my balance and dropped to the ground. I landed on my feet, stumbled backward. The glass slipped to the dirt without breaking and without making any noise. One-Ear jammed a knee my back and propelled me toward the house while Skull-Cap wrested the knife away.

One-Ear toed the unbroken glass aside and motioned me toward the window with his gun. I climbed back up, released the latch, and raised the window. I began to lift my leg into the room, but Skull-Cap poked me with the stiletto and waved me back. One-Ear climbed in first, then beckoned for me to follow. With him and his pistol in front and Skull-Cap behind with his stiletto, I had little opportunity for another maneuver. One-Ear waved his gun toward the safe.

"I need light," I said in a low voice. He clamped his hand over my mouth. I bit his finger. He jerked his hand back and whacked my temple with his gun. I spun, nearly fell, leaned against the safe with my brain foggy. He yanked my head back by the hair while Skull-Cap shoved a handkerchief in my mouth, then followed by tying a bandanna to keep the gag in my teeth. One-Ear pushed me to the desk where he pointed with his gun toward the lamp. I sat on the edge of the desk, still groggy, indicated I needed something with which to ignite the lamp, then pointed toward the living room where I knew matches lay by the fireplace. I stepped toward the office door, but Skull-Cap jumped in front of me. One-Ear pointed to the desk. I shook my head. He pointed again.

I rummaged through the drawers until I found a stray match buried under a blotter and a number of pen nibs. Its head was chipped and nothing was available for a striker. I slid the match across the back of my thigh. Nothing. I attempted it again, pressing hard with my index finger to increase the friction. It flared, sputtered. I cupped a hand to shield it and motioned to Skull-Cap to lift the lamp chimney. He hesitated to do anything but hold his knife to my back, but when I grunted and showed him the diminishing match, he relented. I carefully applied the flame to the wick until it caught and a dim glow spread through the room. I thought to elbow the chimney from Skull-Cap's hand when he moved to replace it, but he waited until I was well clear before he did so. These two had grown much smarter or much more careful since I'd eluded them in Berkeley.

One-Ear pointed to the safe with his free hand. I recalled only a sketchy notion of the combination. I looked to the bookshelf for the volume on Circle M landmarks, but it was gone. Once again I shrugged my shoulders and spread my palms at my sides. They raised their weapons. I stepped to the safe, tugged at the handle, turned the dial, pointed at my head and shook it. They weren't about to accept my explanation. Fragments of the combination returned to me, but the sequence? I thought perhaps working with the dial, would restore them. I knelt and began twisting.

I felt somewhat certain of the numbers themselves—65, 18, 87—or was it 78—19? My experimenting on the night Mother discovered me had carried me through too many variations on the direction and number of the right-left, left-right turns. My captors grew more impatient, shifting and grunting behind me. The more noise they made, the more flustered I became. I'd just tugged the unyielding handle for the third or fourth time when a voice broke the silence.

"Well, Big Brother, you're finally here. I was beginning to think I'd have to burn down the house without you."

CHAPTER SIXTY-ONE

Yellow Squirrel held a pistol in each hand. "Lay those weapons on the floor," he said to the Chinese. "Uh-uh. Slowly," he added when Skull-Cap bent his knees in obvious preparation to spring. "You stay down, Maxwell, till I tell you otherwise." Once all the weapons lay on the floor, Yellow Squirrel instructed us to slide them across the floor with our feet, then had us lie face down. I heard him shuffling about, raised my head to see what he was doing only to have it slammed back to the boards.

Soon, Yellow Squirrel toed me in the ribs and motioned that I should rise. He'd tied and gagged both Chinese with their belts and sashes and anchored them to furniture.

"Take off your belt," he said. "Ain't much of your pants left to hold up anyhow. I did as he ordered and winced as he cinched my hands behind me. "Looks like you had a rough trip, Big Brother. Too bad I need to keep you gagged. I'd like to know what you're doing with a pair of my moccasins." I wondered if Many Clouds had appreciated the irony when she'd given me her uncle's footwear.

He pulled me outside. The moonlight cast ghostly caricatures of the ranch's buildings and fences, like a scene from Poe or Irving. Yellow Squirrel, still limping from the knife wounds, guided me with one hand, clutching a handful of my shirt back, behind the corn rows to the place behind the bunk house where One-Ear and Skull-Cap had accosted me.

"Sit down," he said. "Back to the wall." I hesitated, and he kicked me behind the knees, forced me to drop. "Back to the wall," he repeated. Like the house, the bunkhouse was built by Grandfather's design on a foundation of stone piers. Yellow Squirrel used Skull-Cap's twine to secure me to one of them, then to tie my ankles. "I'll be back shortly," he said. And he disappeared. Round one to the squirrel, but he'd made a mistake by not going for the knockout immediately.

In contrast to the solid log construction of the house, the bunkhouse was a bat-and-board affair. The building's main planks were two feet wide, and the pier to which I was tied was midway between a pair of the one-by-two's that covered the seams between planks. I rotated and leaned my head, planning to hook the back of the bandanna gag below one of the battens and pull the gag down. I came within a couple of inches, lunged once more, then smelled the smoke. I doubled my efforts. Shouts rose in the yard. I still hadn't shed the gag when Yellow Squirrel appeared beside me. He carried a rifle now.

"It's almost finished, Big Brother," he said. "Just like I promised. I want you to see this." He pulled Shelby's knife from his belt, where he had sheathed it after confiscating it from Skull-Cap. He cut the bonds to the bunkhouse pier, leaving my wrists bound, placed the knife in his belt behind his hip, and dragged me just clear of the building. A glow rose from behind the house. Men rushed toward it, some of them with buckets. Yellow Squirrel knelt a few feet from me, his rifle poised.

"Your grandfather was first, Big Brother, and you'll be the last." I yelled my surprise as loudly as I could from behind my gag. "That bull didn't get loose by accident." He grinned at the memory. "It was me. And Standing Oak. Then our old man went soft, then even Standing Oak did too. Now I have to finish it myself. I'm off to a good start, don't you think?"

Amazement at the Indian's revelation pushed aside even my dread of the immediate perils. I thought I'd plumbed the Maxwell history. Yellow Squirrel spoke again. His eyes were fixed on the house.

"You will be last, Big Brother, but before you die, you'll watch. When your ma comes out that door I'll do to her exactly what I did to your father." I don't know what noise or move I made at the words, "your father," but whatever I did turned Yellow Squirrel my way. "You didn't know that nigger was your pa? Well, good. I'd hate to have you go to your grave living a lie."

I at first refused to accept Yellow Squirrel's words, then vivid images rose in my mind—the tears in Shelby's eyes when he left to find his sister, the moment when Amelia gave me his medal, Mother's words on the day Shelby departed on his quest for Amelia. *You couldn't have done better than Shelby,* and my mind whirled out of time and space.

Shelby's pet name for me—mon fils. My son—had been the literal truth. Mother had found love in her loneliness during Father's… during Andrew Stover's… absences. The roving husband had returned long enough to father Julian, then disappeared altogether. Was it discovering the affair that had driven him away forever? I'd thought Grandmother's dementia was the secret Mother could not bear to disclose. But she'd hidden another, one even more painful. She'd taken a black lover, borne a mixed breed child. Illegal, disgraceful, unforgivable acts. And yet, I felt not ashamed, but proud. I'd still find a way to make Shelby proud as well.

Yellow Squirrel turned back to the house and continued. "Father never did appreciate how me and Standing Oak sent that bull your Grandfather's way as a special gift to pay him back for my grandmother. In fact I'm the only one left who really does appreciate it. Well, well, here comes the lady of the hour now, Big Brother."

Mother fled the fire, out the front door, down the steps. He shouldered and sighted his rifle. Gagged though I was, I did my best to yell, at the same time, rolled and bounced my rear into Yellow Squirrel's back just as he fired. I heard the shot, but saw nothing of what followed, being far too occupied with Yellow Squirrel. I'd knocked him flat on his face and now lay back-to-back on top of him. He began heaving like a dozen bronks, and I knew his next bullet was mine if he tossed me off his back.

I managed to grab his belt with one hand and grip the handle of my knife with the other. I drew the knife, but couldn't stab properly, so I twisted and jabbed the blade in every direction I could, much the way I'd done against him in that mountain meadow. Here, my movement even more limited, I couldn't hurt him much, but the pain and surprise were enough to roll him over as he tried to dislodge me.

I continued to work the knife into his backside, but he soon managed to free a pistol, curl his wrist behind him, and point it my way. I released his belt, but kept my grip on the knife. The sudden release caused him to launch himself away from me and his shot plowed into the dirt. I kept hold of the knife. I snaked my way under the elevated bunkhouse until I lay in the shadows. It was a close fit, but roomier than under the rail car. I sawed frantically at the leather strap binding my hands, thanking Shelby—my father—It was both thrilling and discomfiting to think of him that way—for instilling my habit of keeping the blade sharp.

Yellow Squirrel lost track of me for the moment. I saw his feet tramping back and forth in confusion near the far wall of the bunkhouse, heard him calling softly, fiercely, "Where did you go, you Maxwell son of a bitch?"

I worked my hands free, tore off the gag, made short work of the twine binding my ankles, and began crawling toward Yellow Squirrel at the same moment he threw himself on his belly and aimed his pistol at my face. I rolled behind a pier just before the flash and explosion. A bullet slashed the floorboards above me.

"Your mother's gone now, Maxwell. So's your grandfather. Grandmother, too. You're the only one left. Might as well give it up."

I uttered a moan of pain, then rolled to the next pier.

"See? Almost over. Let's finish it off."

"Can't move," I groaned. Then I coughed.

"Never mind. I'll come get you," he said. He began to elbow his way toward where I'd lain when I first moaned. The closer he crawled the deeper the darkness. I could distinguish only light patches, disembodied and scattered, from his face, hands and pistol.

"Give me another whimper, Maxwell," he said. "Let me put you out of your misery." I said nothing, held still, kept my hands under me and my face turned away to avoid reflecting light. Voices approached the bunkhouse.

"I swear the shots came from around here."

"Look how this area's dug up."

He wouldn't use the pistol with men so close unless it was necessary. Perhaps he'd acquired Skull-Cap's stiletto, perhaps carried a knife of his own, perhaps planned to use my own to finish me silently. He inched forward so carefully I thought he'd become too fearful of the crowd milling around the bunkhouse to continue. But he maintained his sporadic crawl until his gun hand finally came in range.

I drove the blade into his forearm with all the strength and leverage I could muster. It glanced off bone, then slipped through flesh and stabbed into the earth. Yellow Squirrel roared like Bahnhof's wounded cougar. I released the knife, dived after the pistol. When I leveled the gun at him, I found him staring at the knife that hung from his skewered arm.

"Arms and face in the dirt, you vicious bastard," I said, "or I'll be the last sight you behold on this earth."

CHAPTER SIXTY-TWO

Yellow Squirrel obeyed. I resisted the temptation to remove the knife from his arm. The man was still too dangerous to touch.

"Under the bunkhouse," I called to the men in the yard. "Bring a rope." Two men knelt and peered at us. One of them I recognized as the watchman, Tom, who had caught me jumping from the roof.

"Who is that?" he said.

"It's Andy. I have our killer here."

Tom moved fast. Within a minute we'd thrown a loop around Yellow Squirrel's feet and dragged him into the yard. A dozen men had formed a bucket brigade between Granite Creek and the rear of the house. I took heart to see no flames leaping from the roof or the front of the house.

"Tie him to a fencepost and assign a man—no, two men—to guard him," I said.

"What about his wrist?"

"What about Mother?" The men looked at each other, shifted their feet. Their eyes wandered to a cluster of people near the front porch. No one said a word. "Ah, no," I said.

I found her lying unconscious, seemingly lifeless, on her side in the dust. Her hair fanned around her head, and a dark stain spread under the side of her nightgown. Part of the gown had been cut away, and a bloodstained patch covered a portion of her bare midriff. Hale Gentry, the blond saloonkeeper, and Ling Chu knelt beside her. What Gentry was doing here in the middle of the night was a mystery, especially dressed for combat as he was in leather and conches, a brace of pearl-handled revolvers at his hips. Ling had raised a knife. Gentry had grabbed the cook's wrist. Two hired hands stood leaning forward as if they wished to intervene, but they held back.

"You're not going to try any of your black arts on this lady, you damned heathen," Gentry said. "We'll wait for a real doctor."

"Be too late," Ling Chu said.

"I'll take Ling Chu over a hundred white doctors," I said. "What should we do, Ling?" Two faces turned to me—Asian, Caucasian—pallid echoes of the hovering moon.

"Mr. Andrew," Ling Chu said. "It is truly your voice under the beard."

"Andy," Gentry said, "You look the wild man of the mountains. And your brain's been addled if you're talking about letting this chink anywhere near Carrie."

I concentrated on Mother, ignored Gentry. "Ling?" I said.

"Take her to bunkhouse. Boil water. Make bandages. I get tools from kitchen."

I placed a hand on his shoulder. "It's burning."

"Maybe not so bad." He tore his hand from Gentry's and began running.

I knelt by her side and scooped my arms under her knees and shoulders. "Please support her head, Gentry," I said. I looked at the other two men, still standing by, hands alternately on hips and in their pockets. "You two light a fire in the bunkhouse stove and find something to boil water in." They rushed off, apparently glad to have a job. I lifted mother and hurried toward the bunkhouse. Gentry scrambled along awkwardly, hands under her lifeless head.

"I'm telling you, Andy, this is a big mistake."

"Please keep her head up," I said. I tipped my cheek toward her lips, tried to feel her breath amid the jostling.

Gentry said, "If anything happens to her because of this—"

"It will be neither your fault nor your affair, sir," I said. I turned sideways at the bottom of the bunkhouse steps, allowed Gentry to back in the narrow door first with Mother's head cupped in his hands. Her hair spilled over them, blended into the black of his shirt so the head appeared to be floating. I felt blood soaking through my trousers, and when we laid her in a bunk, the sheet stained an instant red. The two ranchhands had ignited a lamp and were shoving kindling into the potbellied stove.

"Hand me your knife, please, Gentry," I said. He gave me a silver-handled dagger, sharp at the point, but not particularly keen on the edge. I began chopping and ripping at the hem of Mother's nightgown.

"You can't undress her here," Gentry said.

"You'd rather she die for the sake of modesty?"

After a pause, Gentry said, "Use my shirt." He removed vest and shirt, threw me the shirt, donned the studded leather vest. His furry belly swelled through the lapels and hung over his silver belt buckle. I thanked him and began tearing the shirt into rags.

"Gentry, there were two Chinese gentlemen—thugs, is a better word—bound in the office just before the fire began. I hope they're not dead, and I hope they haven't escaped. Would you go see, please? If they're alive, ensure they're kept tied and under surveillance." He grunted a reply and strode out, hands on his pistol butts. I turned to my doctoring.

There was a dime-sized hole in Mother's side just below the ribs. About the same place as Standing Oak's wound. Yellow Squirrel was at least consistent. I tipped her gently and found a much larger exit wound had ripped her back at a point slightly higher. I tried to remember Grandmother's medical work with Standing Oak, put out of my mind Yellow Squirrel's statement that the older woman was dead, packed both sides of the wound with cloth. My efforts staunched the bleeding somewhat, but I was unsure how long it would hold, even maintaining pressure with both hands.

The rise and fall of her chest was irregular, nearly imperceptible, and she was deeply unconscious. I fought nausea and tears to see her face, slack and pale as a melted candle.

Ling Chu scurried in, coughing and sooty. Bags and bottles filled his arms. He stood by Mother's bed, gazed at her, shook his head. A pan of water on the stove hadn't yet approached boiling temperature. Ling Chu laid his supplies on a neighboring bunk and gestured to the two men who had lighted the stove.

"Go now. Help save house. We're plenty okay here." The two looked to me. I nodded, and they hurried outside.

"What next, Ling?" I said.

"More fire," he said. There was a plentiful stack of stove wood against the wall, and I threw in as much as the stove would hold. Ling began tossing ingredients into the water even though it hadn't begun boiling. "Cloth," he said.

I continued ripping Gentry's shirt into strips. Ling recognized the garment, grunted and shook his head. I thought he smiled, but I couldn't swear it. We followed much the same procedure Grandmother and I had used for Standing Oak, he throwing herbs in the water, me soaking the bandages, he applying herbs and bandages to the wound. Ling also employed a needle and thread. I watched with admiration as he closed the holes in Mother's side stitch by painstaking stitch. I regretted he hadn't been available to help with Many Clouds' mother.

"Couldn't find everything in house," he said. "Too hot and smoky. But I hope enough. Found needles at least. And these." He tossed me a new pair of moccasins. He carefully traced his way to several points where he inserted the magic instruments that had saved me so much pain.

Unlike Standing Oak, Mother didn't recover even a groggy consciousness while we were working. When we finished, we covered her with a triple thickness of blankets, and stood examining her wan face.

"I hope so," he said. "She is a tough lady. But I hope so." I reached over and shook his hand.

"Thank you, Ling. Whatever happens. Thank you."

Then I did something I hadn't intended. I didn't understand then, and I don't quite understand to this day. I knelt, took one of Mother's hands from under the blankets, and pressed it to my forehead. My mind and heart seemed empty at that moment. I don't remember praying or thinking of anything at all, which I know is impossible, or I wouldn't remember it so well. At any rate, Hale Gentry's voice splintered my meditation.

"Well, we got us a real doc now. Carrie'll be okay if that hamhanded cook didn't kill her already."

Doctor Robinson removed his derby, stretched on tiptoes to set it on the bunk above Mother, threw me a swarthy nod, ignored Ling, set his black bag on the floor, and lifted the blankets.

"What the hell are all those spikes sticking out all over her?" he said. He reached out to seize one of Ling's needles. I pulled his arm back.

"We'll leave those until Ling Chu gives further direction."

"Are you insane? They're nothing but superstition, those things."

"They'll stay," I said. He stared into my eyes a few seconds, then lowered his gaze.

"Well, I must certainly remove these bandages to see the damage."

I glanced at Ling, who lowered his eyes. "You'll need to leave them where they are until Ling consents."

"This is your mother, Maxwell. There could be organ damage, internal bleeding."

"Later," Ling said. "Not now."

"Infection could set in. Once that happens—"

"When Ling agrees, I'll welcome your help, Dr. Robinson."

"I won't be responsible," Robinson said.

"There's a prisoner out there who could benefit from your skills," I said. "And my Chinese friends, Gentry? Are they in need of medical attention?"

"They were choking on the smoke, but nothing fatal. Tied them up in the barn." I nodded to Robinson, who grabbed his hat and strode out the door swinging his bag like a weapon.

Gentry stepped toward me, removed his hat, hugged it to his bulging waist with both hands. His belligerence had disappeared for the moment.

"Look, Andrew, I know you're devoted to that Oriental cook, but you're only a boy in spite of your new beard. This situation calls for a man in charge." I began to protest. He held up his hand. "I know you love your mother, but I love her, too—" I tipped my head forward until our brows nearly touched.

"You love her too?"

He shifted his eyes from me to Mother. "And she feels the same way. Oh, she has her reasons for not allowing her feelings to show—the ranch, family, reputation, the business I'm in. But she'll come around eventually. No one can stop what's meant to be." I realized he'd delivered this speech before—over and over perhaps—to her, to himself. I laid my hand on his arm, swallowed an angry and sarcastic reply.

"Ling is a skilled healer, Gentry. And until Mother says nay, the Circle M is an all-Maxwell operation. I hope you understand." He tensed, but I acted as if the argument were settled and knelt once more beside Mother. Her breathing seemed more regular, if still shallow. I looked to Gentry. "Would you remain with her for a time, Mr. Gentry? Ling and I should see to some matters outside."

"I… " He seemed about to object.

"If you don't feel comfortable…"

"No, that's fine."

"Good. Notify me if you see any change. And Robinson is not allowed near her until I grant permission. Ling, please come with me."

CHAPTER SIXTY-THREE

As we emerged from the bunkhouse, dawn was lifting the curtain on a bustling ranch yard. Word of the fire and shooting had spread through the valley. Wagons and horses rattled over the bridge, and a plank-and-barrel table already held a feast of hams and roasts and casseroles. Presiding over the table in an old-fashioned dress with long skirt and high collar was Shelby's sister, Amelia. My Aunt Amelia. Did she know we were relatives? Probably so, but this wasn't the time.

"How is she, Andy?" I looked down to a small group gathered at the foot of the bunkhouse steps. The question came from Bridget Jensen, Julian's flame. Julian had been right. She'd transformed from shapeless and plain to lush and striking in the years since I'd seen her. Her mother stood anxiously behind her. Why would they be so concerned about Mother, the woman who had blocked the romance between Bridget and Julian?

"She's resting peacefully, but—" I stopped to breathe—"still in danger." I began to explain details, but found myself unable to speak.

"What can we do?" Bridget's mother said.

"Nothing right now."

"What about you? Your face looks like someone boiled your skin."

"I'm fine, Mrs. Jensen. If you'll excuse me—"

"It's just that Mrs. Maxwell has done so much for us," she continued. "We'd have lost the café after Horace died. However we can help… "

"Thank you," I said. "I'll let you know." I hurried down the steps toward the house and, working my way through a burgeoning crowd, I heard repeated expressions of Mrs. Jensen's sentiments—the grave concern, the offers of help, testimonials of gratitude, and an eagerness to somehow repay Mother's kindness. I heard tales of ruined crops replenished, burned houses rebuilt, medical bills paid. She'd built a mountain of good will of which I'd been unaware—or perhaps had discounted in my youthful resolve to disdain her.

"Mr. Andy." Ling's voice and his tap on my shoulder gave me an excuse to break away from the pressing throng. "I must enter my kitchen," he said. "Nourishment for Mrs. Maxwell."

"Go ahead. And I must look to my prisoners," I said. I turned back to the surrounding faces. "Thank you for coming, everyone. I'll return soon." I headed toward the barn.

* * *

Tom had chained and harnessed Yellow Squirrel, Skull Cap, and One-Ear hand and foot to the mangers of separate stalls, an armed guard posted at each one. Maintenance had grown lax during the crisis, so I was glad to see the prisoners had plenty of muck to sit in. Yellow Squirrel's smirk had disappeared, but he set his jaw and narrowed his eyes when he saw me.

"He's a tough one," Tom said.

I nodded and squatted next to Yellow Squirrel. "The full moon's come and gone, Michael Yellow Squirrel, and I'm still on my feet."

"That whole 'Frisco jail couldn't hold me," he said. "And you can't either." I was looking down at him, hovering, it seemed, like a hawk poised to dive on a mouse. Owl Feather's parable came to mind.

"I was wrong," I said. "You're the eagle."

"Eagle?" His voice lost resonance, sounded nearly petulant. He cast his eyes at the ground. He knew what I was about to say.

"Owl Feather's vision. I'm the rabbit, or the Maxwells are. The rabbit that turned into a wolf. You're the renegade eagle who endangered your whole family with your bloodthirsty plot. They needn't worry. You're the only one I'm out to destroy."

Yellow Squirrel's air of vulnerability was short-lived. He recovered his glare, his eyes became gleaming obsidian chips. "You're not safe yet, Maxwell."

"How's your arm?" I said. He frowned at the bandage Dr. Robinson had wrapped around his wound, then back at me. Said nothing. "How about your rear?" He turned his eyes away.

"That reminds me," said Tom. "Here." He handed me Shelby's knife, which I had last seen sticking through Yellow Squirrel's forearm. I waved the blade in front of the Indian's face.

"Pray, if you know how, that my mother doesn't die," I said, "or that arm will be the least of your worries."

"Makes me nervous having these rascals around," Tom said. "Sheriff Halstad's off to San Francisco, but we sent a telegram. He ought to return tomorrow so we can lock them up proper."

"You've done a fine job here, Tom. Thank you."

One-Ear and Skull-Cap simply glanced up at me for a moment when I looked in, then returned to a glum squat against the side of the stall. Soot smeared their skin and clothes. Skull-Cap coughed until his cheeks turned crimson under the ashes. When he finished, he became still as if nothing had happened.

I felt both exhausted and energized. For the moment I was in charge of the Circle M, and responsibilities flashed through my brain like images from a thousand magic lanterns. How long before we'd be able to inhabit the house once more? Where would the ranch hands sleep while Mother remained in the bunkhouse? How soon could we turn to gathering hay? Preparing for roundup? Was there time for either or both before the weather turned? And why did I feel such anxiety about turning our prisoners over to Sheriff Halstad?

I decided to assess the fire damage, then return to the bunkhouse in hopes that Mother would have regained consciousness. I asked Tom to come with me and tramped toward the door, my eyes cast toward the ground in hopes of avoiding eye contact and conversation with anyone in the yard. My hopes for solitude dissolved in the low growl of an angry crowd. I stepped into the sunshine and lifted my eyes to see Hale Gentry holding a noose.

CHAPTER SIXTY-FOUR

The hangman's loop framed his black-and-silver vest and hairy paunch, which glistened bronze in the morning sun. Here stood a different man than the moonstruck lover I'd left in the bunkhouse a few hours earlier. Ten or fifteen men behind stood behind and beside him, a collection of upright neighbors and ne'er-do-wells, only some of whom I recognized.

"Who's with Mother, Gentry?"

"Old lady Adams, the midwife. She'll take good care of her."

"This looks somewhat like a lynching," I said.

"It's justice, Andy, is what it is."

"Lynching isn't justice, and it won't happen here on the Circle M."

A voice yelled from above. "Here it is, Mr. Gentry. Heads up." Jesse the insolent stablehand who'd refused to rent me a horse, was leaning out of the hayloft door, grinning, lowering a block-and-tackle. I didn't recall seeing him smile before. The hook dropped to just above my head, and I grabbed it.

"Take it back up, Jesse," I said.

Gentry held up his hand. "Leave it, Jesse." The hook stopped moving. I held it. Gentry went on.

"Look, Andy, this isn't just you or the Circle M, you know. This is the whole valley. These men and their families have a right to be safe."

Harry Hoskins, who owned the general store in Sawtooth Wells, called out. "We can't have all these Chinamen and redskins and niggers running around burning things down and killing decent folks."

"Take care with your language," I said.

"The truth is the truth, Andy. Don't stand in our way, now." Abe Nelson had the nearest place to the Circle M. He favored pigs and goats over cattle and did well with them.

"Let's consider what you're proposing, Gentry," I said. I decided to speak directly to him, hoping I'd have better odds of success negotiating with one man than with a mob. "No one's in danger. The perpetrators are chained, under twenty-four hour armed guard, and Sheriff Halstad will arrive tomorrow."

"They've got to pay, Andy. Besides this ain't your ranch. Not yet." So Gentry was fomenting the notion that I was attempting to seize the Circle M. He'd likely told everyone that I'd chosen Ling Chu's doctoring over Robinson's as part of my grab for power.

"And you believe this is what Mother wants?" He hesitated. "Suppose we allow her to decide."

"You know she can't."

"The doctor says she'll be out of danger soon." He hesitated again. I didn't think he believed I'd talked to Robinson, but he couldn't be certain. I pulled down the block and tackle and placed a foot on the hook. "Hoist me up a few feet, Jesse," I called. At the top of the line, Jesse looked back and forth between me and Gentry. "Only a few feet, Jesse." I motioned up. Jesse pulled. The noose in Gentry's hands swung to and fro.

I stopped Jesse when I'd risen about six feet. I peered over a crowd of thirty or forty, a mix of men, women, children. The rising sun forced me to squint. The rope swayed back and forth, began to twist. I asked Tom to hold me in place by the feet.

"Mother and I thank you with all our hearts for coming this morning," I said. "I trust she'll be able to thank you herself before long. We all want the men who did this to her, to Julian, to Shelby, to pay for their deeds. Some of you believe the way to do that is to ignore the law and lynch them." I was suddenly conscious of the special connotation the word "lynch" had for me now. I heard cheers. I'd taken the wrong tack. If the crowd warmed up to the idea, they'd become an irresistible rabble. I'd been away too long, was still a little boy to most of them. The cheers grew. Gentry waved his hand at Jesse.

"That's enough, Andy," he said.

The hook began to descend. I twisted my foot in the ropes, stopped the pulleys, managed a temporary foothold in the snarled lines, waved my hand and yelled.

"Quiet. Quiet now, friends and neighbors. Please." The noise lowered to a buzzing murmur, but I knew it might erupt again any second. All eyes were on me. "Carrie Maxwell." Her name was enough to purchase near-silence.

"Many of you owe Mother a great deal. Isn't that true?" Complete silence prevailed now. "Is that true?" The murmur this time sounded more akin to cooing than buzzing. "She's lying in that bunkhouse at this moment fighting for her life. Is mob rule what she'd want for the Circle M? For Sawtooth Wells?"

"Carrie doesn't let anybody get away with anything." It was Gentry speaking. The buzzing began anew.

"Let's ask her," I said. The buzzing died. "Simply wait until she can speak for herself. I promise these hooligans will go nowhere in the meantime. And does anyone here have more right to revenge than I do?" People began talking among themselves, and eyes were no longer on me alone.

"No waiting," yelled Gentry. He turned toward the crowd and waved the noose above his head. A few voices answered. Their bodies crowded forward.

"Those of you who don't want Mother to wake up to corpses swinging from the roofbeam," I said, "step over here with me and stop this." I beckoned with as large a sweep of my arm as I could muster. "Come on."

Bridget and her mother began the movement. A few others followed. Then Amelia. The first man was a sheep farmer with a spread close to town.

"Come forward for justice," I said. "Justice the right way."

I counted as they came. In several minutes a group of twenty-two stood between Gentry and the barn door. No more than a half-dozen backed Gentry. The rest refused to commit themselves. I sprang down from my improvised stage and stood face to face with the bare-bellied saloon owner.

"I'd appreciate it if you and your gang would leave the Circle M. Now."

He shook the noose in my face. "You can't get away with this. Carrie—"

"I'm in charge right now, Gentry." I did my utmost to keep my voice low and controlled. "And as of this moment I declare you a trespasser." We stared at one another for a few moments.

"Come on, Hale," said Hoskins. "It ain't right, but leave it alone. For now."

Gentry continued the standoff a few more seconds, then raised the noose as if to whip me.

"I'll be back sooner than you think," he said. He turned in his tracks, stomped toward the house where his horse was tied, bumped aside Hoskins and several others as he went. He rode out the gate on his white stallion alone.

"I think he's more bark than bite, Tom," I said. "But assign men outside the barn as well as near the stalls just in case."

"I was thinking the same thing, Mr. Maxwell," he said.

Mr. Maxwell. At least someone thought I was in charge.

* * *

Three sets of steps entered the house from the rear—one to the kitchen, one to the living room, and one to the billiard room. The billiard room had been one of Grandfather's few afterthoughts. Not included in the house's initial design, its interior walls were full round timbers, originally part of the exterior. Yellow Squirrel's choice of arson locations had guaranteed that a fire had a minimal chance of destroying the building. I didn't believe it was a mistake. He'd wanted to drive Mother from the house where he could shoot her down before my eyes, not cook her in the fire.

I kicked through the ashes, retrieved some of the ivory balls Julian and I had so loved to play with. It was a room Mother seldom entered, and we'd felt like grown men as we circled the table, chalking our cues, calling our shots.

The outside logs were charred, some of them nearly all the way through. The fire had burned through the door into the living room, blackened the staircase. I determined to board the door, repair the living room, decide about rebuilding the rest later. Construction would be a minor problem. I'd always been afraid of fire, but my tour through the house was an education in the ravages not of flame, but of smoke.

Stench was the first culprit. Every window, every door stood wide open, yet no one could remain in the house long without a walk outside for fresh air. Stain was the next foe. Every object, every wall was resin-crusted. Books, clothes, dishes, furniture. I began to wonder whether we would have to demolish and rebuild, even though flames had left most of it untouched.

I found Ling Chu in the kitchen, carrying dishes into the yard behind the house.

"Wash every dish. Every can. Every cupboard. Dishes, curtains, clothes. All thing. Only way."

I glanced at the sun. Halfway to noon. I needed to employ all the available help before everyone left.

"Come with me, Ling, please." I said.

Two men I didn't know stood by the front porch rail chewing on ham sandwiches. Other folks were immersed in obvious chores—slopping hogs, collecting eggs—but nearly everyone else appeared idle or involved in minor activities such as straightening dishes on the table, which was not nearly as heavily laden as earlier. I gathered Ling, Bridget, Mrs. Jensen, and Amelia on the porch.

"I'm afraid I'm wasting everybody's time here," I said. "Can you all help me?"

"Whatever you need, Mr. Andrew," said Amelia.

"Please call me Andy. We're… neighbors after all," I said.

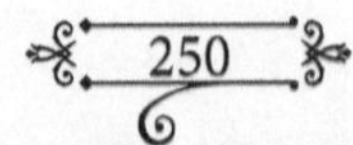

"Yes, sir," she said. I wanted to contradict her "sir" as well, but that was a conversation we'd have later.

You all heard Ling. We need to go through the house and scrub the smoke stains and smell out of everything. Ling can help show you where the cleaning equipment is. Can you do that?"

"We'll set up a lye kettle right out in the yard, Andy," said Mrs. Jensen.

"People are just chomping at the bit to help out."

"Thank you," I said. "Thank you." I thought of the trunk, the account books, the keys, the guns. I pulled Amelia and Mrs. Jensen aside. "There's much here that's confidential," I said.

"Please don't allow anyone to touch anything unless one of you approves."

I'll ask Tom to send a man up here to help keep an eye out."

"Don't worry about nothing, sir… Andy," Amelia said.

"You picked the right folks for this job," Bridget said.

"I can see that. I'm very grateful."

"Mr. Maxwell," a voice called from the yard. Tom ran toward the porch. "They said to come fetch you quick. It's your mother."

CHAPTER SIXTY-FIVE

I grabbed Ling, ran toward the bunkhouse. Mrs. Adams had propped Mother into a semi-sit and was attempting to spoon broth into her mouth. Barely conscious, she closed her lips and turned her chin aside. Then she closed her eyes and sagged back into the pillows. Adams turned toward me and shook her head.

"Too soon. Surprised she's awake so soon, but thought we should call you."

It frightened me more to see her half-conscious and weak than it had to see her passed out.

"Excuse me," Ling Chu said. Adams stepped back, looked at me, wrinkled her forehead in a question. I nodded reassurance, mouthed a 'thank you.'

Ling uncovered the wound. Mother's entire abdomen was swollen and bruised. The bandages were soaked with bloody discharge, It had been only a few hours, but I was glad to detect no odor of infection.

"We'll change now," Ling said. Mother gasped and moaned several times as he probed and dabbed and rolled her aside to care for the exit wounds. The stove was hot, and Ling rebound the wounds in much less time than it had taken to cover them originally. By the time we finished, she was sweating and pale.

"How is she, Ling?" I said.

"No fever. I'll return soon." He ran out the door.

"I didn't know what to think at first, needles sticking out all over her like she's a pine tree," Mrs. Adams said. "But I seen plenty of sawbones in my time, and that old Chinaman's a pretty good hand, I'd say. I'll go see if I can help him," she said. And she left.

I sat and took Mother's hand. It was cool and moist. I felt compelled to talk to her whether she could hear me or not.

"I'm sorry, Mother. I should have prevented all this… somehow. I…" She turned her head an inch, moved her lips, sighed.

"Mother," she said. Her energy drained like air from a balloon, head drooped. Her voice was faint, eyes closed. "Mother," she repeated. I drew a sharp breath.

She said, "Are you there, Mother?"

"I'm here, Mother," I said.

"Shelby," she said. "Thank God. We must find my mother." I leaned forward.

"Shelby's not here, Mother. It's me, Andy."

"Andy?"

"It's all right, Mother. I saw Grandmother. She was fine." Her eyelids trembled, opened a little.

"Andy?"

"Yes. I'm here."

"What did you say?"

"Grandmother is fine."

She peered at me for a moment. Touched my beard. "It is you." I nodded. "So you know." Her voice was barely louder than a whisper. I nodded again. She swallowed, closed her eyes, reopened them wide. "She didn't tell you…" There was no mistaking the unspoken question that filled that next moment. I finally broke the silence.

"I know about Shelby as well, Mother. And it's fine. It is truly, truly fine."

She turned her head away. Tears seeped from her closed eyelids and trickled down her cheeks. It felt odd to see Mother so vulnerable, so in need of solace. And from me. I squeezed her hand, reached to stroke her forehead. She coughed, grabbed at her belly. I dropped from the chair to my knees.

"Shh," I said. "It's all right, Mother. Rest. Please. Get well."

Ling Chu sprang into the bunkhouse, carrying an apothecary bottle. Mrs. Adams shuffled in immediately behind him, a small bag in each hand.

"Found seeds," Ling Chu said. "Make tea."

Mother continued a soft, periodic moaning, but she'd lost consciousness again. Ling and Mrs. Adams worked as a team to help her sip the medicating tea.

"She's doing well," he said.

I shook my head. "But she's so weak."

"She's hurt bad, Andy," Mrs. Adams said. "No doubt about that. But she's better. Not many would have been conscious so soon."

I attempted a smile. "If she survives you'll deserve the credit," I said. I don't know whether Mrs. Adams hugged me or I embraced her, but I suddenly found myself in her arms. I reached behind her for Ling's hand. He was shy about taking mine, but finally did, and we shook. It was the nearest to an intimate moment I had ever shared with him.

"I'd better look to matters at the house," I said. I released them both and stepped toward the door, but Mrs. Jensen blocked my way. She carried a plate mounded with potato salad and a ham sandwich.

"Amelia said she thought you hadn't a bite to eat all day," she said. "Is that true?" I smiled and nodded. "Or a wink of sleep, either."

"I'm grateful for the nourishment, but I've no time to sleep."

"Oh, you think it's a good idea to just run around till you drop dead and you're no good to anyone, Mr. Smarty Pants?" Mrs. Adams grabbed me by the arms and guided me to a chair while she spoke. Mrs. Jensen followed with the plate, which she placed on my lap.

"You eat every bite, Andrew Maxwell."

"And then," Mrs. Adams said, "you can climb right up on that bunk above your Mother. In fact, let's take those moccasins off right now before you get any funny ideas."

"Why, it looks like someone's been at your feet with a razor," Mrs. Jensen said when I'd been unshod. "Ling Chu, come look at this. And your face needs some attention, too."

"Very well, very well," I said. "I'd rather fight Yellow Squirrel than you two."

"Darn tootin'," Mrs. Adams said. "And don't worry, Andy." She patted my head as if I were ten. "You can sleep sound. Everything's under control out there."

"I'll lie down for a short while," I said around a mouthful of ham, "but there's little chance I'll sleep."

* * *

I was digging my way out of a landslide even deeper and darker than the one Standing Oak had dumped on me. I'd used up my oxygen, panicked, gasped and gulped and clawed.

"Hey, hey, Mr. Andy. Just me. Ling Chu." I opened my eyes and saw Ling holding both my wrists. I stopped flailing my feet and relaxed to the mattress.

"Sorry," I said. "It seems I fell asleep after all. What time is it?"

"Not quite dark," he said. "Someone to see you. Said it's very important."

"How's Mother?"

"The same. Mr. Gilligan is outside."

"Feifer Gilligan? That kid Jesse's father?" Ling nodded. "What's he want?"

"Said it's very important."

I swung my legs over the bunk and put on the moccasins. There were dressings on my feet, some sort of liniment on my face. I stepped into the twilight. A fire still flickered under a black pot near the porch, and women came and went in and out of the house, dipped rags, mops, brooms into the pot. Wet clothes hung by improvised clotheslines strung from porch posts and trees, buildings, fenceposts. From the lantern-light in the house, it looked as if they planned to continue their work past sundown. I couldn't allow it. They had their own homes, animals, chores.

"Andy, good. Got to talk to you." Feifer Gilligan was a heavy man with a permanent wheeze and a bulge of tobacco in his right cheek. How he'd fathered such a scrawny son was a mystery, but perhaps Jesse would grow huge as he turned gray also. "Let's duck out of the way, over here by the corral. Don't know who all might be listening."

I spoke as I followed him. "Listening to what?"

"I heard what happened out here this afternoon. Took a lot of guts to do what you did, but you made some enemies, and it ain't over."

"What do you mean?"

"Halstad ain't coming back till tomorrow, so Gentry figures he can pull off the lynching tonight."

"How?"

"Don't know exactly. Damn near had to beat what I got out of that kid, but he can't hide nothing from the old man. All he knows is there's a bunch of them, and there's plenty enough moon to light the way. I can get some help together and between the two of us, we'll stop 'em, by God. Never did like that white-toothed huckster." He spat a brown stream into the corral mire.

"Jesse thought they'd be here around midnight. Calculated things will have slowed down here by then. They don't want no crowd to get in the way this time." Gilligan hitched his pants up, pulled a timepiece from his watch pocket, gazed at the faint halo that still tipped the peaks. "Coming up on eight right now."

The thought of leading a posse against Hale Gentry seemed exciting at first. I looked again at the activity in the ranch yard, listened to the laughing and shouts of encouragement as the group went about its work, cooperating gladly, supporting and helping a neighbor in trouble. To accept Gilligan's suggestion meant asking these people to choose sides, one against the other, with serious—perhaps deadly—consequences. Certainly there was another way. Shelby again. And Grandmother.

"If you will stay, Mr. Gilligan, I can use your help. But I don't wish to begin a war."

"You ain't starting nothing. It's Gentry."

"Mr. Gilligan—"

"Feifer's my name. Fife."

I moved alongside him, reached up to grasp his shoulder. "Perhaps you'd walk up to the barn, tell Tom I asked you to help guard the prisoners, but don't say anything about this lynching. Would you do that?"

"What's this other idea?"

"I'll explain soon, when all the pieces are in place."

"Whatever you say," he said.

"Fife. Thanks for alerting us." I clapped him on the shoulder and hurried back to the bunkhouse.

CHAPTER SIXTY-SIX

Ling bent over Mother. "Well?" I said.

He shrugged. "Maybe a little warm. Maybe not so good."

I stepped closer for a better look. I saw no change except new spots of blood on the bandage. "Infection?"

"Maybe. Hope not. Find Mrs. Adams. Change bandages again." He started for the door.

"We can talk while we walk, Ling." We hurried out of the bunkhouse toward the house.

"Another problem's arisen, Ling. Did you hear Mother discuss sending money to a man named Charley Hung in San Francisco?"

"Bad man." Ling stopped. "That's why Whang and Chin came here. Charley Hung never got Mr. Julian's money."

"Whang and Chin? You mean One-Ear and Skull-Cap." He looked at me, puzzled. "Those two Chinese in the barn? You talked to them? Why didn't you tell me?"

"No time. Didn't matter."

"But it does matter. If Mother sent money, where did it go?"

"She sent wire to lawyer to give to Mr. O'Neill."

"Sheriff O'Neill?"

"Yes, for Mr. Hung. I took the telegram to town for Mrs. Maxwell."

"And do you believe them—Whang and Chin—that Mr. Hung never received the money?"

"I think so. He was very mad after you escaped, but they believe he would not send them here this far if he had five hundred dollars."

"Thanks, Ling. If Mother awakes again, notify me right away."

First, Mother wouldn't talk. Now, she couldn't. My plan to avoid violence depended on retrieving cash from the safe. I was on my own to find or remember the combination.

* * *

It took several minutes to find the contents of the office under a tarpaulin beneath the office window. Someone had done a fine job of transferring everything outside without destroying its order. The ledgers were stacked neatly on boards laid down to protect them from damp earth. The lamp was even in its place atop the rolltop desk. I lit it, determined in a few minutes that the journal with the combination wasn't in the stack on the ground. I turned to the desk, looked through the drawers. Pens, nibs, string, notes, cubbyholes all seemed as they had been before the fire. In a somewhat disorderly stack of discolored envelopes and paper on the desktop, I found an envelope addressed to me in a hand nearly as ornate as my grandmother's. Virginia. Was this a farewell? I was surprised to realize I didn't particularly care if it was. It was the combination I wanted, and that wasn't here.

I stuffed the letter in my back pocket, hurried upstairs to the loft and rummaged through the infamous trunk. but with negative results.

I returned to the office, found a pencil and scrap of paper and knelt at the safe to begin systematically working through possible combinations. I remembered the order of the first two numbers and was sure I remembered the number of left-right turns between them. I was unsure of the rotation sequence, however, and without the journal it seemed trial and error was my only option. I tried one sequence. Failed. Wrote it down. Tried another. Failed once more. Wrote it down once more. I'd grasped the dial to attempt my third pattern when I heard footsteps behind me.

"I never gave no one permission to be up in here," Amelia said. "Oh, Mr. Andy. I'm sorry."

"It's perfectly all right," I said. "I'm glad you're concerned about security, but why haven't you gone home yet?"

"We ain't done yet."

"We? How many people are still here?" I longed to talk to her about Shelby, but she and everyone who remained would be in danger when Gentry attacked.

"I ain't counting, Mr. Andy. Just working. Want to see?"

I followed her into the living room. Lanterns had been set up and a few women labored with pails and rags and brushes over the floors and walls. Curtains, drapes, rugs were all gone. Amelia climbed a step-ladder and began scrubbing the top of the grandfather clock. The clock showed eight-thirty. I rapped on the wall until all the eyes turned my way.

"Please go home, ladies. You've been wonderful. More than wonderful. But you have work to do in your own houses." They looked at each other and shook their heads. It was Amelia who spoke.

"You can be the boss of the ranch, Mr. Andy, but it's for women to be the boss of the household, and you ain't one. Now you just go on about your business and let us do our work. She turned back to her tasks and so did everyone else. Apparently it was easier for Mother to make a mark in a man's world than it would be for me to displace these women from their domain. But safety was more important than a battle of the sexes. I moved close to Amelia, spoke softly.

"I'm expecting trouble—a lynch mob from town coming to hang the prisoners. Perhaps midnight. Perhaps earlier. Don't panic, but please make sure you and the others are out of the way." She nodded and continued her work without looking at me. I mumbled a thanks and returned to the office.

I failed with two more combinations. It was going to take too long to work through all the possibilities. If only Mother would regain consciousness for even a moment. Perhaps she had.

The living room was deserted. Amelia had done a quick and masterful job of clearing the decks. Doors and windows were open to continue the airing out. Outside, twenty or thirty yards of clothesline bowed under the weight of dripping garments. Clusters of furniture, books, pictures lay here and there. The fire under the wash pot had died to a glow, though someone was still stirring the laundry. I found Amelia still working with the provisions at the food table, consolidating empty pots, covering dishes that could be saved. Three of the ranch hands were digging forks into piles of chicken and salad as if this were a Sunday picnic.

I took Amelia's hand between mine, held it gently but firmly. "I'm taking charge now, Amelia, and you and Cooper and the rest must return home. I can't permit innocent people to be caught in a crossfire."

She patted my hand. "We'll just bed down in the barn." She withdrew her hands.

"That would be too dangerous. If you won't leave, come into the bunkhouse."

"Oh, but Mrs. Maxwell's in there."

"There are more than enough bunks. You won't disturb her." She looked at the ground, began to shake her head. "You may even be able to assist Ling and Mrs. Adams." She met my eyes.

"Anything I can do," she said. "I'll do."

I gave her an unplanned embrace. "I know you will." I released her and hurried to the barn, explained the situation to Tom, asked him to assign men to lookout duty, and hurried toward the bunkhouse. I met Ling a few yards from the steps. He walked with a bent head and slumped shoulders.

"Is she worse?" I said. He shook his head and kept walking. I fell in step. "Please, Ling, answer me."

"Need to read my scrolls." He was almost trotting now.

"What's the matter? Can I help?" He didn't answer, but I followed anyway, across the porch and into the kitchen. The shelves were bare, barrels and bins hauled outside for cleaning. Pots and pans heaped on the stove. A cold lamp sat on the chopping block. I lighted it.

Ling knelt before the glass-doored cabinet that housed his medical library, a collection of a dozen or so scrolls he had brought with him from his home village those many years ago when he'd left China to seek the gold mountain, the Chinese name for California of the gold rush days. He reached deep into his tunic and drew forth the key attached to a chain around his neck. A thought crossed my mind. Shelby once told me that a good way to find something was to quit looking for it.

Ling opened the door and pulled forth several scrolls. Behind them, against the back wall of the cabinet stood the log of Circle M landmarks. I said nothing for the moment, concentrated on giving Ling the light he needed to trace his finger down the yellowed parchment. He didn't find what he wanted in the first scroll, unrolled the second.

The living room clock struck the half-hour. Ten thirty. The log pulled my eyes back to the cabinet, and Ling's next words carried an irritated tone.

"Hold light here, please." He scrutinized a passage on the scroll, then stood and pulled two small bottles from the cabinet's top shelf. "Good," he said. "Very good." He began to replace the scrolls. I placed a hand on his wrist to stop him.

"That book, Ling. I need it." The look on his face reminded me of the night he'd seen me absconding with the materials from the safe.

"Mrs. Maxwell said to give it to no one but her." A look of distrust clouded his features. After he'd spotted me sneaking out the office window, I could understand. I tried to allay his hesitation.

"If she could speak, she'd approve." He stared at the book for as long as he'd looked at me, then he reached in and handed it to me. He quickly reshelved the scrolls, locked the cabinet, and trotted out of the room.

* * *

The safe opened easily, but the cashbox was a hundred short of the five hundred I'd planned for. Eleven o'clock sounded from the living room. I had no more time, and Charley Hung would have to be satisfied. I wrote down the combination and secreted it in a corner of the desk, then I locked the safe and buried the log book in the pile of ledgers outside. My next destination was the barn to try my most dangerous task yet.

CHAPTER SIXTY-SEVEN

I found Tom touring the yard with his lantern. "Can you bring a team and wagon to the barn door?"

"Got no one to take my place here. We're short of men with those prisoners."

"I'm going to talk with the prisoners, so I'll send one of those men out here. Hurry, Tom."

Yellow Squirrel slumped on the stall floor, apparently dozing. Feifer Gilligan stood over him, rifle barrel pointed at his head. Gilligan looked toward me as I approached, but the barrel didn't move. "Could be playing possum, you know."

"I hope we'll be rid of him soon."

I sent Skull-Cap's guard into the yard and brought him, still chained, into One-Ear's stall. Both men kept chins to chest and eyes to floor. I showed them the cash.

"This is for Charley Hung," I said. They lifted their chins and fastened their eyes on the pile of bills. "I know Ling Chu told you we already sent him five hundred dollars through Sheriff O'Neill. Is that correct?"

One-Ear nodded. "Mr. Hung never got money."

"I should tell Mr. Hung to go collect it from O'Neill if he wants it, but I want something else from him and you. And I'm willing to pay for it."

"Mr. Hung said bring one thousand dollars," One-Ear muttered, "or we don't come back."

"Oh, I believe Mr. Hung will welcome you with open arms. And I believe you'll appreciate my proposition as well, once you consider the alternatives."

The man I'd sent to the yard ran back into the barn. "Lantern signal from up the hill, Mr. Maxwell. Riders coming."

"Thanks," I said. "I'll be there shortly." To One-Ear I said, "A gang of vigilantes will arrive in no more than fifteen minutes. They intend to hang you. If we somehow stop them, Sheriff Halstad will escort you to jail when he returns tomorrow. Or you can take this cash, a team of horses, and—this is the most important item—transport Yellow Squirrel back to Chinatown with you. Mr. Hung can sell him to one of those China-bound ships he's always talking about. After that, if I see or hear of Yellow Squirrel again, neither you nor Charley Hung will know peace this side of the grave." I almost smiled to feel the confidence that prompted my next words. "And by now you should know I mean what I say."

Skull-Cap spoke in Chinese to his partner. I waved the money in their faces. "The offer is good until I count to ten. After that, you take your chances with the vigilantes. One… " I got to six before One-Ear interrupted.

"Indian very bad man. Long way to Mr. Hung. He can escape. Or maybe lawmen will stop us."

I smiled down at him. "Growing up around Ling Chu taught me a few things about your people. I know you can count on help from Chinese in every town along your way. They'll protect you and keep your journey secret." I held up the money again. Skull-Cap nodded. Then One-Ear did the same, held out his hand for the money. I returned it to my pocket.

"I'll give it to you due time."

I gathered Gilligan and the guards and briefed them on my plan to chain Yellow Squirrel to the wagon bed, supply One Ear and Skull-Cap with water and food, and lead them the back way through the homesteads and pastures to the road west of town. Tom was to drive the wagon—leading a horse to ride for his return to the ranch—and give the Chinese money, pistols, rifles, and knives only when their journey to the coast was well under way.

"Gentry and his gang must see nothing," I told Gilligan. "Keep down and use the outbuildings for cover."

"You'll do, Andy, you know that?" Gilligan said. "Come on, men. Let's move."

I took one last look at Yellow Squirrel, in chains again, just as I'd seen him behind bars.

"You're going to wish you'd finished me off," he said.

"You don't know when someone's doing you a favor," I said. "You're not welcome anywhere in these parts, even by your own family. You may as well try China. I'd love to see you hang, Yellow Squirrel. But I won't allow anyone else in Sawtooth Wells to die because of you."

I hurried into the yard, directed the guard to remain concealed behind the house, to keep his gun quiet unless I signaled for help. "We've had more than enough shooting," I told him. Then I walked toward the Circle M archway to await the arrival of the vigilante who said he loved my mother and sought to seize command of my family's ranch.

CHAPTER SIXTY-EIGHT

Moonlight captured Granite Creek's ripples and splashes as it ran under the bridge. I pulled out Shelby's knife, kissed it, resheathed it. I looked across the road and up the trail to the Cedar Spring overlook. Soon, I vowed, Mother and I would ride up that trail again, gaze over the ranch as partners rather than adversaries.

Approaching horses shuddered the bridge before I could hear them. I walked out from under the archway and planted my feet on the far side. Shadows darkened the sky above the rise, gained detail and definition as they approached.

Gentry led about ten men. His silver conches on a fresh black shirt flashed moonlight. Harry Hoskins, the store owner, rode behind him. I didn't recognize the others. Hoskins pulled a rifle from a saddle boot, several of the other men followed suit. Gentry reined up about ten feet from me. The others remained behind him.

"Stand aside, Andy."

"They're not here, Mr. Gentry." The crowd muttered. Gentry nudged his horse near me, reined it sideways so he could talk directly down to me.

"What do you mean?"

"They're gone." I stepped back toward the bridge, uncomfortable staring up at a steep angle. "No farther, now. You'll be trespassing."

"We're gonna see for ourselves," Hoskins said.

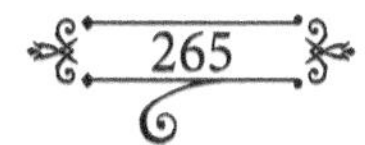

"You'll have to ride over me, Mr. Hoskins. And the only weapon I have is this little thing. I held up the six-inch blade of Shelby's knife. Then I'll have to talk to Sheriff Halstad not only about trespassing, but assault as well."

"How's Carrie?" Gentry said.

"I'll let you know if anything changes. Please leave now." He moved his horse a few steps closer. Hoskins crowded behind him. The rest hung back.

"Something's moving back there, Hale. By the outhouse," said Hoskins.

I didn't dare turn to look. "Of course it is, Mr. Hoskins. We'll be working day and night for the next week to clean up."

"Tell us where they are, or we're coming in."

I pointed a finger at him. "I've lost my brother and my… and a man who was like my father, and my mother's close to death. Do you believe I'd free those men?"

"We want to see for ourselves." Hoskins looked over my head, raised in his stirrups, and heeled his horse forward. I grabbed my knife with one hand, Hoskins' bridle with the other, and sliced one of his reins. His left hand flew in the air, leather strap dangling. The tension on the right rein pulled the horse around in a tight circle. While he attempted to straighten himself, I raised my voice to address the entire contingent.

"You'd all best return home and allow us get on with our work."

Hoskins leaned over his horse's neck and grasped the short length of bridle strap that remained after my cutting. "We're going in. Come on, Hale."

"You'll go without me," one of the men called.

"And me," another said. Both speakers turned their horses toward town. Others began to follow.

Gentry turned to Hoskins, spoke softly. "Looks as if we're losing our help, Harry." Then he turned back to me. "You'd better hope you play as good a game as you talk, Andy, or the next crowd won't quit so easy."

"Good night, Gentry. You, too, Hoskins." I waved them in the direction of Sawtooth Wells, and they trotted after their comrades. I watched them ride up the hill and around the bend. I felt a presence behind me, recognized the wheeze.

"That was slick, Andy." Gilligan still had his rifle in his hand and was backed by three other armed men.

"The wagon's on its way?"

"You bet, and Tom's going to take them around by Shingle Lake to make sure they don't get spotted."

"It will be essential to keep watch the rest of the night. I'm not satisfied those men will keep their word." They walked toward the barn. I jogged to the bunkhouse for my first visit to Mother in many hours.

* * *

Inside the bunkhouse, the lamp was low, the mood subdued. Ling Chu was nowhere in sight. In the shadows, I discerned the slumbering forms of Mrs. Adams, Amelia, other women who had worked so hard and so late. And beside Mother, holding her hand and crooning a soft comforting tune sat the crazy Indian woman I'd come to know was my grandmother.

CHAPTER SIXTY-NINE

Seeing them together for the first time brought a smile to my lips and puddled my eyes. After Yellow Squirrel's insinuations about her death, I nearly felt I was seeing her resurrected a second time.

"Hello, Grandmother."

She returned my smile, but said nothing. She wore clean buckskins, and she'd rebraided her hair and woven red and blue ribbons into the plaits. Her full cheeks and lips mirrored the face on the pillow.

"How is she?"

"With prayer and Ling's doctoring… " She stroked her daughter's hand. Mother's color seemed better now, but she still appeared flushed. I wasn't sure whether she was unconscious or sleeping. I found another chair and sat beside Grandmother.

"What does Ling say?"

"Very little."

"How are the others? Owl Feather?" Grandmother passed Mother's hot, dry hand to me, rearranged covers and pillows as she spoke.

"I believe Owl Feather will be at peace soon. Unless he has other work on this earth to accomplish. That's not for me to know."

"And Standing Oak?"

"He walked a few steps. He'll return to the reservation soon."

"Mother's injury is very similar to his. Perhaps…" She'd finished adjusting the bedding, looked at me.

"Yes."

I smiled again. Patted Mother's hand. "I wonder where Ling is."

"Resting, no doubt. He needs to remain strong."

A gunshot sounded outside, followed by two others. Grandmother took Mother's hand from me, and I ran out the door, keeping my head low. I heard another explosion, saw a flash from the direction of the barn. I circled behind the bunkhouse and bellied up to the barn door. Gilligan stumbled into the yard, dropped his rifle, gripped his thigh, and sat in the dust. Hale Gentry walked out after him, both silver pistols drawn.

"Goddamn it, Feifer. Why'd you make me do that?"

Harry Hoskins emerged behind him, rifle at his shoulder. "They're not in the barn, Hale. Couldn't be far, though."

I ran to Gilligan. "How is it, Fife?" He looked at the sky and sucked in a breath.

"Had worse, but it hurts like hell."

I stood and called. "Ling. Ling, come quick." A shadow leaped from the porch outside the kitchen, and I knew Gilligan would be taken care of. Gentry spoke next.

"Someone's got to do things the right way, Andy. Sorry about Gilligan, here, but we can't let killers—"

I interrupted him. "This has nothing to do with justice, does it, Gentry?"

"Of course—"

"You want to bring those crooks to Mother like a cat brings a dead bird to the door. Leave the Circle M, sir. Do not. I repeat, do not return. Ever."

He pointed his pistol at me and waved the barrel. "Carrie'll have something to say about that."

"Mother will support me completely. If… when she gets well." I stepped toward him. He holstered his pistols and smiled.

"You can't tell a grown man what to do, Andy. I think you need a good whipping." He reached for the buckle on his gunbelt.

"Fighting. Your usual answer, Gentry. It won't change anything. Win or lose, you're leaving. I'm staying."

"I won't lose, and I won't leave." He unbuckled his guns, dangled them from his right hand.

"I won't fight, and you will leave." I felt like I was trapped in a melodrama. Gentry jerked one of the pearl-handled revolvers from its holster and snapped off a shot that raised dust two feet in front of me.

"Maybe you'd rather lose a toe or two than a fight," he said.

I raised my hands. "You don't believe—"

Another shot, this one closer. I stepped back. He tossed the gunbelt to Hoskins and advanced on me, thumbs in his sliver-riveted belt. I stood my ground. "Your mom never did care much for you, you know, Andy. Called you—" He was sneering now, inches from my face—"the worm."

Gentry was no more than an inch taller, but he outweighed me by at least thirty pounds. Everything around me seemed to have stopped. It seemed combat had become inevitable.

I widened my stance and clenched my fist, preferred Gentry to make the first move. I was prepared for a kick or punch, but I wasn't prepared for him to rush me like a bear, wrap his arms around me, crunch his knuckles into my spine, butt his head under my chin, and lift me from the ground. I flailed like a snared cat, and blood filled my mouth, salty and warm, poured down my chin and neck. Gentry grunted and squeezed. He smelled like beer and unwashed armpits. I couldn't draw a breath, felt on the verge of blacking out.

I attempted to shove my hand under his chin, punch his face, but he tucked his forehead into my chest and left me with nothing to pound but shoulders and the back of his head. Finally, I collapsed his knee with a kick of my heel and sent us both sprawling. He tried to maintain his grip even as we rolled in the dust, but I slipped away and gained my feet, lightheaded and gasping. He rose as quickly as I and rushed me like a bull.

I clenched both fists, sidestepped, and clubbed the back of his head as he charged, but I was off-balance and dealt him only a glancing blow. His skull missed my belly, but banged my hip and spun me around. He stumbled past, and I rushed to seize him while he was staggering. Again, he recovered quickly, turned, stepped aside, swung a foot and took my legs from under me. I flew to the ground face down, remembered my fight with the trooper in Lander, expected him to jump atop me and begin pounding. I began to roll over, but the point of his boot caught me in the ribs and tossed me on my back.

I used my momentum to keep rolling and spun myself back to my feet. He rushed me again, threw his weight behind a roundhouse right. I stepped inside the punch and began pummeling his gut. This time, he was the one left with only shoulders and the back of the head as targets while I thrashed at his midsection. He started gasping for air as his saloon life began to take a toll.

Unable to dislodge me with pushes and punches, he leaned over my back, grabbed me under the arms, and fell backwards. My impetus carried me past him, and I smacked into the dirt once more, this time on my back. I lurched to my feet. So much punching had leadened my arms, and I let them dangle, wriggled them to stimulate blood flow. He lumbered toward me, swaying paws big as shovels. One of his haymakers could finish me. I skipped away, raised my fists, circled to one side, then the other, alert for an opening. He spread his arms.

"You going to dance or fight, Andy? You know you can't lick me. Let's get it over with."

"Fine with me." I jumped forward, dodged inside another of his right hooks, and landed one of my own to his eye. The punch opened a cut on his brow, and blood streamed down his face. He pushed me away, shook his head, bearlike, sent droplets into the moonlight. Swung again. This time with his left hand.

I tried to step inside this punch as well, but he anticipated my move. My head exploded with the same burst I'd felt when Standing Oak shoved me into the San Francisco street. I was face down and groggy, but this time I knew what Gentry would try.

I rocked back to my knees just in time to slap down his kick with both hands. I crawled forward, wrapped my arms around his knees, jerked up, and dropped him to his back. I heaved myself to a seat on his belly and fired blows to his face, suddenly confident of victory. Then I felt a sharp sting in my shoulder. I grabbed at the pain, spilled backwards, and fell across his feet. As he kicked himself free, I clutched one of his ankles and held on. He struggled and squirmed, and all at once loosed himself, leaving me holding a silver-pointed, snakeskin boot.

We reached our feet simultaneously. The knife in his right hand explained the pain in my shoulder. I dared not look, but I felt a warm flow down my side and feared the fight would soon drain from me along with the blood. His blade flashed in the moonlight, headed for my belly. I swung hard with the boot I held in my left hand, deflected the thrust, dropped the boot, and grabbed his wrist.

Somehow, I ended with my back to Gentry, my hands locked around his knife hand. I slammed the hand to my knee, but he maintained his hold on the knife while his other fist battered my ribs. I pounded his hand to my knee once more with no success, so I dropped to my knees, jerked and twisted to the right, threw him to the ground. I lifted a knee and dropped onto his wrist with my full weight. He loosed the knife at last, and I kicked it toward the bunkhouse.

I turned back toward Gentry just in time to see him lunge at me, the errant boot lifted like a tomahawk. The pointed toe with its silver tip hit the top of my head. I lost control of my legs and slumped to the ground. He landed a frenzy of sharp-toed blows on the hands I'd wrapped around my head. I rose to my knees and woozily attempted to crawl away from the beating until my knees slipped and I was once more flat and face-down, my brain mired in pain and confusion.

"Try it again when you grow up, Andy." Gentry's gasping whisper sounded distant, though it came from just above my head where he knelt, one hand resting on the ground on each side of my face. Even in this humiliated and defeated position, I entertained no thought of losing the battle. Outrage stormed through me, and I swung an elbow into his jaw, and we rolled, wrestling for the boot. I weathered some hard kicks in the back, but my head cleared somewhat, and I finally won possession of the boot. I clung to it like St. George to his lance, though I remained on my knees and had no idea what to do with it.

Gentry supplied my answer when he turned his back and leaped toward the knife a few feet behind him. I stumbled to my feet, threw the boot at his back, and ran at him. Gentry didn't realize the whack on his rump had come from the boot instead of me, and he turned before he reached the knife, fists clenched. Before he gathered himself to launch another swing, I drove an elbow to his throat. He grabbed his neck with one hand, choked, and I clenched my hands into a single fist, slashed back and forth at his head like Paul Bunyan swinging an ax, until I battered him to the ground. I believed I'd finished him then, but he began striking again as I straddled him. We both continued, neither of us punching with great impact, but I was on top, had clear shots at his head, and he at last lay quiet.

I stood over him, exhausted and bleeding, and it occurred to me that I had a knife of my own, but there was no need for it now. Gentry was conscious, eyes locked on mine, but still.

I spoke quietly. "Take your friend home, please, Mr. Hoskins." One of the Circle M hands led Gentry's white stallion forward. He helped Hoskins drape the big man across his saddle.

"Please escort our guests a mile or so down the road," I said to the cowboy. "Make sure they're well on their way before you return." None of us spoke as we watched them head out the archway toward town, watched until they became dark lumps on the road. Ling Chu began probing my shoulder.

"Lot of blood, Mr. Andrew. Let me look."

"You finish with Mr. Gilligan, Ling Chu. I must return to Mother.

Amelia and Mrs. Adams met me at the bunkhouse door, ushered me to a chair, and began washing my wounds.

"Where's… Crazy Lu?" I said.

Amelia stopped dabbing at my shoulder and drew back. "How would I know?"

I chuckled. "You wouldn't. I apologize. I suppose Gentry addled my brain a little."

Mrs. Adams pressed a hand on my forehead. "If you don't keep that head tipped your nose never will stop bleeding. Now allow us do our work so you can get to bed where you belong."

"Yes, ma'am," I said. But more than I wanted sleep, I wanted another conversation with Grandmother. The gunshots had interrupted us and prevented me from asking about one more person in Wyoming.

AUGUST 15

CHAPTER SEVENTY

Mother's fever broke at mid-morning. Ling Chu prodded me awake, and I climbed down from an upper bunk to see her resting peacefully, color pale, but approaching normal.

"Hello, Mother." Her eyelids lifted for a moment. She smiled slightly.

"Andy." She coughed, winced. "That hurts."

I reached down to take her hand. Pain from my left shoulder stopped me. "I understand what you mean." She smiled again.

"Tell me all," she said. "Ling Chu would say not a word."

"It appears you'll recover. That's what's important."

"You know what I'm talking about, Andy." Her voice carried a dose of her customary sternness, then softened. "Please, now."

"Grandmother was here."

Water filled her eyes, but no tears spilled. "So it wasn't a dream."

"The house will be fine. The neighbors and hands have been hard at work. They believe you're an angel."

"I suppose I nearly was, wasn't I?" We were silent for a few moments. She closed her eyes, and her head drifted down. Then she righted herself with determination. "They wouldn't believe me so angelic if they knew the truth, would they?"

"About me and Shelby and Grandmother and Grandfather? Maybe not."

"Grandfather?"

"His murder." She raised herself from the pillow, cried out and fell back. I rose to my feet, gave her some water. Again she seemed to drift away.

"I thought you knew," I said. "We'll talk later."

She lifted her hand. "Now."

"Jerome III was no accident. It was Standing Oak and Yellow Squirrel who set him loose to gore Grandfather. They thought they were paying him back for the way Owl Feather was treated. And Lolo."

"You know about Lolo?"

"Grandmother's journals were very complete. At any rate, Owl Feather rebuked them instead of thanking them for killing Grandfather. Standing Oak accepted the scolding. Yellow Squirrel's rage just got stronger over the years."

"So it was a vendetta. Just as you thought. I'm sorry, Andy."

"But it was all Yellow Squirrel." I smiled. "So we were both right, and we both survived the full moon."

She fell back on her pillow, spoke with closed eyes. "About Shelby…" She was so exhausted, I wished again to tell her to rest, but when I began to speak, I had no voice.

"We so loved… but we just couldn't… and you… I still don't know… "

"We'll have time to talk it all through, Mother. Later. Please." She nodded and lay back.

I knelt and brushed her warm cheek with my lips, placed her hand on the cover, and watched until her breathing became soft and regular and her face relaxed.

I stepped to the bunkhouse door and looked out. The fire under the lye pot was ash. The clotheslines were still laden, but apparently everything that could be washed had been. The hands sat in clumps, smoking, talking. I raised my hand to wave. My shoulder protested. My face was torn and bruised, my head pounding. But I felt invigorated.

I thought of Virginia's letter in my back pocket, spotted Tom sitting on a pile of bales outside the barn, half asleep in the morning sun.

"Did our little company get on their way?"

"My God, Andy, the way you look. And they said you won that fight."

"It was a narrow victory."

"I took them thugs halfway to Placerville, I reckon. Gave them weapons and the money and bid them good riddance." He pulled a Bull Durham sack and packet of cigarette papers out of his shirt pocket.

"You think they'll deliver the cargo?"

"Way they were talking about how happy this Charley Hung's gonna be, no doubt about it." He sprinkled tobacco on the curl of paper.

"You did a fine job, Tom. Mother and I appreciate it."

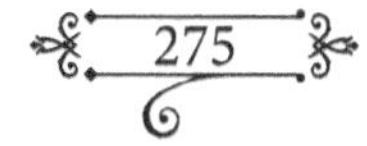

"How is she?"

"For the first time I can say I feel pretty sure she'll make it." Tom looked over my shoulder and spilled the tobacco. "Uh-oh," he said. I turned to see Sheriff Halstad crossing the bridge under the Circle M arch.

"Good. I'd rather not go all the way to Sawtooth Wells to talk to him. That tobacco's pretty expensive to be throwing it on the ground, Tom." He smiled and poured a new supply into the paper.

I met Halstad at the hitching post in front of the gallery. We stepped into the shade of the porch and sat in a pair of overstuffed leather chairs that had been pulled out of the house for scrubbing. Virginia's letter crinkled in my back pocket as I settled in. We traded pleasantries, general information, then approached the real reason he'd come.

"The way Gentry and Hoskins tell it, you been harboring fugitives out here and stopping law-abiding citizens from doing their bounden duty, Andrew."

"So that's what he claims? What do you believe?"

"I don't think nothing till I have some facts in hand." Neither of us looked at the other, simply watched the peaks bathing in the summer sun.

"The main fact, Sheriff, is that justice has been served." He shifted in his chair, turned toward me, stroked his moustache.

"I'd appreciate a few more details, if you don't mind."

"Gentry and Hoskins raised a lynch mob. Right-minded citizens wanted no part of it. If shooting began, we'd have engendered grudges that'd persist for generations. I arranged for Yellow Squirrel and the Chinese to be transported to San Francisco."

"To O'Neill's custody, then?" It was the question I'd feared. I wished to tell Halstad as little as possible. If he knew too much, he'd be compelled to act like a lawman, track down the wagon, and turn the fugitives over to the dubious jurisdiction of the San Francisco sheriff. I turned toward Halstad.

"Sheriff Halstad, I've learned a great deal about the capricious nature of big city law enforcement in the last few weeks, and I'm sure you know far more than I ever supposed. Am I correct?" He looked at me, combed his moustache again.

"Talk plain, Andrew."

"Was there ever a cent that passed through your office and didn't go where it was intended? Was there ever a citizen complaint that you didn't investigate as thoroughly as you're investigating Gentry's right now? I'm saying it isn't always that way in O'Neil's bailiwick."

"You're asking me to overlook a deliberate dodge of the legal process."

"I'm asking you to avoid a corruption of the legal process."

"Against my principles and sworn duty." He stood, turned his back to the peaks, and looked me in the eyes. I met his gaze without flinching.

"Just because a man wears a badge," I said, "Doesn't mean he signifies the rule of law."

"That Squirrel fella committed cold-blooded murder in my territory. I'm going after him. You helping or obstructing?" I stood and crossed the porch to him.

"All right. I'll tell you everything. Then it's up to you." He leaned against the porch rail, crossed his arms.

"Damned right it's up to me."

So I told him about the carelessness that had allowed Yellow Squirrel's San Francisco escape, about Charley Hung and his henchmen, Julian's debt, the missing five hundred, and the deal I'd negotiated.

"Then those Chinamen get off scot free, and there's no guarantee that Injun's going to end up in China," he said.

"Yellow Squirrel's their ticket back into Charley Hung's good graces," I said. "That and the money. If you bring them back here, you'll have a mob on your hands. And what guarantee do you have with O'Neill that Yellow Squirrel will get what he deserves?"

He stared at the peaks. The sun had wrapped them completely in light, drawing pinks and greens from their rocky shoulders.

"As for the Chinese, they do deserve some punishment. But do they merit hanging? That'll be their certain fate in Sawtooth Wells after a very unruly trial. And I wager the anger will last quite a while after."

The silence was long. He seemed to be memorizing every detail of the peaks.

"Glad to hear Carrie's better, Andy. Thanks for heading off the little range war. We don't need none of that." He shook my hand, returned to his horse, mounted and looked toward me across the railing. "Reckon I better get to rounding up my posse."

"Thanks for stopping by, sheriff." I could barely utter the words. He waved and headed out the archway. I couldn't control what Halstad did now, but I could do nothing more at the moment. I decided it was a nice day for a walk, made sure Virginia's letter was still in my pocket, and headed for Cedar Spring.

* * *

Berkeley, August 1, 1908
Dear Andy,

I hope this finds you safe at home after a successful struggle with all the difficulties you have been facing so courageously.

I am writing to express my sincere regret for the way we parted. Father and I had a long talk on the way back to San Francisco—about you and about the way he humiliated you in front of your mother. I asked him if it was he himself who had seen you and Julian in that place. He told me he had been there, but as part of a legislative investigation. He was lying. It was his last chance.

In short, Andy, I have severed relations with him and mean to make my way in the world as an artist. He thinks my action is merely another of my girlish flirtations with Bohemian ideas; but I am determined, and I will never go crawling back to him as he expects me to.

I do not know how you will receive this, and I know it is forward of me. However, I wish to assure you that should you contact me in the future, you will find yourself in the company of a very different girl than the one who treated you so rudely in the past.

With my best wishes and warm regards,
Virginia

Cedar Spring lay clear in its granite bowl. Water skippers dimpled the surface, cast bulbous shadows on the gravelly bed. I folded the paper, ran my fingers over each crease several times before I returned it to the envelope. It was not the reproach and farewell I'd expected, but what was it? My mind turned toward some of my old fantasies. Grand dinners at the Circle M or in some San Francisco hotel, Virginia on my arm. Mother looking on proudly. Odysseus returned. Penelope waiting.

"How is the patient doing?" Grandmother approached from above, sat on a rock next to me. I was becoming so accustomed to our unexpected encounters that I wasn't startled.

"Her fever's broken, Grandmother. She'll recover."

"The Great Spirit is pleased." She knelt by the pool, cupped water in her hands, bathed her face, and raised her arms to the sky. "All thanks." She stood, reached out to me. I rose and took her hands. "The one you didn't ask about, Andy. She's waiting. She doesn't think so, but her heart knows." She smiled, dark eyes shining from amid honeyed crinkles. I pictured Many Clouds plaiting her hair in the desert, smiling at me from the firelight, imagined her standing by the Wind River looking west. Emotion poured from my heart like water from Moses' rock, an affection I hadn't known—or perhaps simply hadn't acknowledged—was there.

"Take care, Andy." She began one of her humming chants and danced downhill into the cedars.

"And you, Grandmother." I surveyed the ranch—charred timbers, scattered, desultory figures resting around the barn and porch. A scene of disorder neither Grandfather nor Mother would tolerate. Nor would I. I needed to organize, repair, rebuild. And roundup was approaching. Everything fell to me, at least until Mother recovered.

AUGUST 22

CHAPTER SEVENTY-ONE

Mother walked slowly, one hand on a cane, the other on my arm. We stopped several times to rest between the house and the graveyard, a distance she was accustomed to covering in five minutes on a slow day. It had taken her a week to gather this much strength, and I was afraid she'd pay dearly for our little journey. But she'd insisted. And when that hadn't worked, she'd pleaded. And I'd relented at last.

Halfway there, Tom and Ling Chu rolled across the bridge on a buckboard with a load of supplies from Sawtooth Wells. Tom, jumped down, and trotted toward us, digging something from his shirt pocket.

"You have a note from Sheriff Halstad." He smiled, tipped his hat back while I opened the envelope.

"What's so funny?" Mother said.

"The full story's in there," Tom said. "But I'm busting to give you the gist. Halstad, Gentry and Hoskins as his posse, led them all over the hills for three days, dry-camping and such till they was so sore and hungry they had to admit there wasn't no more use trying to track that wagon. I'm sure they was ready to give up the first day, but—nossir—Halstad didn't want them claiming he took no half-measures."

Tom had given an excellent summary of the note. And Halstad included as well the text of the telegram he'd sent to San Francisco—

* * *

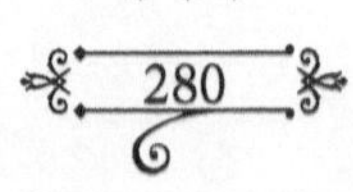

O'NEILL STOP YELLOW SQUIRREL CAME THROUGH LAST WEEK STOP LOST HIM STOP HE HEADED YOUR WAY STOP.

* * *

Mother lifted her cane and waved it like a club. "O'Neill hasn't heard the last of that five hundred dollars, either."

I stepped back and raised my hands. "Careful with that cane, Mother. It may go off." She smiled and swatted me on the hip.

"Hush, your smart aleck mouth. Thank you, Tom. Did you finish that little task I asked you to do?"

"Oh, yes, ma'am."

"What task?" I said. But Tom just touched his hat brim.

"Ma'am. Andy." He headed toward the wagon, which Ling Chu had begun unloading.

I decided not to inquire further and offered Mother my arm once more. "Are you certain you're strong enough for this?"

"I can say what I must in only one place, Andy, and I'm bursting like Tom was. Let's go."

Even if Mother hadn't fully regained her stamina, she possessed all her resolve, and the second half of the little journey went more quickly than the first. The four headstones now took on an entirely new meaning than they'd had the last time I'd visited. They now seemed, like the crests above us, separate peaks grown from a single mountain. Grandfather, Shelby, Julian—victims of Aeschylian vengeance, avenged in turn with some measure of truth and mercy.

I followed Mother's lead. We knelt first at Grandfather's grave, then at Julian's. Our prayers and meditations there were silent, solitary. Then came Shelby. She knelt on one side, gestured for me to kneel on the other. She took my hands, much as Grandmother had at the spring a few days earlier. This time, I couldn't hold the pose, but dropped to my hands and knees and gripped the earth to stifle my sobs.

"I can't erase the hurt I've caused you, Andy. I can only explain." She waited. I nodded, shifted my knees, breathed and looked up. She gazed at the earth a moment, then raised her eyes. "You might know the line from Twelfth Night—'Love sought is good, but given unsought is better.'" I nodded. Her eyes drifted from mine to the headstone. Shelby… your father… and I never sought each other's heart, but we found that in one another's presence we became inseparable parts of the same element—like the light of fire, and the warmth of it. Yet, there was no place for us as a couple in this world. We yearned for some tangible expression of our love, and that was you. We needed you here with us, where we could both love you in the open, even if we couldn't do the same with one another. That's why I didn't want you to leave the ranch."

"But it was just to school, Mother."

"No. I knew that school would become like a second home to you. Remember, my little bookworm."

So there it was. Worm. Bookworm. Gentry had taken a term of endearment and twisted it into an insult. A curse which had no power to hurt the Maxwells or anyone else ever again. I felt one more surge of resentment for the villain.

Mother went on, "You'd eventually… I'd suffered through such a thing once, with someone I didn't care for nearly as much as I care for you. I couldn't bear to repeat it."

I wished I could sooth her anguish, make the promises I knew she craved. But they were promises I didn't yet trust, and I knew she wouldn't trust them either. "And now?" I said.

"I know I can't control you, Andy. I hope you'll want to stay. I want you to."

The obligations I'd collected during my Wyoming trek lined up in my mind like entries in an account book. All those horses—Ira's, Zeke's, the shepherd's, Sailor. And what of poor Theodore in Evanston? And where did graduate school fit in? Not to mention Virginia and Many Clouds.

"I believe I've proved I'll do everything I can to care for you and the Circle M," I said.

She looked at me with a tremble in her lip, brought our hands together and kissed them. "That's as good an answer as I can expect for the time being, I suppose. Please help me up. We must see to your grandmother."

She tottered to Grandmother's headstone, stood behind it. I wondered at the small, fresh-dug trench around it. Mother caressed the top of the tombstone as she spoke.

"She created so much trouble for Father with all her letters to senators, assemblymen, and governors demanding justice for the Indians, making outrageous comments at legislative dinners. He wished so to get on in government and thought she held him back. In truth, I think everyone believed she was so daft they simply ignored her. But she and Father had terrible rows, and I didn't help matters by taking his side in everything.

"When she finally decided to run with the natives, he couldn't bear the disgrace. He concocted the tale about discovering her fallen from a cliff, carved a headstone, and pretended to bury her. I believed him. I was fourteen, not nearly as heartbroken as I should have been.

"She revealed herself to me just after he died. I was eighteen by then, devastated by Father's death. I didn't believe I could run this place alone. I thought I'd be forced to sell or submit to an overseer. Mother insisted I mustn't let it go. I begged her to return and help, but she said she was happy as she was and that I could accomplish it all on my own."

"And you did, Mother."

"And what a mess I've made. But perhaps it's not too late to repair a few things. Help me, Andy." She began pushing on the headstone, and I now understood the trench she'd instructed Tom to dig. Her efforts were feeble, but together, we soon laid on its face the stone that had marked a living woman's resting place for more than twenty years.

"And let that mark an end," Mother said, "to all these years of lies and secrets. Let's return to the house, Andy. There are still a number of items in that trunk you should know about."

"And I have some sharing of my own to do," I said. I was thinking of Shelby's medal, of course.

This time I wrapped my arm around her waist as I helped her cross the yard. About halfway to the porch, she placed hers around mine, and we climbed the steps together.